THE SECRET DIARIES OF
MISS ANNE LISTER

Edited by
Helena Whitbread

VIRAGO

This paperback edition published in 2010 by Virago Press

5 7 9 10 8 6

First published in Great Britain in 1988 by Virago Press, as
I Know My Own Heart: The Diaries of Anne Lister, 1791–1840

This selection taken from
Anne Lister Journals held by Calderdale District Archives,
reference numbers SH: 7/ML/E/1–26 and RAM: 52–76, 78–9.

Permission to reproduce the page from the diary by
Calderdale District Council is gratefully acknowledged.

Introduction, selection, editorial comment and notes
copyright © Helena Whitbread 1988, 2010

A CIP catalogue record for this book
is available from the British Library.

ISBN 978-1-84408-719-8

Typeset in Goudy by M Rules
Printed and bound in Great Britain by
Clays Ltd, Elcograf S.p.A.

Papers used by Virago are from well-managed forests
and other responsible sources.

Virago Press
An imprint of
Little, Brown Book Group
Carmelite House
50 Victoria Embankment
London EC4Y 0DZ

An Hachette UK Company
www.hachette.co.uk

www.virago.co.uk

'I know my own heart & I know men. I am not made like any other I have seen. I dare believe myself to be different from any others who exist.'

Rousseau, *Confessions, Volume I*

'I might exclaim with Virgil, *In tenui labor*, but I am resolved not to let my life pass without some private memorial that I may hereafter read, perhaps with a smile, when Time has frozen up the channel of those sentiments which flow so freshly now.'

Anne Lister, Friday, 19 February 1819

CONTENTS

ACKNOWLEDGEMENTS

It is to Dr Betteridge and his excellent team of archivists that my first debt of gratitude must be paid. They have given unstintingly of their time, expertise, good humour and friendly advice throughout the period I was engaged in actively researching this book. My grateful thanks to them and also to the staff of the Reference Library, next to the archive department, whose help was as willingly forthcoming when the archives were closed.

To my many friends and colleagues in secondary education in Calderdale whom I have met whilst working as a supply teacher, I can only say thank you for your interest in the Anne Lister saga. Support and encouragement has come from many quarters, not least from language teachers when I was struggling with some rather puzzling quotations in French, Latin and Greek which occur in Anne's scholarly journals. My own deficiencies in those areas have been nicely camouflaged, thanks to their help.

To Ruthie Petrie and Rosalind Smith I extend my thanks and appreciation. As my editors and advisers at Virago Press they have guided me and helped to shape the book into a manageable publication.

A special thank you to Caroline Davidson whose own work on *The World of Mary Ellen Best* brought about our friendship. Her constructive advice, her scholarly interest in my work, and her professional expertise in, and knowledge of, the publishing world have been immensely beneficial to me.

My immediate family, of course, have been intimately involved in the whole proceedings from the start. To Rachel and her friend, Ruthanne Gregory, I give my thanks and love for their patient research undertaken in York on my behalf. To my son, Philip, for his work in Calderdale archives at times when I was unable to go myself and for his continuing interest and support in my literary activities, many thanks are due and my very best hopes and wishes for his own literary work. To my two other daughters, Claire and Elizabeth, go my thanks for their patience and tolerance. Immersed as they are in busy family and business lives, with all the attendant problems such lives bring, they have nevertheless been a willing and sympathetic audience when I have expounded on my literary problems, of which there have been not a few. Lastly, a very special thank you to my husband, Bob, whose role in the whole undertaking has been of crucial importance in enabling me to work as freely as I have done. Role-reversal situations are no longer a novelty in these times of mass unemployment and the professionalization of women, but degrees of willingness and efficiency must vary. I can only say that the smooth running of the domestic scene has, for the last few years, been entirely due to his efforts and has been the most important factor of all in enabling me to embark, somewhat belatedly, on my writing career, the first fruits of which lie in the present publication.

My thanks go to my editor at Virago, Donna Coonan, and my agent, Caroline Davidson, for their help and guidance in the preparation of this new edition. It remains for me to say that throughout the whole undertaking, historical and textual accuracy have been an over-riding concern; I have placed it equally in importance with my desire to elucidate the life of a courageous and extraordinary woman.

To my daughter, Rachel, whose love, care and support throughout the 'Anne Lister years' has been, and continues to be, invaluable.

INTRODUCTION

When this book was first published in 1988, it was the first to openly record Anne Lister's lesbianism, previously suppressed or just hinted at. This edition of the 1816–1824 diaries prompted wider interest in Anne Lister and many scholars and writers have subsequently expanded on Anne's life. I particularly recommend Jill Liddington's *Presenting the Past*, which reveals much about the complex history of the diaries.[1] The journals are contained in two thin blue exercise books and twenty-four small hardback volumes. They evolve over a number of years: although they begin in 1806, it isn't until 1808 that the entries become more detailed and Anne introduces the rudiments of what is eventually to become an elaborate code – her 'crypthand' as she called it – the use of which allowed her the freedom to describe her intimate life in great detail.

The idea of using an esoteric code appears to have had its roots in Anne's burgeoning knowledge of the Greek language: she mingles Greek letters with other symbols of her own devising. She felt safe in the belief that no one would be able to decipher the coded passages, and as her confidence grew, they became longer and much more explicit when dealing with those aspects of her life which could not be written about in 'plainhand'.

The history of the concealment of the journals is a story in itself. Whether or not Anne Lister intended to destroy them before her death is a debatable point. In 1840, her premature death in Russia, at the age of forty-nine, precluded any such decision on her part. Her journals remained intact at Shibden Hall for a period of almost sixty years until, in 1887, John Lister, the last remaining member of the Lister family to occupy Shibden Hall, decided to publish some of the plainhand extracts in the local paper under the title 'Social and Political Life in Halifax Fifty Years Ago'. The crypthand passages had not yet been deciphered and their content was still unknown.[2]

However, the secrets buried within Anne's cryptic code were about to be discovered. John Lister and his friend, Arthur Burrell, a Bradford schoolteacher and antiquarian, decided to set themselves the task of attempting to unravel the code. What they found was, to them, so disturbing that Burrell thought they ought to burn the journals immediately. What was it that so shocked these two educated Victorian gentlemen? Arthur Burrell put it into words some years later when he wrote that: 'The contents of this cipher . . . is an intimate account of homosexual practices among Miss Lister and her many "friends"; hardly any one of them escaped her.'

It was not merely the revelation of his predecessor's sexual activities with members of her own sex that so dismayed John Lister. He also worried that local scandal about his own sexual orientation would be brought to the notice of the higher authorities.[3] In that era, the late 1890s, homosexual acts between men were punishable by law, as the trial of Oscar Wilde in 1895 demonstrated.

Despite Burrell's advice that the journals be burnt, John Lister was reluctant to destroy such an important historical document. His antiquarian instincts could not allow him to countenance such an act of vandalism and, instead, he replaced the journals behind one of the panels in Shibden Hall, where they remained until after his death in 1933. He never published another word from what he now saw as the infamous document which his predecessor, Anne Lister, had left behind.

Shibden Hall fell into the possession of Halifax Town Council after John Lister died. He had become bankrupt some years before.

A friend and Halifax philanthropist, Mr A. S. McCrea, purchased the estate and gave the grounds to the people of Halifax as a public park, but stipulated that John Lister could remain in the Hall for the remainder of his life, after which it would revert to the Borough of Halifax for the enjoyment of the townspeople.

Prior to its opening as a museum in June 1934, an inventory of all the Lister documents was made and the journals made the transition from private hands to public property. Inevitably questions were raised about the coded passages. The town clerk of Halifax wrote to Arthur Burrell in an attempt to clear up the mystery, but he received a reluctant reply. The only person who could provide the answer was initially unwilling to reveal the clues to the code: 'You must excuse my hesitations: I am not in full possession of what old Halifax scandal knows about Miss Lister; and as I say, I do not want to be the means of allowing a very unsavoury document to see even a partial light.' He did, however, have scruples about withholding the information and went on to say: 'At the same time I have, as a student, the feeling that someone (and preferably someone in Halifax, and a Librarian) should be, so to speak, armed with a knowledge of what the cipher contains.' A copy of the key to the code was placed in the possession of Edward Green, Halifax's chief librarian at the time, who kept it locked in his safe.

The task of cataloguing and indexing the Shibden Hall muniments fell to his daughter, Muriel, a young woman who was working towards her librarianship qualifications. Her father had given her a copy of the key to the code used by Anne Lister in her journals but for her dissertation Muriel chose to work on the letters of Anne Lister instead. As she said in an interview with Jill Liddington:

I don't think my father knew much about Anne Lister, that she was a lesbian or anything. And I never mentioned it. We didn't talk about it much in those days. It would have cast a slur on the good name of the Lister family if it were known then, so I didn't put it into my Letters at all. It doesn't come into the Letters really.[4]

A twenty-year period of comparative silence followed until 1958, when Dr Phyllis Ramsden, a historian who lived in Halifax, and her London friend, Vivien Ingham, obtained permission to work jointly on the journals. No major publication resulted from their research, although Phyllis Ramsden did attempt to write a book about Anne's travels. Vivien Ingham focused on Anne's adventurous mountain-climbing, 'Anne Lister in the Pyrenees', while Phyllis Ramsden wrote a more general paper entitled 'Anne Lister's Journal (1817–1840)'.

But, here again, the secret of Anne's sexuality, although known to the researchers, was carefully concealed. The authorities in Halifax, worried about scandal, insisted on vetting any material which Ramsden and Ingham might wish to publish. Dr Ramsden herself cooperated in the cover-up by stating that that the coded passages in Anne's journals were 'excruciatingly tedious to the modern mind ... and of no historical interest whatsoever.' Ramsden's dismissal of what has since been recognised as a unique contribution to the history of women's sexuality in the early nineteenth century was somewhat redeemed by her colleague, Vivien Ingham, who wrote that anyone who wished to undertake serious work on the life of Anne Lister could not afford to ignore the contents of the coded passages in her journals.

The history of the secret sexual life of Anne Lister remained behind an iron curtain of conspiracy by those 'in the know' – a handful of Halifax town officials and one or two scholars.[5] That situation was about to change. The liberalising decade of the 1960s saw the introduction of the Sexual Offences Act (1967),

xvi

which legalised homosexual activity so long as it was conducted in private and between consenting adults. The following two decades saw an extension of this climate of toleration and, as the homosexual community became more visible and vocal in their demand for equal rights, it became possible to speak, or write, openly about the lives of lesbian or gay people.

It was in the early 1980s that I first came across the Anne Lister journals, a serendipitous discovery that radically altered the course of my life. I had completed my degree and wanted to carry on studying with a view to publication. Due to work and home commitments I decided to look close to home for a suitable subject – one which I could fit around the other demands in my life.

Anne Lister of Shibden Hall was vaguely familiar to me as a woman of some importance in Halifax during her lifetime. I also knew that some of her letters had been published from time to time in the local newspaper. Apart from these scanty facts, I knew nothing about her. I thought it would be interesting to know more about her life, so I visited the archive department of my home-town library. The Anne Lister letters were available on microfilm and, given my incompetence with machines of any kind, the young archivist obligingly placed the reel on the reader for me.

What I saw made me consider the complexities of the work I was about to undertake. On many of the letters Lister had used up every bit of available space by turning the paper around at a ninety-degree angle and writing across the original lines of the page. This technique formed a trellis-like effect which, in addition to the small handwriting, looked rather daunting. As I sat staring dubiously at the difficult material before me, the archivist asked, 'Did you know she kept a journal?' It has since amazed me how those seven small words set me on a literary and academic journey which, to date, has lasted almost three decades.

The microfilm reels were changed over and the next sight to meet my eyes was a coded page of Anne Lister's journal. If you turn to the example included in this book, you might be able to gauge what my feelings were when confronted with those lines and lines of unintelligible symbols – a sight much more puzzling than the trellised letters. But I was hooked. Curiosity, allied to the thrill of an intellectual challenge, gripped me. What was this woman, living in the early nineteenth century, hiding? I there and then decided that, if at all possible, I would unravel the mysteries concealed in the pages of Anne Lister's journals. I had found my research project!

The extant journals, so I believed in the initial stages of my research, began in March 1817 (I was to discover earlier journals some years later).[6] Finding that the key to the code was available, I obtained a copy of it and photocopied the first fifty pages of the 1817 journal to take home with me. From then on, for the next three years, I visited the archives weekly, collected fifty pages each time, and made it my next week's work to read and decode the material. As I worked through the journal I became very aware that Anne Lister's life, which was so rich, historically, and complex, was far too valuable to be buried in the archives, hidden in an esoteric code. But there were many textual difficulties to overcome if I wished, as I did, to place Anne Lister's journals before a reading public.

When I began the collation of the two types of scripts, I found Anne's handwriting almost as difficult to decipher as the code had been. This was particularly the case when she wanted to economise on paper by cramming the pages as fully as possible with very small handwriting, or when she was writing in a hurry or in a state of great emotion. Her usual method, especially whilst travelling, was to jot down memoranda in small notebooks, on odd pieces of paper or, occasionally, a slate and then write it up in her journal wherever she happened to be lodged. I endeavoured to place her at the time of writing by putting the location at the head of each entry along with the date.

Anne's spelling of some words can be seen, by today's standards, as idiosyncratic; for example, 'shewed' for 'showed'; 'sopha' for 'sofa'; 'poney' for 'pony', etc. Where each of these spellings first occurs, I have indicated this by 'sic' and thereafter left her spellings as they are. Anne also used to vary the spellings of some of her friends' names; for instance, Miss Brown/Browne. I have left these unchanged.

Almost every other word written by Anne in plainhand is abbreviated, a habit which, while economical on paper, makes the reading of the text difficult. There have been other obstacles to surmount in presenting the diaries; for instance, the use of a dash in place of a full stop at the end of a sentence; the lack of paragraphs when Anne passed from one subject to another in the same diary entry; the non-use, on many occasions, of the personal pronoun, and other small difficulties too tedious to enumerate.

The coded sections posed different problems. A superficial scrutiny of these texts gives no indication whatsoever of any form of punctuation and, to add to the obfuscation which Anne obviously intended, there is no space between individual words. Only when every symbol in each extract had been decoded could a sense of what was written emerge. Even then, it had to be the decision of the decoder to impose a structure on the sequence of words that emerged – to define where words and sentences begin and end. Italics have been used throughout the text to distinguish the 'crypthand' passages from the ones written in 'plainhand'.

After five years hard, albeit enjoyable and intellectually stimulating, work I felt that I knew Anne Lister well enough to venture into print. I wanted to share with the reader the fascination I had experienced on reading Anne's own words: the small, local world of Halifax and, eventually, a wider world beyond that, spring vividly to life in the pages of her journals. What we read is an authentic depiction of the fictionalised scenarios provided by writers of her day: Mrs Gaskell's small town of *Cranford*; Jane Austen's genteel society novels; and, given the wildness of the Yorkshire countryside around Halifax and Anne Lister's passionate love affairs, Emily Brontë's *Wuthering Heights*.

Anne Lister's writings, in their mixture of sophistication and gaucherie, demonstrate a tension in her life that she attempted to resolve by committing her thoughts to her journal. The use of her code involved a great deal of labour, but its worth to Anne as a means of expressing that 'disguised & hidden nature that suits not with the world' was invaluable: 'I tell myself to myself & throw the burden on the book & feel relieved.' [31 May 1824.]

Her conservatism generated a fierce pride in family, a stubborn adherence to church, king and country, and an inability to empathise with the sufferings of the poor or admit the justice of the democratic spirit which was abroad in the years of the French Revolution. Nevertheless, in education, travel and not least in her determination to live her later life openly as a lesbian with a woman of her choice, Anne can be seen as a trail-blazer for the emancipation of women from the mores of her day. She became the first woman to be elected to the committee of the Halifax branch of the Literary and Philosophical Society because of her academic contributions to that society. She managed her estate, dealt with the business of farming, and developed coal-mines on her land. Much of her working life was spent out of doors, supervising workmen and, at times, tackling some of the physical tasks herself.

The romantic element in her nature drove her to explore the wilder parts of the world, to see things for herself and commit her travels to the pages of her journal for future reference and her own enjoyment. Whatever social approval or disapproval Anne earned in her lifetime and, indeed, since her death, her journals will surely guarantee her a place in history as a woman of outstanding courage, fearless enough to approach life on her own terms and fashion it to her liking, according to the nature which, as she saw it, God had endowed her.

Anne was born on 3 April 1791 in my home town of Halifax, West Yorkshire, during that turbulent period of history when revolutionary and radical ideals and actions were changing the nature of political and economic structures in Western society. Her father, Captain Jeremy Lister, had served in the American War of Independence and was wounded at the battle of Lexington. In 1788 he married Rebecca Battle, a young heiress from Welton, a small village near North Cave in the East Riding of Yorkshire. They had four sons, three of whom died at early ages, and two daughters, Anne and Marian. In 1813, the fourth son, Jeremy, died from drowning at Fermoy in Eire, whilst serving in the army there. It was as a result of his death that Anne was to inherit Shibden Hall and its estate. Anne had spent many happy childhood days there and in 1815, at the age of twenty-four and as the putative heir to Shibden, she went to live there permanently with her Uncle James and Aunt Anne, unmarried brother and sister. She was relieved to escape her parental home at Market Weighton, where she had been unhappy for a long time.

During the early adult years of her life at Shibden, Anne was dependent financially on her uncle and aunt with only occasional help from her father who was usually insolvent himself. The work involved in helping to run the estate was not particularly onerous for her and the liberal attitude of both her uncle and aunt towards their talented and unconventional niece allowed her a great deal of freedom to follow her own inclinations. She was able to spend a great deal of time on self-education, travel and her hobbies of walking, riding, playing the flute and shooting. To those who did not know her well, and even to some who did, she appeared eccentric. That her nickname, amongst the rougher elements of Halifax, was 'Gentleman Jack' is indicative of the fact that her masculine appearance and behaviour was sufficient to cause comment.

Anne's status in the town, as a member of the only land-owning family in the district, gave her a distinct social advantage over enterprising local families who had grown wealthy from profits made through opportunities provided by new advances in the manufacturing industries. Although they were by many degrees wealthier than the Listers, these entrepreneurs could not lay claim to the ancient lineage enjoyed by the owners of Shibden Hall, which reached back to the early fourteenth century. Anne was snobbishly aware of the high status she and her family enjoyed in the town and considered it a great condescension on her part if she socialised with the less elite, but eminently respectable, middle-class families in the town. The trenchant remarks she confided to her journal indicate the dissatisfaction she felt in having to seek company among those who were not, as she saw it, her social equal.

Anne compensated for the limitations of Halifax social life by embarking upon improving her education under the tuition of the Rev. Mr Knight, the Vicar of Halifax, studying Greek, Latin, French, mathematics, geometry and history, as well as setting herself a demanding list of English literary texts. Her masters of style were Gibbon and Rousseau, the latter of whom she particularly admired, and her journal, in its qualities of honesty and explicitness, was an emulation of his *Confessions*. Indeed, in her journal entry for Wednesday 20 August, 1823, she quotes from Rousseau: '*Je sens mon coeur et je connais les hommes. Je ne suis fait comme aucun de ceux j'ais vus; je croix n'etre fait comme aucun de ceux qui existent*'. [I know my own heart and understand my fellow man. But I am made unlike anyone I have ever met. I dare to say I am like no one in the whole world.]

For this volume of excerpts from Anne Lister's journals I have concentrated on the years 1816–24, the most emotionally dramatic period of her life, during which the development of two of her most significant relationships with women, Mariana Lawton and Isabella Norcliffe, is chronicled in detail. What is also brilliantly depicted is the social milieu in which she moved, particularly in the town of Halifax and the city of York. The people in Anne's circle are brought to life by her accounts of their day-to-day lives, their intrigues and the petty gossip-mongering that was endemic amongst such closely knit communities.

In 1816, the date at which this book commences, Anne was twenty-five and had come to terms psychologically and emotionally with her own sexuality, her 'oddity' as she called it. Her journal entry for Monday 29 January, 1821 expresses her feelings about her sexual orientation: '*Burnt Mr Montagu's farewell verses that no trace of any man's admiration may remain. It is not meet for me. I love and only love the fairer sex and thus, beloved by them in turn, my heart revolts from any other love than theirs.*'

This is an explicit statement of lesbian love and one to which she remained true to the day she died. It was also the case that she was 'beloved by them in turn'. Throughout her life she had no difficulty in attaching to herself the passionate and jealous affection of a number of women whose love she returned in varying degrees of intensity.

There was, for Anne, an element of suffering during these

years which stemmed from her relationship with M— (Mariana Lawton née Belcombe), daughter of a York medical practitioner. The two women had first met in 1812, when Anne was twenty-one and M— twenty-two. Anne had quickly fallen passionately in love with M—, who returned her love, and for four years they had enjoyed an idyllically happy sexual affair, finding as much time and as many opportunities as they could to be together. In that era two women friends sharing a bed was not uncommon, no eyebrows were raised, no sly insinuations expressed. The prevailing culture of 'romantic friendship' provided the perfect cover for love of a much deeper kind between women.

This idyll of lesbian love was shattered, however, when M—, in order to satisfy the conventions of the day and to enjoy the material comforts his wealth could provide, accepted a proposal of marriage from Charles Lawton (C— of the journal), a wealthy widower of Lawton Hall, Cheshire. Although Anne was bitterly hurt by this betrayal, the two women kept up a clandestine relationship for several years, as well as maintaining a lengthy correspondence, much of it in the esoteric code invented by Anne to disguise her intimate life with women.

The other love of Anne's life during these years was Isabella Norcliffe, whom Anne met in York c.1809–10. Isabella (Tib of the journals) born in 1785, was six years older than Anne. She was the eldest child of Lieutenant-Colonel Thomas Norcliffe Dalton and his wife, Ann. Their country home was Langton Hall in the small, picturesque village of Langton, near Malton, a market town situated between York and the east coast town of Scarborough. They also had a town house in York. Like Anne, Isabella was never to marry and at one time she had entertained hopes of becoming Anne's life-partner. However, she had been instrumental in introducing M— to Anne and, in so doing, quickly found that the intensity of the new relationship precluded any realisation of her dream of a future life with Anne.

The point at which Anne's story begins in this book, 14 August 1816, has not been an arbitrary decision on my part. The early journals, from 11 August 1806 to 22 February 1810, were written before Anne had met Mariana Belcombe. The journals that would presumably have covered the period from 23 February 1810 to 13 August 1816 are missing. Therefore, 14 August 1816 is the first available extract in which Mariana appears. She is now the wife of Charles Lawton and Anne Lister has been left broken-hearted.

Mariana Belcombe and Charles Lawton were married on 9 March 1816 at the small medieval church of St Michael-le-Belfry which nestled in the shadow of its bigger sister church, York Minster. Masochistically, Anne not only attended the ceremony but, together with Mariana's sister, Anne (Nantz) Belcombe, accompanied Mariana to her new home. They were to be with Mariana for the first six months of the marriage, following the custom of the day, in certain social circles, of helping a new bride to settle in the marital home where all might be strange and unfamiliar to her.

The newlyweds and their entourage left York after their wedding and their first night was spent at the Bridgewater Arms hotel in Manchester. Later, in recounting the details to a friend in Paris, Anne recalled the anguish she felt at the thought of the sexual union between Charles and Mariana: *'I arranged the time of getting off to bed the first night. Left Mrs Barlow to judge what I felt for I had liked M— much.'* [10 December 1824.]

In August 1816, five months after their marriage, the Lawtons, still apparently on their protracted honeymoon and still accompanied by Anne Lister and Anne Belcombe, were in Buxton, a spa town in Derbyshire famous for the restorative powers of its spring waters.

Helena Whitbread, 2010

Tun. 21 Aug.t 3 ½ p.m. 1822.

How! a cow! love g.t dear! et.c 6
kpt. watch! it stunk away — How few & high! feel! on g.t c.l ha. in
u were bush! away — yet stile one melanc.? point of union un!.
in devol.t ; a time she ha. died! it do swet.?, my heart stile linger
t. do. did. not blows this? & screach.t memory is disturb! — At oh! i
k.– "Je sens mon cœur, et je connois les hommes. Je ne suis fait
n'être fait comme aucun de ceux qui existent."

1816

Wednesday 14 August [Buxton]

You descend to Buxton down a very steep narrow road with an ill-fenced off precipice (the case in many other parts of the road) on your right. The appearance of the town is very singular – surrounded by rude, bleak, barren lime-stone mountains covered with lime-kilns. The Crescent[1] is situated so low & so hid from view, you hardly see the chimnies till you drive round the back & come into the area in front. We went to the Great hotel[2] – had a sitting-room downstairs. C— preferred it on account of seeing the people as they walked along the Piazza. Ordered dinner immediately and devoured a brace of Moor-game which were excellent but dear (6s) in consequence of the moors being so strictly preserved ... Anne [Nantz Belcombe, Mariana's sister] and Watson [Mariana's maid] have a double-bedded room – I a tolerably good single one opposite – 10s per week – up I know not how many flights of stairs. All rather tired & went to bed early. Anne sat by my bedside & lay by me upon the bed till 3 in the morning – *I teasing & behaving rather amorously to her. She would gladly have got into bed or done anything of the loving kind I asked her.*

Thursday 15 August [Buxton]

[After an exhausting day's sightseeing] ... We got back at 7. All delighted with our day's excursion. C— hardly spoke as we returned & would have been very much hors de queue if we had not coaxed him out of it. He told us how faint & sick & quere [sic] he had felt in Speedwell mine – he thought he should have died while he was in the boat. It certainly was very vaultish & the atmosphere not agreeable. *Anne sat by my bedside till 2. I talked about the feeling to which she gave rise. Lamented my fate. Said I should never marry. Could not like men. Ought not to like women. At the same time apologizing for my inclination that way. By diverse arguments made out a pitiful story altogether & roused poor Anne's sympathy to tears.*

Friday 16 August [Buxton]

A very rainy day & Buxton looked very dull. Took a few turns every now & then under the Piazza. Tasted the well-water – & it has nothing at all unpleasant to the taste but the mouthful I took made me rather sick. Went to Moore's circulating library in the Crescent – found nothing but novels & some of them none of the best nor least exceptionable. Saw the ball & card rooms which are in the house which are both very handsome & well adapted to their respective purposes. There was a ball in the evening but we did not think it worth the trouble going – the fuss of dressing at 9 to break up, according to rule, precisely as the clock strikes 11 . . . Anne came in to my room at night & staid perhaps an hour. *I contradicted all I said last night. Argued upon the absurdity & impossibility of it & wondered how she could be such a gull as to believe it. She said she had really been very sorry for me & said she thought I hardly behaved well to make such a fool of her. I begged pardon, etc.*

The party left Buxton on 17 August and returned to Lawton Hall. There are no journal pages to cover the next few months but Anne's index for that period indicates that on 20 August she and Anne Belcombe finally left Charles and Mariana to begin their post-honeymoon life together at

Lawton Hall. They spent three days at the Newcastle-under-Lyme home of Mariana's brother, Dr Steph Belcombe, and his wife Harriet, before returning to their respective homes – Anne Belcombe to her parents' house in Petergate, York and Anne Lister to her uncle's home, Shibden Hall, Halifax. It is obvious from the cryptic index entries that Anne Lister had continued to woo Anne B while at Newcastle-under-Lyme, for on 21 August she enters a line in code in her index, which states: '*All but connected with Anne*'. In November, Anne Belcombe had been staying again at Lawton Hall with Mariana and Charles. On her way back to York, she broke her journey at Halifax to spend some time with Anne at Shibden Hall. Her visit lasted three weeks.

Thursday 7 November [Halifax]

Anne arrived by the evening coach at the Union Cross & got here about 7. She brought me a kind letter from Mrs H[arriet] S. B[elcombe] & one from M— (Lawton) *with a couple of white muslin morning waists* [a slip or underdress] *made by M—*. Anne looking well. It snowed & was stormy all the way as she came from Manchester . . . On getting up in the morning [I] found the ground covered with snow an inch or two thick – the 1st we have had this year or rather this winter.

Friday 8 November [Halifax]

Nantz [Anne Belcombe] and I walked over to Pye Nest, & sat with Mrs Edwards an hour. On our return met my Aunt Anne at Mrs Veitch's & got home to dinner at 3. In the course of conversation Nantz told me, M— now thinks it would have been better if C— & she had gone to Lawton tête-à-tête after the wedding. *Anne & I lay awake last night till 4 in the morning. I let her into my penchant for the ladies. Expatiated on the nature of my*

3

feelings towards her & hers towards me. Told her that she ought not deceive herself as to the nature of my sentiments & the strictness of my intentions towards her. I could feel the same in at least two more instances & named her sister, Eliza, as one, saying that I did not dislike her in my heart but rather admired her as a pretty girl. I asked Anne if she liked me the less for my candour, etc., etc. She said no, kissed me & proved by her manner she did not.

The atmosphere between the two women in snow-bound Shibden was becoming intense. Nantz, or, to give her her full name, Sarah Anne Sherson Belcombe, was not an eighteen-year-old ingénue. She was a thirty-one-year-old unmarried woman, six years older than Anne, and probably had no experience in matters of sex. She was intrigued by Anne's pleading of her cause – but at the same time could not help but be worried about the finality of going, as Anne Lister put it, '*to the last extremity*' in lovemaking with another woman. Her hesitations began to wear Anne Lister down and she decided to talk to Nantz in a very straightforward way – a tactic which proved successful.

Saturday 9 November [Halifax]

Talking to Anne almost all the morning telling [her] she should either be on or off, that she was acting very unfairly & ought either to make up her mind to let me have a kiss at once or change her manners altogether. I said she excited my feelings in a way that was very unjustifiable unless she meant to gratify them & that, really, that sort of thing made me far from well, as I was then very sick, languid & uncomfortable – not able to relish anything.

Monday 11 November [Halifax]

Had a very good kiss last night. Anne gave it me with pleasure, not thinking it necessary to refuse me any longer.

Anne Belcombe's conscience, however, was bothering her. She was concerned about the question of whether or not sex between members of the same sex was counted as sinful.

Wednesday 13 November [Halifax]

She asked if I thought the thing was wrong – if it was forbidden in the bible & said she felt quere [sic] when she heard Sir Thomas Horton[3] mentioned. I dexterously parried all these points – said Sir T. H.'s case was quite a different thing. That was positively forbidden & signally punished in the bible – that the other was certainly not named. Besides, Sir T. H. was proved to be a perfect man by his having a child & it was infamous to be connected with both sexes – but that [there] were beings who were so unfortunate as to be not quite so perfect &, supposing they kept to one side [of] the question, was there no excuse for them. It would be hard to deny them a gratification of this kind. I urged in my own defence the strength of natural feeling & instinct, for so I might call it, as I had always had the same turn from infancy. That it had been known to me, as it were, by inclination. That I had never varied & no effort on my part had been able to counteract it. That the girls liked me & had always liked me. That I had never been refused by anyone & that, without attempting to account for the thing, I hoped it might, under such circumstances be excused.

Anne Belcombe accepted Anne's rationalisation of the fears she had expressed although secretly Anne Lister felt that the sin, on her part, was more in deceiving Mariana by having sex with another woman, a thing which she had promised faithfully not to do. Her guilt, however, was soon assuaged in the face of further temptation and the affair continued.

Thursday 14 November [Halifax]

Just before tea I told [Nantz] the anecdote of the ancients using lead plates to prevent pain in their knees – the expression which I use, &

*which she understands, to mean desire. She said I wanted them. I
said she would soon take them off. She said yes, perhaps she should.*

As the visit wore on, it became obvious that Aunt Anne was
fretting about the length of her stay. Anne, although embar-
rassed at having to hint to Nantz that it was time for her to
return to York, was nevertheless also relieved.

Thursday 28 November [Halifax]

Anne & I had a good deal of conversation just before we got
into bed. She evidently wished to stay till after the musical festival [at York]. I said she ought, by all means, to go to it. Said if
this was my house I would not let her leave me these three
months, etc., but that it was not. That I did not feel myself
<u>quite</u> at home. That I could not feel quite so much so with my
uncle & aunt as I could have done with my father & mother. I
gave no encouragement to the idea of her prolonging her stay
but very gently hinted advice to the contrary.

Friday 29 November [Halifax]

*A long prose just before getting into bed. Talked of the abuse I had
had for romance, enthusiasm, flattery, manners like those of a gentleman, being too particularly attentive to the ladies, etc. That in
consequence I had resolved to change & had succeeded in becoming
much more cool & cautious in my general intercourse with people &
much less lavish of cordiality & civility . . . I asked her if, after all this*
[their lovemaking], *she would own being in love with me. She said
no, she did not like the term but clasped me in [her] arms. We kissed
& fell asleep.*

Anne and her Uncle James walked into Halifax with Nantz
the following day and saw her safely into the Highflier
coach. The experience had left Anne in no doubt that Nantz

6

would never be able to take Mariana's place in her life. Nantz had done everything she could to ingratiate herself with Anne and Anne was appreciative but her charms did not match up to those of her sister, Mariana. However, as Anne cynically recorded, '*I ought not to complain. Superior charms might not be so easily come-at-able on such easy terms*'.[4]

The return to her daily routine at Shibden Hall brought on a fit of restlessness in Anne. During December the snow fell relentlessly and Anne began to plan a method of securing her independence. On Christmas Eve she and her aunt had a long, confidential talk during which Anne expressed her frustrations about her dependency.

Wednesday 25 December [Halifax]

Sat up last night talking to my aunt. *Talking of my father's* [financial] *affairs. That I seemed, as it were, a log upon my uncle & aunt, who had so much to do for me. Wished I could persuade my friends to let me try & do something for myself. [I] said I was sure I could make two or three hundred pounds if I might go off for 5 or 6 months & do as I liked, hinting, or rather covertly alluding, as I have often done before, to my scheme of rambling, begging, and eventually gambling . . . I steadily persisted, of course, in not telling what I thought of doing but said it would require much nous & much spirit & was quite a speculation which I would breathe to nobody unless it answered. I said I knew my aunt & my friends would say no if they heard what it was but that it was nothing against my conscience or that I could not afterwards think of with pleasure. I talked till my aunt said she was not averse to my doing anything that was likely to answer but advised telling my uncle, which I said was impossible. She guessed I meant to go on the stage or sing for a few months in the season. I said no. She then said perhaps I meant to take pupils or get to be a clerk in some office. (She must have some idea I should not scruple to throw off my petticoats.) I said I had no thought of either of these. Neither would do at all. Together with much more of this kind of conversation, I think I could gain my point if I chose.*

It was a wildcat scheme which never came to fruition but the mere fact of going so far as to discuss it with her aunt showed Anne's desperation to escape her dependent situation. The next day, Christmas Day, sanity prevailed. The family, including Captain Lister who had arrived at Shibden Hall on the twenty-third of December, went sedately to morning church and all 'staid the sacrament'.

1817

Friday 21 March [Halifax]

In the afternoon, *mending my black silk petticoat & black worsted stocking*. In the evening, wrote a letter to Marian,[1] Market Weighton. A fine, cold, frosty day . . . The flute for ½ hour after tea.

Wednesday 2 April [Halifax]

Began this morning to sit, before breakfast, in my drawers put on with gentlemen's braces I bought for 2/6 on 27 March 1809 & my old black waistcoat & dressing-gown.

Tuesday 15 April [Halifax]

Did not sleep well last night & was, besides, disturbed about 4 by the cook, who awoke me to say a shabby-looking man was stealing the hens. She spoke to him out of the Green room window & the hens escaped for the time . . . In the morning, walked to Halifax, put my letter into the post, bought a horse pistol (pr.16/6) at Adams & Mitchell's; a lb of very large shot, 4d., & 2 ozs powder, 3d. . . . Not much sun. The wind exceedingly high & the dust blown about so violently as to make it almost impossible to face it.

Tuesday 22 April [Halifax]

Walked with my aunt to Halifax & went with her, shopping. Called at Northgate.[2] Went to Whitley's, the stationer's. Got

Droiiet's 'God Save the King' . . . Then to the library . . . The flute ½ hour before tea & also ½ hour after, trying Droiiet's variation, which I think I can soon play. Mr Whitley told me that Sugden is reputed a very good player & the best hereabouts. Said it was too difficult for him & he durst not venture on it. I never heard him play & this gives me no great opinion of him. By the way, Whitley told me that this Droiiet, a Frenchman, had made 20 guineas a week all last winter by his flute playing in London.

Thursday 24 April [Halifax]

My uncle Joseph & I had a good deal of talk on family affairs. *I advised him to make his will . . . He gave me five pounds. I told him it was acceptable for that I had very little from my father, & that my uncle & aunt gave me nearly all I had . . .* Very windy as I came home & the dust blown in my face most terribly. After supper, read aloud.

Saturday 26 April [Halifax]

Had a letter from M—, Lawton. All going on swimmingly. *As yet C— all attention. Gives her all her strengthening medicines & washes her back with cold water every morning, & in spite of home concerns, going to the sea for two months. All this in hopes of a son & heir.*

Tuesday 29 April [Halifax]

In the afternoon, took my uncle's letter . . . & after seeing it marked in the office, gave it to the boy who was just setting off on horseback with the London post. Staid half an hour at the library. Called at Whitley's, the booksellers, to pay for a blank book &, saying I should like to hear Sugden play on the flute, Mr Whitley said he was sure he would be happy to play any time I liked if I would fix a time, & next Tuesday afternoon was named. *I repent this, uncertain how far the thing is quite correct. That is, how far it is sufficiently keeping up my dignity. It is fixed now & I must make the best of it, resolving not to buy music at this rate any more.*

Wednesday 30 April [Halifax]

Had a letter from Marian (Market Weighton) *directed by my father & containing an inclosure* [sic] *of five guineas, East Riding bank notes. I read my uncle & aunt the letter & shewed* [sic] *them four of the notes but said nothing of the fifth. This is a sort of dissimulation which my heart does not approve, & I already repent having practised it, but it is not pleasant not to have a sixpence but what they know of, as I may occasionally want a pound or two extraordinarily* . . . Dawdled away the afternoon *looking over & unripping some old gowns & petticoats for my aunt to make into wearable petticoats for me.*

Friday 2 May [Halifax]

Immediately after breakfast, walked to Halifax (Betty being cleaning my room) . . . Sat an hour with Mrs Rawson.[3] She mentioned the great alarm now prevailing at Leeds & other places about vaccination, several children having, not withstanding, been seized with the smallpox. Many were having their children inoculated & in many instances the infants had been taken in spite of previous vaccinations which had been pronounced perfectly good at the time. It seems, however, to be observed that those who have been vaccinated have the smallpox more favourably & much more mildly. Mrs Rawson also mentioned Mr Rawson having been in York at the Assizes where, &, when, tho' he had heard the thing before, it was the common topic of conversation that M— was parted from C— & returned to her father & mother; that she & C— were the most miserable couple in the world, & that, in fact, he had little or nothing; that he had killed his first wife; had not the very best character; in short, the old [story] all over again. I pretended to smile at the strange incongruity of reports & made the matter look as well as I could but surely, in spite of anything I can say, people must think there would not be all these reports afloat without some reason or other.

Saturday 3 May [Halifax]

Had a letter from M— . . . I am to begin my letter to M— as usual but not send it till the latter end of next week, or the Monday of the following week instead of next Monday. C— 'has taken it into his head lately to go for the letters & sometimes we do not get them till 12 or 1 . . . Till this whim ceases, perhaps a little irregularity may be as well.'

Monday 5 May [Halifax]

After supper, firing off the pistol, that had been heavily charged above 3 weeks, out of my room window. The report was tremendous. It bounded out of my hand, forced itself thro' the window, & broke the lead & 2 panes of glass. My hand felt stunned for some time.

Tuesday 6 May [Halifax]

Had a note from Miss Caroline Greenwood (Cross-hills) to ask me to drink tea (quite in a free way) tomorrow. Wrote a note back to accept the invitation, thinking I could not well do otherwise. In the afternoon, went to the library. Paid a bill for my aunt to Miss Stead, the matua [*sic*] maker & called at Whitley's. Bought 3 sticks of sealing-wax, & then Mr Sugden came. Went upstairs for five minutes & heard him play a couple of airs without book. He said he was a very bad player without book, that his flute was dry, he had not touched it for 3 weeks. I complimented him highly &, as far as I could judge, he deserved it. His tone & taste both good, particularly the former. I asked his terms for teaching. A guinea a quarter for 1 lesson a week & a guinea & a half per quarter for 2 lessons per week. He is quite self-taught. He was a fustian-cutter by trade, but this grew so bad he gave it up &, being a single man, supports himself by teaching singing, the flute, or French horn, & writing out music for anyone. I rather think his living is but spare. *This adventure has passed off more satisfactorily than I expected.*

Wednesday 7 May [Halifax]

A ¼ before 6, went to drink tea at the Greenwoods' at Cross-hills . . . Music after tea. Several hits on the musical glasses by Miss Caroline Greenwood. A single song by Miss Susan Greenwood. An Italian duet by Miss Susan Greenwood & Miss A. Staveley. The 2nd of 'See From the Ocean Rising', with Miss Susan Greenwood. 'The Bewildered Maid' & the 2nd to one of Braham's [sic] ditty with Miss A. Staveley by myself. Miss Susan Greenwood sings very fairly but was frightened. Miss A. Staveley is said to be very scientific both in playing & singing. Of the former I could not judge. In the latter she is tame, not always in the best tune, & appears to have slender vocal powers from nature, i.e. not much naturally good voice. Miss Caroline Greenwood enlarged on the value she set on my notes & rally'd me on the shortness of my last. She would like to have long ones from me & longs to see some of my letters. Regretted the 'invisible enchantment' that kept me so closely at Shibden. Often longed to put on her things & join me when she saw me go past, & threatened to do so some time or other. In fact, she makes a dead set, to all which I return no encouragement, but am very civil. Miss S. Staveley made several bold pushes for me to sing with her sister & to bring on a visiting, but I took not the smallest notice of any of them . . . They were a vulgar set & I was [glad] to get home a little before 10. I had a pleasant walk, the night was so fine & warm. Miss S. Staveley was in anxious expectation of seeing something from my pen, as she & everyone made sure of my intention to publish. The people seem wonderfully impressed with the idea now that I keep myself so snug at home.

Monday 12 May [Halifax]

5 chaises, a stagecoach that commonly runs between Leeds & Halifax, the Blackpool mail (a long coach, so called in derision), the Wakefield car, a sort of tea-cart topped something in the same way as a sociable to keep off the rain, all passed here this morning, filled with voters for the Registrarship of Wakefield. The contending parties, Mr Frank Hawksworth & Mr Fenton Scott. The report of this evening is in favour of the former. 2 more chaises passed to Wakefield in the afternoon.

Tuesday 13 May [Halifax]

Between 1 & 2, the 1st 7 propositions of the 1st book of Euclid, with which I mean to renew my acquaintance & to proceed diligently in the hope that, if I live, I may some time attain a tolerable proficiency in mathematical studies. I would rather be a philosopher than a polyglot, & mean to turn my attention, eventually & principally, to natural philosophy. For the present, I mean to devote my mornings, before breakfast to Greek, & afterwards, till dinner, to divide the time equally between Euclid & arithmetic till I have waded thro' Walkingham, when I shall recommence my long neglected algebra. I must read a page or 2 of French now & then when I can. The afternoons & evenings are set apart for general reading, for walking, ½ an hour, or ¾, practice on the flute.

Anne's plan of study and self-education was three-fold: first, in an age when university education was denied to women,

Anne wished to educate herself up to, and above, the standard of most men, particularly in the Classics. Secondly, she did have ambitions to write, as Halifax society had suspected and, therefore, wished to equip herself for a career in letters. Thirdly, she needed to keep her mind occupied whilst living in virtual seclusion at Shibden Hall. Until she inherited the entire estate and became financially independent, she was financially dependent on her aunt and uncle who were becoming aged and needed her support in dealing with its management. Anne's move to Halifax cut her off for long periods from her friends in and around York, the Belcombe family, the Duffins and the Norcliffes. She was thus a lonely young woman, particularly as she could find no one in Halifax whom she deemed to be her equal, either socially or intellectually. She moved as little as possible in the limited social milieu of the small Pennine town of Halifax, and she often disparaged the rather unsophisticated female company available to her. She began to get a reputation as a snob and a 'loner', and people began to resent her standoffishness. At the same time they stood in awe of her undoubted intellectuality and her reputation as a *bas bleu* or bluestocking. As the Listers were of very good social standing in the town, it was deemed a compliment if one could be on 'calling terms' with them, or include them as guests at social gatherings. There was great rivalry amongst the young ladies of the town to be counted as an intimate friend of Anne Lister's.

However Anne – except for one or two instances – refused their offers of friendship. Her emotional life was closely involved with Mariana Lawton (one of the Belcombe sisters, now married to Charles Lawton of Lawton Hall, Cheshire) whom she called M—, in the journals. The two women had enjoyed a deep friendship and sexual liaison for a number of years. Originally they had planned their future together, but M— had married Charles Lawton (C— of the journals), a man much older than herself and a widower, who was rich enough to give her a comfortable style of life. Anne was, and remained, deeply hurt at M—'s betrayal but, despite this, continued the relationship in the hope that C— would die, leaving M— a young widow with perhaps one or two children. The two women would then combine fortunes and lives, and bring up the children together.

However, in January 1817, C— had found a letter from Anne which hinted at this arrangement and he became extremely jealous and suspicious of her. This put obstacles in the way of the women's friendship but despite this the two carried on a correspondence and were able to meet from time to time, although it was not possible for Anne to visit M— at her home at Lawton Hall, Cheshire. M—'s family, the Belcombes, however, lived in York and Anne was a regular visitor to their home when M— contrived to visit at the same time.

Thus, Anne was playing a patient waiting game until M— was free to set up a domestic household with her at Shibden, where they would live together for the rest of their lives. Meanwhile, she continued her day-to-day routine of study, walking, limited social visiting, and writing long letters to M—, for which she devised an esoteric code in order to prevent C— from reading the contents. Anne also used this code in her journal to pour out her feelings in privacy.

Monday 19 May [Halifax]

C— continues terribly jealous of me. M— thinks we had better be cautious lest he should forbid her writing to me, & therefore desires to hear from me every other Tuesday, as there will be little comfort for her & me as long as he lives & God knows how long that may be.

Thursday 22 May [Halifax]

I shall write to M— this morning & send it on Saturday or Sunday. She wishes to hear from me every other Tuesday till C—'s jealous fit subsides a bit, till he gives up fetching the letters himself & till we can, therefore, write in more security. *At present we are in constant fear of him forbidding her writing to me at all.* God help those who are tied to such people. Wish the day was over . . . If I was once to give way to idleness I should be wretched. Nothing but keeping my mind so intent upon study can divert the melancholy reflections which would constantly prey upon me on account of M—. Alas! They are even now a source of bitterness & disquiet that words can ill describe. Wrote 2½pp. to M—, chiefly in our secret alphabet which I have lately, in my letters to her, used a great deal.

Wednesday 28 May [Halifax]

Had a note from Mrs Edwards (Pye Nest), to ask me to a supper party and to stay all night on the 4th of next month. Wrote an answer, to be ready for the post in the afternoon, declining parties, but saying I hoped to spend a day with her in a friendly way as soon as my aunt returned from Harrogate . . . *Sat up talking to my uncle till 11 o'clock about getting married . . . I took care to say, however, that I never intended to marry at all. I cannot make out whether he suspects my situation towards M— . . . I begin to despair that M— & I will ever get together.*

Sunday 1 June [Halifax]

Spent the afternoon in mending some of my things for the wash. After tea, read aloud sermons 13 & 14 of Alison's. A fine day, the pleasantest we have had this year, & the first time I have thrown aside my winter things, *having changed my black cloth spencer and straw hat for a black silk spencer and common straw hat.* I have almost made up my mind always to wear black.

Monday 9 June [Halifax]

Read . . . Demosthenes & . . . Leland's Translation. This is the 4th Greek work I have read thro' & I certainly feel considerably improved. But I am dissatisfied with myself for not having lately got up in a morning so early as I thought. It grieves me that I am ever in bed after 5.

> In June of this year (1817), Anne begins to mention Isabella Norcliffe, a friend of even longer standing than M—. The Norcliffe family lived at Langton Hall, Langton, Malton near York, and were wealthy landowners. Anne visited them regularly as they were part of the York society in which Anne moved when she was there, along with the Belcombes, the Duffins and Miss Marsh, another old friend.
>
> Isabella Norcliffe and Anne had been particularly close until M— had been introduced to Anne by Isabella, after which M— took first place in Anne's affections. After M—'s marriage, Isabella's friendship resumed much of its old importance for Anne, but she soon became disillusioned with Isabella's heavy drinking habits. Anne's commitment to Isabella weakened as time went on, but in 1817 Anne's enforced estrangement from M— caused her to turn her affections temporarily towards Isabella.

Monday 16 June [Halifax]

Had a long letter . . . from Isabella Norcliffe (Naples), dated 25 May 1817. They were to leave Naples the following day for Rome, thence to proceed to Florence, Nice, Berne & Bruxelles on their way home. I am to write by return of post and direct my letter to Turin. She gives a tolerable account of herself &

writes as affectionately as ever. *Ah, my Isabel, you have indeed loved me truly &, after all, perhaps it may be fate that you & I shall get together at last. But on this subject, I dare not think. God knows what is best.*

Monday 23 June [Halifax]

At six o'clock, had some cold veal cutlets, cold new potatoes & cabbage brought in & made a good dinner, after which took 3 cups of tea & enjoyed my late meal exceedingly.

Saturday 28 June [Halifax]

In the evening, between 6 & 7, my father arrived, having come on horseback from Market Weighton. Brought no letters. Walked down to Northgate. Found my Uncle Joseph not quite so well & in low spirits.

Monday 30 June [Halifax]

Had a letter from M— (Lawton) of the 2nd excursion she and Lou[4] made into North Wales the week before last . . . They very much admired Lady Eleanor Butler & Miss Ponsonby's cottage in Llangollen.[5] M— *wished we had such an one. I now begin to think seriously that she & I will never get together. Strange to say, I seem as if I was weening [sic] myself from wishing it . . . I have no fault to find with M— as to her conduct but her letters have ceased to be those best calculated to keep alive my affections, & the present impossibility of our seeing each other may have made a wide difference in both before we meet again.*

Friday 11 July [Halifax]

As I was getting into bed I began thinking how little confidence I had in M— & how little likely it was that we should ever get together. I was very low. I felt that my happiness depended on having some female companion whom I could love & depend upon & my thoughts naturally turned to Isabella. I got out her picture & looked at it for ten minutes with considerable emotion. I almost wished to persuade myself I could manage her temper as to be happy with her.

Anne, while on the whole despising much about Halifax and the people who lived there, was nevertheless sensitive to the social niceties and to the opinion of the townspeople. She was aware that there was much speculation about her in the town, mainly because of her pronounced masculinity in appearance and manner. On her daily walks people wondered aloud whether she was a man or a woman. Her own circle, eager to form social connections with the Lister family, viewed Anne's tendency to 'take up' serious, almost obsessive friendships with young women with scandalised amusement. There was something malicious in this attitude and Anne was fully aware of the tendency to 'bait' her on the subject of her favourites. Most of the time she was able to shrug off the scandal and petty gossip, but there were moments when she was undeniably hurt by it.

On the other hand, the York circle in which she moved (members of which had known Anne since childhood), provided her with an atmosphere of security, tolerance and affectionate acceptance. York was a place of refuge where she could relax away from the critical gaze and speculation of the people of her newly adopted home town. It must also be borne in mind that Anne, herself, could be extremely cutting and at times exhibited a degree of snobbery which inevitably made her enemies in Halifax.

Monday 16 July [Halifax]

My uncle & aunt drank tea at Mrs Prescott's (Clare Hall) to meet a large party. My father & I staid at home. Indeed, I was not asked, I suppose from its being known that I decline parties.

At all events, they ought to have given me the option of refusing. Flute ¼ hour between 9 & 10. My uncle & aunt got home a little after 10. Neither Mrs nor Miss Prescott made an inquiry after me that probably their not inviting me was an intentional omission, & indeed, I know not what for.

Tuesday 12 August [Halifax]

About 11, my father walked with me to Mr Knight's,[6] where we parted . . . Mr Knight, being going out to dinner, I had not time to get a satisfactory answer about the method of treating fractional sums. On mentioning my wish to become his pupil again, he said he could not take me till after Michaelmas (10 Oct.) but would then let me have an hour from 3 to 4 every other day, according to my desire.

Monday 18 August [Halifax]

My uncle Joseph rode up & sat on horseback at the gate near ½ hour. My father gave me seven pounds which led me to reckon up my money & I found I had altogether twenty-eight pounds, seven shillings & fivepence. Such a sum I have not had together of years, never since I went to Bath in 1813. I take good care to let nobody know I have so much. Had no time for Euclid but looked into Emerson's mechanics for ¼ hour, as I wish to prepare myself a little for Dalton's lectures which are to begin on Wednesday & which I mean to attend.

Tuesday 19 August [Halifax]

Just after tea read aloud to my aunt the very favourable review of *Lallah Rookh; an Oriental Romance* by Thomas Moore . . . The extracts from this poetic romance are very beautiful. John Oates of the Stump came between 7 & 8, & staid till near 10. His errand was about a pair of spectacles for my aunt. I was surprised to find him so good a workman & optician – entirely self-taught.

Tho' the wonder is lessened by the discovery of his having had so liberal an education. He learnt Latin & a little Greek at Hipperholme school & afterwards became a good arithmetician & algebraist as well as pretty well versed in Euclid under the tuition of Mr Ogden, then of the charity school at Boothtown. What a pity that such a man should [have] been put apprentice to a cardmaker, then, this not answering, have turned tanner & should now be bankman at a coalpit. The pit, to be sure, is his own. At least, he & John Green of Mytholm have jointly taken it off my Uncle Lister . . . John Oates only took up the study of optics & mathematical instrument-making about a dozen years ago. He was then a tanner & had little time to spare – frequently kept at his work till 12 at night &, even then, got up at 3 in the morning to pursue his favourite occupation. He has made several telescopes, electrifying machines, etc. His family have been tenants to our family for several generations. He now lives in a neat house that he built some years ago at the Stump & is comfortable in his circumstances owing to the frugality of his parents who saved their money at the Mytholm public house & by his own prudence in keeping what he had. He has taught himself optics chiefly from Martin's works.

Wednesday 20 August [Halifax]

Just after breakfast received a small box (carriage 1/6) by the coach from York . . . containing the little alabaster Cupid on a bed of roses which Isabel mentioned having sent me, in her letter from Florence. It's an elegant little figure & I am most pleased with it. Poor Isabel, she never forgets me. Her thoughts & affections are constant & my heart keeps a faithful register. *In spite of all, I think we shall get together at last.*

About this time, Anne began to attend a course of lectures in Halifax and there met a young woman called Miss

Browne. She became infatuated with her and this was to dominate her emotional life almost entirely for the next two years. At the same time as Anne wished the friendship to become more intimate, she was also very conscious of the differences in their social background, considering Miss Browne's family to be inferior to the Listers – Miss Browne's father was a self-made businessman. It was this discrimination on Anne's part which incurred the disapprobation of those who were of sufficient standing to be on calling terms with the Listers.

Wednesday 27 August [Halifax]

Went to the lecture at 7. Having all the 4 preceding nights admired Miss Browne, daughter of Mr Copley Browne of Westfield or West Cottage, sat just before her. Handed her several things to look at & contrived to get into conversation with her after the lecture was over. The lecture being longer than usual & I staying a good while afterwards to look at the apparatus, or rather at Miss Browne, did not get home till near 11.

Thursday 28 August [Halifax]

Did nothing but dream of Miss Browne &, tho' I woke at 6, yet had not resolution to get up but lay dosing [sic] & thinking of the fair charmer. She is certainly very pretty. She seemed evidently not displeased with my attention & I felt all possible inclination to be as foolish as I ever was in former days. In fact, I shall be much better out of the way of the lovely Maria (for such is her name) than in it. Mended the leather covering of my stays till breakfast time.

Anne was prevented from furthering the acquaintanceship with Miss Browne as the latter went on a prolonged visit to Harrogate and the friendship was not resumed until the spring of 1818.

An interesting aspect of Anne's self-presentation was her secretive attitude towards discussing or writing about her clothes. She obviously felt reticent about her dress and appearance and was constantly the subject of criticism from her friends for her shabby and unfashionable wardrobe. She always used her cryptic code in her journal when referring to her clothes. Eventually she came to a decision to wear only black and, apart from a few touches of white on the odd social occasion, she kept to this rule.

Tuesday 2 September [Halifax]

Spent the whole of the morning in vamping up a pair of old black chamois shoes & getting my things ready to go & drink tea at Cliff-hill. As soon as I was dressed, went to drink tea with the Miss Walkers of Cliff-hill. Went in black silk, the 1st time to an evening visit. I have entered upon my plan of always wearing black.

Later in the month of September, Anne visited some friends, the Priestleys, at Haugh-end, just outside Halifax. She had previously paid a visit there with M— before her marriage, and her return there evoked some painful memories.

Saturday 13 September [Halifax (Haugh-end)]

A thousand reflections & recollections crowded on me last night. The last time I slept in this room & in this bed, it was with Mariana, in 1815, the summer of. *Surely no one ever doted on another as I did then on her. I fondly thought my love & happiness would last for ever. Alas, how changed. She has married a blackguard for the sake of his money. We are debarred all intercourse. I am not always satisfied with her. I am often miserable & often wish to try to wean my heart from her & fix more propitiously. There seems little chance of our ever getting together. Tho' I believe she loves me as yet exclusively, the misfortune is, my confidence is not invulnerable.*

Sunday 14 September [Halifax (Haugh-end)]

Before breakfast, props. 24 & 25 lib. Euclid. Mary [Priestley] & I went to Sowerby church in the morning in the carriage with the old people . . . Returned after drinking tea at White Windows . . . Mary & I had a little music. I played & sang a little. *In conversation about economy & keeping house, she told me they last year spent above seven hundred pounds, tho' it was not an expensive year & did not appear that they could live as they do for less.*

Saturday 4 October [Halifax]

Hous'd a couple of loads of oats this afternoon, the 1st corn we have got in this year. My throat & chest better, but not enough to play the flute.

Sunday 5 October [Halifax]

All went to morning church[7] & staid the Sacrament . . . My aunt dined at Northgate. My Uncle Joseph very poorly today . . . told my Aunt Anne he felt he could not live long and mentioned several things respecting his decease – what bills he owed, etc. My Uncle Lister called in [on] his way from afternoon church. My Uncle Joseph gave him his will to bring home. Read the psalms & lessons to myself. After tea, read aloud sermon 15 & . . . my aunt read aloud Sermon 17, Polwhele.

Friday 14 October [Halifax]

Wrote the whole of my journal (except the 1st line) just before getting into bed. Had a cup of strong green tea as I was undressing.

Thursday 16 October [Halifax]

In the evening, looked over an old portfolio of papers, extracts, letters, copies of letters, etc. Began directly after tea & did not leave off till ½ past 10 . . . A wildish, showery day – very cold & thick in the evening. No time for the flute. The general rummage among my letters & papers takes a great deal of time & puts me sadly out of my way – but as I have never had my things fairly set to rights as they ought to be, 'tis high time to begin if I mean to get it done in my lifetime.

Friday 17 October [Halifax]

Spent the whole morning in rummaging out & siding my great canteen that stands in the landing place leading to the upper kitchen chamber.

Monday 3 November [Halifax]

Called to inquire after Mr Knight, whom I supposed not yet recovered from an inflammation in his bowels. Agreeably surprised to find he had preached on Sunday nearly as well as ever again, not having had an inflammation but a tedious passage of gall-stones. He was in agony for 20 hours . . . Finding him afloat again & my Uncle Joseph being going on so well, resumed the subject of my studies – of how much I had forgotten & how little he was to expect, & it was agreed that I should recommence my attendance on him tomorrow at 3 o'clock. I am to go Tuesdays, Thursdays & Saturdays – be there each day at 3 & stay there till 4. I feel happy at the idea of getting into a proper train again & only hope I shall be able to make good progress . . . In the evening, writing out the rough draft of an index to the 3rd vol. of my journal. A remarkably fine day. Beautiful afternoon & evening. The air as mild as new milk . . . Brought my flute home (the newer one) that Whitley has got Sugden to clean up for me. It is much improved & I can now play with pleasure. Flute 20 mins during supper.

Tuesday 4 November [Halifax]

Got to Mr Knight's ¼ after 3 & was with him full an hour & a half. I was silently astonished at myself as well I might. I know not that I was conscious of feeling agitation but something or other seemed to steal away my wits. These questions were all asked as soon as I had done reading Latin. By the time I began with Lucian, my mind was a little recovered & I construed Greek, Mr Knight said, pretty well – a proof, he added, of what he expected, that I had lost less Greek than Latin. He confessed, however, he had not given me the easiest Latin to read. The real fact is Mr Knight does not well remember what progress I had formerly made. I am just now a better Grecian than I ever was in my life. Indeed I have read more Greek within the last year & a half than all I ever read before – & as for Latin, whatever I may have lost is certainly not in construing. It is perhaps in writing it & this was always the worst thing I did, but I had had hardly any practice, having never got ½ through Willymott's particles. Algebra is to come on Thursday. I have lost nothing in this unless a few rules about simple quadratic equations which I had got by rote. I knew nothing, in fact, about the extraction of algebraic roots, should I have stumbled at an algebra long division sum or the regular reduction of algebra fractions. Arithmetic I knew very superficially indeed. Very little of vulgar fractions & nothing of decimals, unless it was to add cyphers in extracting square roots. I think I could hardly manage a cube root. I had done the 1st 6 books of Euclid twice over & just begun mechanics. I have lately done the 1st 6 books of Euclid twice over &, in addition, 30 propositions of the data. However, I have forgotten the little I knew of mechanics, though probably a few days, perhaps hours, will be enough to regain it. Just asked Mrs & the Miss Knights how they did, thinking it civil to do so the 1st time of my going.

Thursday 6 November [Halifax]

Before breakfast, looking over the Greek grammar & Bonnycastle's algebra . . . Went to Mr Knight at 3. The 1st sum he set me was in algebraic addition. Finding I made light of this [he] set me some sums in algebraic long division & fractions. Gave me a couple of algebraic theorems to work. Very easy, & here my examination ended. He said nothing to this effect but I was evidently much better than he expected. It was agreed that Tuesday & Thursday should be mathematical days & Saturday dedicated to the Classics. I am, however, to take him a Latin exercise every time I go. Went to the library & staid near ½ hour, reading Southey's letter (about 40 8vo pp.) to Wm Smith, Esq, MP, on the subject of the speech he had made in the House of Commons, that Southey should be prosecuted for republican sentiments contained in his poem entitled 'Wat Tyler', written when Southey was about 20 (since which time, he says, he has learnt better) & surreptitiously published without his knowledge or consent. The letter is a severe but a very good one.

Anne's plan of serious study with Mr Knight suffered serious interruptions due to the ill-health and eventual death of both her mother and her Uncle Joseph. She was not able to resume her studies until after the New Year, 1818.

Saturday 8 November [Halifax]

Before breakfast, from line 36 to 86, Sophocles' *Electra*. Thomas[8] came up about 9 to say my Uncle Joseph died a few minutes past one this morning. My Aunt Anne went to Northgate immediately after breakfast. My uncle & I followed at 11. Staid till 8 in the evening & returned in a chaise. My Aunt Lister & Aunt Anne had got the meeting over before we got there. My uncle went into the room to them directly, but was so overcome, he was obliged to hurry out again & was several minutes alone in the dining-room before he could compose himself to return. My Aunt Lister has really shewn a great deal of fortitude &, tho' very much affected, was quite as well as one could expect. She said she liked to talk of my uncle & told us very particularly how he had gone on since yesterday evening. Wrote a few lines to my father by this morning's post to announce the melancholy event & say, if he could leave my mother, there was no time to be lost, as I feared, from the state in which my Uncle Joseph died, the funeral must be soon . . . At 3 o'clock Milne, the undertaker, Casson, the joiner, & the sexton came. Matters being arranged with these people . . . Miss Stead, the mantua-maker came & bombasines & stuffs were sent over from Milne's & bombasines from Butters. Chose mourning for the 2 women servants from the former place, & from the latter, 50 yds (a whole piece) bombasine at 4/9 for ourselves. The servants had each 8 yds, 6/8 wide twilled stuff at 2/4, & 3½ yds of the same for a petticoat. Once thought of returning home for dinner but a little rain came on & besides, on 2nd thoughts it seemed better to stay. Well I did, as I was the principal person to choose the mourning & give orders to Miss Stead. Just before coming away, Fanny[9] went with me to see my uncle. He was laid out in the north room where he died & looked quite as well as he did when I saw him last, about 5 in the afternoon of last Tuesday. It was very rough, windy & stormy at the top of the bank, as we returned . . . My Aunt Lister told us in the afternoon that, while putting her flannel petticoat over her head, one morning about 2 months ago, as she was preparing to get up, she for a moment saw, very distinctly, a black figure, large as life, standing at the foot of the bed – that the fright made her almost sick, but she had never mentioned it to anyone till now, tho' she had, in her own mind, from that moment given up all hopes of my uncle's recovery. She said she had not been thinking of anything of the kind, nor was she just then thinking even of my uncle. She mentioned, however, that just before the death of her brother, Oswald, she as distinctly saw a black figure of the same appearance rush past her, in broad daylight, as she was going along one of the passages in her father's house at Frimley (about 20 miles from London). This, & the sight of my uncle, literally left such an impression on me, that all the while I was undressing to get into bed, I kept almost involuntarily looking round, as if myself expecting to see some apparition standing by. Whatever people may say, I believe there are few minds at all times capable of resisting impressions of this kind. What must be his terrors whose conscience is forever upbraiding him with acts of villainy? We had hardly got to Northgate this morning before Fanny brought in the melancholy intelligence of the Princess Charlotte of Wales having died a few hours after being brought to bed of a still-born male child on Thursday.[10]

Sunday 9 November [Halifax]

Before breakfast, wrote a couple of pp. to Miss Marsh[11] (Micklegate, York) to tell her of my Uncle Joseph's death . . . Wrote also 2¼pp. to M— (Lawton) & was just going to seal it when William[12] brought me a letter from her saying she had been distracted with the toothache. Durst not let Wolfenden draw the teeth, they were so broken. C— had made her an offer of going to York to have McLean & asking my advice whether to go or not. To this I hastily replied, 'Self-preservation is the 1st law of nature. I see no objection to your going to York – but remember that you have Louisa at your elbow.' Added also, 'The same post has brought a letter from Marian to say my mother has been confin'd to her bed since Tuesday with an inflammation on the lungs. I look at those around me & see that all the fortitude & presence of mind I can command are necessary.' . . . My uncle & I went to Northgate . . . Just before tea, had Fanny into the sitting-room & wrote down the following (on a scrap of paper, from which I am now copying it) verbatim as she told it . . . 'My Master was very restless till 12, throwing his arms about & saying, "Oh, I'm sick – I'm very ill – talk to me. Is not it what they call drawing away." About 12 he said, "Off, off – stand off – a little air." Then my Mrs came in & went up to him & said, "Must I come to you, Joseph?" & my master answered, "Yes! Do!", putting out his hand. "Oh, I'm very ill" & my Mrs said, "Call up the Lord, Joseph – he'll hear us – he'll help us – he'll comfort us in our time of need, love – he will." "That's what I want, to deliver myself up to the Lord." Then my Mrs said, "Now, Joseph, you're easier – you're comforted – are you not Joseph?" & he answered, "Yes." "Shall I read by you, dear Joseph?" "Do! Do!" Very eagerly & turning on his left side to listen, gave my Mrs such a heavy look & said, "Read slow that I can hear you." My Mrs then began the prayers for the sick & he made great efforts to say something (to make the responses) but he could not. When my Mrs had read a little he said, "Stop! Stop! I'm all in a perspiration. Have you done? Shut the book." These were the last words my master said & he spoke them very plainly. This was about 10 minutes after 12. He was ever after quite composed & went off without a groan – one would have thought he was only falling asleep at exactly 5 minutes past 1 by his own watch that was hanging up in the room.' . . . My uncle Lister & I returned in a chaise & got home a little before 9. During supper, wrote down on a slate my journal of yesterday. Just before going to bed, drank Isabella's health & happiness, it being her 32nd birthday. [Anne, herself, was twenty-six.]

Monday 10 November [Halifax]

My father arrived about 8 this [morning] in the mail from Market Weighton. He & I walked to Northgate between 10 & 11, & my uncle & aunt soon followed (my aunt on horseback). We all dined there . . . Had mourning sent over from Farrar's & bought for our own 2 women servants 17¼ yds (the cook being so big takes 9¼ yds) at 4/6 & twill'd stuff at 1/8, it being very good & there being no better. My uncle also ordered at Milne's the same mourning for his 3 men as he had done for William Weeder & Peter. Thomas is to have the best superfine cloth. Miss Ibbetson just before dinner, & sent hats or rather, bonnets, in the afternoon. She sent Miss Tennant to speak about them. I made a point of being civil to Miss Tennant (whom, by the way, I had never seen before) as being the daughter of Dr Belcombe's sister.

Tuesday 11 November [Halifax]

Got to Northgate before 1. As we were sitting after dinner, my Aunt Lister mentioned her intention of having a hatchment put up.[13] My uncle & I staid till after 8 in the evening. They had just got my Uncle Joseph put into his coffin before we came away. My uncle & I saw him soon after dinner. The discoloration [sic] was more decidedly all round the mouth, & the smell in the room certainly stronger than yesterday. This was, perhaps, occasioned by the closeness of the room; as there has not been a breath of fresh air let into it since my poor uncle died. This, they say, is the practice now, & that the corpse keeps better in a confin'd room than a ventilated one. They have once or twice burnt paper in the room, previously steep'd in a strong solution of saltpetre & water & then dried. This is what the new cook, a Bradford woman, says the doctors ordered to be done in the rooms at Bradford a little while ago to prevent infection from a bad, putrid fever that prevailed. The smell left by this burnt paper was certainly so powerful as to overcome everything else. Besides this, there has been a tarpot in the room every now & then.

There are pages missing from the journal which cover the period from Thursday, 13 November 1817 to Friday, 21 November 1817. During this time, the funeral of Anne's Uncle Joseph takes place. Also, her mother dies and Anne has to make a hurried journey to Market Weighton for the funeral. She stays in Market Weighton until 7 December 1817, when she sets off for York to visit her friends there. M— is still at York, at her mother's, to have some dental treatment carried out.

Sunday 7 December [York]

Got into the coach [at Market Weighton] a little before 6. There was only one inside besides myself, a traveller from a house in Birmingham (in the Birmingham trade, iron goods), a civil, intelligent sort of young man who paid me a high compliment on the intelligent kind of questions I asked, & answered them very well. He was on his way from Hull ... Speaking of the iron bridge at Sunderland, my companion said that the toll for a foot passenger was 3d. on a week day & 6d. on a Sunday – that the common toll for a gig was 2/6, for a chaise, 4s. & a chaise & 4, I think, 7s. I asked him his travelling expenses. He said that when travelling in his gig, he charged the firm (he himself was a partner, & son to 1 of them) a guinea a day – but that when travelling by coaches, he charged 17s. a day & coach-hire. Breakfast, tea & supper each 1/6, dinner 2s. besides wine, of which every traveller was expected to take at least a pint at 6s. or 6/6 a bottle. Waiter, 6d. a day – chamber-maid, 1s. a night, & boots, 2d. For a gig cleaning, 1/6 – 6d. or

1s. a night to the ostler, I think 6d. Keep of a horse would be about 4s., or rather more. Any gentleman might travel on these terms, if he chose to go into the travelling room & was sure of being well received so long as he did not give himself airs, but behaved like a gentleman. Indeed, he said, many gentlemen did travel this way . . . Stopped at the White Horse, Coppergate [York] a few minutes before 9. Took a chair to Miss Marsh's lodgings at Hansom's in Micklegate. She was at Mr Duffin's & she & Mr Duffin[14] came to give me the meeting . . . Sat up talking about my poor mother[15].

During this short visit to York, Anne had to make an effort to get herself back in favour with the Belcombes. There appears to have been some coolness on their part over Anne's attitude to M——. People had been somewhat scandalised by the lover-like attentions Anne had lavished on M——. Anne was staying at Miss Marsh's because the Belcombes had been reluctant to offer her a bed at their house. M—— came to see Anne the first morning after her arrival at York.

Monday 8 December [York]

M—— came about ½ past 9, to breakfast. She came to me into my room as soon as I was dressed. Felt a good deal agitated at seeing her, but behaved very well. A double letter from my Aunt Anne (Shibden) enclosing a £10 Bank of England note, the remaining ½ of the legacy left me by my Uncle Joseph. Mr Duffin came before 11, sat about an hour with us & made us all promise to dine with them at 4.

Tuesday 9 December [York]

Breakfasted at the Duffins' . . . Miss Marsh came in just as I was taking my leave . . . & we went together to the Belcombes'. Met

Dr Belcombe in Micklegate. Called at Todd's & bought the last & 5th edition just come out, of Thomson's *Chemistry*, 4 vols. 8vo. Met Eli[16] & Lou rather formally, Nantz[17] & Mrs Belcombe cordially. Studiously avoided shewing any warmth to M—. Had a few minutes tête-à-tête with Mrs Belcombe. We got upon the subject of romance. I said I had changed my manners to M— as soon as I was properly told of the folly of them; but that my regard for her was still the same as ever. *I am not quite so certain of this.* M— & I went out. Ordered Parsons to come [and cut] my hair at 11 tomorrow morning . . . In the evening I was purposely very civil to Eli, who seemed by no means displeased at my civility . . . She played some little airs to me & appeared well inclin'd to be agreeable . . . Mr John Swann drank tea with us & sat by Mrs Milne[18] all the evening while she, Mrs Belcombe, Lou & Col. Milne played Boston. Went home in a chair at ¼ after 11. Sat up talking to Miss Marsh.

Wednesday 10 December [York]

Nantz, Lou, M— & I walked out of Monk Bar and went as far as the 1st turnpike on the Malton road. Sitting over the drawing-room fire just before dinner, it came out that Eli had been buying ½lb barley sugar kisses. We all asked for some & she refused. M— said she longed & I instantly went & got her a lb (2/6), 2d. abated on account of the quantity taken. Eli refused to take any & look'd ashamed. I again offered her some in the evening & she refused. I mentioned the thing to her just before I came away, & said I was sorry she had refused. I perceive, tho', we were very good friends – getting rather cordial . . . Mr & Mrs Bury drank tea with us & played whist with Mrs Belcombe & Col. Milne. I flirted with Harriet then played 3 rubbers with Milne against Mrs Belcombe & Mrs Bury & came off winning 4 shilling points. Mr Duffin & Miss Marsh, returning from a party, called for me to walk home. Fine, soft day.

Thursday 11 December [York]

Went to the Belcombes. Nantz took me upstairs to tell me M— had had her three stumps of teeth out soon after breakfast; that Husband, the apothecary, had drawn them exceedingly well; that she had got over it better than she expected, was lain down on her mother's bed & was to be kept quiet. I was just going in to see her when Mrs Belcombe prevented me. I briefly expressed my opinion that it was not good judgement to prevent my going to her for a minute or two but that I would, at any rate, comply.

Friday 12 December [York]

Breakfasted at the Belcombes' . . . M—'s face bad, worse than yesterday & she had a bad night in spite of 65 drops of laudanum & did not get up till 12. However, a little before 11, *she herself suggested our having a kiss. I thought it dangerous & would have declined the risk but she persisted & by way of excuse to bolt the door sent me downstairs for some paper, that she was going to the close-stool. The expedient answered & she tried to laugh me out of my nervousness. I took off my pelisse & drawers, got into bed & had a very good kiss, she showing all due inclination & in less than seven minutes the door was unbolted & we were all right again.* Just after breakfast, Mrs Belcombe said as she had just heard that Miss Bland, the friend she had been expecting, could not come, she desired & hoped I would take a bed with them in Petergate. M— & I talked it over. I did not like a bed to myself in the room next the drawing room, *on account of Nantz, that is Anne Belcombe.* I should petition for the little turn-up bed in M— & Lou's room. I mentioned this to Mrs Belcombe & would consent to stay with them on no other condition & it was at last so settled.

Sunday 14 December [York]

Walked into Petergate . . . Sat with [M—] till 3 & then went back to Miss Marsh's to be ready to dine at the Duffins' at 4 . . . Sat talking till 11 when the chair came to take me into Petergate. Walked to Miss Marsh's to put up my things. Took all with me in the chair & got to Dr Belcombe's as the Minster clock struck ½ past 11. The passage door locked. Rapped & rang to no purpose & was just going back again when James[19] let us in, Dr Belcombe, accidentally sitting up in the drawing-room reading, having heard us. Apologized for being so late . . . Slept in the same room with M— & Lou . . . in the little turn-up bed by myself, M— being afraid of Lou getting cold, as there were not so many clothes on it as she had been accustomed to in sleeping in the great bed with M—. A rainy, wet, dirty, disagreeable day.

Monday 15 December [York]

Anne, Eli & Lou went to the rooms,[20] the 1st time of their being opened this winter on a new plan & a good one, by subscription. To be opened once a fortnight. Stewards, Mr Dixon (the reverend) Mr Tweedy, Junior, etc. Dancing to conclude at 1. They want 70 subscriptions or the rooms would or could not be opened at all, but they got above 100, at a guinea each. There was to be one quadrille set tonight & perhaps they might muster another by & by. M—, not feeling quite well, stayed at home. Dr Belcombe & I had a good deal of conversation about . . . general subjects at & after tea e.g. the edition of Malthus's *Essay on Population* just come out – farming, etc. The girls went home from the rooms (at 1) with Captain & Mrs Wallace, 1st Dragoon Guards. Had a hot supper & did not get back till 3. *I slept with M—.*

Tuesday 16 December [York]

All of us at home this evening. I wanted to read to M—, Nantz & Lou, Cuvier's theory of the earth, but Mrs Milne, having no penchant for literature on such occasions, M— thought I had better shut the book, & I amused myself by getting Lou to write me down, in pencil, the Hebrew alphabet & asking her questions about it. Mrs Milne, having nobody to talk to but Eli, looked glum. M— was in bed an hour & ½ at least before Lou & me, who sat up talking very cosily.

Wednesday 17 December [York]

Lou & I sat perhaps a couple of hours together in her mother's sitting-room, & she gave me my 2nd lesson in Parkhurst's Hebrew grammar . . . The language seems very easy & I think I could soon get a tolerable knowledge of it. Lou is certainly a quick, clever girl & seems remarkably *au fait* at Hebrew considering the little attention she has been able to pay to it & the few lessons she has had from Mr Jessop, curate to Mr Greyson at St Martin's Church, Micklegate. She can read a chapter in Genesis by herself with the assistance of a lexicon.

Thursday 18 December [York]

M— went with me & . . . had my name booked & paid a shilling for an inside place in the True Blue heavy coach that sets off from the Black Swan in Coney Street every day at 2p.m. for the Golden Lion, Leeds, where it should arrive at, or a little before, 6 . . . Got home a little before 5, only just in time to dress for dinner. As soon as we left the dining-room, went upstairs into our own room (over Mrs Belcombe's sitting-room) & sat talking very cosily to Lou about M—, Lawton, C—, & one thing or other till 8 o'clock. *She, as well as Anne, strongly suspects that neither M— nor I would much regret the loss of C—, but that we look forward to the thing and, in the event of it, certainly mean to live together.* Lou and I have joked about it several times, *I asking if she thought I might hope to come in possession of M— in ten years.* A decade. Both Lou & Nantz think I may say five years instead of ten & half a decade is becoming quite a joke among us . . . On going down into the drawing-room, & speaking to M—, found her very low & in tears. *She wondered how I could leave her so long the last night & said she should be jealous of Lou.* Tho' I laughed at the thing at first, I soon perceived it more real than I had imagined. It however passed over. M— & Nantz went upstairs with me to try on the new things I had got & a little after 11 we all retired.

Friday 19 December [Halifax]

Busy packing all the morning. M— sat by me. Talked over my adventures in former days. M— said had she known them, she would never have been introduced to me . . . At 1, took a hasty luncheon. Said goodbye & got out of the house by ½ past. On my way to the Black Swan, in Coney Street, called at Todd's to inquire for a Hebrew Bible to give Lou. Met with a thick, 8vo 2nd-hand edition of Simon's at £1 8s., but, this not suiting my purpose, called at Mrs Marshall's . . . *Bought Anne & Louisa each a mother-of-pearl knife with two blades, corkscrew, etc & at the end, a pair of small scissors contained in a silver sheath, price fourteen shillings each. As [they] had not another of the same size, I got a smaller one for M—, price eight & sixpence. Got a silver pencil with a magnifying glass at the end for Mrs Belcombe, price fifteen shillings. Hastily directed them and desired they might be sent immediately to Dr Belcombe's.* Just got to the Black Swan in time. Took my seat in the True Blue heavy coach & drove off for Leeds as the Minster clock struck 2. Two ½ ladies from Hull, 2 schoolgirls & a great horsedealer who, during the war had supplied almost the whole of the British Cavalry, & who had been at the great York fair which ended yesterday, were my companions . . . It turned out a rainy afternoon. We reached Leeds & stopped at the Golden Lion at ½ past 6. Got a porter to take my luggage & led the way to the Rose & Crown in Briggate. After at least ¼ mile's wet walk thro' dirty, busy streets, they told me I could not secure a place in the Mail till 4 in the morning, & that they were so full they had not a bed to spare me, nor an unoccupied room for me to sit down in. Sent for my friend, the chambermaid & made my little arrangement with her. Then, while tea was ready, went to Radford's (just over the way) to order rings in memory of my poor mother. For the family . . . ordered 7 embossed hoops at 42s. each (Marian's having, in addition, a box head with hair which made it 2 guineas & ½) 'To the memory of' embossed in gold black-letter on the outside & in the inside, 'Rebecca Lister, ob^t 13 Nov –aet 47.' For Mrs Inman, a jet-headed ring, 20s. For Mr Inman, Mr Alderman Dales of York, the 2 Misses Trants of Leeds & old Mrs Wetherhead of Halifax, mourning hoops, 36s., giving directions for the sending them as my father desired. My friend, the chambermaid, put me into a parlour that would not be wanted till 10, had got me tea & everything comfortable & let me have a snug little bedroom, no. 18, at the extremity of the house on the 3rd floor. She shewed me upstairs a little before 10, lighted me 2 mould candles on my dressing-table, brought me a rush-light, as I thought the room too small for a fire, assured me I had *really* clean sheets & hoped I should have a good night. I paid 3s. for my tea & lodgings & gave this civil chambermaid 2/6. Washed my hands, untied my neckkerchief [sic], took off my boots & got into my little camp-bed which I certainly found very clean & comfortable. Just before coming upstairs, Mr & Mrs Webster (from Halifax, she a stay-maker), the occupiers of my sitting-room, came in. I thought it proper to stay a short while & she amused me with an account of the roguery practised in coach offices about luggage & charges, saying they would take advantage where they could, & that, being commonly clerks & understrappers, greedy for all they can get, they would charge more both for luggage & the fare than they ought & that strangers should always look at the bill of fares posted in the office before they paid what was demanded.

Saturday 20 December [Halifax]

After a few hours disturbed sleep, Boots called me ¼ before 4. Got up immediately, washed my face & hands, buttoned on my boots, etc., gave Boots a shilling & got into the mail at 4. A decent kind of woman & 2 decent kind of tradesmen my companions. Got to Halifax a little before 8. Saw after my luggage. Just called at Northgate to send my love to my aunt & say I was arrived. Walked to Gradon's, the shoemaker's, at Haley-hill, to order a pair of strong shoes & reached Shibden a little before 9. My uncle & aunt not having expected me till one (by the Highflier) were agreeably surprised to see me & I felt glad I had not been persuaded to wait & come with M— next Friday.

Sunday 21 December [Halifax]

Wrote to M— (Dr Belcombe's, Petergate, York) to announce my safe arrival here & say I had ordered 4 horses at the Rose & Crown (Briggate, Leeds) to be ready for her at one next Friday.

M— was to call in at Halifax on her way home to Lawton from York and stay a day or two with Anne at Shibden Hall.

A remarkably fine frosty day. My uncle & aunt were at church in the morning. Mr Wilmot, curate of the church, gave a most impressive funeral sermon to the memory of our late vicar, Dr Coulthurst,[21] who was buried in the choir of the old church last Thursday (18), aet 64. The church, I understand, was handsomely put in mourning for the Princess Charlotte but now, in addition, the galleries are hung round with black cloth, bordered with broad black fringe, and escutcheons of the Dr's arms hung round the pulpit, & a few in other parts of the church.

Tuesday 23 December [Halifax]

In the morning, writing out a rough draft of my journal of last Saturday, Friday, Thursday, Wednesday & Tuesday. Did nothing in the afternoon but count over my money & see what I had spent while away. After tea, wrote the rough draft of my journal of Monday 15 December. My aunt gave me an account of what she had paid for my mourning, which amounted to £8 6d., the 6d. being abated. I paid her £8, she having first given me £5, & my uncle also having [given] me £5.

Thursday 25 December [Halifax]

The Listers appear never to have engaged in any Christmas festivities and Anne's entries on almost every Christmas day are usually brief, merely outlining the religious duties which they undertook.

We all went to morning church & staid the sacrament. Assisted my aunt in reading prayers in the afternoon. In the evening, read aloud sermons 8 & 9, Hoole. A remarkably fine, frosty day. Roads very slippery. Barometer 1½ deg. above changeable. Fahr. 29° at 9p.m.

Friday 26 December [Halifax]

Went without dinner today, not having felt well since I came home (bilious & heavy) which I solely attribute to dining at 3p.m. & which certainly never agrees with me. Went downstairs to dessert & then walked to meet M— on her way from York to Lawton, thro' Leeds by Burstall & met her (& the cook,

Elizabeth, she had hired in York) in the landau, a few yards beyond the Hipperholme bar. I was pleased to find she had very good horses and very civil drivers from the Rose & Crown (Leeds) & which were in readiness according to my orders at 1, exactly the time she reached Leeds. M— arrived here at 5 by the kitchen clock, ¾ past 4 by the Halifax, & ¼ past 4 by Leeds & York.[22] She brought me a small parcel from Nantz, containing a very kind note from herself and one from Lou, and a pair of cambric muslin sleeves with broad wristbands to be worn as linings, which she (Nantz) had made & another pair which she had altered for me. After tea, M— & I played whist against my uncle & aunt & won a rubber of 4 & a game. Very fine, frosty day . . . Came upstairs 20 mins before 11, but sat up talking till 12. *After all, I believe M—'s heart is all my own.* M— told us, after tea, what a narrow escape Mr C— L— [her husband] had just had the other day of being shot. In getting over a hedge, something caught the trigger, the gun went off & the contents only just missed. A similar accident, I understand, occurred to him just before M— & Louisa left Lawton, & his glove & waistcoat were a good deal burnt.

Sunday 28 December [Halifax]

Just as the dinner things were going out, John Morgan, the coachman, arrived with a letter from C—, dated Albion Hotel, Manchester, saying he was happy to find M— so unexpectedly on her journey (their letters had crossed on the road & he fancied she might stay in York till the day after New Year's Day) that he had set off from Lawton the morning he received her letter (yesterday) &, that she might not be detained on the road, as the horses could not get to Halifax in any reasonable time to take on today, he had sent John forward by the coach to tell her to take 4 posters, set off immediately & travel as fast as she could to meet him in good time at Manchester this evening, adding that if she had been in any other direction, he believed he would have met her there himself, tho' the distance had been twice as far. It was after 2 before John got here. He had his dinner to get & go back again to the White Lion to order the carriage, we not having room for it here. The poor fellow, however, his frost-bit face all colours, sent in a message to say, his mistress must go. It was bitter cold, the roads dreadfully slippy, Blackstone Edge to cross,[23] and no moon – but his mistress understood the necessity. All was got ready and they were off from our door a few minutes before 4.

Wednesday 31 December [Halifax]

In the evening, wrote out, in my journal book, my journal of Sunday 7 & Monday 8 December. My uncle, who had been at a turnpike meeting (of the Wakefield road) this afternoon, & called at Northgate, heard at the latter place . . . that Mr James Edward Norris, of this town attorney, & the petition he took up to Lord Liverpool, signed by Mr Knight's friends & congregation, had succeeded in getting Mr Knight the promise of the vicarage.

1818

Wednesday 7 January [Halifax]

Tried on a pair of drawers Marian sent me & some black raw silk stockings (cotton tops & feet) like which my father brought me 3 pairs, he having bought them for Marian, for whom they are too small, & not choosing them to be returned.

Thursday 8 January [Halifax]

After breakfast . . . dawdling away the morning in looking over medical mss., weighing out powders for Betty, the housemaid, etc., till ½ past 12, when I got ready to go to Halifax . . . Called at Whitley's, the booksellers, & staid ¾ hour at the library. Went to congratulate Mr Knight on his promotion to the vicarage. Sat near an hour with him & Mrs & Miss Knight (his sister). Sat ½ hour at Northgate & got home at ½ past 5.

Friday 9 January [Halifax]

Mending my stockings & an old shift . . . Staid downstairs till 11, talking to my father. Entered a little into affairs. Found the tenants had paid their rents better than I expected.[1] Barker, at the Low Farm only half a year behindhand. Marshall will pay up in a week or two. Porter, at the Grange, who has always been able to pay but who had given notice to quit, likely to stay. However, my father has taken from him 18 acres of the hold field, along the Shipton Lane side, & let it off to a man at Shipton at 2 pounds an acre, the tenant to pay taxes. Porter did not pay quite 22s. an acre for it, at which rent he has all the rest of his farm. My mother's funeral expenses (already paid) are upwards of £90, everything included . . . My father is looking remarkably well, is grown fatter & seems in high glee. *He said he has got his pocket full of money & shewed me his pocket book full of bills. I asked if he had got them all in rents. He said how else should he get them? I hope this means that he has not been borrowing.* My father says he thinks he shall now be able to get his rents &, if he does, he & Marian will not spend more than half.

Saturday 10 January [Halifax]

Walked to Halifax . . . Read 1½ hours at the library[2] . . . No books delivered out today nor are there to be till next Tuesday 3 weeks, 3 February, when the new room adjoining the theatre[3] will be opened. They are calling in the books to see what repairs are wanted & are to begin to remove to the new room next week. In the meantime the old library room will be open as usual & tho' you may take no books away, you may read them.

Monday 12 January [Halifax]

Dined at 1 o'clock. My father & I walked to Halifax a little after 2. Called at Whitley's & left my flute piece for Sugden to repair the D key while my father went to Rawson's bank & paid their £50. We went to see the new library room which was just finished & a woman was washing it. We were both instantly struck with the awkward, ugly, inconvenient manner in which the entrance is contrived. A complete glass box from the ground floor to the floor above, which is the library, & no communication whatever to the rooms above (2 heights of chambers consisting of 4 very good rooms & which will soon be wanted for books) except for a common ladder, stuck up between a window & one end of the glass box & by which ladder you are to creep up thro' a square hole cut in the floor above!!! A committee of 4 gents were appointed to superintend the fitting up of the rooms. These agreed to leave the thing entirely to Mr Norris, and Mr Norris has, by a stretch of brilliant genius which the glazier will value at about £30, contrived to throw 2 rooms into one by means of the stairs, enclosed in an oblong glass case, in the centre of the room!!! The staircase that (instead of the ladder) used to communicate with the 3rd floor being taken away, & no support left, & the partition walls have been so shaken they are visibly cracked in several places.

Wednesday 14 January [Halifax]

Before breakfast, writing out the rough draft of an index to this volume of my journal . . . Did not come upstairs till 11, & soon after . . . Mrs John Waterhouse (Well-head) & Emma Saltmarshe (George Street) called . . . Poor Emma looks very thin & ill. Engaged to rout parties every evening, except next Tuesday, for the next three weeks to come. Emma Saltmarshe, a bride last summer & Emma Stansfield, a bride 3 or 4 weeks ago, make the town quite gay. Thank God I have nothing to do with their parties, nor do I intend it ever. My morning sadly broken into.

Anne was having a rather quiet time at the beginning of 1818. M— was firmly ensconced in Lawton Hall under the watchful eye of her jealous husband. The Norcliffes had not yet returned from their travels on the Continent, and besides, they were undergoing a period of mourning for the deaths of their daughter Emily and their son-in-law, Charles Best, married to another daughter, Mary. Both had died within a short time of each other during their travels abroad, and this, along with the deaths of Anne's mother and her Uncle Joseph, had given Anne a great deal of despondency.

Friday 16 January [Halifax]

Most boisterous, tempestuous night . . . At last, I have brought up the time I lost in York & have got right again to my journal as usual. I will never get so behindhand again, I am determined. In fact, I shall write my indices[4] as I go along & shall be upon a better plan, I hope, altogether.

Monday 19 January [Halifax]

Mrs Wm Priestley called & walked with my aunt & me to Halifax . . . My aunt went to see the boa constrictor & wild beasts. I should have gone in with her but they would not admit me without paying a shilling, even tho' I paid 2 on Saturday, so I walked about on the outside stage of the caravan till my aunt returned. We then went & paid the bride-visit to Emma Stansfield . . . in Aked's Rd & sat ½ an hour. She shewed us over the house which is very neatly furnished & made the most of, but it is a cold & comfortless looking situation & I should be sorry to live there . . . Emma is an insignificant looking bride.

Wednesday 21 January [Halifax]

Wrote out the list of books, pamphlets & periodical works contained in this volume [of her journal] up to today & was the whole of the remainder of the time, before breakfast & afterwards, from 10¾ till 2¾, adding up & arranging on a new plan my expenses of last year, i.e. classing them under the following heads – Clothes, Hair-cutting, oil & brushes, washing, sundries, Postage, Parcels, Stationery, Books, music, Charity, Presents, servants, chair-hire, Travelling expenses, 2 courses of lectures, shoe bill at Hornby's of last year. Balance of account with M— from Sept. 1815 to 25 February 1817, paid on my mother's account – so that I can see at a glance what I have spent during the year in each department. I mean to pursue this plan in future &, to save myself all the trouble I have now had in having the items of the whole year to separate & class all at once, I shall do it as I go along, regularly every month. In the afternoon & evening, going on with the rough draft of an index to vol. 1. of my Extracts [from her journal]. From 5.25 to 5¾, played the flute without book.

Thursday 22 January [Halifax]

Puzzled over my accounts. Could not make the sum total of the different heads under which I had classed them agree with the sum total of the year. There was a difference of 8d. . . . In the afternoon, did not feel quite well (indigestion, my hands swelled a good deal, my head a very little & felt much heated) in consequence of eating ¼ of a fine American apple.

Friday 23 January [Halifax]

Till time to get ready for breakfast (9.40) working over my accounts to make up the difference of 8d. and, at last, after adding them up all over again, got them, to my great joy, quite right. I was determined not to be mastered and determined, let them take what time they would, my patience should not be wearied. There had been snow in the night . . . During breakfast it came in thick & soon began to snow a little & turned out a thoroughly winterly, snowy day.

Tuesday 27 January [Halifax]

At 11, my aunt & I set off to Halifax . . . walked forward to Pye Nest & sat ½ hour & 5 minutes. Mrs Priestley (White Windows) there. They had a fine bulldog die of hydrophobia on Monday night having been taken ill the night before. It was bit ten days ago by a mad dog which was unfortunately at large in the town & neighbourhood, bit one of Mr Edward's workmen, 2 or 3 other men, several dogs & did much mischief. Among the rest, Mr Edward had also a cow bit, which is still kept up.

Thursday 5 February [Halifax]

Could not do so much, my eyes were so very tired, particularly the right. I have read too much by candlelight lately & neither managed day nor candlelight properly. I have sat with it too much in my face & not thrown properly on the paper . . . In the evening did nothing at all, on account of my eye which is quite bloodshot. Besides other things, I have got cold in it.

Thursday 5 March [Halifax]

Left my letter to M— at Northgate for Thomas to put into the post office. Mrs Bagnold, the postmistress, had bailiffs in her house again yesterday & consequently, changed her abode.

Thursday 17 March [Halifax]

Crossley cut my hair this morning which, as usual, hindered me full ½ hour. Besides, I have not felt very brilliant this morning. I am quite vexed at myself for not having got into a regular train of getting up earlier. I ought not to be in bed after 5. In the afternoon, went with my uncle & George Robinson to Lower Brea . . . to see what repairs would be wanted before George & his wife could get into the house. Found it in a sad, dirty, forlorn, pulled-to-pieces state. The roof must be taken off & £200 laid out – besides a new barn that will cost about £150. Were 2½ hours looking about in spite of the cold & boisterous wind & flying showers. In the evening (Chas. Howarth having brought me the box I ordered some days ago) sorting out & arranging the minerals Isabella Norcliffe sent me from Switzerland . . . Flute 20 minutes during supper.

Sunday 29 March [Halifax]

Soft, damp morning with small rain, but we should none of us have gone to church, at any rate, as they are scraping the walls

& going to have it newly whitewashed, I believe. Most of the pews are covered over with pack-sheets or something or other to keep them clean, but we understood there was still to be a service. My lip too much swell'd & inflamed to allow of my helping to read prayers aloud . . . During dinner, walked ½ hour on the terrace. In the afternoon, Fanny came from Northgate & brought my aunt a parcel from York – a box of sweetmeats forwarded by Fisher[5] & sent to my aunt by Isabella from the South of France several months ago . . . My lip so painful came upstairs to bed at 9, as I did on Friday.

Anne had spent a very quiet winter, concentrating on her studies, her letter-writing to her friends, helping to run the estate, getting into town when weather permitted, and generally leading a rather restricted life. She did go visiting when the occasion demanded it, but otherwise did not join in the social activities of the town. The month of April was to see a change in her life in that Miss Browne returned to Halifax and Anne began to cultivate a relationship with her.

Thursday 16 April [Halifax]

Wrote a note to Mrs Briggs, Savile Green, excusing myself (as I declined all parties for the present) from her party next Wednesday, the 22nd inst . . . At ¼ before 4, set off & walked to Stoney Royde. Found Mrs Rawson alone. Told her I now dined at 6. Had some excellent cold fillet of meat & drank tea with her. She was glad to see me. I staid with [her] till ½ past 7 & spent the time very pleasantly. Speaking of the death of the Princess Charlotte, she said she understood from good authority that . . . as soon as the labour was over, about 7 in the evening, H.R.H. sent away the nurse, Mrs Griffiths, saying the Prince (Leopold) would stay with her, that they were accordingly left entirely to themselves, & he sat by her 3 hours before he perceived any change, when he immediately called Mrs Griffiths & the physicians, but it was too late. Everybody thought the poor princess was lost for want of proper care. Dr Simms was not called in till they sent for him to see if he could restore animation to the child. I observed it ought to have been destroyed. When this was named to Sir Richard Croft, he said he was not authorized to use instruments without the Prince Regent's leave. Why then, replied the people, was not the Prince Regent there? Mrs Rawson observed it was singular that the medical attendant (Sir Richard Croft) had not even taken with him (which is common with all practitioners) an instrument for inflating the lungs of the infant, if necessary . . . As an anecdote in proof of the universality of the opinion that the poor princess was lost for want of proper care, Mrs Rawson mentioned 2 poor women (beggars) being overheard talking about it in one of the London streets, & one said to the other, 'Ah! poor crater, if she had only had a sup of gin, she'd a' done.' Sir Richard Croft was never happy afterwards. Mrs Rawson asked after M— & if they went on any better than they did, adding significantly, 'You have never been there since the 1st time.' I smiled (I could not help it) & carelessly answered, no, I had not & that I had heard the same remark made before, but that this was nothing.

Tuesday 21 April [Halifax]

Called at Cross-hills (to ask the Miss Greenwoods to tea) where I was persuaded to stay tea, amused tho' uneasy at the vulgarity of the party the whole time. Yet they are certainly very good & worthy & very obliging. I suppose such a thing is quite out of the question but from mere appearance & conversation, one might have fancied Mrs Greenwood had had a drop too much. Speaking of Miss Browne, I said I should like very well to meet her if there was nobody else asked, & it was agreed to give me the opportunity.

Tuesday 28 April [Halifax]

Miss Greenwood & Miss Susan Greenwood called, but would not come in, between 2 & 3, to ask me to tea to meet Miss Brown tomorrow. Walked back with them very near to the top of the bank.

Wednesday 29 April [Halifax]

Mending my gloves, the trimming of my black bombazine petticoat and all in readiness for this afternoon . . . At ½ past 5, went to the Greenwoods' (Cross-hills). Miss Brown & her 2 friends, the Miss Kellys from Glasgow, arrived in about an hour . . . Considering her situation in life, Miss Brown is wonderful – handsome, or rather, interesting, gentle in her manners, entirely free from any sort of affectation & much more ladylike than any girl I have seen hereabouts. From conversation, I made out she is 23 & her sister 17. *I wonder what she thinks of me? My attention to her is certainly sufficiently marked to attract her notice. Is she flattered? I think she is. I have thought of her all the way home, of writing to her anonymously and (as she said, when I asked her if she liked Lord Byron's poetry, 'Yes, perhaps too well') of sending her a Cornelian heart with a copy of his lines on the subject.*[6] *I could soon be in love with the girl.*

Sunday 10 May [Halifax]

Had tea at ½ past 5 & my aunt & I walked to the lecture at the old church . . . Mrs Browne & her daughters & her visitors, the Misses Kelly from Glasgow, were there. My aunt & I waited for them as they went out, for her to get a peep at Miss Browne, who looked very interesting. Fair as a lily, with the loveliest rose upon her cheek.

Tuesday 12 May [Halifax]

In the afternoon, walked with my aunt to Halifax. We went to the library. Miss Browne & her friend, Miss Kelly, came in . . . Talked to them a few minutes (till 5) & then walked with them as far as Barum Top, making myself very agreeable. Miss Browne evidently pleased & flattered. When I met her at Cross-hills she said she never went to the library . . . They inquired for the 5th canto of *Childe Harold*. It is not in the library & I have been thinking ever since (for, somehow or other, this girl haunts my thoughts like some genius of fairy lore) how to get it & offer it for her reading.

Wednesday 13 May [Halifax]

Slept very ill last night. Did nothing but dream of Miss Browne; of being at their house; hearing her play on the piano & witnessing the vulgarity of her mother. I wish I could get the girl out of my head. However, there is one comfort; let me think or scheme what I may, I shall never allow myself to <u>do</u> anything beyond the folly of talking to, & perhaps walking a little way with her, now & then when I happen to meet her.

Saturday 23 May [Halifax]

Went to Mr Knight's & sat ½ hour. Mentioning my despair of getting on with my studies, he proposed my giving up altogether the thought of pursuing them. This, I did not think it necessary to dissemble, I scouted entirely.

Monday 25 May [Halifax]

In the afternoon, *cut off the feet of a pair of black silk stockings. Hemmed the legs & sewed [them] to a pair of cotton socks I have just got made for the purpose.* At ½ past 5, my aunt & I set off to walk to Horley Green. Drank tea & spent a pleasant evening with

Mrs, Miss & Miss Sarah Ralph & got home at 9 . . . The Ralphs very civil. Miss Ralph mended me my gloves & offered to make the waist of my gown fit better.

Wednesday 27 May [Halifax]

Miss & Miss Sarah Ralph called. *Miss Sarah undid the bombazine waist Mrs Stead made me & pinned it how it should be altered . . .* I had to get ready to dine at Mr Tom Rawson's at 3. Went (walked) down the old bank & got there 3 or 4 minutes before [by] the church clock. Mrs Catherine Rawson & Mrs Tom's cousin, Mr Holdsworth (curate of the old church, pro tempore) dined there besides myself. In the evening, played & won a rubber of 2 points with Mr Tom Rawson against his aunt & Mr H. (sixpenny points). After supper, Mrs Catherine & I joined at one hookah while Mr Tom smoked another. Remarkably fine tobacco brought by Mr Stansfield Rawson from Turkey last year. Spent a pleasant day & got home at 11.

Monday 1 June [Halifax]

Dined at 5 & walked immediately afterwards to drink tea at Mr Drake's in Northgate. Found my uncle & aunt already there. Whether from having walked too fast (in 17 minutes) or from the heat of the room & smell of drugs, I was hardly settled before I felt a bilious sickness come on &, hastily leaving them, went to my Aunt Lister's, threw myself on Fanny's bed in my aunt's room &, after being very sick, fell asleep & remained so till 8, when my Aunt Anne awoke me & soon we all set off to walk home & got back at 9 . . . Had coffee as soon as it could be made (which settled me a good deal) & got into bed at 11½.

Tuesday 2 June [Halifax]

For near an hour & a half, sewing fast the crape trimming round the bottom of my gown and getting ready to go to Halifax . . . Sat near an hour at Cross-hills. *Talked about Miss Browne. They rallied me on the subject of my great admiration & Mrs Greenwood said we must have another meeting. To this I made no reply but, speaking of singing, joked & declared I would sing for nobody but Miss Browne & that to have been obliged to refuse her what she asked me at their house had made me ill ever since of a refusal fever. They said the admiration was mutual; that Miss Browne thought me very agreeable & that the younger Miss Kelly & the younger Miss Browne had gone one afternoon to the library on purpose to see me there* . . . (Miss Caroline Greenwood & her mother as vulgar as ever. Miss Greenwood is certainly less vulgar than either of them.) Got to Well-head a few minutes after 5. Mrs W—, in her way one of those people who profess to 'tell your mind', very agreeable, seemed desired to make my visit pleasant. *Speaking of what would be my choice in men, I said above all things, after good sense and good temper, good family and remarkably elegant manners. She mentioned Philip Saltmarshe. I said no; I think they all have some idea of Sam Waterhouse, but I told her that even if he could make up his mind to ask me to say yes, I should instantly make up my mind to answer no.* The party was Mr & Mrs Waterhouse, the governess, Miss Green, & Mr Waterhouse's brother, Mr Samuel Waterhouse, whose long visage & tardy utterances are anything but jocose.

Wednesday 3 June [Halifax]

The weather gets hot & my room, in spite of its being heightened, is too warm to brace the mind for study. However, I must do as well as I can . . . Looking over some songs, writing out 'The Bay of Biscay' & 'Said Eve Unto Adam' & dawdling literally quite in a perspiration, the sun full on my room & very hot . . . Drinking whey from the curds this morning. *Lolling over songs, determined to have one ready if I should meet her again and she should ask me to sing, unless the number of the party present, as was the case before, again prevents me . . .* I hardly remember spending such an idle morning & may I not soon, or ever, do it again, but I am hot & unnerved & unable, as it were, to attend much to anything. What should I have been if my room had remained as it used to be – about 2½ yds high & the pigeon-cote over it!

Anne's obsession with Miss Browne grew. Each time she went to town she made some excuse to go past the Brownes' house. The two women began to meet on a regular basis at the library and also at church, as well as taking walks around the outskirts of the town. The friendship became the target for gossip, particularly as Anne refused to put the relation-ship upon a proper social footing, with the two families calling formally upon each other. Miss Browne was at first puzzled, then hurt at Anne's attitude and Anne, herself, was uncomfortably aware both of her own snobbishness and of the town's gossip.

Sunday 7 June [Halifax]

My uncle & I went to morning church . . . *Took my letter to put into the post as an excuse for walking up Horton Street & talking to Miss Browne. Followed her party out of church but she was not there, nor had she been in the morning. Met with the Misses Staveley, Bessy & Sarah, & walked to the top of Horton Street with them . . . Spoke or moved to Mr Browne & Miss Isabel Kelly, but she seemed to return the salutation rather coolly. Tom Rawson spoke to her & then to me (for I was just before her). I made an attempt to enter into conversation with him & asked which way he was going. He said home, but somehow left me, tho' our roads were the same . . . Why was Miss Browne not at the lecture last Sunday, nor at church this morning or evening as usual? Why did Miss Isabella Kelly appear to give a cool salutation? Miss Browne told the*

Greenwoods I was very agreeable and Miss Isabel Kelly told them she & Miss Maria Browne had gone to the library on purpose to see me there. Perhaps I am fanciful but I cannot help having some idea Miss Browne observes my singular attention and, as I do not call on her, wishes to avoid me, and Miss Isabella takes her queue [sic] from this. I wondered at Tom Rawson's not joining me and did not much like walking with the Staveleys. In fact, I was disappointed altogether and felt as if I wished to hide my diminished head. I said in my head, "Tis well. I deserve it. Miss Browne is right. It will do me good. I will think no more of her and, instead of throwing myself in her way, keep out of it as much as possible for the future and make myself scarce to everyone.' Determined to devote myself solely to study and the acquirement of that literature which may make me eminent and more decidedly above them all hereafter. Is my admiration of this girl generally observed? . . . But I will think no more of Miss Browne. This night shall be a lesson to me and I will profit by it. My mind was intent on these reflections as I walked along and I resolved to stick diligently to my watchword – discretion, & next to good, devote myself to study.

Sunday 14 June [Halifax]

My aunt & I went to morning church. She rode the young black mare (that was my Uncle Joseph's) for the 1st time . . . Had tea at 5 for me to get to the lecture . . . *Walked from church with Miss Browne . . . Offered Miss Browne (Kallista, as I shall call her)[7] my arm at the bottom of Horton Street and we two walked together by the side of one division of their party . . . Having the two keys in my hand belonging to the seat [in church] I smiled and told Kallista if they were the keys of heaven I would let her in. She made no reply. I observed she never does to anything the least bordering on a compliment. She told me she walked a great deal in the garden and she liked it by moonlight for it made her melancholy. She owned to being a little romantic and said she admired a little romance in* people. I quite agreed & said a very sensible woman had once told me she thought a slight tincture of romance made a character more amiable . . . She wished she might ever meet me at church. I had looked into her prayer-book & excused the impertinence by saying I wished to find a name, as I had often inquired hers. She told me Elizabeth & thanked me for the interest I had taken in doing so. She goes to the baths, Dr Paley having ordered her warm bathing. She was not well last Sunday & therefore did not go to church. I think Miss Isabella did not mean to look coolly last Sunday . . . I asked Miss Browne if she had been to see Shibden valley. She said they had been to see Scout Hall but meant to come again to see more of the valley and asked me what way they should go. In explaining I said I should have been most happy to see them at Shibden but that my uncle & aunt visited so little, I feared so large a party would look alarming. She seemed to think this a thing of course with elderly people but was certainly pleased I had made the speech. Perhaps she may, in her own mind, give this reason for my not calling on her.

Friday 19 June [Halifax]

Anxious to awake very early this morning, attempted to sleep last night on the floor, then on the bare ticking, wrapping myself up in the sheet & blanket, but feeling my back very cold, lay across the bed, putting the pillow on a chair. This did not do. Did not awake till 7 & was so vexed to find it so late, I lay dozing till 9.

Saturday 20 June [Halifax]

In the evening, walked down the old bank & called at the vicarage to inquire after Mrs Knight who [was] suddenly taken dangerously ill about 1p.m. yesterday with a violent pain in her head, and pressure of blood on the brain, for which Dr Paley had her bled in the temple with a lancet, then 12 leeches put upon the place, a blister on her head & a mustard plaster on the back of her neck. He gave no hope of her yesterday but she is rather better today, tho' they can't keep her awake 2 minutes together.

Sunday 21 June [Halifax]

Had tea at 5 in the hope of my going to the lecture, but it was too wet. Having myself proposed making it a rule to have the pedigree [family tree] brought down & read aloud the 21st days of every June & December, began the thing this evening.

Tuesday 23 June [Halifax]

There being a wedding in the town today, not a chaise to be had. Mr Wriglesworth's carriage came to convey us to dine at Whitwell place . . . General Fawcett & I walked to Elland. My uncle rode Diamond. Mr Wriglesworth & my 2 aunts in the carriage . . . Mrs Veitch gave us a good dinner & we had a tolerably pleasant visit. Drove home in an hour . . . my aunts & myself inside. The General with Thomas on the box . . . My father & Marian arrived (by the Highflier coach from Market Weighton), both looking very well – having slept last night at the Tavern in York. Singing different songs for 20 minutes before getting into bed.

Saturday 27 June [Halifax]

As we were coming up the new bank, at the top, met the whole party of Brownes & their friends, the Kellys . . . Miss Brown, in a white gown & green velvet spencer, looked Kallista. I stopped & kept her talking till my father & aunt, who [were] some several yards behind, came up. My aunt also admired her.

Sunday 28 June [Halifax]

The people generally remark, as I pass along, how much I am like a man. I think they did it more than usual this evening. At the top of *Cunnery Lane, as I went, three men said, as usual, 'That's a man' & one axed* [sic] *'Does your cock stand?'* I know not how it is but I feel low this evening. *I don't think quite so much of Miss Browne but still too much . . . I wish I could get her out of my head.*

Monday 29 June [Halifax]

Sewing till twelve ... This seems to have been a lost day. Visiting hereabouts gives me no after satisfaction & wasting my time in bed in a morning disturbs my happiness for the day. My only pleasure is in the thought of having employed myself profitably &, deprived of this, my spirits are unable to support themselves. I have felt low (tho' I have not seemed so) all the day, nor am I less so now.

Tuesday 30 June [Halifax]

Finished my morning's work a few minutes before 2. Made an extract or 2 from Lord Byron's *Childe Harold* & the lyrics at the end of the book in readiness to take it back. Set off down the old bank a little before 4. Staid at the library above an hour looking out a couple of books with proper prints for the children to copy at Pye Nest. Returned up the new bank & walked up & down the little lane towards the west, very nearly an hour. *What led me there was to have a view of Mr Brown's house & to see if I should be able to distinguish Miss Brown walking in the garden. I could do it very well with a telescope & I thought of getting one.* Found the wind so bracing & the situation so suited to reflection & so happy in point of prospect, that I almost made up my mind to walk there often. Mused upon the practicability of aiding my classical studies under the tuition of Dr Carey. I should like to be at least 6 months with him. I 1st thought of this some time ago – soon after I began to study his elements of Latin prosody.

Thursday 2 July [Halifax]

Marking linen & petticoats & all sorts of things with permanent ink & looking over my things in readiness to go to Langton.[8]

Friday 3 July [Halifax]

From 2 till 3 & afterwards from 4 till 6, putting a new blue paper lining into my travelling trunk.

Sunday 5 July [Halifax]

Had tea at 5 &, it being the 1st Sunday in the month, when Mr Knight generally lectures, my aunt went with me . . . Sat in my aunt's seat in the north aisle. *Don't much like going with her on this account as I cannot see Miss Brown & feel as if I were quite out of the way. Got a distant glimpse of the girl as she went out. Felt inclined to be grave all the way home because I did not see more of her. Never uttered her name but thought of little else. I wish I was with Isabella & was happy with her. I will try to be so, if possible.*

Wednesday 22 July [Halifax]

In going down the old bank, a littleish, tipsyish-looking, young man stopped me. Fancying I was going to strike him with my umbrella, he stepped back, saying, 'If you do, I'll drop you'. I quietly walked off, adding, 'I should like to see you.'

Thursday 23 July [Halifax]

Had tea at 5 & all set off to walk to South-holme at 6½. Got back at 10¾. A very hot walk, hardly a breath of air . . . Just as we reached the opposite side of the hill to South-holme, a good band of clarinets & horns & a big drum (perhaps there were 10 or 15 or 20 tho' not all were players) struck up & we staid to listen 5 or 6 minutes. Hemingway had just sold all his peas, except a few strikes that were to get at 16d. or 18d. per strike. He has already had 150 strikes. He planted 2½ days work.

Sunday 26 July [Halifax]

Had tea at 5 & went to the lecture ... Walked out of church ... Joined Miss Browne & her sister ... *Miss Browne said so much to me about calling & how happy her mother would be to see me that I told her at once, by way of excuse, I should have great pleasure in doing so, but that my uncle & aunt visited so little we never made any new acquaintances. She still said, 'But you might call,' & I heard her mutter something about, 'I should not trouble your uncle much.' Immediately begged she would not think of such a thing as troubling my uncle, but that he was elderly. 'Oh,' said she, 'I can enter into your feeling.' ''Tis well,' thought I & added, 'I have not said I will never call. Never is a long time.' We then proceeded to chit-chat ... Rejoiced she was better for warm bathing, complimented her on looking better. She had a lovely colour, was clad in robes of virgin white & looked altogether beautiful. But soon after I got home, beyond the pale of beauty's fascination, the words, 'I won't trouble your uncle much,' & the manner of them, occurred to me & gave rise to the question, 'Is she good-tempered?' It is not to be expected she should know much of the world. If she had, she would have said less about my calling, assured that I should call if I chose. Besides, she would recollect it is my place to offer the thing, not hers to ask it.*

Monday 27 July [Halifax]

Letter from Isabella Norcliffe (dated Bruxelles, 21 July 1818) ... Isabella desiring me to write immediately, I filled a sheet before dinner ... *My letter of today is certainly more affectionate than any I have written her of long ... I have always loved her in spite of all & now that circumstances have so far alienated me from M—, Isabella's fondness, fortune & connections, if her temper be grown rather more tractable, will make me happy. I almost begin to feel that we shall get together at last.*

Saturday 1 August [Halifax]

Set off to Halifax . . . to Mrs Tom Rawson's. Mrs Tom's sister & cousin, Anne Holdsworth, are staying with her. The latter sings well &, after tea, gave us 'Auld Robin Gray', Moore's 'Wilt Thou Say Farewell, Love?', & an Italian song. I sang, 'Early Days', blundered thro' the 2nd of a duett [*sic*] at sight, & croaked 'Fite Gustace'. Staid supper &, after a couple of glasses of excellent Madeira, sang Scott's 'Hail to the Chief' to everyone's satisfaction. Tom walked home with me & I got in just before it struck 11.

Saturday 8 August [Halifax]

Had dinner at 5 & my uncle & aunt & I set off immediately to drink tea at Haugh-end. Met there Mr & Mrs Page from Gosport . . . old Mr & Mrs Priestley, George & Dr Busfield. The latter sings and plays on the piano scientifically & accompanied himself in 2 songs, the latter 'Listen, Listen to the Voice of Love', & sang 'Salley [*sic*] in our alley' without music. I sang 'Early Days' & 'Hail to the Chief Who in Triumph Advances'. Dr Busfield & I afterwards sang a chant together & tried one or two sacred things. I then sang 'Pray Goody' & made an attempt at the last words of Marmion, but could not manage both to sing & play at the same time. The evening passed very pleasantly & we did not get home till ½ past 10.

Monday 10 August [Halifax]

Got home 25 minutes before 9. Found my aunt at the harpsichord. I tweedled & sang near an hour . . . Having had no dinner, indeed nothing but bread & butter at Lightcliffe, & fancying myself peckish just before I got into bed, went down into the cellar & ate a little cold veal.

Wednesday 12 August [Halifax]

In the morning, till 12, writing out, from notes on a slate, my journal of Monday & yesterday, settling my accounts up to this day, & siding my drawers . . . In the evening, at 8½, my aunt & I went to the top of Bairstow to see the fireworks played off from the piece-hall.[9] They not seeming to be beginning, we returned home, resolving to go again by & by. At 9.20, my aunt, & Marian & I set off. Finding we saw little or nothing from the top of Bairstow, we left the people (& there were a good many, tho' several went before & with us) & dashed straight down the hill. My aunt, unable to keep her feet, slid down on her honourable part, Marian ditto, & we all laughed exceedingly. We hurried down the old bank & got to the hall door (with our shillings in our hands, determined to go into the servants' gallery) just as the business was over & all the smart people were coming away. We instantly turned back & retraced our steps & got home at 20 minutes after 10, having only been an hour away altogether – my aunt a bit tired with the exertion & Marian red as a turkey cock with heat. Never said we had been further than the top of Bairstow. Had something hot & came up to bed at 11, when I wrote my journal of the evening.

Saturday 15 August [Halifax]

Called & sat ¾ hour at Cross-hills. Saw Mrs & the 3 oldest Miss Greenwoods. They introduced the subject of Miss Brown & we talked a good while in her praise, touching my admiring her, etc. They wanted me to call on her, but this I said I could not do, lamenting at the same time, that her father & mother's vulgarity was such a disadvantage to her. *I said we never visited new people & that, tho' I would make an exception in Miss Brown's favour, I could not expect or think of my uncle & aunt doing so. But if Miss Browne would consent to come to Shibden Hall without my going to Westfield, it would make a difference. I said the last time I saw her was the twenty-sixth of July, & talked altogether as if I admired her exceedingly.*

The eyes of the town's society were now on the ripening friendship between Anne and Elizabeth Browne and a subtle process of baiting began, with the Greenwoods being the chief instigators. The Brownes, of course, were pleased to think that a leading Halifax family, or a member of that family, was going out of her way to cultivate their daughter and they probably hoped to be introduced to a more select social circle through their daughter's friendship with Anne.

Sunday 16 August [Halifax]

Spoke to Miss Brown in going out [of church]. She was walking with her mother but the good woman slunk aside to her husband directly & left the fair one & myself together. Both the Greenwoods darted off to the Staveleys & I never did see two people left more tête-à-tête in my life. In this, I was obliged to offer my arm & we had our own chit-chat as far as Harrison Lane, when the Greenwoods & I turned homewards & they walked with me to the first cottages in the bank. I told them they ought not to have left us so pointedly together. Caroline said Mrs Staveley asked her if she was not jealous for fear all the friendship I had for her should be transferred to Miss Browne. She said no, she knew my heart was large enough to admit them all. I told them I would drink tea with them on Tuesday, so they may possibly ask the girl, for I think they seem to be in her interest. I am sure Kallista has no dislike to me & her not speaking last Sunday was politic bashfulness. She seems determined to let all the notice come first from me. Sensible girl. She knows how to play her part.

Tuesday 18 August [Halifax]

Called downstairs to try on a new bombazine waist my aunt is making for me ... In the afternoon ... went down the old bank . . . to Cross-hills to drink tea there . . . *I should not have gone but for the hope of meeting Miss Brown & not seeing her at any of the windows as I passed Westfield deluded me into the idea that she was already set off. I afterwards bore my disappointment as well as I could but my nose began to bleed a lot about an hour after tea & Mrs Greenwood observed more than once she had never seen me look so dull.* The Greenwoods . . . soon introduced the subject of Miss Brown . . . *Talked as if Miss Brown was lessened in my estimation & as if I should gradually shirk the acquaintance. Miss Caroline, in spite of my arguments, called me fickle. All declared the lady a perfect pattern of propriety & retiring modesty &, tho' they did not seem to believe me, I declared I was satisfied & she was higher in my esteem than ever, tho' I said her society was out of my reach as I could not call. They talked of pride, etc. However, I gained my object for I learned she was greatly pleased & flattered, as well as papa & mama, by my attentions; that she had doubtless a growing regard for me; had reason, after my conduct, to call me a friend (which term I would not admit but substituted acquaintance) & to believe that I could not visit her on account of my uncle & aunt, but that I should certainly do it as soon as I could. They all wished me to spend some days at Cross-hills in the winter. I would not be hired to do it. Surely Caroline has a sneaking partiality for me.* Got home as the kitchen clock struck 10. Had a slice or two of cold beef, not having had anything at Cross-hills but tea & bread & butter . . . *Thinking of Miss Browne all the way home & while I was getting into bed.*

Sunday 23 August [Halifax]

Awoke last night by the dogs' barking & the cook told me 3 shabby-looking men were about the house. Got up, charged the pistol to be ready & had scarce got into bed when roused again by the dog. Followed the cook into her room (the Green Room), put my head out of the window &, seeing 2 men leaning against the wall below, declared I would blast their brains out if they did not immediately go about their business. Talked to them a minute or two & they almost provoked me to fire but the cook said these were not the same men she saw before. They said they had done, & meant to do, no harm & went away down the lane. Such is the fruit of a footpath so close to the house. Kept a lighted candle in my room but fell asleep a little after 2 & was no more disturbed.

Sunday 24 August [Halifax]

In the afternoon, *mending my black silk legs to which I tack cotton socks & wear them under my boots.*

Wednesday 26 August [Halifax]

Got to the old church this evening a few minutes before the lecture began. Managed this on purpose in the hope of seeing Miss Browne, who generally goes. Alas! I was doomed to disappointment & . . . I concluded she must have set off to Harrogate according to her mother's desire. I either am, or fancy I am, in love with the girl. At least, I think more of her than ever & felt quite low & vapourish at not seeing her. I wonder if she ever thinks of me, or if she has the least spark of anything like regard for me?

Friday 28 August [Halifax]

Called & sat an hour with the Misses Caroline & Susan Greenwood . . . Miss Susan soon mentioned Miss Browne. They said she set off to Harrogate for a week . . . & then she & her sister are going to spend 5 weeks in the neighbourhood of Chesterfield & a month at Sheffield . . . *The Greenwoods said she was likely to marry well at Sheffield. I said I should rejoice at it & declared I would call & see her. I said I would have done it long ago if I had twenty thousand a year, etc, of my own but that, as it was, what could I do? Speaking of her looks, I said I thought I had never seen her look as little like herself as when I met her there at tea & that surely she looked the best in a walking dress. We all admired the modesty of her manners. They particularly admired her conduct towards me, not at all pushing but always waiting for me to make the advances . . . They were astonished to think I should think so much of anyone. They fancied me quite taken up with Miss Norcliffe. I said that was quite a different thing.*

During Miss Browne's week of absence at Harrogate, Anne turned her thoughts towards her other absent friends. She began to analyse her feelings for M—.

Monday 31 August [Halifax]

Letter from M— . . . Her letter breathes little of affection & indeed I do not estimate her feelings towards me very highly. She has not, she never had, the heart that Isabella has. I suppose she is more comfortable now than formerly with C—. She has her carriage & the luxuries of life & thinks proportionately less of me. Mrs Featherstone said, 'Give her these things & these are all she wants.' M—'s conduct to me has certainly been as strange a mixture of weakness, selfishness & worldly-mindedness. Consider her conduct on our first acquaintance; before her marriage; about her marriage; & ever since. An unfaithful friend to Isabella, a weak & wavering companion to me. On calm & mature reflection I neither much admire her nor much esteem her character. But she is specious, very specious, with much female vanity. I do not accuse her of premeditated deceit because perhaps she deceives herself as much as anyone else. She always seemed religious & talked piously. She believed herself, or seemed to believe herself, over head & ears in love, yet she sold her person to another for a carriage & a jointure, still keeping her intercourse with the one she loved & was seriously desirous of executing the prostituting of herself in disguise to any man who could make up the deficiencies & get her with child for the sake of fixing her importance by being the mother of an heir to Lawton. I know the scheme was originally my own proposing but she persisted in it till I utterly disclaimed it, shocked, as I said, at the serious idea of such a thing. Wherewith her morality? But I have acted very foolishly & wickedly. Oh that I may repent & turn me from my sin. Lord, forgive & help me.

Saturday 5 September [Halifax]

Went into the market-place & ordered the Elland basketmaker to make me a wicker box about ¾ yd by ⅜ and ¼ deep, to be covered with oil case & to carry my hats & light things in when I travel . . . Spoke to Furniss, the sadler [sic] about covering my wicker box with oil-cloth.

Sunday 6 September [Halifax]

Went to Pye-nest today for nothing in the world but to see Miss Browne . . . I wonder what she thinks of me & what she thought of me tonight. Surely female vanity cannot seriously be offended at my so particular attention? As soon as I got home I asked my aunt seriously about calling on the girl & declared I would joke no more about her, for that I really liked her in good earnest . . . My aunt looked a little surprised, but I had taken her by surprise & she behaved very well . . . Came upstairs. Ten minutes afterwards brought my aunt up with me. Talked about Miss Browne. Said how foolish it was, but I really liked her & expressed a serious wish to call. After half an hour's talk, my aunt consented . . . As soon as she was gone, thought the matter seriously over. Lamented, prayed God to have mercy on me & to help me & resolved never more to mention Miss Browne & to avoid her entirely. For the last time I will allow myself to try to meet her tomorrow.

Monday 7 September [Halifax]

At 11¾ set off to Halifax . . . *looking about me in every direction for Miss Browne . . . Spied a suspicious bonnet in Royston Road. She came a good yard or two out of her way to speak to me . . .* She had been having a warm bath & dinner was ready but I asked her to walk & we went almost to Willowfield . . . *I think I succeeded in making myself agreeable . . . Paid her beauty several compliments & told her she was the best-dressed girl in town or neighbourhood . . . She thanked me for my good opinion. I said I wondered I had told it to her so freely as surely it was so evident from my conduct that saying anything about it was quite unnecessary. She said she was afraid of me, tho' she declared I suited myself to her as well as anyone with my talents could possibly do. I assured her she had often frightened me so as to make me quite nervous . . . brought about an agreement to meet at the library at 4 tomorrow afternoon . . . How changed since last night when I declared to seek after the girl only once more. This once has done the business. I like her & this morning's walk & having told her to meet me tomorrow have certainly made me, shall I call it, happier, than I was before. At any rate, she does not shew any antipathy to my attentions.*

Tuesday 8 September [Halifax]

This meeting with Miss Browne seems to have stimulated & roused me altogether. I cannot live happily without female company, without someone to interest me . . . In the afternoon at 3.40, set off to Halifax. Went down the old bank & up Horton Street to the library . . . Miss Browne, not making her appearance, walked towards Westfield & met her at Blackwall. Turned back with her to the library . . . Asked her to walk. Found she had promised her mother to be back at 5; that her time was seldom her own; that 'mama' always inquires where she has been; that she did not like to see her poring over books in the daytime, but that she was kept stitching & attending to domestic concerns . . . Miss Browne is the most modest, unassuming, innocent girl (yet not wanting good sense) I ever met with. She is not brilliant. In fact, she has other things to do & reads by stealth. She said her mother, she believes, was thought a sensible woman by those who know her; that she had a most high opinion of me & told her how much she was honoured by my taking notice of her. *My whole strain of conversation was complimentary & calculated to impress her with the idea how much I was interested about her. Desired her to bring her heart safe back from Chesterfield & Sheffield – that I thought it was a heart worth having & begged her not to throw it away. She seemed much pleased at my telling her she must walk with me some afternoon & drink tea at Shibden. Just before we parted I asked if she believed all I said. The poor girl said no. I begged her, at any rate, to be persuaded that I myself believed it, as she would not hesitate to allow if she knew how little given to flattery my conversation was to people in general . . . She modestly said, 'Well, I must understand you' . . . looked modest & seemed rather at a loss . . . If I mistake not, she is more than flattered. What girl under such circumstances would not be flattered, & more interested than she might possibly be aware. I shook hands with her cordially. She modestly walked up to the house without once looking aside.*

Wednesday 9 September [Halifax]

Sat 20 minutes at Northgate. A sad parting [from relatives who had been staying with Aunt Lister]. They got off 10 minutes before 11. Got to the Albion at Manchester by 4. Bitter complaints of the dirt & uncomfortableness of the house. A great many soldiers there & the town full of military in consequence of the late disturbances made by the cotton spinners to have their wages raised, & yet many of these very men can earn 3 guineas a week.

Thursday 10 September [Halifax]

At 3½, my aunt & father & Marian & I set off to Halifax. Took them to Furniss, the sadler, to look at my basket I ordered on

Saturday. Made an inch every way larger than the order, & even the order too big for my purpose. Set off to Elland to order another (24 in by 14, and 8 in deep inside) and desired it to be sent to Furniss on Saturday. Had a pleasant walk, tho' a few drops of rain on my return. Went the low way to Salterhebble but came back along the high road & a little on this [road], a very civil, well-dressed traveller, I suppose, in a neat gig, offered me a seat as it seemed so likely for rain. This, however, I civilly declined &, having parted with my aunt at the top of Horton Street at 4.25, walked from thence to the basket-makers in Elland & back to my Aunt Lister's at Northgate in an hour & 40 minutes, a distance of more than 6 miles. Staid a little while at Northgate, walked from there with my Aunt Anne & got home at 6.40. Told her I met Miss Browne on Tuesday & walked with her to the 1st milestone beyond Salterhebble & repeated a part of our conversation in as much as it told to Miss Browne's credit. *My aunt expressed no dislike nor surprise at the thing.*

Saturday 12 September [Halifax]

Letter from Mrs Norcliffe (Langton, Malton) . . . Kindly desires me to fix an early day for going . . . Looking over my things to see what I should want doing & at 1.40 set off to Halifax to see if my basket was done. Paid the man 6s. for it & got him to take the other back by giving him 4s., so that the charge being 7/6, I have lost little more than half.

Sunday 13 September [Halifax]

Set off at 6 . . . to the lecture . . . *Walked out of church with the fair one, meaning to have turned down by the vicarage but she said she was afraid she should not have seen me & wished so much that she had the courage to walk up the bank with me that I then said I would walk a little way with her. She envied my courage. This, I said, like all other qualifications of the mind, might be gained at last by practice ... Miss Browne then asked me if I should be in the library on Tuesday. I said yes & in spite of the great deal she had to do, she offered to meet me at 4. In fact, she now begins to shew that she is as much pleased with me as I can wish. When she told me she was afraid I had not gone to the lecture for she could not see me on account of the number of people between us, I said I knew her & her sisters by their bonnets, particularly the drooping flowers in them, both which, together with the ribband [sic], I thought the prettiest I had seen. She seemed pleased, saying she thought I did not notice such things as these. I said no, not in general. Some people might have sacks about their heads & I not know, but there were some whose ribands I could count over for the last seven years.*

Anne makes preparations to go to the Norcliffes' house, Langton Hall, arranging to stay overnight at York with the Belcombes.

Monday 14 September [Halifax]

Till 7, writing my journal of yesterday, all but the 1st 9 lines, & wrote a couple of pp. to Mrs Norcliffe to thank her for her letter & fix the day for coming. 'The mail, I suppose, gets into Malton about 4 in the morning. Now, if people at the inn had a chaise ready for me, I should be at Langton about 5 and if Burnett[10] or some one would quietly let me in, could go to bed for an hour or two & disturb no one else.' After breakfast wrote a note to Parsons [in York] to desire him to be at home to cut my hair between 9 & 10 on Thursday night. Gave it to my father to put into the York P.O. as also (to save her the postage so far) my letter to Mrs Norcliffe, Langton, Malton. Walked with my father & Marian to Halifax ... Never had so disagreeable walk in my life. A high wind blew clouds of dust full in our faces, & small rain made it stick like plaster ... Went to the White Lion

& saw them both off in the Highflier (for Market Weighton) at 11½ by the church clock.

Anne undertook a round of farewell visits to her friends in Halifax, as she would not be back there until towards the end of December. She met Miss Browne for the last time until her return; Miss Browne also went on extended visits to relatives.

Tuesday 15 September [Halifax]

At 3½ set off to Halifax again. Went to a shop or 2 & got to the library as the church clock struck 4. Miss Browne came in a minute or 2 after & just escaped a heavy shower which kept us prisoners some time. *She said she had left her sister making shoppings, who wondered what could induce her to run up to the library in such a hurry. She said she had promised her mother to be back by half-past four, but she made no difficulty about taking a walk, even tho' it exceedingly threatened rain & she would not leave the library before it was quite fair because of spoiling her green lustre gown. I said if she did I would offer to give her another but it would be so impertinent. She replied, not impertinent but unnecessary. We walked by Blackwall . . . to King Cross. About 100 yds from here it began to rain. She wanted to turn back but I said we had better go on & take shelter in the inn. She consented after a few 'hems' & 'hahs' & the woman civilly shewed us into a room by ourselves where we staid about 12 minutes, not at all to the lady's annoyance. I told her her gown sleeves were rather too wide & that her frill was not put on straight. I took it off & put it on again, taking three trials to it before I would be satisfied. She did not seem to dislike the thing, nor to be unhappy in my society. I think if I chose to persevere, I can bring the thing to what terms I please . . . I observed, however . . . that she had dirty nails & that her gown sleeves were not lined & she had no loose sleeves on. Is she very tidy? But she is pretty & I thought of what I should not . . . They are to set off for Sheffield tomorrow at 5 in the morning . . . In the evening, as also last night after supper, making a bag of oiled cotton to hold my sponge & toothbrush.*

Wednesday 16 September [Halifax]

Busy all the day about getting my things ready. Mending, & in the afternoon & evening, making a lining for my basket. Came upstairs at 10½. Counted over my money, etc. Began packing about 12 & had all quite done at 3½ . . . Dawdled so long that I was not in bed till 5.

Thursday 17 September [Langton]

My aunt, having determined to go with me as far as York, to put herself under the care of Mr Horner, the dentist, we set off at 11, & my uncle walked with us to Northgate. *Tired of sitting at Northgate, I went to the White Lion &, tho' I had an inside place in the Highflier, mounted the box with the coachman.* It began to rain a couple of miles from Halifax & came on so heavily that I got inside at the inn on Clayton Heights . . . Set off from Halifax at 11.40. Got to Leeds at 3, where we had a wretched dinner, to Tadcaster at 6 (I on the box from Leeds to Tadcaster) and reached the Tavern, York, at 7½. Stopped & left my aunt's luggage at the George Inn in Coney Street as we passed . . . I hastened to make 1 or 2 shoppings, to get my hair cut, inquired if Mr Horner was at home & ordered about my aunt's rooms at the George. Preferred going alone &, tho' at this early hour, (about 8), one could not walk about unobserved. *Some men & women declared I was a man.* Did all my jobs to my satisfaction & then went to Parsons who, as he cut me close behind, & curled my hair like the crest of a helmet at the top of my head, as they wore it 8 or 10 years ago, amused me with an account of his month's visit to Paris last June. He went in the cabriolet of the diligence &, excellent provisions, was franked from the White Bear, Piccadilly, to Paris, for £3 18s. He said he found

Paris *very* expensive; that with one thing or another, it cost him 22 or 23 francs a day, but he could manage better another time, for, not being able to speak a word of French, he had gone to the hotel frequented by the Duke of Wellington & all the English, Meurice's, one of the most expensive hotels in Paris. The Hotel de Suede [Tuede?], near the Italian boulevards, he understood was a very good one. Speaking of the shameful badness of the police of York, he said tho' there was certainly a great deal of vice in Paris, yet it was kept so entirely out of the way of all those who did not seek for it, that no one would be annoyed in the streets of Paris at any hour unless they chose it, for the bad women were only to be distinguished by looking behind them or on one side, since they durst not speak first. Got to the Belcombes' at 9. I had tea & my aunt went away in ½ hour. Thinking of meeting the Norcliffes rather agitated me[11] & my spirits were anything but buoyant. Anne, however, soon assured me that no fault was to be found with the spirits of the party at Langton. Mr & Mrs Norcliffe looked as usual. Charlotte[12] had stayed all night there with Harriet [Milne née Belcombe] & Isabella had given them imitations of Talma.[13] Anne & I had about 20 minutes tête-à-tête after the rest went to bed . . . Left Anne a few minutes before 12 & James went with me to the Black Swan in Coney St. where he had secured me a place in the Whitby mail . . . There were several bad women standing about the mail. They would have it I was a man & one of them gave me a familiar knock on the left breast & would have persisted in following me but for James. Paced about one of the front parlours at the Swan till 20 minutes past 12, when we drove off . . . Got to Malton at 3. Found a note from Mrs Norcliffe, who had ordered a bed to be ready for me & said it would be soon enough if I ordered the chaise at 8½ in the morning. In about an hour, just as I was dropping asleep over the kitchen fire, the chamber-maid, seemingly in her teens, made her appearance. She shewed me into a large, double-bedded room which, however, on examination, she found to be preoccupied. She then took me into a small back room, where the bed was literally smoking from some gentleman who had just left it. This, however, I was too sleepy to mind &, seeing that it was, in good truth, clean-sheeted, ordered up my luggage, jumped into my friend's birth [*sic*] which needed no warming, & slept soundly for a couple of hours & a half.

The house party at Langton Hall consisted of the family – Mr and Mrs Norcliffe, Isabella, Mary (now the widowed Mrs Best), Mary's two little girls, Rosamond, aged ten and Mary Ellen, aged nine, Charlotte Norcliffe and Anne herself. There was also a friend of the Norcliffes staying, Miss Mary Vallance, a brewer's daughter, from Sittingbourne, Kent. The Norcliffes had spent some time touring Europe and Anne was both apprehensive and excited about her meeting with Isabella, after almost three years' absence. Earlier in the year, thinking about their impending reunion, Anne had indulged in a little fantasising. On 12 February, 1818, she had confided her thoughts to her journal: '. . . *Lay in bed thinking & building castles about Isabella, as in fact I did last Saturday. How fond she would be, what sort of kisses she would give. Whether Miss Vallance would find us out.*' However, later in the year, when she arrived at the Hall around nine-forty on the morning of Friday 18 September, the romantic dreams were soon dispersed. That first night together, about which Anne had fantasised earlier, was not a success.

Friday 18 September [Langton]

I had been asleep about 2½ hours when the chamber-maid awoke me at 7½. Ordered a chaise to be ready a little before

9 . . . The hostess, very neatly dressed, came to the door to see me off & I was on my way here at 9. The man drove me by the wold in 40 minutes. Nobody downstairs. Isabella Norcliffe in her dressing-gown waiting to receive me in my own (the blue) room. She seemed a good deal agitated at 1st, but when this went off, I thought her fatter than when I saw her last & looking remarkably well . . . Took off my pelisse & went down to breakfast a bit before 11. Mr & Mrs Norcliffe seemed glad to see me & I very sincerely rejoiced to find them in spirits so much better than (before seeing Anne Belcombe) I fancied they would be.

Saturday 19 September [Langton]

Tried for a kiss a considerable time last night but Isabella was as dry as a stick & I could not succeed. At least she had not one & I felt very little indeed. She was very feverish, quite dry heat & seemed quite annoyed & fidgeted herself exceedingly at our want of success, saying she had grown fit for nothing & asking what could be the matter with her. It was certainly odd as she by no means seemed to want passion. I carried the thing off as well as I could, that is to say very well, tho' I confess I felt surprised & disappointed. Went to sleep in about an hour. Tried again just before getting up & succeeded a little better, tho' far from well.

The next night saw an improvement but by the third night Anne was beginning to have reservations.

Monday 21 September [Langton]

[Isabella] *dotes on me & her constancy is admirable & her wish to oblige & please me overcomes every other, yet her passions seem impotent without the strong excitement of grossness & her sentiments are very far from being those I most admire. But so far she is improved in temper. She has seen a great deal of vice abroad & heard a great deal of loose conversation. Her mind is not pure enough for me, but time must tell the event of our connection* . . . Just before dinner, Isabella gave me a prayer book in 14 languages which she brought me from Venice.

Tuesday 22 September [Langton]

Mr Norcliffe, Isabella & I . . . went a coursing at 2 & were out a couple of hours. After ranging about almost an hour, found a couple of hares on the wold. The dogs worried them almost to their seats. Went into the stubble fields – worried another poor thing, & killed 2 more after 2 fine runs, the greater part of which, to my sorrow, as we did not follow, we could not see. *I rode Butcher Bob's poney* [sic] *& was exceedingly tired from not having ridden of so long. Charlotte lent me her habit.*

Saturday 10 October [Langton]

Soon after breakfast, Miss Albinia Dalbiac [one of a family of new arrivals who had joined the house party] stole away by ourselves into the drawing-room & sat down to chess. I lost 1 & won 2 games.

Monday 12 October [Langton]

Walked with Miss Vallance a couple of hours on the wold. After supper, Isabella Norcliffe put on the dress in which she had acted at Florence, & gave us the part of Constance in the Earl of Warwick. Very well done – and a most spirited &, Mr & Mrs Norcliffe agreed, most like, imitation of Talma in Hamlet on the French stage. Isabella's talents for the stage are certainly first-rate.

Anne leaves Langton Hall on 2 November to visit an old Halifax friend, Ellen Empson, now living at Elvington. The Norcliffes left their home also, to travel south for the winter in order to improve Charlotte's health.

Monday 2 November [Elvington]

All of us set off from Langton . . . at ¼ before 12 . . . Arrived at Fisher's door in York at 20 minutes past 2 . . . Set off in Mr Empson's gig a little after 5 & reached Elvington a little after 6. Ellen seemed very glad to see me & she & Mr Empson were looking well. Put by all my things before getting into bed.

Tuesday 3 November [Elvington]

Three walnuts after dinner must have disagreed with me. About 7½, felt a universal sensation of pricking & swelling, & went in a hurry to bed. Crimson all over me. Every feature double its size & much pain in my head & stomach. Lay till 10½ when, being better, (tho' still very crimson & swell'd) . . . added a page to my letter to Marian & wrote 2½ pp. to Miss Marsh, Micklegate, York, leaving the letters at my door to go early in the morning.

Wednesday 4 November [Elvington]

Had a tolerable night but rather swell'd & headachy this morning. Read the 1st four letters of *The Fudge Family in Paris*. 1 vol. 12 more lately published. Edited by the author of the 2 penny post-bag. In verse. (Amusing & ridiculous enough.) Mr & Mrs Empson went to York in the gig at 11 . . . brought my trunk & the golden gage plum tree Mr Norcliffe had given me & which ought to have been sent to Shibden immediately.

Tuesday 10 November [Elvington]

Walked along the river side (the Derwent) . . . Came up to bed at 10.20 & Ellen staid talking till 11.35 . . . *Ellen & I had a long confab. Told her I was often in low spirits & she owned I had some reason – my father's managing his estate so ill & living in that quere [sic] sort of way at Weighton. I said I often wanted a companion –*

someone to take care of me & now she was gone there was nobody I cared about. Said she, very innocently, 'Why did you let me marry?' 'What could I do? You never asked me'. 'Well,' said she, 'That is true enough. I never asked anybody.' She seemed to feel a good deal interested about me. Said I was odd but hoped I would not change. I had before told her of having walked two or three times with Miss Browne, that I thought her a nice [girl] & had some thoughts of calling on her. She bade me tell her if I did do so & also if I heard of anyone whom I could go to for a little while for the sake of study, I having also told her my great wish to pursue my studies with some- one or other for another year, Mr Knight & his son, James, being both out of the question.

Wednesday 11 November [Market Weighton]

¼ hour tête-à-tête with Ellen & at 11½, went to pack. Quite ready at 1. Ellen then came to me & we sat down to luncheon & had near an hour's tête-à-tête. 'You never knew me so well before, Ellen, as you do now.' 'No & I like you better.' 'I am afraid I cannot say so. I loved you so much from the first, I hardly left room to like you better. But you said it would not last.' 'I remember I did, for I could not understand why you should like me, I was so unlike you – so uncongenial.' She pressed me very much to accept her grey cloth cloak & seemed really fond of me . . . The groom drove me in the gig . . . Got to Market Weighton a little after 5 . . . My father & Marian looking well. Had a mutton chop & tea.

Wednesday 18 November [Market Weighton]

Walked about in the garden. At 12 set off walking with my father & got back at 4½ . . . Called at all my father's 3 farms & walked full 7 miles. Today, what they call the statutes – for hiring servants – the town full of people & stirrings. A sort of merry andrew [clown or buffoon performing in public] shew in the market hill . . . Just before tea, backgammon with my father.

On Saturday 21 November, Anne left Market Weighton for York where she stayed with the Duffins at the Red House. Miss Marsh was in constant attendance and Anne employed her time by paying social calls, particularly to the Belcombe family, walking around York, and writing her journals.

Saturday 21 November [York]

Packing most of the morning. *My father asked how my pocket was & gave me five pounds besides four sixpences for change, having paid my fare, five shillings, & three shillings for postage.* Left Market Weighton about 6½ & got to the Tavern, York, at 9 . . . The people at the Tavern very civil. The waiter immediately shewed me into a private room &, for the short time I staid, lighted wax-lights. Got into Micklegate about 20 minutes after 9. The Duffins very glad to see me. Miss Marsh staid till near 11. Went upstairs at 11. Put by my things, that I did not get into bed till one. No fire which [made] the room look rather comfortless.

Wednesday 2 December [York]

At 11¼, Mr Duffin & I called for Miss Marsh. Went to the national school (in part of the same building as the Manor School,[14] the great room that used to [be] called King James's drawing-room). 449 boys, Mr Danby. Everything in excellent order. 4 or 5 of the boys in Hutton's mensuration. Mr Danby 1 of the best masters at any school on this plan. To the national school, Merchant Taylor's hall in Aldwark. 239 girls, Mrs Danby, wife to the master at the boys' school. She had every-thing also in good order & seems as clever in her department as her husband in his. 1 of her own children, not quite 3, was knit-ting a stocking. To the Bluecoat school, Peasholme Green. 18 neat beds (without any curtains) in the sleeping room, plaster floor, and 56 boys – Mr Ward. Most of the boys were at their looms weaving chiefly coarse calico when we went in, which was just before dinner. To the Merchant Hall in Fossgate, an odd-looking old building. There are 2 large rooms, in 1 of which the Bible Society holds its meetings. There is a charity here for 5 old widows & 5 old men. The widows have a living-room with 5 little fireplaces in it, & a sleeping ditto with 5 beds, placed round 3 sides of the room, as it were in wood closets each just large enough to hold 1 bed, and 4s. a month. The old men have their living room divided with boards into 5 equal compartments with each a little fireplace, table & chair, leaving a wide passage along the front of them that admitted light for the whole through one or 2 windows. They had also 5 beds in 1 sleeping room & seemed, on the whole, more comfortable & more contented than the women . . . Tho' today is the funeral of the queen,[15] yet there is a dinner party at the Richard Townends' at 5 & a rout in the evening . . . A rout also at the Revd Mr Dixon's, Minster Yard. As we walked along in the morning, all the shop windows shut, but hardly any of private houses, tho' we have been told they were all shut during service (which began at 3) at the Minster. There was service also at Belfries – but at no other church. The Coney Street bells rang a dumb peal at intervals during the day. But as for the people, I must say, no one appeared to care anything about it. Mr Duffin dined at the Townends' & Miss Marsh went in the evening at 8. I walked with her & went to the Belcombes'. The streets full of people returning from the different chapels for, to the shame of the church clergy, there was service at, I believe, all the different places of worship in the city . . . Sat talking to . . . Lou. Said I was vapourish, could not live comfortably without a female friend & companion . . . Said Lou, 'You should not have let Mariana marry.' 'That, Lou, I would not have prevented for worlds, unless I had worlds to give in exchange.' Mr Duffin & Miss Marsh were to call for me. We were just sending to see if they had forgotten me when they arrived at near 1.

Thursday 3 December [York]

Went with Mr Duffin into the Shambles, where he made a contract with butcher Wilson to have the choice of the best joints of beef, mutton, veal & now & then, if he chose, a joint of pork at 7½d. per lb. Went thro' Thursday market & came out by the Tavern, down Coney St. & home at 4. At 6½, the Duffins & Miss Marsh & I went to tea & supper at the Swanns'. Played 2 pools at commerce . . . The supper, sweetbreads white, pheasant, scalloped oysters, mashed potatoes out of small moulds, hot apple-tarts, & stewed pears. Afterwards, toasted cheese. Got home at 10½.

Tuesday 15 December [York]

Miss Salmond came in & brought some ripe strawberries & a bunch of ripe raspberries just come out of the kitchen garden at Swinton, nr Bedale . . . The strawberries looked like chillies & were a good size – the raspberries small. Met the Milnes, Anne Belcombe & Lou at the end of the passage. Lou went with me to Bramley's in Blake St, to order a pair of boots to try if he can do for me instead of Hornby to whom I had just paid 21s. per pair. She & I then walked thro' the crowded horse fair, out of Micklegate Bar, as far as the white house. Took another turn, then left her to join her sisters, who were before us. Got home at 3½. Dined at the Belcombes' at 5. Mr Duffin & Miss Marsh came at 7 to play Boston . . . *When I said, as we walked home tonight, how much I would like to stay two or three months, Mr Duffin never said a word. I cannot make out whether he would like to have me a winter or not. I have more than once given him an opportunity of saying but he never uttered.*

Thursday 17 December [York]

Lou & I got off a walking by ourselves. Walked to the 2nd milestone on the Malton Rd, & got back at 1¾ . . . *Talked of M—'s*

match, I persisting it had answered, & about the state of my affec-
tions, that I must have somebody to dote upon. That, however I was
changed in appearance, my heart was warm as ever. Lou plainly said
she liked me &, in telling my sentiments towards her, when I talked
of esteem & high opinion, she said she would rather have my love
than esteem. I told her she did not understand my love & that she
was too cold for me. She owned she appeared so but said she could
convince me to the contrary but would not – felt she could not tell
me. She fancied from my conversation, I wished to invite her to
Shibden (in reality, no such thing ever entered my head) & said noth-
ing would give her more pleasure but she could not leave home.

Saturday 19 December [Halifax]

Got comfortably washed & dressed, buckled up my basket, ate
a crust of bread, & drank a glass of Vidonia, & was in the
Highflier which drove off from the door as it struck 6 . . . To
Leeds, where we arrived about 9 – took no breakfast – arrived at
Halifax about 1½ . . . Spent the afternoon & evening in conversation. Came upstairs at 9. From then till 12, putting by my
things.

Wednesday 23 December [Halifax]

Set off my usual walk up Royston Rd etc. *Miss Browne joined me*
as I passed. From her quickness she must have been on the watch . . .
She looked very pretty but I begin to think that, except her good looks
& her character for amiability, she has little to boast, little to say for
herself, & a stupidish companion. She seems innocent & unknowing
as to the ways of the world. I wonder if I can ever, or shall ever,
mould her to my purpose.

Friday 25 December [Halifax]

We all walked to morning church. Mr West of Southowram
preached . . . Afterwards wished us 'A merry Xmas'. All staid

the sacrament. *I fear I never received it with less feeling of reverence. Was thinking more of Miss Browne than anything else. She was there opposite me at the altar table.*

Saturday 26 December [Halifax]

Went down the north parade & sat ½ hour at Cross-hills. The whole kit of them at home & vulgar as ever. Miss Caroline's head like a porcupine. Surely Mrs Greenwood must drink . . . During supper, fired the pistols.

Monday 28 December [Halifax]

My aunt & I set off to Halifax at 2½, she having, just before, gathered out of the garden for my Aunt Lister, a nosegay of 15 different sorts of flowers – laurustinus, chrysanthemums, yellow jasmine, pink-tree flower, dwarf passion-flower, heart's-ease, double primrose, purple stock, auricula, sweet allison, Venus's looking-glass, gentianella, roses, larkspur, & pheasant's eye – & 3 or 4 more sorts might have been added, such has been this uncommon season.

1819

Friday 8 January [Halifax]

Miss Browne met me at their front gate . . . *I was rather in a com-plimentary strain & rather more inclined to be a little jocose than usual. I asked if she was still afraid of me. She said she could not help feeling a little so sometimes . . . She told me she thought I had a very penetrating countenance. She did not observe it so much at first, but she had thought so of late and very often did not like to look at me. I said I was, at some times, more anxious to be penetrating than at others. 'Oh, oh,' thought I to myself, then, 'I have sometimes looked rather unutterable things.' I wonder what she feels. Thinking of me so often & not liking to look at me augurs well. I said I should always be happy to give her any information [in] my power & begged she would always ask me anything she wished to know. I said I would notice everything she said that wanted correction.*

Saturday 9 January [Halifax]

[Miss Browne] came about four . . . Walked past Clare Hall[1] . . . *Told her when she did not hear a person, not to say 'Ma'am'. Asked her not to cover her face so much with the cap under her bonnet & shewed her how to shake hands, that is, not to keep shak-ing, or hold one's hand so long . . . She wonders why I like her so much. I begin to wonder too, for I fear she is stupidish & has very little in her – no warmth, I fear. I told her never to mention the* observations I made to her, as they were made for her alone . . . Never did I feel as little satisfied with her . . . I thought as I came along, Well, at all events, I will never call on her. What sort of a connection am I forming without anything to repay me? I could almost see her tomorrow at the lecture & excuse myself on Tuesday. I seem well inclined to think & care less about her in future. I have seen a great deal of her lately & they say, 'Give a dog rope enough & he will hang himself.'

Thursday 14 January [Halifax]

After supper, gave my father, to take to Marian, a green & yellow shot Italian gauze evening gown, a muslin ditto, a blue satin waist, a plaiting of buff satin riband for the bottom of a gown, a light drab kersey, more spencers trimmed with swansdown, very little worn – got for M—'s wedding, & a pair of cleaned, white kid shoes.

Saturday 16 January [Halifax]

All the morning, preparing clean stays, covering the steel busk, etc. & putting my hoard, forty-four pounds & Tib owes me six, which will make fifty. I never was so rich before.

Sunday 17 January [Halifax]

Sat up downstairs talking to my uncle about making his will . . . I said I should wish to have all the estate here, ultimately. 'What, all?' said my uncle, smiling. 'Yes, all. Isabella will be left in the entail for all the Langton estate & if I had any power, I should hereafter leave all to one.'

Saturday 30 January [Halifax]

In the afternoon, at 3¼, down the old bank to the library . . . walked up & down . . . with Miss Browne ¾ hour. She said she had been in great trouble, had almost cried her eyes [out] & often thought of telling me but could not make up her mind to do so till this *afternoon. Mr William Kelly, who has lately been staying at Westfield, & she are mutually attached &, it seems, have been ever since she was staying at his father's, 3 or 4 years ago. Mrs Browne is quite against it & Kallista cannot determine to give him up . . . She is in love, it seems, & this gives me little hope of making much impression on her in the amatory way. Besides, I have not enough opportunity & dare not make any serious tempting offer. This would never do for me. Besides, penchant is of a lighter nature.*

Monday 1 February [Halifax]

Wore my night cap both all this morning & the 2 preceding ones on account of shading my right eye which, from some cause or other, is becoming unable to bear any draught of air, & I am obliged to sit with my door open on account of my chimney's smoking.

Tuesday 2 February [Halifax]

At 3½, down the new bank to the library . . . Went . . . to the Greenwoods', Cross-hills. Staid tea, as was my intention, thinking I ought to do so as they would fancy from my never going, I was offended. Mrs Greenwood & all the 5 young ladies at home. The 2 youngest scarce spoke a word. Mrs Browne called there this morning. A repetition of her conversation about cooking & eating, etc. An account of Miss Browne's unbecoming dress at the Assembly. A sort of quiz upon her excellence & practice in domestic matters, spoke of her in a sort of general style of ridicule. Her unassuming quietness & constant attention to propriety cannot be supposed to suit the Greenwoods. Account of a party 10 days ago at Miss Pollard's. Played 'rural games', French blind man's buff, etc. Mrs Pollard (of Greenhill) set as a forfeit, that Miss Greenwood should sit down on the floor with the man she liked best & they should kiss 'wheelbarrow fashion'. All this going on when the servants brought in wine & cakes!! *The Greenwoods said they heard I was going to be married to Mr George Priestley. They little know me. Talking afterwards of society, I said how very much I preferred ladies to gentlemen &, when each was to choose a walking companion for each day in the week, I said Miss Browne should be mine at least six days out of the seven. Married ladies were not to be named.* The Greenwoods vulgar as ever. I felt thoroughly ashamed of my company and upon the whole, I know not when I have paid a visit that has displeased me so entirely. It was a few minutes after 10 by our clock when I got home. I could not resist saying I thought, without my mind changed, I should not drink tea at the Greenwoods again in a hurry. I know not how it is, I can less than ever get over the vulgarity of all the set of them & shall waste few hours at Cross-hills in future. Having had no dinner except a little tea & muffins, had a couple of slices of cold veal & some bread & butter just before I came upstairs. The Miss Greenwoods, while they were in town this afternoon, met Mrs Mitchell in great distress about her son, Daniel, concerning whom there had been a letter from London to say he was so much worse (of a fever caught in the dissecting room) that he could not survive many hours. 2 of the students were already dead of the same kind of fever caught at the same time & place.

Wednesday 17 February [Halifax]

Met the Misses Caroline & Margaret Greenwood (Cross-hills) ½ way between Westfield & King Cross. They did not seem inclined to stop, therefore just spoke in passing. I think I shall have no more notes from Miss Caroline Greenwood. I shall probably owe this good thing to the shew of my preference for Miss Browne. She came out to meet me – took 2 or 3 turns with her up & down 'Kallista' Lane . . . *said she would meet me tomorrow at the library or in passing their house.*

Thursday 18 February [Halifax]

At 3½, down the old bank to the library. Staid only a few minutes. As I was going out, met Miss Browne at the door . . . *She
said she had thought of me last night but so much that it prevented her
sleeping & she must not think so much of me after going to bed in
future. Miss Bessie Staveley asked her how she & I agreed together.
'Why, certainly, we did not quarrel.' Said Miss Staveley, 'I know
you are of a peaceable disposition, but Miss Lister is very whimsical
& I expect soon to see you not speak to one another.' I replied I did
not think that likely but time would tell . . . I said I seldom did a thing
without consideration but when I did, once made up my mind as to
the propriety of a thing, I was not easily turned from it. I thought
Miss Staveley alluded to Miss Caroline Greenwood when she said I
was whimsical. She asked Miss Greenwood some time ago if she was
not jealous . . . & I fancied she really was so now, but gently hinted
it was no fault of mine; for whatever she might have said or thought,
I had never made any professions & only went there four or five times
a year, which I should always do as their father had been very civil to
mine about some business. At all events, I thought Miss Browne had
nothing to fear. She had thought over last night what Miss Staveley
said. Owned she would be sorry to find it true & said she had strange
thoughts but could not help thinking she wished I had been a gent; that
perhaps she should not have known me. 'Oh, oh,' thought I. I replied
perhaps she had not more strange thoughts than other people & that,
if I had been a gent, I thought Mr Kelly would have had a poor
chance. She had wondered what I saw in her & thought perhaps it
was her vanity that made her believe I liked her. 'No, no,' said I. 'I
have given you reason enough.' Mentioned my going to the lectures
on purpose to see her, walking up from church with her, etc., which
surely she could not mistake. I had often wondered what she thought
of all this. She somehow brought on the subject of my calling. Said
they talked to her about it at home & her mother said she must have*

very little influence & very little eloquence not to be able to persuade me to call. She mentioned what I had said about my uncle & aunt (allowed to be good). Her mother answered I might go in sometimes & get a cup of tea. It would help me up the bank. She wondered I stood so much upon formalities. I smiled to myself but gravely said I had often thought of the thing & wondered whether, as I did not call, she would still continue our walks together, adding that I felt convinced, if she was the sensible girl I took her to be, she would never notice the thing . . . 'If, however,' said I, 'you would like to give up our walks, whatever self-denial it may be to me, I will do anything in the world you like & should I not see you for twenty years, I shall neither forget you, nor feel less regard than I do at present.' She thanked me. 'But long before that time you will be Mrs Kelly & settled in Glasgow. Then, of course it will be different, yet I only wish you happy &, tho' I would rather, if possible, be in some degree instrumental to your happiness myself, for we all value the work of our own hands, I shall be satisfied to know you are happy, by whatever means.' Miss Browne; 'Perhaps you will be disappointed in me. I may turn out very wicked.' I; 'That is more likely for me to do, but we have all of us our weak side.' Miss Browne; 'I have many.' I; 'I fear you have not such an one as I should choose you to have if I could choose. At any rate, I know mine &, tho' I always endeavour to be guarded at all points, it does not always answer, for one is sometimes taken by surprise & the business all over before one had thought of danger . . .' I begged if she ever thought of anything I said or did with displeasure she would name it & hoped she would take all I had said this afternoon as she liked & make the best of it. She said she could not always think what she liked. 'Sometimes,' said I, 'I know you do not know what to think.' Miss Browne; 'You are right. You seem to know my thoughts whether I tell them or not.' I; 'Well, I care not what Miss Staveley says. I can any time talk away the impression in five minutes.' Miss Browne; 'Yes, I think you can. I do not know how it is, you could make anything of me.' I; 'Why should you not *believe what I say? It is always truth & you only shew your penetration in discriminating it so soon.' We parted at the top of George St. There were people near & I did not shake hands. I shall explain this on Saturday & say how sorry I was I had not time to set her nearer to me. I see how it is. She begins to like me more than she is, perhaps, aware . . . I must mind I do not get into a scrape. Wishing I was a gent; I can make her believe anything, etc; bespeaks my influence, & a few more walks & perhaps she will understand her feelings better. She mentioned on the moor my taking off the leather strap put through the handle of my umbrella, which made it look like a gentleman's. I said I would do if she asked me but not otherwise. She asked & I did it instantly. Surely she must like my society & would be more or less than woman were she unmoved & unpleased by my attentions. She was twenty-five last Thursday week.*

Friday 19 February [Halifax]

Wrote in this book the journal of yesterday. I might exclaim with Virgil, 'In tenui labor!' But I am resolved not to let my life pass without some private memorial that I may hereafter read, perhaps with a smile, when Time has frozen up the channel of those sentiments which flow so freshly now.

Monday 22 February [Halifax]

In the afternoon, at 3.35, went by Benjamin Bottomley's to John Oates, at Stump Cross. Staid there 35 minutes. Saw a large electrifying machine he had just finished. Received one very slight shock, the first I ever had in my life.

Tuesday 23 February [Halifax]

Sadly disappointed at not meeting Miss Browne. I had little pleasure in my walk. Wondered whether she was ill or whether, as I would not call, she meant to give up seeing me. Felt the want of some companion whom I could love & the thought made me very vapourish. It was some comfort to ejaculate a prayer for God's mercy. For the last month, or six weeks, I have generally, through the grace of the Almighty, contemplated his mercy during my walks.

Thursday 25 February [Halifax]

By Blackwall & Royston Rd to King Cross. Miss Browne joined me as I passed their house . . . *Whether I call on her or not, she could not easily make up her mind to give up our walks. At a party the other evening at the Greenwoods' of Bankfield, Miss Browne not there, Mrs Browne overheard Miss Ramsden & Miss Caroline Greenwood talking of Miss Lister & Miss Browne. The latter, among other things, said I should think it too great a condescension to call on Miss Browne. All this makes the subject become very tender with Mrs Browne. She said, 'Elizabeth, I will not have you talked about.' . . . I said . . . that I would think about the thing & really would call, by & by. She said she should be very much obliged to me, that she did not deserve it but should be very much obliged. Of course, I bade her not to talk in this way, said I could not withstand that, & only gave her to understand how exclusively my call would be on her . . .* Called at James Crossley's for some toothbrushes & at Metcalfe's about getting my old umbrella covered.

Tuesday 2 March [Halifax]

In the afternoon, at 3¼, down the old bank to the library. Miss Maria Browne there. Came up to me to say her sister had so bad a cold & cough & was so unwell, she could not possibly stir out today or, indeed, she scarce knew when. Expressed my sorrow, staid a few minutes & set off my usual walk, musing whether to call or not. I had made up my mind to call sometime, perhaps soon. If you do a thing, do it with the best grace possible & deserve all the merit you can. In the early stage of Johnson's dictionary, Lord Chesterfield refused his patronage. Some time afterwards, seeing the good fortune of the work, he offered it.

Said the Doctor in his letter of reply, 'Had it been earlier, it had been kinder ...' I walked slowly up Royston Rd, stopped a moment at the gate; *felt, I know not how, nervous*; went in, found Miss Browne, not perhaps quite so unwell as I expected, sitting on the sopha [*sic*] reading the last canto of *Childe Harold*. Would not let her send for her mother till I had sat 40 minutes tête-à-tête with herself. Obliged & pleased by my calling. Well she might! Sat ½ hour after Mrs Browne made her appearance. A good sort of looking woman, who may possibly fill the office of grand-conversationalist of the family & not vulgar as I expected from the accounts of the Greenwoods, whose own mother, by the way, is by very many degrees the worse of the 2.

Wednesday 3 March [Halifax]

Spent all the evening talking to my aunt ... *about going to France, perhaps by myself in the autumn or with Tib [Isabella] in the spring of next year. My aunt is really good in giving in to all my wishes & says she will save money. No objection to my going by myself but the fear of my being ill. May perhaps go with me herself. I calculate forty pounds for our travelling expences [sic] & twelve or fifteen for three weeks in Paris ... Talked of my ambition in the literary way, of my wish for a name in the world, all which she will second. She really is very good & is surely fond & proud of me. Talked of my fancy for Miss Browne. Told her I had gone to the lectures for no other purpose than to see her. She said she knew very well & that I should like Miss Browne better than Tib or M—, if I durst. No, that, I said, is a different thing. If I had had M— with me I should probably not have known Miss Browne at all, tho' I should have & felt, & said I admired her notwithstanding.*

Wednesday 10 March [Halifax]

In the afternoon ... to Well-head ... Mrs W— received me very civilly. Talking of Mr Knight's father having been a collier employed both at Shibden & by the Walkers of Crow Nest led us to religious subjects & I was surprised to find Mrs W— apparently much less tainted with unitarian principle than I supposed, her mother & all her mother's family being Socinians. Mrs W— asked after Miss Browne, as she did also the last time I saw her, & wondered how it was I had taken a fancy to her. I said she was just the mild, modest, unassuming sort of girl I always did take a fancy to & told how [I] had scraped acquaintance at Dalton's lecture & had walked with her from church on a Sunday after morning service & after the lecture in the evening. *Mrs W— thinks me very odd & asked if it was owing to education. I said no, I had not begun the sort of education she meant till my native character was sufficiently developed. I was fifteen when I first went to Mrs Knight. Was always a great pickle, never learnt anything at school. Was always talking to the girls instead of attending to my book. Talked a little of my being whipped every day at Ripon.*[2]

Thursday 11 March [Halifax]

At 3.35, down the new bank to the library . . . Miss Browne came in, fancying me later than usual . . . *Her brother is returned from Glasgow & he is not so averse as he was to her marrying Mr William Kelly. I see it will be a match. I told her to tell me in time as I should have to go immediately to the waters of Lethe.*[3] *She hoped not. She hoped to see me when she was far away from here & it would be my own fault if she did [not]. I said she should not call it my fault but I should make up my mind never to behold her again & I must try to forget her as soon as I could.*

From this point, Anne's interest in Miss Browne dwindled. The marriage between Miss Browne and Mr Kelly did indeed take place on 28 September 1820. The references to her grow less and less frequent as the time approached.

Thursday 18 March [Halifax]

In the evening, between 8 & 9, read from pp.263 to 307, vol.1, Gibbon's *Miscellaneous Works*. He died in London ¼ before one p.m. 16 January 1794 ... Was born in 1737. His remains deposited in Lord Sheffield's family burial place in Sussex. Fine day ... (Fire in the hall.)

Saturday 20 March [Halifax]

Called at Whitley's & got the blank book which is to form the next volume of my journal. Sat near ¾ hour at Northgate. My aunt has been told by several people of my attentions to Miss Browne – she comes out & joins me as I pass & we walk arm in arm in the most earnest conversation, yet I have only called once – when she was very ill. My aunt would not believe what they said at first. Walking, etc, with Miss Browne was so unlike me. The thing seems to be the talk & admiration (wonder) of the town.

Sunday 21 March [Halifax]

All went to morning church ... Came out of church ... & Miss Caroline Greenwood, to my astonishment, offering her hand. Shook hands with her. What could make the lady so much more complaisant than she has been ever since my return from York? Did her jealousy of Miss Browne & her mimic dignity of indifference to me slumber awhile? Foolish girl! I never thought of her unless to think that she, like the whole kit of them, is too vulgar to be endurable ... My aunt & I read prayers ... The screen put before the fireplace in the hall that there will be no more fires this season.

Monday 22 March [Halifax]

Did not take my walk as usual on account of dining at 5½ & going to Webster's lecture in the Assembly room, Talbot Yard, in the evening ... Mr Webster is a great, stout man, 6ft 2 or 3 inches high, at least. He seemed to understand his business as a lecturer & performed his experiments very neatly but his oratory is disfigured by frequent instances of bad grammar and an unpolished pronunciation ... His explanations were clear & easy of comprehension, I should suppose even to Miss Watkinson's young ladies[4] who lined the front bench. Speaking of the aggregation of chemical elements; 'Let us take a gr. of shot, for instance, for the sake of obtaining some tangible idea' – what would Locke[5] have said of *some tangible idea*? However, after reading Mr Webster's book on chemical & natural philosophy & not remembering or observed in it any heinous sins against grammar, I did not expect that his oral language would be so thickly strewn with the misuse of the person of his verbs.

Saturday 27 March [Halifax]

In the afternoon at 3.40, down the old bank to the library ... No Miss Browne. I could have said, changing only the gender, (as Gibbons wrote to Deyverdun, vol. 1. 604/703), 'Êtes vous mort? Êtes vous malade? Avez [vous] changé d'avis? Est-il survenu des difficultés?'[6] I wished to see her for, as Gibbon afterwards observed ... 'Such is our imperfect nature that dissipation is a far more efficacious remedy than reflection.' My mind dwelt on M— ... *It struck me, if we should not meet for years & then, when she expected our being together, if I should be disappointed with her looks, etc, seen her grow old in the service of another, could I then cordially wish to realize the scheme of early days? If I should, by & by, meet with anyone who would quite suit me, could I refuse & still lose a substance to expect a shadow?*

Wednesday 31 March [Halifax]

Went to ... Mrs Stansfield Rawson's, Savile Green. Got there a few minutes after 4. I was just thinking I should be obliged to tell Mrs Rawson I was afraid of needing an introduction (I only remember having seen her once, at a party at Mrs Ramsden's 7 or 8 years ago when I think I was not introduced & I met her walking with her husband one evening last summer & we moved to each other) when she herself opened the door for me, held out her hand & said she was delighted that anything had induced me to go there. This gave me my queue [*sic*]. We all talked away as if we had been in the habit of visiting for years. The forms of etiquette need not involuntarily trouble anyone here . . . Miss Rawson (Catherine) put on the costume of the island of Mycone [Mycene?], white, reaching only to the knees, as if to shew the red worsted stockings & slippers down at the heels of the ladies of the island. A curious sort of dress but in which Miss Rawson looked uncommonly well. She is pretty, a handsome, elegant looking girl.

Saturday 3 April [Halifax]

At 4.35 set off to call at Cross-hills on Miss Ellen Greenwood from Burnley. Mrs Greenwood opened the door for me. As I entered the little room, saw at least one of the young ladies making her escape down the stairs. After sitting a good while with the old lady (she seemed to have dined & to clip the King's English a little), Miss Greenwood & Miss Susan made their appearance. Miss Ellen & Miss Caroline were dressing for a party at Dr G. Alexander's. They are a sad, vulgar set & heaven forgive me if I wrong the *mater familias*, but I verily believe that, when I have seen her, she has often been more diligent in the potion way than, for her spirit's sake, was necessary. I really must shirk the whole squad somehow or other.

Monday 5 April [Halifax]

As it seems now fixed for my aunt & I to set off to Paris on the 12th, next month, it is time for me to attend to French in earnest ... In the afternoon, at 5.35, down the new bank to the Saltmarshes' ... Mrs Waterhouse called for us & we 3 went to the lecture ... Mr Jeremiah Rawson came in soon after us & Mr Waterhouse when the lecture was ½ over. All went away together. In passing Mrs Smurfitt's door, Emma proposed having some hot meat pies. We all went in, sat round the kitchen fire, ate a hot veal pie (price 3d.) & had 6d. worth of ale, the greater part of which & one pie, fell to the lot of my uncle's man, William Green, who wondered, doubtless, what was become of us all &, I not liking him to stand starving at the door, was called in. Heating & eating the pies took up 25 minutes. We all walked home with Emma. She wanted to go in & sup, & the rest might & would apparently have been persuaded, but I said I was the steadiest of the party & thought we had much better let her go to bed & go home our-selves. *Emma wanted to rap at their aunt Catherine's window & frighten her as we passed & they would have done so, but I said, 'No, that would be too giddy a trick.' Jerry Rawson joked about who was to pay for the pies, etc. Mr Waterhouse paid. Jerry threw down a shillling saying, 'Come, I will give you that towards them;' He is a sad, vulgar dog.* Returned down the north parade & got home at 10.20.

Friday 9 April [Halifax]

[Good Friday] All went to morning church & staid the sacra-ment ... Walked from church with Miss Caroline & her cousin, Miss Ellen, Greenwood, & they accompanied me over the bridge to the bottom of the bank. *Miss Caroline introduced the subject of Miss Browne by observing how much I staid at home* [Miss Browne was away from home just then] *&, on my saying I went out every day but got home from my walks as soon as I could, she said, 'No, not always. I have seen you when you have not seen me, walking very leisurely in that shady lane near Mrs Wilcock's.'* [Anne's usual walk with Miss Browne.] *'Oh,' said I, 'That is when I am settling the affairs of the nation with my prime minister.' She caught at the term. I* said it was inconsiderately made use of as it expressed a subordinate situation. I asked her to choose a term for me. She replied, 'Angel.' I answered I should have many orders of angels & as she had invented the term for me, begged she would take the first rank. She should be called Angelica, the other Ministeria. She told me my mind was so engrossed with this new object it effaced all others & I forgot old ones. I said she never made a worse hit, for that my mind was the most convenient, capacious concern possible. It admitted new impressions without crowding or incommoding old ones & that all things keep their proper places. She said the last time I saw her I would not have the word friendship made use of. I answered I was wrong then, that it was friendship. She denied this, saying it could not be, for I should think of circumstance & situation. I said I never minded these. She asked me to give my sentiment a name. I answered it was perfect esteem, but desired her to give it a name. She replied, 'Enthusiasm. A passion that would only last a short while.' I said that, in consequence of hearing a report of my choosing to walk with Miss Browne, yet not to call on her I had called & sat half an hour with her & meant to do myself the honour of calling again as soon as she returned. She seemed astonished & incredulous, but I confirmed the thing. She asked if the ladies had returned the call. I answered Miss Browne had been ill. She asked how I liked 'scrawk', Mrs Browne. I said better than I expected. Very well, for I had heard so much of 'slobbering in the pot', etc, I scarce expected to find her presentable. Miss Caroline likes me certainly, after all, & did not seem to dislike the opportunity of saying all this to me. I never offered my arm but walked by the side. Miss Ellen Greenwood apologized for not having called but waited for Miss Caroline to accompany [her] who had no shoes till she got some (expected) from Leeds.

Thursday 15 April [Halifax]

In the afternoon, at 4, set off to Lightcliffe to call on Mrs Priestley after the death of her mother-in-law, 3 weeks ago.

Mrs Priestley was dressing to go to Cliff-hill, that Miss Griesdale & I had to introduce ourselves. I daresay we were 20 minutes together tête-à-tête & got on very well, but, after hearing so much of her, of her talent, of her spending 2/3 of her time in courtly society at Lowther Castle, etc, I was inwardly surprised to see a fat, rather untidy, vulgar looking woman, apparently on the wrong side of 30, & whose manner of speaking & pronunciation were far from the most elegant, or, occasionally, from the most proper. However, Mrs Priestley never set up her manners, on the contrary, mentioned her as a proof that first-rate society cannot always impart to those around them the first-rate polish which they themselves possess.

Friday 16 April [Halifax]

Talking to my uncle about his keeping a carriage, having 2 out of his 3 horses, carriage horses, & 2 men in livery, a house servant & William Green, as groom & coachman, for £100 per annum.

Saturday 17 April [Halifax]

Letter from M— (Lawton). A good deal better. Has been bled with leeches & taken an emetic which did her more good than anything. *'As long, my dear Fred, as I reign undisturbed over your heart, I am satisfied. 'Tis the only kingdom in the world that I covet &, assured that no rival can have power to dethrone me, I am fully & entirely satisfied. Tell me this, however, sometimes, & then perhaps I shall not doubt again'* . . . *She complains of suffering much from the piles. Alludes to our living together at the end of the letter.*

Monday 19 April [Halifax]

Inadvertently setting down my writing desk on the table, broke the watch-key M— gave me in 1814. *If I were at all superstitious, I might think this ominous. I had certainly never less idea, hope, or rather wish, of our being ultimately together than I have at present. Now, poor soul, she has got the piles. She will indeed be worn out in the service of another & she has not talent enough to blind me to the discovery or charm me from the remembrance of all this.*

Thursday 22 April [Halifax]

At 10½ . . . down the old bank to see [Ellen Empson] . . . *Ellen was very agreeable. She hears a great deal of me. 'The people say, "And do you really like somebody?"' But Ellen would not give up her authority. 'It is no great compliment for Miss Lister to single out any-body after being intimate with Mrs Tom Rawson and Miss Browne.' Miss Browne, they say, is my shadow. I laughed & said I was amused. At any rate, the people knew nothing about me for I never went to their parties or mixed with them at all, & I only hoped Ellen never enlightened them about me, giving her, at the same time, to understand that I thought myself of that importance that I might choose my own society, that I always consulted my own inclination & comfort & should feel at perfect liberty to walk with a chimney-sweep if I chose. Before all this, Ellen had asked me not to study so much. She said I should be going mad. She had thought so often, for I was certainly odd. I laughed & said I was sane enough yet, I hoped, & people might be odd without being mad, adding that, if I was mad, I would beg to go to Elvington[7] to show her what I was like . . . Ellen seemed to say the people would willingly lay hold of anything against me if they could but that I gave them no opportunity. I certainly will not put myself much in their way . . . Said Ellen, 'I wish you did not live at Shibden Hall. They will never appreciate you there.'*

From Monday 10 May 1819 to Saturday 12 June 1819, Anne was in Paris with her Aunt Anne. She did not inform her friends where she was going, merely telling them she was going away with her aunt on account of the latter's poor health.

On her return, she settled back into her routine of visiting the local families, going to the library, attending church on Sunday, catching up with her studies. She found life in Halifax rather tedious after her travels abroad.

Tuesday 22 June [Halifax]

Got to the Saltmarshes' about 5 by the church. Staid till about 10 by the same & got home in 20 minutes by our clock. Great deal of talk about France. Told them we travelled in the coach; were in the 3rd or 4th story [sic] in Paris; conversation about paying servants at inns, waiters, etc . . . Emma had a bad toothache. *I fancied I staid too late & came away unsatisfied with my own conversation, & feeling somehow or other unsatisfied altogether. I seldom pay a visit hereabouts that is not afterwards the case. I seem as if I had not kept up dignity enough & yet how can I do otherwise than I do? I never feel to have been in good society when I have been with them. All this must continue for a time but I will get out of it as soon as I can.*

On Thursday 24 June 1819, Isabella Norcliffe came to stay with Anne. The visit was not a success and Anne discarded any longterm plans for her own future which might have included Isabella. She also became tired of her attempts to woo Miss Browne in view of her impending engagement to Mr William Kelly of Glasgow. Also, M— seemed more unobtainable than ever, with reports from her sister that she grew more happy in her marriage each year, although this was not the impression given in M—'s letters to Anne. Anne's emotional life had reached an impasse.

Monday 26 June [Halifax]

In the afternoon at 4, took Isabel down the old bank with me to the library. Staid till 5. *Tib's manner there fidgetty & a little impatient. Would try to kiss me. She shall not go with me often again.*

Sunday 27 June [Halifax]

A letter from M— (Lawton). She could not write on Thursday, *unhinged by a letter telling her Isabel was to be here on that day. Cannot bear the thought of her being here. This looks like jealousy & as if she loved me.*

Tuesday 29 June [Halifax]

After tea, at 7.20, took my aunt & Isabel down the new bank to see the giant & giantess – he from Norfolk, aged 18 and 7ft 5 ins high, she from Northampton, aged 16 and 6ft 5 ins high; a dwarf with them, a native of Strasbourg, & aged 36 . . . In passing Edwards's (the bookseller)[8] he said the giant & giantess had been married in the morning . . . I walked from Northgate to Cross-hills with the Misses Caroline & Susan Greenwood. Never introduced Isabella.

Thursday 1 July [Halifax]

The Misses Caroline & Susan Greenwood called & staid ½ hour – the former grinned & talked, the latter scarce uttered. They must have got wet in returning . . . In the evening at 7¾, went with my aunt to Halifax. She ordered a white & black livery for James at Milnes'.

Monday 5 July [Halifax]

Fine air this evening. I think Isabella much less tired than she has been before. She gets to bear walking better & better. *Poor soul! She little thinks how things are. She feels secure. I scarce can bear it. I wish she knew all & all was settled.*

Saturday 10 July [Halifax]

Conversation with Isabella. *If Charlotte does not marry, she must live with Tib, whether Tib ever has Langton or not. Then I could have no authority in Tib's house nor therefore, she in mine. But if she had not Langton, then she can live with me if I will take Charlotte, too. 'But,' said she, when I hinted this would not do, 'we might always be together. You visit me six months & I visit you the same.' When I hesitated she said, 'Well, but I can visit you six months & the other six, you can get somebody else.' I said little but that I must have someone who had the same authority in my house as a wife would have in her husband's house . . . When I hinted that I could not have Charlotte, she said, 'I cannot forsake my sister. Surely you would not wish it.' 'Surely not,' I said immediately.*

Sunday 25 July [Halifax]

[On going down to church] *I was last. Not halfway up the Cunnery Lane, a little-ish, mechanic-like, young man, in a black coat, touched his hat, stopped & said he wished to have some con-versation with me. Suspecting the subject, 'What about, sir?' said I, sternly. He looked rather dashed but said he wished to ask if I would like to change my situation. 'Good morning, sir,' said I, turned on my heel & walked on. Just heard him repeat, 'Good morning, Madam,' surprised, perhaps, at the cool dignity of my manner. I could not help thinking of the thing most of church-time, mortified, tho' why should I be? Everybody else is liable to the same. I will be stern enough & care nothing, & certainly say nothing, about it. Surely it is meant as an insult. To annoy is all such fellows want & they shall not succeed with me.* They were reading the Psalms when we got to church. Miss Browne there. Took my glass to look back after the sermon. Saw Miss Caroline Greenwood, on a broad grin, looking towards me. In the afternoon, my aunt read the lessons & Isabella & I the prayers.

Monday 26 July [Halifax]

Followed a girl I rightly guessed to be Miss Caroline Greenwood down George Street into Whitley's shop & thence gave her my arm & ½ my umbrella to her own door. Told me 'my belle' was returned. Thought they 'should never see me at Cross-hills again'. She began to think she 'must subscribe to the opinion she had heard'. What was that? 'That one favourite set aside all the rest.' Begged her to believe that could not be the case. They had had many invitations to Shibden, any one of which we should be glad if they would accept. Had not fixed a day, thinking they would like best to fix one for themselves. She never went without a day fixed, thinking people would say when they wanted her.

Tuesday 27 July [Halifax]

Called on Miss Browne. Found her at the door (4.50) just coming out to meet me & had been on the lookout . . . In about 5 minutes who should come but Miss Greenwood. All seemed to look oddly – I, stiff & formal. She came for some flowers. Presently, all went into the garden to get them. Miss Maria Browne came, & went also. I could scarcely help smiling at the significance of Miss Caroline Greenwood's manner & the consequent effect on the rest. About 10 minutes before 6, she thought she must be going & preferred the back way. For Miss Browne's sake, I was willing to bother myself with shewing her the utmost attention & we set off to walk a part of the way with her. She led us past the Staveleys' (Savile Green). Saw them in the window & laughed & spoke. All walked separately. Nothing could have persuaded me to offer my arm in such a case. Managed to get quit of the fair intruder in Harrison Lane. Would walk back with Miss Browne & turned up by Blackwall. *Immediately gave my arm & explained why I had not done it before, that I could not do it without also doing it to Miss Caroline. She understood & seemed to take it in very good part. She said she had interrupted us sadly. She had thought of me often & wondered when she would see me again . . .*

She had made up her mind to care nothing about her mother's cross-ness to Mr Kelly. She met him in one of the streets in Hull & he had gone to see her at Selby. It was all settled . . . She did not know how to tell her mother. He wisely thought he would come & tell her himself but she would not see him. They could make no objection to him but his religion, Kirk of Scotland . . . It gave me an odd sort of feel to hear all this & to find her really engaged . . . I felt, & really feel, I know not how about it. Prudence says it is well for me. I might have got into a scrape & yet do not feel to rejoice at her being thus lifted so entirely out of my reach. Felt grave all the way home & never uttered but 2 or 3 commonplace observations which I felt as if I must make.

Wednesday 28 July [Halifax]

At last I have worked thro' this fag of a journal! I have been at it almost incessantly ever since our return from France. I have been able to do little or nothing else & have scarcely opened a book. I long to begin my studies again, yet dread to find out how much I may have lost. Yet I have still our French accounts to settle & the index to this volume wants continuing from 9 May, p.21, to here. How difficult it is to make up for neglecting to do things in the proper season. How hard to redeem lost time! Let this be a warning to me, & let me never so involve myself again. I see I write, on Saturday 19 June, on the margin of my pencil journal of Wednesday 12 May, 'It is as extravagant to borrow time as to borrow money; every delay involves us more deeply, till the accumulation of interest is in either case ruinous.' How true! May I never forget this and always profit by its remembrance.

Friday 30 July [Halifax]

Miss Kitson came in the morning to try on Isabella's gown-waist. *Asked her to have beer. My aunt said wine & water. Tib*

*wondered how I could ask such a nice woman to have beer – wine,
certainly. Her father always asked Willoughby, the master-builder
at Malton, & even Tomlinson, the master-joiner, to have wine.
Much more should I have asked such a woman as Miss Kitson to
have wine.*

Saturday 31 July [Halifax]

Met Mr Rawson (Christopher) & Miss Richardson on the moor –
he on horseback, she on a very pretty little mule. Stopped &
talked 2 or 3 minutes. Told her I should never forget her speech
at Stoney Royde [Friday 6 July], 'that there was no living without
kissing & she kissed Mr Rawson all the day' (he is her godfather),
to the latest moment of my life.[9] She hoped I should forget. It
made her quite uncomfortable to think I should not. She should
get no sleep tonight. Poor girl! I only said so to tease her a little
& 'twas a pity. She looks good-tempered.

Sunday 1 August [Halifax]

Joined Miss Browne at the church gates . . . *She said Mr Parker,
at whose house she had been staying, knew my father, and that his
brother, Mr Parker of Altencoat, asked her if he (Mr Lister) had not
a very extraordinary daughter. He had heard of me in Lancashire. I
smiled & said I thought the epithet 'extraordinary' unjustly applied.
I should deserve it better without the 'extra'. 'Oh, no,' said she. 'You
cannot think so.' I wonder what she really thinks of me? At all
events, she likes me. Now I know she is positively engaged I begin to
care & think less about her, nor would I have gone last night but for
Isabella's impatience to have me fix a day for her going to the library,
so anxious is Tib to see her. We were talking of her just after we came
up to bed & Tib wanted me to take the first opportunity of giving her
a kiss to see how she liked it & how she behaved on the occasion. I
laughed & said, 'If anything particular happens, Tib, you will be
more to blame than I.'*

Thursday 5 August [Halifax]

In the afternoon at 4.20 down the old bank to the library. Isabella came (on horseback, double) soon afterwards &, in a minute or two, Miss Browne . . . *Tib did not say much to her. She looked too like a gentlewoman for Tib to launch out all at once. Tib admires Miss Browne. Meant to have made a good story of all we said, etc, but she, Miss Browne, was so like a gentlewoman she could not.*

Thursday 12 August [Halifax]

In passing Westfield, Miss Browne met me. Prevented going to the library, her father & mother not yet returned. *Commonplace conversation. Nothing very interesting. Indeed I thought her looking less well, less pleasing, than usual & felt her company dullish. I do not feel the same interest in her I did before I knew she was positively engaged. She is out of my reach. Knowing this makes all the difference in the world & her leaving Halifax will give me no sort of uneasiness. I begin to think her dullish & shall not, perhaps, be sorry to get rid of her.*

Monday 16 August [Halifax]

Dined at 5¼ & set off in ½ hour down the old bank to drink tea at the Saltmarshes'. Took a couple of turns round the garden with Emma before Isabel arrived (rode behind William). Isabel, much to my annoyance, mentioned my keeping a journal, & setting down everyone's conversation in my peculiar hand-writing (what I call crypt hand). I mentioned the almost impossibility of its being deciphered & the facility with which I wrote & not at all shewing my vexation at Isabella's folly in naming the thing. *Never say before her what she may not tell for, as to what she ought to keep or what she ought to publish, she has the worst judgement in the world.* Spent a pleasant evening. Walked by the side as Isabella rode & got home at 9¼ . . . My aunt sent a note this evening to Cross-hills to ask Mrs & the Miss Greenwoods to drink tea here any day of the week & William called for an answer . . . My aunt read the note which turned [out to be] a long rigmarole from Miss Caroline to me, taking no notice of my aunt's invitation. A ½ sheet more foolishly filled I have not seen for some time & my aunt & Isabel, as well as the rest, laughed exceedingly. *Surely the girl must like me in spite of all the stiffness of my manners to her. In fact, her jealousy of Miss Browne shews something unlike absolute indifference.* Came upstairs at 11 . . .

Anne brought Miss Browne to visit Shibden, as the Listers were having a rare social evening.

Thursday 26 August [Halifax]

Miss Browne & I walked leisurely along & got to Shibden by 5. Sat 10 minutes alone in the drawing-room. Then my aunt came & afterwards, Isabella. Staid with them (excused 10 minutes for my dinner) till Miss Inman & the Miss Knights rapped at the door. Then dressed in ½ hour & went into tea. Walked a turn or two in the garden, shewed Isabella's prints, etc. & the evening went off pleasantly, I taking care to pay rather more attention to Miss Browne than the other young ladies. Her brother & Mr William Knight came for their sisters at 8. John Oates brought a small instrument to procure a light by the compression of air enclosed in a tube. All pleased with it . . . They all went about 8½ . . . *Just before we came in from the garden, contrived to be a few minutes alone with only Tib & Miss Browne. The former gave me a kiss & I made it an excuse to kiss Miss Browne on her lips, a very little, moistly. She looked shamefacedly. Were, a few minutes afterwards, us three in the hall. Miss Browne said kissing was an odd thing & people made quere [sic] remarks about it. 'These,' said I, 'none of us understand.' But I think she did not very much dislike it after all.* Miss Browne looked very neat, pretty & like a gentlewoman. They all thought so & could not do otherwise.

Sunday 29 August [Halifax]

All went to morning church . . . *In passing Miss Browne, smiled very graciously. I fancied she looked rather sheepish. What has she thought of my kissing her when she was here on Thursday? Tib said she pulled her bonnet over her face the moment after I had done it.*

Thursday 2 September [Halifax]

In the afternoon dined at 4½ & at 5.35, my aunt, & Isabel & Marian & I set off in a chaise to drink tea at Cliff-hill. My uncle & father walked. Nobody there but ourselves, except Mrs W. Priestley, who very civilly asked Isabella & me to spend a week with her, which we left undecided. She wished she could get me to like the Miss Hudsons of Hipperholme but they were frightened of me – my Latin & Greek, etc. What nonsense!

Friday 3 September [Halifax]

Tho' I shall not be sorry when Tib is gone & I am settled, yet it made me low to hear her talk of going & I have been so all morning . . . I feel towards her differently, more coolly than I did . . . Does she see me changed or, rather, does she think of it? Years make a difference. She does not suit me. I cannot feel that she is, or ever can be, all to me I want & wish. Oh, that I had some kindred spirit & by whom, <u>be</u> loved. I have none & feel desolate. How sweet the thought that there is (still) another & better & happier world than this. M— could once have made me happy but could she now? Yet she is lost to me & it matters not to inquire. The having written this seems a relief to my mind & I feel rather less low & cheerless.

Tuesday 7 September [Halifax]

Drank tea & had a mutton chop at Well-head. Staid till 7½ & got home (up the old bank) a little before 8.

Thursday 9 September [Halifax]

Down the old bank to Whitley's. Ordered the 8vo edition of
Lallah Rookh[10] (by Thomas Moore, Esq.) with the illustrations
to be bound in crimson morocco, richly guilt [*sic*] & the inside
of the binding lined with green satin as a specimen of Halifax
bookbinding, & a present to Isabella.

Friday 17 September [Halifax]

*Tib sat in my room all morning, writing & trying on a pair of stays.
She interrupted me desperately & I shall not be sorry to have my
room once more to myself. I am never much good at study when she
is with me & I am weary of this long stoppage I have had to all
improvement . . . I only hope to make up for lost time when she is
gone. Besides, she has no idea of keeping up her dignity, professes to
have no pride, not that of family; would associate with anyone she
thought pleasant & by no means would relish the sort of elegant society I covet to acquire. She is the image of her father in everything &
I think does, & will often, let herself down. This, besides all other
things, does not suit me.*

Sunday 19 September [Halifax]

In the afternoon, my uncle & I read the prayers. Mr Sunderland called in the midst to see my aunt & staid near ½ hour.
She is, by & by, (Tuesday, perhaps) to have 2 leeches set on
each foot to ease the noise & swimming in her head. They calculate an oz of blood to each leech including what the animal
sucks & as much as can be made to run afterwards, & he has
sent her a bolus[11] & opening mixture. Asked him the price of
his gig – grasshopper springs, no top to it – £70. Built in
London, at Blackfriars, I think he said – but if he lives to have
another he will have a top to put on or take off, & curricle
springs.

Monday 20 September [Halifax]

My aunt had the leech-woman from Northowram this afternoon. 2 leeches on each foot. Her charge, 6d. each leech, as is common, & my aunt gave her a shilling over, for which the woman seemed exceedingly obliged. They seem to have done, my aunt says. She fancies she felt her [head] relieved immediately after the bleeding.

Tuesday 21 September [Halifax]

Crossley cut my hair. About ½ hour's job . . . In the afternoon, down the old bank to the library . . . Called to tell the sexton to cover my uncle's pews as they are going to sweep the interior of the old church . . . A Mr Preston, now of London, sold my uncle his 2 sittings in a pew no. in the old church (let to Martha Ingham & her husband) for £15 . . . Now my uncle has all the pew. It formerly belonged to John Howarth's farm.

Wednesday 22 September [Halifax]

At 11.20, set off to walk to Lightcliffe . . . found Mrs W. Priestley & her sister, Miss Ann Paley, at home . . . Miss Ann Paley seems a nice enough woman (girl) but lolls her arm over the chair back or sticks her elbow out with her hand akimbo in rather too masculine a manner, but this both her sisters, Mrs W. Priestley & Mrs Dr Paley, do. From Lightcliffe to Cliff-hill. Sat ½ hour with the 2 Miss Walkers. I half promised to go & drink tea some time soon in a free way as I do at Lightcliffe.

Friday 24 September [Halifax]

Great many people out of work. A very creditable looking woman, who had been obliged to sell all their furniture & all the clothes but what she had on, applied to me, & afterwards, 2 weavers.

Sunday 26 September [Halifax]

Wrote a note to Mrs Cooke (Coney St. [York]) to order a black hat and a note to Hornby (Blake St. [York]) to order a pair of black cloth boots . . . *Often as I have thought I should not be sorry when Tib went, I felt a sinking at my heart this afternoon as I thought how soon she would be gone & I left all alone, none to love, to turn to, or to speak to. All will be dreary & forlorn. Oh, that I had a fit companion to dote on, to beguile the tedious hours. But I must study & never think of love & all the sweet endearments of life.*

Friday 1 October [Halifax]

Just before going downstairs the post brought a letter from a William Townsend, purporting to be of King Cross & the man who spoke to me one Sunday some time ago. The letter is dated the 28th of last month. It annoyed me a little at first sight but now, just after coming upstairs, I care little about it & only expect some row in meeting him some time or other. However, I will never fear. Be firm. Learn to have nerve to protect myself & make the best of all things. He is but a little fellow & I think I could knock him down if he should touch me. I should try. If not, whatever he said I would make no answer. Never fear. Pray against this & for God's protection & blessing, & then face the days undaunted. It is always a relief to me to write down what I feel & after I have done, I am, as it were, satisfied.

Tuesday 5 October [Halifax]

At 12, set off with my aunt to Halifax & up the North Parade to call on Mrs & her sister, Miss Ann Paley. Saw there Dr Paley . . . Sat ½ hour. The Dr talked away facetiously about the meeting of radicals[12] yesterday & their vote of thanks to Mr George Pollard for his opposition to raising a troop of yeomanry & thus perhaps preventing Halifax from being turned into a scene of blood. Mrs Paley looked untidily dressed; the room seemed untidy, & I was not much charmed with what I saw.

Wednesday 13 October [Halifax]

The morning clearing up, my uncle & aunt determined to go to the Oratoria in the new church at Southowram . . . The 4 Miss Walkers of Walterclough were in the pew next to us. Miss Delia made a dead set at conversation with first one & then another of us, but fastened on my uncle. I never saw a more impudent woman. All looked forlorn &, except Miss Walker, who could look grave, seemed hardly as respectable as they should be.

Saturday 30 October [Halifax]

Letter from M— (Lawton) . . . [She] will accompany her mother & sister as far as Manchester on their return [to York] & wishes me to meet them there that she may get a sight of me. *If C— is not with them this is very well, but I am too forlorn in spirit & in wardrobe. Besides, my uncle & aunt would think it foolish. They would think of the money it would cost & they would not approve. I would do many things if I could but at present I must be as careful as I can & study only to improve myself in the hope of a possibility of making something by writing. I know not how it is, I feel low. My eyes filled with tears as I read M—'s letter. Indeed I am generally low on hearing from her. There seems to be no real or, at least to me, satisfactory sympathy between us. We seem to have no mutual affairs & little mutual confidence. Is then this the person with whom I must hope to spend the evening of my days? I am very low. The tears gush as I write but, thank God, I generally feel relief from thus unburdening my mind on paper . . . Oh, how my heart longs after a companion & how I often wish for an establishment of my own, but I may then be too old to attach anyone & my life shall have passed in that dreary solitude I so ill endure.*

Friday 12 November [Halifax]

Got home at 5¾, my aunt having ordered dinner at their hour for me to dine with them on a hare Hannah Button sent. Tea at 7 . . . Afterwards did nothing. Felt sleepy & uncomfortable. My usual way (dining at 6 & having a little dinner & tea at the same time) suits me the best.

Tuesday 16 November [Halifax]

Staid at the Saltmarshes' perhaps near ¾ hour . . . *They seemed glad to see me & Emma asked me to stay tea, but I fancied it more faintly done than some time before & when I said I used to go every week, not much notice was taken. But perhaps I am sometimes more nice about these things than I should be.*

> On 18 November, Anne decided to go to Manchester after all to meet M— and spend a night together without the presence of M—'s husband, C—, to inhibit them.

Thursday 18 November [Manchester]

Did not get off from here till a few minutes after 9 by our church, but after all, had to wait 10 minutes & the coach drove off at 9½ by the old church. Very fine, mild morning & I left my place in the inside to sit behind the coachman next to a blind fiddler, having given his companion, a blind flute player, 6d. for the seat in front. By & by, the gentleman with the coachman exchanged with me to be a better safeguard to the fiddler while he played & we had music thro' the villages & up the hills nearly the whole way.

Stopped at the Moseley Arms, Manchester, at 2¼. Went in & got my boots cleaned. Had a thorough washing & brushing &, being near an hour altogether, did not get to the Albion Hotel in Piccadilly till a little after 3. They were all arrived

(M—, her mother, Anne & William Milne[13]) about an hour ago. Had just gone out & had not ordered dinner till 5½. Called for a newspaper – read a little while but, fidgetty & tired of waiting in the house, sent for someone to shew me Petersfield & its environs, the scene of the late meeting and dispersion of the Manchester radical reformers by the yeomanry and troops.[14]

Went out at 3½ & made a ¾ hour circuit . . . On coming in . . . went upstairs into Mrs Belcombe's room & presently, tho' it seemed an age, came M— & the rest. They passed the Moseley Arms as the Defiance was at the door but somehow missed me in getting out. Never dreampt [sic] of my not going immediately to the Albion, & quite gave me up. M— sadly disappointed. *She met me affectionately enough & seemed rather nervous. Dinner was ready. In taking off my hat and front, the firelight did not let M— see my hair was in paper. She thought it cut close to my head & started back, saying I was not fit to be seen. She could not make it look decent. I said Anne could & sent for her. I was before, when I saw M— nervous, beginning to be a little pathetic, but this little incident cured me. I laughed it off, said M—'s horror had done me a great deal of good, put on a neat waist & went down grinning & looking the neatest of the party . . .*

Not much conversation before getting into bed. C— made no objection to her coming to Manchester when he heard she was to meet me, tho' before he did not wish her to go farther than Wilmslow, he hurried them off before seven in the morning that she might have more time to be with me, & on this account, would give her till eight o'clock to be at home tomorrow . . . Asked how often they were connected &, guessing, found might be at the rate of about twenty times a year. Got into bed. She seemed to want a kiss. It was more than I did. The tears rushed to my eyes. I felt I know not what & she perceived that I was much agitated. She bade me not or she should begin too & I knew not how she should suffer. She guessed not what passed within me. They were not tears of adoration. I felt that she was another man's wife. I shuddered at the thought & at the conviction that no soffistry [sic] could gloss over the criminality of our connection. It seemed not that the like had occurred to her ... (I said, just before we got up, 'Well, come, whatever C— has done to me, I am even with him. However, he little thinks what we have been about. What would he do if he knew?' 'Do? He would divorce me.' 'Yes,' said I, 'it would be a sad business for us both, but we are even with him, at any rate.' 'Indeed,' said M—, laughing, 'indeed we are.' Shewed no sign of scruples ... What is M—'s match but legal prostitution? And, alas, what is her connection with me? Has she more passion than refinement? More plausibility than virtue? Give me a little romance. It is the greatest purifier of our affections & often an excellent guard against libertinism ...) From the kiss she gave me it seemed as if she loved me as fondly as ever. By & by, we seemed to drop asleep but, by & by, I perceived she would like another kiss & she whispered, 'Come again a bit, Freddy.' For a little while I pretended sleep. In fact, it was inconvenient. But soon, I got up a second time, again took off, went to her a second time &, in spite of all, she really gave me pleasure, & I told her no one had ever given me kisses like hers.

We talked over different circumstances. I, she said, I had every comfort at home & elsewhere, alluding to Sarah Binns.[15] She had not. I said it was dull work. Mentioned Tib's being fond of me as ever & the deceitful game I was now obliged to play as, of course, I could say nothing of my engagement to her. 'Indeed,' said I, 'Is there, or can there be, any engagement at present? Was not every obligation on my part cancelled by your marriage?' She acknowledged that it was. I said Tib had told me of this, that I had never thought of it till she reminded me that, whatever might formerly be the case, I was quite at liberty from any tie to M— now. She seemed pleased to hear me say that, tho' Tib seemed fully to expect living with me, yet, at all events that would not be, for I neither did, nor could, feel anything like love towards her ... Speaking of my being at liberty, 'Well, but,'

said she, 'You might make another promise now.' 'Oh, no,' said I,
'I cannot now.' I said Tib would really willingly marry me in disguise
at the altar but, I said, a promise made anywhere would be equally
binding to me & I would not make one.

Friday 19 November [Halifax]

Went shopping in St Anne's Square (Manchester). Some
excellent shops. *Nantz saw some flowers she admired. Said I would*
give her a bunch. I did & she, not having silver, I had to pay also for
one she bought herself. This made nine shillings. I never expected to
be paid again, & M— made me give her a bunch at five shillings,
that altogether I spent fourteen when I could ill afford it. At
Oliphant's too, said I wanted a clasp for a coral necklace got in Paris
which I meant for M— or Miss Browne. M— chose a coral clasp for
herself. It so happened I did not pay for it as it had to be made & was
sent to the Albion when we were out, but I expect it will be half a
guinea at least. I told M— I had just got The Pleasures of Hope[16]
beautifully bound for Miss Browne, but she should have her choice
between the book & the necklace. She said she had The Pleasures of
Hope & would take the necklace . . . We made 2 or 3 more shoppings & drove off from the Albion at 2½ (a nice situation &
apparently what might be called the 1st or genteelest house in
Manchester but where we had bad eatables or cooking). Only
10 minutes changing horses at Rochdale & got home at 8¾
after a good journey.

Anne's life settled once again into its even tenor. The only
disturbance arose from a practical joke played on her regard-
ing an advertisement supposedly put into the *Leeds Mercury*.

Monday 29 November [Halifax]

Halifax letter, just opened it, beginning, 'As I understand you adver-
tised in the Leeds Mercury for a husband . . .' Saw no more but

reclosed, three drops of sealing-wax & sent it back to the post office.
I begin to care not much about these impertinent insults. Their
intended shafts of annoyance fall harmless & I shall never read them.
What the eye will see not, the heart will grieve not.

Tuesday 30 November [Halifax]

From the library . . . to the Saltmarshes' . . . Miss Pickford (Mrs
Wilcock's sister) a *bas bleu*. Emma had heard a discussion of her
merits & the honour done to Halifax by her presence. *She was*
compared with me, which Emma would not allow, however. She said
I gained the palm. Above all, I was allowed to be very good-hearted.

Thursday 2 December [Halifax]

Miss Browne met me at their front gate . . . Thanked me for the
splendid book. Talked a little of Miss Caroline Greenwood, who
told Mrs Browne it was my custom to make choice of some who
were rather silly &, when Mrs Browne stared, said perhaps she
should not have said so. Told how little I either admired or liked
Miss Caroline & complimented Miss Browne who certainly is very
fond of me & said she should not know what to do without me . . .
She had heard me compared with Miss Pickford but would not allow
it & convinced her sister Maria how much I was in every respect
superior.

Friday 3 December [Halifax]

Went to Mrs Saltmarshe's. Sat there, all of us, a good while, listening to Emma's amusing account of the Assembly. Mrs
Walker had the annoyance to see her daughter, tho' on her first
appearance, stand the 7th couple, placed below the Misses
Bates & Elizabeth Watkinson, who had precedence as being
bridesmaids to the reigning bride, Mrs Turney, Miss Hannah
Watkinson that was. Next to her, Mrs Frederic Norris, another
bride, then Mrs Pollard then Lady Radcliffe's sister, Miss

MacDonald. Emma thought all the old Assembly-goers seemed like intruders among the new ones. A motley set.

In her political outlook, Anne was a staunch Conservative with very decided views about the positive role of monarchy, the church and Toryism in Britain. She abhorred the movement for reform which had grown out of the radicalism of the French Revolution and her journals contain many outbursts of indignation against the people who espoused the cause. This was the year of the Peterloo Massacre and the north of England was greatly roused by the radical speakers who moved from town to town, making speeches and whipping up support for their cause. Halifax, itself, was a town in which radicalism appeared to have gained a firm foothold and on Friday 3 December 1819, Anne went to see 'the barracks just made out of a warehouse of Mr Taylor's at Ward's End & calculated for 208 men. 210 are coming tomorrow, 4 companies of the 6th Foot. Mrs Tarleton, wife of one of the officers, happened to be standing near the door, & Mr Jeremiah Rawson introduced us all. He is one of the Constables & therefore has the management of all this preparation.' It is apparent from that excerpt that trouble was expected in Halifax and troops were being moved in as a precaution.

Monday 6 December [Halifax]

This morning's post brought me (from York, directed by Anne Belcombe, Petergate) the *Manchester Observer; or Literary, Commercial & Political Register* . . . 2 sheets of 4 columns each, one of the most inflammatory radical papers published. When in Manchester I said to Dr Lyon I should like to have one to see what it was like, but should be ashamed to ask for it. I suppose, therefore, he has begged them to forward it after they had read it in Petergate. Read a little of it aloud just after breakfast, p.4, col.2, under the title of 'Important Communication to the People of England', decorated with a banner at the head, inscribed, 'Reform in Parliament', the flagstaff surmounted by a cap of liberty[17] & the flagstaff appeared to grow out of a united rose, thistle, & shamroc [sic] – is a most seditious, rousing article occupying near 2½ columns, shewing by short quotations from their works, 'Sir William Jones, the Duke of Richmond, William Pitt, Home Fooke, etc., Postlethwaite, Milton, Lord Trevor, & Locke' to have been of radical reform principles. p.2, col.4, 'Rights of Women' is a curious list of authorities in support of the rights of women to take part in these reform meetings – to vote for representatives in the House of Commons &, in short, to be in every sense of the word, members of the body politic. What will not these demagogues advance, careless what absurdity or ruin they commit!

Thursday 9 December [Halifax]

Before breakfast & afterwards, from 11 to 1, making minutes & extracts from Hall's *Travels in France* (it must go to the library today) . . . He is an arrant republican in politics & would, perhaps, style himself a philosopher in religion. Consequently, his sentiments & mine on these subjects, who [as] a limited monarchist & a Protestant Christian according to the established Church of England, are opposite almost as the poles. However, there is some information useful to a tourist.

Friday 10 December [Halifax]

Met Miss Browne . . . *Said nothing particular. Very kind but quite commonplace, at least as far as my manners can be so. I wonder [if] she perceived any difference or whether she felt as much interested as ever? I am sure I did not. It seemed very flat & now that all nonsense & one sort of sentiment is forever at an end, my interest is* gone. I care not twopence whether I see her or not & in truth, would rather not & only keep up the intercourse for appearance's sake. It will be deadly stupid but I must carry the thing on till she goes & I shall not be sorry to get out of the way a little after Christmas.

Monday 13 December [Halifax]

Notes (to my aunt & myself) from E. Saltmarshe to ask us to the ball & sandwiches on Tuesday, 21st inst . . . In the afternoon . . . called at Northgate . . . my Aunt Lister told me the soldiers had [been] alarmed on Thursday by the sound of a bugle in the middle of the night & that they had, in consequence, been under arms the rest of the night that, in expectation of a rising of the radicals, they had never gone to bed at all on Saturday night. Thomas heard all this from the soldiers themselves . . . Called at Whitley's &, change being so scarce there is hardly a sixpence to be had, left him a pound note, on my uncle's receipt, in payment of 15/6.

Wednesday 15 December [Halifax]

Lighted my fire this morning for the 1st time since last winter. 'Tis high time to begin to get up a little sooner & I hope to go on improving from this morning . . . *Another of those letters with a red wafer half out & the Halifax postmark. Just looked at it when Betty[18] brought it upstairs & bade her send it back again. She has brought it back saying it is directed to Mr Lister, my uncle, therefore sent it down to him . . . On going downstairs after dinner found the letter was signed, William Townsend, King Cross Lane, who had had the impudence to write to my uncle restating his impertinence & saying he had written often to me but could get no answer. My uncle read it all but I would not let him or my aunt tell me the contents. Put a wafer into it & gave it back to the postman. My uncle proposed redirecting the letter & sending it to the writer that he might have to pay the postage. To this, however, I of course objected. I was hot & said what I would do with my umbrella if I met him. My uncle laughed & said, 'You had better take the pistol & tell [him] you will blow his brains out if he plagues you any more.' 'I would,' said I, 'if I could do it without being known, but it would be all over the town directly & that would never do.' Is it not want of judgement in my uncle to think of sending him [his] letter back? Would not this be stooping? He thinks him a madman. He must be insane, surely he must, to have the impudence to write to my uncle also.*

During the last few months Anne had been hard at work on a descriptive work about her visit to France. The Duffins had requested it and she had written exhaustively about the sights she had seen whilst touring the city.

Wednesday 22 December [Halifax]

Looking over the last 30pp. of the letter to Mr & Mrs Duffin & wrote a note to Mr Duffin giving the dimensions of the Louvre gallery, account of the Diana, etc . . . so that, after all, this letter of 96pp. was to have been sent off at 1, but I was hurried & did not get it dispatched till ½ past. I am heartily glad it is finished & gone. It has been a sad, tedious concern but I hope I have learnt something during the time spent in writing it. At least I have gained a valuable turn towards a habit of patient reference & correction which, should I ever publish, may be of use to me.

Thursday 30 December [Halifax]

Miss Browne met me at the gate . . . *No conversation interesting to me. Talked chiefly about Mr Kelly & her anxiety to see him. She had often thought of my telling her he had been gay.*[19] *She had nothing to do with what he had been. Should make allowances, etc. Descanted on the weakness of our nature & that we should all be liberal . . . Bid her, in no case, raise her expectations too high. As I returned over the bridge, could not help reflecting for a moment how little I thought or now cared about Miss Browne. This girl who not long ago was so much in my mind, after she goes to Glasgow I shall never care to behold her again. She says she shall always remember me. Well, it may be so, but it is more than I shall do towards her.*

Friday 31 December [Halifax]

Looking over the *Annals of Philosophy* for November last. Population of Moscow – effect of bathing in the Dead Sea – M. Bouillon Lagrange's recommendation of carrot juice or rather carrot poultice as a remedy for cancer . . . In the afternoon . . . to the Saltmarshes'. Staid rather above an hour & got home at 5.10. *Better satisfied with my visit than usual. Thought them glad enough to see me & I said nothing I wished unsaid. From Emma's account their ball must have been a riotous concern. The Greenwoods & Miss Mary Haigue danced riotously & Tom Rawson took Mrs Prescott & danced her on his knee before them all, having before as publicly tickled her daughter, Elizabeth, on the soffa [sic]. She & Miss Mary Haigue afterwards went into another room. Tom kissed them both. Emma was obliged to leave them & Mr Saltmarshe & Mrs Walker of Crow Nest unluckily went in together & caught them. He had his arm round Mary Haigue's neck, but she looked nothing abashed. Mrs Christopher Rawson took Miss Astley with her, the Unitarian Minister's sister. Tom said, 'It is a long time since I have had a kiss of you.' Mr Christopher gave her one, said the ladies will think it rude if it does not go round, & tho' he had never seen Miss Astley before, put his arm round her neck & kissed her also* . . . A good deal of snow fell last night & the morning was snowy till after 10.

1820

Tuesday 4 January [Halifax]

Gave the librarian five shillings as I said, last September, I would do every half-year on condition of his managing to let me have as many books at a time as I wanted. Not, however, that I think of exceeding the regulated allowance by more than two.

Wednesday 5 January [Halifax]

A man civilly asked if it was going to thaugh [sic] as I came up the new bank. Whether it was the same or not, I am uncertain, but a man in a greatcoat made like a soldier's followed me down our lane & asked if I wanted a sweetheart. He was a few yards behind & I said, 'If you do not go about your business, sir, I'll send one that will help you.' I heard him say, 'I should like to kiss you.' It annoyed me only for a moment, for I felt, on coming upstairs, as if I could have knocked him down. But I ought not to have spoken, nor should, but being so near home I was at unawares provoked to it.

Monday 10 January [Halifax]

Another of those letters. The direction apparently in a better hand than usual & directed for the first time, Miss Anne Lister. However, I scarce looked at it but sent it back unopened. That people should be so impertinent annoys me yet, perhaps, a little at

the moment, but it is soon over & I think the writers will tire, by
& by.

Tuesday 11 January [Halifax]

My usual way to King Cross & back & got home at 5½. *About
midway between the two sets of cottages in the new bank as I returned,
a man, youngish & well enough dressed, suddenly attempted to put his
hands up my things behind. In the scuffle, I let the umbrella fall but
instantly picked it up & was aiming a blow when the fellow ran off as
fast as he could & very fast it was. I did not feel in the least frightened,
but indignant & enraged. Knew not till the moment afterwards that I
at first said, 'Holo' & then immediately, 'God damn you, but I'll –'
but he was soon out of sight down the hill & I walked quietly home.
Told them during tea. My uncle & aunt think it is the man who writes
these letters. At any rate, I think not William Townsend.*

Sunday 16 January [Halifax]

Walked from church with the Stansfield Rawsons & went in for
a few minutes to tie up my garters. Then past Bull Close & up
Callista Lane to King Cross. *As I returned, met two young women
& two boys. Walked by their side, one of whom said, just before they
came up with me. 'That's her that lives at Shibden Hall & advertised in
the paper for a sweetheart.' It immediately occurred to me that somebody must have had some advertisement of this kind inserted in the
Leeds Mercury . . . Had a longish talk as soon as I went home about the
advertisement. They were for having me make inquiries & get to see it
& have the editor contradict it . . .* Stood talking to my aunt by the
kitchen fire, after my uncle went to bed, ¾ hour, *about the people
calling after me, being like a man & about people's being insulted.*

Monday 31 January [Halifax]

*Another queer Halifax letter. Thought of nothing but its being from
William Townsend. Resolved therefore to go immediately to consult*

Mr Horton.[1] My uncle very hot & indignant & was for sending somebody to ask if he wrote the letter & if he owned it, to stop it into his mouth. I was vexed & enraged but said little or nothing & got off to Halifax at eleven & a half. Stopped Mr Horton near Edwards, the booksellers, & we walked together to the Sessions House near the theatre. He could do nothing without the letter. Could be construed into a breach of the peace. He opened & read it (I did neither). Not from William Townsend but some man saying he was a native of Bolton &, I think, named Lomas (to be directed to at the White Horse public house, as my uncle told me on his reading it when I got home). Of course, I could do nothing. At least Mr Horton advised my taking no notice &, in the case of Townsend, I must not take the law into my own hands by any violent measure. The only thing to be done was to desire him to desist, which would be best done by an attorney. And, in case the man did not, it would be a misdemeanor [sic] & Mr Horton would summons, issue a warrant against him &, unless he found bail, send him to the House of Correction at Wakefield, binding over my uncle or myself to prosecute him at the Sessions. He said there had been no advertisement respecting me in the Leeds Mercury. He was very civil & I went away satisfied at having consulted him & almost resolved to let them write on in future till they were tired.

The affair of the mysterious letters faded into the background as Anne became caught up once more in York society. On 1 February, M— arrived at Shibden Hall to spend the night there, before going on to York accompanied by Anne. They did not return to Halifax until 30 March. They were joined by Isabella Norcliffe for part of the time during their stay in York.

Tuesday 1 February [Halifax]

About 4 M— arrived having left her nephew, William Milne, & her servants at the White Lion . . . Looking better than I expected & in good spirits. We are to sleep tomorrow night at the Chaloner's at Newton Kyme, near Tadcaster.

Wednesday 2 February [Newton Kyme nr Tadcaster]

M— & I off from Shibden at 10. Walked to the White Lion. The carriage ready & after taking us thro' the town & Haley Hill (Watson & William Milne had walked on before) we walked a couple of miles up the hill & took them up 3 miles from Bradford. Stopt there at the Sun (on account of the horses) ½ hour. Got to Leeds (the White Horse, Boar Lane) about 3½. While the coachman looked after his horses & ordered about leaving them there, M— & William & I went to the mus. room in Albion St to see the newly invented carriage impelled by the feet of the person going in it. Very simple mechanism – like a small gig on 3 wheels. Price of that, £35. One to carry 2 people, £45. Off from Leeds with 4 posters in less than ¾ hour & got out at the Chaloner's . . . a few minutes before 6, the hour at which M— had fixed to be there for dinner.

Thursday 3 February [York]

Down to breakfast at 10½ & off to York at 12½. A pair of posters brought us in 1½ hours (12 miles) & I got out here at the Duffins' in Micklegate at 2. Mr Duffin came in about 3½ from the procession in honour of the proclamation of George the 4th which began at 1.[2] Mr Duffin thought there might be a concourse of about 5,000 people. *The Duffins & Miss Marsh really seem glad to see me.*

Wednesday 9 February [York]

M— & Eli & I stayed at home . . . *Just before Harriet* [Milne, née Belcombe] *went, happening to talk a little to her in the complimentary style, M— & Eli remonstrated. M— & I talked about an hour after we got into bed. A very little would make M— desperately jealous. Speaking of my manners, she owned they were not masculine but such was my form, voice & style of conversation, such a peculiar flattery & attention did I shew, that if this sort of thing was not carried off by my talents & cleverness, I should be disgusting. I took all in good part. Vowed over & over, constantly, etc., & M— gave me a good kiss.*

Tuesday 15 February [York]

At 9, M— & Anne & Eli & I went to the Macleans in Coney Street. A rout party, but a quadrille or 2 danced to the piano, & a nice supper. Lost a rubber of 4 shilling points . . . A pleasant evening & got home at 12½.

Thursday 17 February [York]

In the evening . . . *would not have the girls in our room & had a comfortable, cosy conversation. M— loves me. Certainly her heart is wholly mine. If I could have allowed her twenty or thirty pounds a year in addition to what she had, she certainly would not have married. But what could she do on her allowance of only thirty pounds a year? Passed an affectionate hour or two.*

Wednesday 1 March [York]

A little before 7, walked to the Belcombes' to dress & go from thence to the Officers' Ball at the Assembly Rooms. Went in with Dr Belcombe. Soon joined Mr Duffin & never left him till 2¼, when he went away soon after. The most elegant supper I ever saw. All managed by Mr & Mrs Barber of the Black Swan, who had a confectioner down from London. The tables in the little Assembly room beautifully ornamented. At one end of the little middle table, fronting the sideboard, a large & beautifully done boar's head of brawn. At the other end, a large swan swimming on jelly &, in the middle, a beautiful windmill near a yard high. At the two ends of each of the other tables, a couple of soups, white & brown. Altogether excellent & beautiful. Mr Barber was to furnish the supper at £150, exclusive of tea before supper, & wine & negus, etc. 'Twas said the whole would probably cost about £300. According to the list of the company taken by one of the sergeants, there were present 340 people. The benches were taken away that used to disfigure the pillars. The room was tastefully decorated. Flags at the four corners (the arms of England, the Union Jack, the arms of Scotland & of Ireland). The entrance to the room was through a tent lined with soldiers. The Egyptian Hall looked finely imposing & the whole thing was uncommonly well-managed & went off most uncommonly well. Only 2 or 3 country dances, all the rest, quadrilles . . . I came away at 5. M— staid with Anne & Lou, who remained till the finale at a few minutes before 6. Terribly bad night. Wind, rain & snow.

On Friday 17 March, Isabella Norcliffe joins the house party at the Belcombes'.

Saturday 18 March [York]

Slept with M— in Anne's room upstairs over the drawing-room . . . Little tiff with Tib . . . Said taking snuff & lying in bed did not suit me & she knew it. Answer; I never found fault with M—, & proceeded to it. It was a pity I let her marry. M— advised me last night to tell Tib every now & then she did not suit me & not to let her dwell so on the idea of our living together . . . *Told Louisa I should not like to be long in the same house with M— & Tib. Lou is sure I like M— the best.*

Tuesday 21 March [York]

At 8, Miss Marsh & I went together in the same chair to Mrs Copley's . . . The latter part of the evening entirely with M—.

2 glees by Mr & Mrs J. Rapier & Mr Howgill & a sing-song by the first. Quadrilles, & supper at 12 for those who remained. *Very odd concern. Half a large cold pigeon on one side & a piece of roast beef at the bottom, one of the ribs laid bare at some previous meal. Only one bottle of port & ditto of white. No malt liquor, no servants. No Mrs nor Miss Copley. The former desired M— to do the honors [sic] & left us all to ourselves. M— ashamed of the thing & did nothing.* Miss Marsh & I returned in the same chair & got home at 12.50.

Wednesday 22 March [York]

Mrs Simpson came unexpectedly at 9 . . . *[She] told M— this morning she could not bear me, that I was the only woman she was ever afraid of. Wondered how anyone ever got acquainted with me. Mentioned my deep-toned voice as very singular. The girls said they were afraid of me but could like me because M— did.*

Thursday 23 March [York]

Someone who did not know me said to Mrs John Raper of me, 'One must not speak to her. She is a bluestocking.' 'I don't know,' replied Mrs Raper, 'but she is very agreeable.'

On 30 March, Anne returned to Halifax taking M— with her. M— stayed at Shibden until 14 April.

Sunday 2 April [Halifax]

Wet morning, sun, rain & wind. Had a chaise & my aunt & M— & I went to morning church . . . *Miss Browne at church. M— rather nervous, I suppose at seeing her. At least, we talked about her on our return. M— said she did not like the thing & shewed her fondness for me by her care & quiet tears about it. I will not doubt her love any more.*

Monday 3 April [Halifax]

M— said, very sweetly & with tears at the bare thought, she could never bear me to do anything wrong with . . . anyone in my own rank of life. She could bear it better with an inferior, where the danger of her being supplanted could not be so great. But to get into any scrape would make her pine away. She thought she could not bear it. I never before believed she loved me so dearly & fondly. She has more romance than I could have thought & I am satisfied . . . I thought of its being my birthday, but let it pass without notice. How time steals away! What will the next year bring to pass? May I improve it more than the last!

Tuesday 4 April [Halifax]

After coming up, M— was to look over some of our old letters. In getting them, happened to stumble on some memoranda I made in 1817 on her conduct, her selfishness in marrying, the waste & distraction of my love, etc. Began reading these & went on thoughtlessly till I heard a book fall from her hands &, turning round, saw her motionless & speechless, in tears. Tried very soothing & affectionate means. She had never before known how I loved her or half what her marriage had cost me. Had she known, she could not have done it & it was evident that repentance now pressed heavily. I endeavoured, & successfully, to prove it to have been done for the best. She said she had never deserved some of the remarks made, but it was quite natural in me to make them. She grieved over what I had suffered & would never doubt me again. I am indeed persuaded & satisfied of her love.

Wednesday 5 April [Halifax]

Came upstairs at 10½. Sat up talking about my manners being too attentive; having too much of the civility of a well-bred gentleman, that I unintentionally spoilt people. Shewed her Emma Saltmarshe's last note before my leaving. She said it proved that I gave rise to an interest which people did not understand, or why they felt [as they did]. I promised to make my manners less attentive. She convinced me that my society was no advantage to Miss Browne as it might unfit her for that of others. M— said, after we got into bed, that if she did [not] believe me bound to her in heart as much as any promise could bind me, she should not think it right & certainly would not kiss me.

Monday 10 April [Halifax (Haugh-end)][3]

In the evening Captain & Mrs Priestley & Lou [who was staying at Haugh-end together with Anne & M—] went to a dance & sandwiches at Mrs Rawson's (Hope Hall)[4] & got back at 4. Mrs Rawson had, thro' the medium of a note, to Mrs Edwards, invited M— & me, also, in spite of the awkwardness between us, but we were delighted to have a snug evening to ourselves. *I was on the amoroso till M— made me* read aloud the first 126pp., vol.2, of Sir Walter Scott's (he has just been made a baronet) last novel *The Monastery*, in 3 vols., 12mo. Stupid enough. Tea at 7½. Went upstairs at 11. Sat up lovemaking, she conjuring me to be faithful, to consider myself as married, & always to act to other women as if I was M—'s husband.

Thursday 13 April [Halifax (Haugh-end)]

Walked (we 4) by Brockwell to Sowerby church . . . & as we returned, just went into the public school for the children of the lower classes . . . Walked & sauntered about after dinner. All four went up & saw a cow calve in a field, several people being present, men, women, & children After supper, read aloud (took me 40 minutes) Canning's[5] speech to his constituents at Liverpool on his election for this present parliament. Fine day. Went upstairs at 11.20. *M— & I had a good deal of talk. She again conjured me to be faithful & let the rule of my conduct to ladies be – what would a married man do? ... She was very low after we came upstairs. As soon as Watson went & even while Lou was lolling on the bed, she cried a good deal & seemed very miserable at the thought of leaving. I said & did everything that was kind. Told her I believed she loved me most fondly & faithfully & I loved her better & had more confidence now than ever before. I said I would do or promise anything, but that she needed no further promise than my heart, at that moment, gave her. (I made no promises.) I am indeed satisfied of her regard & I shall now begin to think & act as if she were indeed my wife.*

Thursday 20 April [Halifax]

Miss Browne met me at their farther gate, turned down 'Callista Lane' on to the moor ... Parted after about an hour & a half. Behaved kindly. Said nothing about ever seeing her in the future, but bade her to think that, if I should not see her of twenty years, I should be equally interested in her welfare ... Just after getting thro' Skircoat Green, she asked me if my watch riband was worn out. I shewed it her & she said it was not. I told her I guessed her intention & she hoped I would do her the honour to accept one she had made for me, tho' it was very ugly & she was much dissatisfied with it. She meant it to be purple but it was scarlet. Certainly I would not wear the thing but admired it & thanked her very prettily & excused my not wearing it by saying I should value it too highly & would put it by with several other presents that I thought too valuable to wear. She seemed pleased ... How different my feelings now & formerly. I felt rather ashamed of being seen with her. Felt sorry for myself. Would be glad to see her no more & regretted that she would have to return [to Halifax before her marriage]. *I said I was sorry at her going several times over & I think she believed me. Yet I was only anxious not to seem inconsistent or less kind than usual & to appear as I wished, or rather as I thought proper, was an effort to me. We met Miss Maria Brown & Mr Higham, one of the officers of the Sixth*

Foot, & Mrs Lees & Miss Tipping & Mrs Louis Alexander. I was sorry for myself & ashamed of my company. Poor girl. How little she thought this. I rejoiced she could not know, she could not think it. I am indeed glad she is going. Told my uncle & aunt she was going to be married. Very good match, I said, & we were all glad . . . Yet I believe she likes me very much & feels grateful for all my attention. This has its effect on me. Her heart is unvitiated by the world. I would gladly do anything in the world to serve or give her pleasure.

Monday 1 May [Halifax]

All sitting quietly downstairs when (a few minutes before 10) we were roused by a loud rapping & screaming of female voices at the door. In came Mrs Walker of Crow Nest & her 2 daughters, the former almost fainting, & all ½ dead with fright, having just been overturned into the field in taking the sharp turn at the top of the lane. The reins had broken, the coachman lost all [control?] from the top of the hill. The horses came down full speed & were lying as if dead. None of the ladies, fortunately, much hurt. The footman did not happen to be on the box (not having been able to mount after walking up the new bank). The coachman had sprung a bone in his left ancle [*sic*] & bruised the hip a little. The horses did not appear at all the worse. After a glass of wine & being furnished with cloaks & a lantern, the ladies set off in ¼ hour to walk home. The carriage (very much broken) was brought here & the man sent off on one of the horses in about an hour after the rest. What a mercy they were no worse. How provident that the mischief was, in fact, so small considering the greatness of the accident.

Wednesday 3 May [Halifax]

Musing on the subject of being my own master. Of going to Buxton in my own carriage with a man & a maidservant. Meeting with an elegant girl of family & fortune; paying her attention; taking her to see Castleton; staying all night; having a double bedroom; gaining her affections, etc. Mused on all this but did not let it lead to anything worse.

Thursday 4 May [Halifax]

Sewing leather on to my clean stays . . . It was near 1 before I could get upstairs & it is now more than ¼ past before I can sit down to write to M—, *having been obliged to finish mending my bombazine petticoat* . . . Told M— that 'Miss Browne went some days ago to town & Chepstow for 2 months or perhaps 3 or 4, at the end of which time she was to commence her *travail* in the holy state.'

Friday 5 May [Halifax]

In stopping a moment or two, as I often do, to look down the valley from the top of our lane, a carter overtook me, accosted me by name & asked civilly, which I answered, some questions about how the Walkers' carriage was overturned. I had wished him goodnight & had not gone more than 2 or three yards before he called out, 'Young woman, do you want a sweetheart?' 'What!' said I angrily, 'I never listen to such impertinence but I shall know you again, & mind you never speak to me again.' He muttered something, I know not what. Did the man mean to be impertinent, or was he encouraged by my talking to him? It will be a lesson to me to take care whom I talk to in future. One can hardly carry oneself too high or keep people at too great a distance.

Tuesday 9 May [Halifax]

All the morning till very near 3, copying notes from loose papers into Extracts, vol. B., & writing out an index to my volume of poetry & scraps for which, by the way, I must find out some more tractable name. One thing occurs to me after another. I have now thought of looking over all my extracts & making a universal index of similes, e.g. strong as Hercules;

licentious as Tiberius; modest as Daphne, etc., & to make this index extend thro' all my future reading. It would certainly be useful; for when one wants a good simile, it is often astray.

Wednesday 10 May [Halifax]

All the morning till after 3, looking over Extracts, vols B, C & D & finished the rough draft of an index of similes. I know not whether I can make the thing answer i.e. be worth the time & trouble. *All the afternoon altering the tying & drawing of my velvet spencer after Miss Kitson's letting down the hem, & mended one of my black cloth boots.* From 7.35 to 8.10, walked to the shoe-maker's & back at the top of Hayley-hill.

Friday 12 May [Halifax]

At 11¾ down the new bank to Mr Saltmarshe's . . . Mr Garlicke has this morning (at 9) pronounced Emma Saltmarshe's house-maid in the scarlet fever & the girl is crimson with the irruption [*sic*] & can scarce speak for sore throat. Emma Saltmarshe seems pleased to find it the scarlet instead of rheumatic fever as she yes-terday feared, & is not, apparently, apprehensive of the infection spreading, so that we both made ourselves very comfortable . . . 'Tis the custom here for physicians to send in their bills. When an illness is over, the family desire to have the bill. But some, it seems, have been so dilatory that Mrs Paley has sent in 1 or 2 bills of a hundred pounds each & already dunned the people 2 or 3 times!!! 7s. a visit in the town. 10/6 one mile beyond, & 2 guineas she believed the physicians some time ago agreed to have for going as far as Millhouse. Ellen (Mrs Empson) had told of Dr Belcombe's taking £15 from a blacksmith at Elvington for 3 visits, which she seemed to think enormous. But the doctor was said to have behaved handsomely in telling the man after this that he could do him no more good . . . Felt a sick headache coming on (perhaps from eating a little at dinner & taking two very small oranges without sugar). Very poorly at Well-head & walked ¼ hour by myself in the garden, after having eaten biscuits & drank cold water to keep off sickness . . . Talked a good deal. Told Mr Saltmarshe my opinion of *Don Juan*. *Emma told me afterwards she had read it at Elvington but durst not own to Kit that she had read more than a part of it . . . Just before coming away, Emma told me the story of Mrs Empson's, the old mother's, cook & housekeeper, who had slept with her, rubbed her all over, for two years & whom she recommended to her son, John Empson, turning out to be a man.* 'Mrs' Ruspin was an excellent cook & housekeeper but unluckily fought with the footman which made the place so uncomfortable 'she' could not stay. The housemaid therefore left, to whom 'Mrs' Ruspin had shewn great attachment. They both went to London. 'Mrs' Ruspin married her. They keep a cook's shop in London & Ruspin has taken his proper name & dress. Told the story before a family party after dinner. 'Indeed,' said —, 'I did not know this.' 'No,' said —, 'If you had, I'm sure you'd never have parted with her.' A laugh.

Monday 15 May [Halifax]

Called at Well-head & thanked Mrs Waterhouse (at the door) for her attention to me on Friday afternoon when I was sick. Left a message of thanks & inquiries at the Saltmarshes' (the manservant beginning in the scarlet fever this morning).

Friday 19 May [Halifax]

Emma Saltmarshe rather poorly & her 2 servants, the man particularly, has been worse in the scarlet fever this last day or two.

Sunday 21 May [Halifax]

All went to church & staid the sacrament . . . *During dinner, as is generally the case on a Sunday, sewing, mending my worsted stockings* . . . James having been sent to Halifax immediately after tea yesterday & not returning till 9.35, & having, on Thursday, not come in till 9.25, in spite of all that was said to him about being in at 9, my aunt gave him warning this morning & told him he would be at liberty in a month. He was in at 9 tonight.

Monday 22 May [Halifax]

'Tis now high time to resume my regular course of study . . . I have done nothing since going to Paris last May & this excursion has lost me, as it were, a whole year. I must manage better in future. I am heartily sick of the way in which this last 12 months has passed & am as heartily rejoiced to get back again to my former habits & pursuits. May the event be prosperous . . . Came upstairs, after being with my aunt in the garden planting out some seedling sycamore trees . . . *My aunt told James's father of his son's going. He answered it was right, in a way that was not very pleasing & as if he took his son's part. My aunt & I were vexed at such want of civility & gratitude, & both declared he had no more favors [sic] to expect. I should, if I had any influence, [see] he should not [have] Willroyd Farm* . . . The thought & feeling of having recommenced my regular studies has afforded me a pleasure & happiness I have not experienced of long.

Wednesday 24 May [Halifax]

Letter . . . from Mrs Norcliffe (London) wishing me to inquire the character of a servant that has lived with Mrs Prescott & has offered to her (Mrs Norcliffe) as housekeeper . . . The woman was turned off for giving away great quantities of bread & meat & will not do for Mrs Norcliffe at all.

Thursday 25 May [Halifax]

Wrote 3pp. to Marian (Market Weighton) to ask her if their servants have not a brother who would suit us in James's place

& to make inquiries about one . . . At 2, down the new bank to Mr Sunderland's. Waited ¼ hour, & then Mr Sunderland extracted from me (very well) the farmost [*sic*] low tooth on the right side. It was very fast & a very small portion of the jaw bone came with it between the fangs.

Friday 26 May [Halifax]

My gum bled very much & my mouth was very sore & uncomfortable all yesterday afternoon & evening. Towards night my throat began to feel very sore. Nor could I sleep much till this morning . . . A little after 8, the Saltmarshes' groom brought me a note from Emma Saltmarshe thanking me for mine she received this morning, & saying Mr Saltmarshe began to be ill of the scarlet fever on Saturday. The disease increased so much on Sunday & Monday that he had been in great danger, but was now rapidly recovering. Poor Emma, I am heartily sorry for her . . . My throat worse again this evening. A little headache all the day & a little pain at my chest, & heavy & unwell in the evening. *My aunt put it into my head & for a moment or two, I have thought whether I have caught the infection from Emma.*

Sunday 28 May [Halifax]

My uncle went to morning church but my aunt staid at home with me. Heard her read the psalms & chapters & then came upstairs & lay down most of the day. In a good deal of pain from both the upper & lower jaw on the right side. That side of my face much swelled & my throat very bad. Mr Sunderland came between 4 & 5 in the afternoon. Ordered 6 leeches to be applied immediately & sent me some opening mixture, an embrocation & a gargle. If the inflammation could not be stopped, I should have a quinsy. Betty Wood, the leech-woman of Northowram, came at 7. In 10 minutes I was in bed & had 6 leeches just underneath my right jaw. They were on rather more than an hour. Rather sick but not to fainting. Hot flannels dipt [*sic*] in the embrocation applied, then lastly, a white bread poultice sprinkled with it. My aunt sat up with me till 5 in the morning. At 11, thought of gargling with vinegar & water (Mr Sunderland's being altogether too smooth) & till 3½ gargled every 10 minutes. This relieved me exceedingly. Gargled twice afterwards & my aunt left me very much better. Dozed a little tho' unable to sleep & got up at 11.30.

Monday 29 May [Halifax]

Very much better for my aunt's attention & kindness which I verily believe was a great means of arresting the inflammation, the leeches, however, doing their part. The orifices bled a great deal in the night & since the cloths were changed, at 5 this morning. Gargled with vinegar & water 4 or 5 times today. Mr Sunderland should have come at 12 but was prevented till about 4 this afternoon. Surprised to find me so much better than he expected. Said not a word of the gargle.

Monday 5 June [Halifax]

[Letters] from Miss Marsh (Micklegate) & one from Anne Belcombe both . . . to announce the melancholy tidings of Mr Norcliffe's death, in London, of an inflammation of the lungs . . . How melancholy! How shocking! Poor Isabella! . . . A thousand terrible anxieties beset me. I wish I could set off instantly to meet her. How sad! How melancholy! How bitter thus to weep another's woes.

Wednesday 7 June [Halifax]

Very affectionate letter from M—. A remarkable dream about my being found dead seems to have made a great impression on her. She heard of the death of Mr Norcliffe on Monday & was exceedingly shocked. 'My Fred, *will this melancholy event make any difference to you or me? I shall not lose you, my husband, shall I? Oh, no, no. You will not, cannot, forget I am your constant, faithful, your affectionate wife.'* . . . Wrote to M— . . . *very affectionate. Asking what made such a thought about Isabel arise, saying it cannot be, & holding out much promise of the future, but all in a way none but M— can understand & I think the letter might be seen & do no harm.*

Thursday 15 June [Halifax]

My aunt had a letter from Marian. The character of George Playforth so far satisfactory . . . that he is to come on Monday as soon as he can.

Monday 19 June [Halifax]

George Playforth came (from Market Weighton) a little before 11. With a blue groom's coat, & his breeches knee-ribands down to his shoetops (having, as I suppose, [been] all night in the mail), his appearance was not scanned to advantage.

Thursday 22 June [Halifax]

My father & Marian arrived from Market Weighton by the mail & were here by 7. Both looking very well *but vulgar. Marian in a light-blue sort of lustre with as long a waist as any my aunt & I saw last year in Paris. Very unbecoming &*, as yet, *out-Heroding too much for Halifax* . . . In the afternoon at 4½ (my father walked with me), down the old bank to the library. *In returning, near Whitley's, met Mr Jenkinson of the White Lion. To my dismay, my father shook hands with him. Near his ironworks, met Job Brook who, still more to my surprise, accosted my father very familiarly & then clapped him on the back. Shocking! I thought to myself, & will mind how I walk with you again to Halifax* . . . *Told my uncle & aunt of my father's shaking hands, etc, & how I was shocked. They evidently wondered & were shocked, too.*

Saturday 24 June [Halifax]

In the evening, went with my aunt & Marian looking for seedling trees in the little field to plant out in the garden.

Sunday 25 June [Halifax]

All went to church except Marian who staid at home on account of her bonnet. Mr Knight preached 28 minutes from St Luke. ch. 19. v. 41 . . . Sat down & put my legs up – slept a little.

Friday 7 July [Halifax]

In the evening (from 7½ to 9½) walked with my aunt to Halifax to see a very good collection of whole length waxwork likenesses of eminent personages by Madame Tussaud, a Swiss who left her country (Berne) 38 years ago & has not been there since. I saw her collection (tho' a different one from the present) 8 yrs ago in York. Admittance tonight, 1s. each.

Friday 14 July [Halifax]

Gave Marian some old muslin frill, a pair of chamois shoes, my fur cap & the green silk skirt, low waist, & spencer of the same that Mr Charles [C—] bought at Congleton for me in exchange for a much better & [rich?] thing M— made for me. Gave my aunt the pair of brown silk shoes, the stuff for which M— gave me at Lawton & that were made there. Mended my stockings, etc. All the morning till after 3, looking over my things . . . George got his white livery tonight.

Saturday 15 July [Halifax]

Mrs Rawson (of Stoney Royde) & Mrs Empson called. In about ½ hour came Mrs Greenwood of Cross-hills & her youngest daughter. In a little while, went out with Mrs Rawson & Ellen (without taking leave) to shew them the way home over

Bairstow. Stood a minute or two viewing the country from the lane above the Cunnery field, & then met Mrs & Miss Greenwood at Benjamin's Gate. Was sorry they had left Shibden. Mrs Greenwood said they had made a long visit, & seemed to be in dudgeon. I am glad of it. She is passing vulgar & disagreeable.

Tuesday 25 July [Halifax]

In the afternoon at 4.50, down the old bank to the library, thence to the Saltmarshes'. Mrs Rawson, Mrs Waterhouse, & Mrs Empson there to tea. *As I had, on first going, said I meant to stay tea, there was no retracting tho' I soon felt sorry for myself & as if I was in the way. Ellen rather boisterously talkative & she & Mrs Waterhouse had all the conversation, which they turned rather towards double entendre. Emma or I scarcely uttered during tea &, what made it worse, she observed a little too gravely that, indeed, we could not get a word in. Mrs Waterhouse asked me afterwards if I had read Don Juan. I would not own it. Emma said nothing, not a word on the subject. I thought Ellen quite vulgar. Well might Mr Bilton think her rather a romp if these be her manners. At coming away, Emma came to the door. 'When,' said she, 'will you come again after this specimen?' I am sure she guessed what I think ...* Came away early. Met George (going for me) in the town. Got home at 8.50 ... *Talking to my uncle & aunt about Ellen's vulgarity.*

Friday 11 August [Halifax]

In the afternoon, at 5¼, all set off over the top of Bairstow & Becon [sic] Hill to walk to Stoney Royde to drink tea. Got there in 43 minutes. Spent a tolerably pleasant evening. Ellen wondered I had not been again to breakfast, or to spend a day & *feared something or other had happened which had offended me. I said I had been very busy.* They were at Manchester on Tuesday

& Wednesday. Went over to Mr Falconer – the dentist, said to be one of the best out of London. He told them nothing was so good for the toothache as rubbing behind the ear on the side affected, till the skin was off, a mixture composed of equal parts of hartshorn, opium & sweet oil, & that the very best sort of toothpowder was powdered charcoal sifted thro' muslin. Get it in the stick & bruise it yourself. This will entirely correct the effect of any acid you may have taken. Got home in 38 minutes, along Church Lane & up the old bank, the typhus fever being very bad by the waterside about Bailey Hall.

Monday 14 August [Halifax]

Looking over & settling my accounts. I am minus one shilling & twopence, which has possibly arisen from some transaction with Whitley when he could not make up change & which I have forgotten, or perhaps the velvet brush I got the other day for George's breeches I have not been paid for. I am, at this moment, worth sixty-one pounds, thirteen shillings & tenpence farthing.

Wednesday 30 August [Halifax]

Very affectionate letter from M— . . . *She seems to consider my last letter as containing a promise on my part. Now this I certainly did not mean & she ought not to take it so far. I still feel myself as much at liberty as ever. But I have kept a copy of what was in crypt hand on this subject.*

Thursday 31 August [Halifax]

Wrote [to M—] . . . *of all the crypt hand kept a copy, disclaiming very gently having given her a promise & bidding her send me back my letters & be careful, for a discover [sic] would be ruin to us both. Said nothing could excuse our present connection in our own eyes but a reference to former circumstances. Otherwise our intercourse might bear an epithet that would alarm us both. But wrote very kindly. I wonder what she will say? I know she loves me & I am attached to her. After all, perhaps we shall get together at last.*

Sunday 3 September [Halifax]

From two till four, trying things on – my old pelisse, a spencer & waist. Studying how to improve my chest by stuffing, etc.

Wednesday 6 September [Halifax]

Letter from M— (Lawton). An account of her stay at Buxton. Mrs Siddons,[6] (whom she met at Stoke, nr Matlock) not at all what she expected. 'There is none of that grace & ease of manner which I expected would shine forth so conspicuously; & what certainly surprised me infinitely at dinner, she ate everything with her knife ... her daughter has neither grace nor manner, she has a fine complexion with black hair & brown eyes & would be handsome were it not for her mouth which is wide, thick & unfeminine. Her figure, too, is little & her size about the bosom, most immense. I do think I never saw anyone so large.'

Thursday 14 September [Halifax]

To Well-head at 4¾. Staid tea. Mr Samuel Waterhouse came in for a little while just afterwards. Came away at 8.35 & got home at 9. *They were very civil & Mrs Waterhouse made a great deal of me, but she looked as if something had been the matter. I do not think Mr Waterhouse appears well & this seemed to have made him a little crossly, or peevishly inclined in his manner to her. After all, he is vulgar & tho' very attentive to me, I have no enjoyment in such society & I had better go & sit with her now & then in the afternoon & come home to dinner than stay there a meal. I will not do this soon again, not of six months to come.*

Friday 15 September [Halifax]

Dressed & dined at 6 (having waited ½ hour). All went to Hipperholme to drink tea at Mr Hudson's. Asked to meet the party from Crownest & Cliff-hill, & found the room full of people. A vulgar clergyman & his wife of the name of Wasney, staying in the house & Mr & Mrs Wm Moore, of Northowram & their visitor, a vulgar young man, a Mr Smith from Liverpool. Mr Watson there & Mrs W. of Crownest & the 2 ladies & Mrs E.P. of Cliff-hill, & Mrs W. Priestley. Talked a good deal to the latter & fixed to sit an hour with her on Tuesday afternoon. *She said something about having given up asking me to dinner as it was ridiculous. She might, thought I, give me cold meat at six. I do not quite understand her* . . . Spent a disagreeable afternoon. Told Mrs Priestley I was in dudgeon at being so taken in with the party & in these cases seldom subjected myself to the thing a second time.

Saturday 16 September [Halifax]

Talking about Isabella, my aunt said a good deal about her being no companion for them, being stupid when I was not downstairs, about her pulling my face, etc., & being so unmindful of these things before my uncle & herself & my father, & indeed, James – such a lad as James – a servant! Indeed, she never felt so little in her life. Wondered Miss Norcliffe should let herself down so. I said what I could. Laid it on the manners of the world. My aunt said I did not understand her. In fact, I would not seem to understand. Tib was too fond, I know, tho' I cannot well choose to appear to know. She observed how different M— was. Said I, 'They are such different characters they cannot be compared, but M— says she has just as much regard for me as Tib.' My aunt seemed to doubt I believed she had just as much or more, however diffident her manner of shewing it. My aunt seemed still incredulous. I wonder if she smokes Tib? Surely she has not nous enough, tho' Tib is, indeed, shockingly barefaced. I must manage things better in future.

Friday 22 September [Halifax]

They took 2 men last night at Stoney Royde, stealing the fruit in the garden & sent them to the black hole[7] to stay till tomorrow morning. 'There is nothing to be done,' says Mr Jeremiah Rawson, who is constable, 'but making them pay the value of the fruit they have got & a penalty of 5s., unless you prosecute & put them in danger of transportation.'

On Wednesday 27 September, Anne travelled to York where she stayed with the Duffins for a few days and then went on to pay an extended winter visit to the Norcliffes at Langton Hall.

Wednesday 27 September [York]

Off . . . in the Highflier coach to York . . . Arrived here at the Duffins' (Micklegate) to tea about 7. Very glad to see me yet, tho' I said I had not dined, Mr Duffin mentioned cold meat only slightly & I had the bread loaf brought in . . . Heard at Leeds that the Leeds London Union coach in coming over the wooden bridge over the Trent at Newark, about one last night, or rather this morning, lost the coachman. He had driven too near the side of the bridge. Perhaps the side gave way a little, but the guard was thrown off on one hand & the coachman on the other, into [the river] where he was seen, by the moonlight, to float on his back perhaps 3 minutes & then, his clothes being full of water, sank & was drowned, leaving a wife & 5 children.

Wednesday 4 October [York]

During dinner, marrying happening to be mentioned, I declared my determination against it & Mr Duffin understood. 'I fear it,' said he, '& more the shame.' 'Shame,' said I. 'I see no shame in consulting your own happiness,' & the subject was soon ended. Both Mr Duffin & Miss Marsh would very evidently have had it otherwise

but I care not & they must see their efforts are vain. They were
beginning to joke a little about it this morning but my grave silence
stopped them. Mr Duffin walked over the bridge with me. *Staid*
a little too long at Miss Gledhill's &, tired of waiting in the street, he
walked home in a hough [sic] & when I got back at four, he shewed
his temper pretty plainly. I thought it right & best to conciliate but I
don't relish this sort of enduring & never leave this house with much
regret, or stay in it with any great pleasure. But it is convenient to be
here &, at any rate, I am less selfish than Mr Duffin & Miss Marsh,
who take care to make me pay for the convenience by reading &
dancing attendance . . . Went to the Belcombes' & got home at
10½, *luckily just before Mr Duffin. Rather agreeablizing to Eli who*
looked pretty. I think Anne observed my doing so with rather jealous
eyes. She thinks me making up to Eli. Am certainly attentive to her
but cautiously, without any impropriety that could be laid hold of. Yet
my manners are certainly peculiar, not all masculine but rather softly
gentleman-like. I know how to please girls.

On Thursday 5 October, Anne left York to pay her visit to
Langton Hall. The Norcliffes were still in a period of mourning following the death of Mr Norcliffe. The visit, therefore,
was of a rather subdued character. The company was made
up of Mrs Norcliffe, Isabella and Charlotte Norcliffe, Miss
Vallance[8] from Sittingbourne, Kent, and Anne. Later, they
were visited for short periods by Anne Belcombe and her
married sister Harriet Milne.

Thursday 5 October [Langton]

Before breakfast, packed up my things. Had my hair cut . . . Mr
Duffin went off shooting. Took leave of Mrs Duffin . . . Paid 2 or
3 bills. Went to the Belcombes' & staid with them till 1, then
to Fisher's, took leave there of Miss Marsh & set off for Langton
at 1¼. Arrived at 4. Found them all in good spirits & looking

very well. Dinner at 5. Miss Vallance gave us a little music in the evening.

As the weeks wore on, the routine began to pall on Anne. Apart from walking on the wold, going to church on Sundays and an occasional jaunt to Malton in the gig with Isabella, there was very little else in the way of distraction. Inevitably, the atmosphere between the women became a little strained. Small jealousies and bickerings grew up, particularly when the Belcombe sisters (Anne & Mrs Milne) joined the party.

Sunday 5 November [Langton]

A quantity of treacle with Hasty pudding at dinner yesterday gave me a little pain in the stomach & I went to 'my uncle' twice . . . Service at church in the afternoon, but a slight complaint in my bowels kept me at home tho', independent of this, the badness of the weather would have been enough. Rainy, stormy, windy day. Came upstairs at 10.25. ¼ hour with Miss Vallance, then wrote the above of today. Felt a bad cold coming on towards evening. *Sat up getting my things ready for the wash.*

Tuesday 7 November [Langton]

Walked near 1½ hour with Miss Vallance in the garden & low garden. At 1½, Isabella & I set off in the gig to call at the George Stricklands' . . . tho' they were fortunately not at home to us & we did not get out, it was after 5 before we got back, so bad were the roads. No regular road to the house. Obliged to drive over the green sward, a very solitary looking place – in a hollow among the high wolds, but a few thousand might make it well enough. In the evening, Charlotte began to do a little Latin with me & I made my 2nd attempt at a little Italian with her.

Friday 10 November [Langton]

Did nothing all the evening. Should have given the world to read. Tired of hearing or saying nothing worth a straw. Having such company is a desperately bad lounge & I am heartily sick of it. Gave Charlotte ½ hour's Latin lesson.

Saturday 11 November [Langton]

At 12¼, Isabella & I set off in the gig . . . to Housham, to see a woman having a patent for a particular sort of straw-hat manufacture whom, together with eight young women Mrs Cholmley has just sent down from London to settle at Housham & teach her business to the children of the village, about 30 of whom she has taken under her hand. The hats are not sewn but platted [*sic*] all of a piece & very light. Will wash with soap & water & bear crushing. The straw is from North America & from its length & appearance might be split from some sort of reed. A round hat with a deep brim that would fit me was 24s. A children's ditto, 12 or 15s. The patenter, a plain, elderly woman, speaking low London.

Friday 17 November [Langton]

Not long with Miss Vallance but long enough to say, in brief, that Tib & I . . . had had a rowe [sic] . . . about drinking so much wine. Tib was very violent after she came into bed at night. We renewed the conversation & she was a good deal more violent than before . . . I stood by the fire, talking very calmly, I daresay an hour, while she was in bed, repeating what I had said before. She still swore by all that is sacred she never took more than five glasses a day; one at luncheon, one at supper, one at dinner & two at tea. I repeated that I could, if I chose, mention a time (alluding to when she was last at Shibden) when, for several days she not only took more than five but more than six or seven glasses. She called God & all the angels of heaven to witness it was a lie & wished herself at the devil if it was not false. I still quietly persisted that I knew the thing to be fact. She declared it an infamous lie, that I would not mention the time & place where, because I could not . . . I told her a great many home truths. When the converse ceased, I began to curl & get into bed. She was soon snoring & we never spoke after my getting into bed.

Saturday 18 November [Langton]

Lay so long in bed talking seriously to Tib above an hour. She was quiet & calm this morning & would attend to what I said more than I expected. I again gave her to understand that her taking so much wine was generally known & lamented by all her friends . . . Miss Vallance said the servants here began to talk of Tib's taking so much wine. I told Tib she did not know the injury she did herself. She was now twenty years older in constitution than she was ten years ago &, in fact, much more an old woman than she ought to be at her age. I saw that this made an impresssion . . . She was afraid I must be tired of her & could never like to be with her. She had rather do anything than cease to be loved & desirable to me.

Tuesday 5 December [Langton]

Just before dinner, Tib very kindly told me I was beginning to be too pointed in my attention to Miss Vallance: that observations might be made & I had better take care. Indeed, Charlotte joked & told me, a while before, she supposed the cronyism had now got to such a pitch I could not live without the sight of Miss Vallance. Consequently, went to Anne's room after dinner & Charlotte came & we staid an hour. In the evening did nothing but read the 1st 14pp., vol. 2, Blackwall. Rainy day, came upstairs at 11. Only a few minutes with Miss Vallance & then went to Anne, *a little before twelve & staid two hours. At first, rather lover-like, reminding her of former days. I believe I could have her again in spite of all she says, if I chose to take the trouble. She will not, because it would be wrong, but owns she loves me & perhaps she has feelings as well as I. She let me* kiss her breasts but neither she nor her room seemed very sweet to my nose. I could not help contrasting her with Miss Vallance, & felt no real desire to succeed with her. At last she said, 'Now you are doing all this & perhaps mean nothing at all.' Of course I fought off, bidding her only try me, but I felt a little remorse-struck.

Saturday 9 December [Langton]

Wrote 3pp. & the ends, letter to my aunt (Shibden) & Isabella drove me to Malton to put it into the post. Terribly windy over the wold. Dawdled away the evening. Asleep on the sopha an hour. Fine day with high wind. Came upstairs at 11. *Only five minutes alone with Miss Vallance, the girls staid so long in my room. Charlotte came first & said, in substance, that I was always praising M——. Thought her all perfection & liked her much better than Tib, which was very unfair on poor Tib, who preferred me to all the rest of her friends. I rather fought off about M—— but Charlotte persisted it was plain enough. Tib came in. She does not suit me. I began to feel very low & said I had a headache. It was a heartache & I know not when I have felt a feeling so dispirited, so lorn & miserable, yet the thought of M——'s most affectionate letter came across me & I wondered that, after such a one, I could be so uncomforted.*

Saturday 16 December [Langton]

Very high wind last night. The ground thinly covered over this morning with strong frost, & high wind. Too cold & windy for anyone but myself to walk. From 3 to 3.50, went across the wold, thro' the Malton gate & back. Hard tugging against the wind on my return. In the evening, Anne Belcombe played a little on the piano.

Wednesday 20 December [Langton]

One and a half hour, just after tea, with Anne in her room. In low spirits. Mentioned, as frequent causes of this sort of thing, my father's having so lost the manners of a gentleman, the bad luck of his estate at Weighton, &, above all, M—'s marriage, etc. Anne must and does think me very much attached to M— & must guess our hopes of eventually coming together. One and a half hour with Anne after she was in bed. Talking, at first, much in the same style as in the evening, just before, but then got more loving. Kissed her, told her I had a pain in my knees – my expression to her for desire – & saw plainly she likes me & would yield again, without much difficulty, to opportunity & importun[ity].

Friday 22 December [Langton]

From 3 to 4, walked with Anne Belcombe in the East Balk field. *In the evening, Mrs Milne played. Hung over her at the instrument. Afterwards, sat next to her & paid her marked attention . . .* Came upstairs at 10.40. Near ½ hour in Mrs Milne's room. Near an hour with Anne Belcombe. *She told me of my attention to Mrs Milne & that I had taken no notice of her or Miss Vallance & that she was sure Miss Vallance had observed it & felt as she did. Said I could not help it. Mrs Milne was fascinating. Then went half an hour to Miss Vallance. Got out of her that she had observed me to Mrs Milne & was a little jealous. Anne then came to my room, having expected me again in hers, & staid almost till I got into bed. Her love for me gets quite as evident as I could wish.*

1821

Sunday 7 January [Langton]

All up late & none of us went to church. From 3 to 4, packing. *Miss Vallance put, in one of my drawers, a sealed parcel of spills to light candles with & a note enclosed, half sheet full, very affectionate. She certainly likes me & is very low & nervous about my going . . . Gave her the crypt hand alphabet which M— has . . . but was not very tender. Indeed, I get lukewarm about her. Tib low. Anne curled & saw me in bed.*

Monday 8 January [York]

All seemed low at our going. Dawdled till 2 when Mrs Milne, Anne Belcombe & I set off in a chaise (from the Tavern, York, at a shilling a mile) & got into Petergate about 5 . . . *All seemed glad to see me. Eliza very civil & kind to me but hardly spoke to Harriet [Milne]. Observed this afterwards to Anne, whom I easily persuaded to sleep with me.*

Anne stayed with the Belcombes until 15 January, when she travelled back home to Shibden.

Monday 15 January [Halifax]

Got to Halifax at 6½ [a.m.] . . . In the evening, played whist with my uncle against my father & aunt . . . They seemed glad to see me.

Tuesday 16 January [Halifax]

Wrote, & sent, 3pp. to Miss Marsh to say how I got here, but principally to give an answer to William Cawood, whom I saw & inquired about in York as a footman, that it is out of the question to think of him now as George will stay his year out, 5 months, at least. Miss Marsh highly recommended the man.

Wednesday 17 January [Halifax]

Mr Sunderland came to see Betty (who is ill with a sore throat & has been bled with leeches) & staid tea . . . Have not had such a comfortable evening of reading for long.

Friday 19 January [Halifax]

Letter . . . from York about the Friendly Society there, of which I have been an honorary member (12s. a year) ever since 1810 or 1811 but, during my last stay in York, I asked Miss Marsh to withdraw my name from their books. Whatever I can give in charity, my uncle & aunt have long said should be given here, to which Miss Marsh readily agreed.

Saturday 20 January [Halifax]

My Aunt Anne not in the best humour today. Mentioned my Friendly Society letter & not begrudging me shoes if I had not doctor's bill to pay, etc., making me feel that I wished she had less to do for me & this brought on a sort of sentiment of disquiet & unhappiness which usually besets me on these occasions. Better, however, & my aunt seemed quite right in the evening.

Thursday 25 January [Halifax]

Met with Mr Edward Priestley about Whitehall, standing by the men mending the road. We began talking of roads, the new wall falling & one thing or other that he came as far as Shibden but could not come in. Perhaps his chief object was to ask me if I would be a subscriber to a book society they wished to establish. About 12 subscribers at one guinea per annum each, the books to be disposed of every year to the highest bidder of the subscribers, but if none wished to purchase, the recommender of the work should take it at half-price. I said I should be sorry their plan fell through for want of a subscriber but that such a thing was quite out of my way who went so often to the Halifax library & had there as much reading as I had time for. The thing originated with the young ladies at Crownest, tho' Mr Edward Priestley had long ago thought of it, it was so long before they could get popular new works from the Halifax library; but I have no difficulty of this sort . . . George took my letter to M— (Lawton) to the post this afternoon. Came upstairs at 11. *After curling, was an hour adding up each page of my last year's accounts & examined all the totals of every month. There was an error of a shilling in that for April. Set all right & ready to balance.*

Friday 26 January [Halifax]

At 11½, my aunt & I set off to walk to Cliff-hill & Crownest.[1] Sat about ½ hour at each place & got home at 2¼ . . . Shook hands with Mrs W. Priestley but bowed formally to Miss Paley in consequence of her not having returned the call I made on her a year or 2 ago at Dr Paley's & not thinking much of her manifold apologies sent by Mrs W. Priestley . . . *but my relish for going to Halifax making calls is very much on the decline.*

Saturday 27 January [Halifax]

Dawdling over my accounts & one thing or other. I had a balance of ninety pounds, twelve shillings & twopence three farthings, & have now seventy-four & one shilling & ninepence farthing. I am in a pretty prosperous way altogether . . . Letter from Miss

Marsh, (Micklegate, York). *It seems they have been angry about [my] not taking William Cawood. He had* 'walked here & back twice, 32 miles, & all for nothing, & from your cool manner of putting an end to the business, I am sure you could not have thought much about it, or your natural kindness would have softened the disappointment by some expression of concern.' *Lord bless me! What could I do? I told the man how uncertain the thing was, that my uncle had not given warning to our present manservant, etc., & if he thought it worthwhile to inquire after such a place, as he must do after others, what was I to do? To pay him for his walking?* Expressions of concern in such a case are mere nothings. I never thought of them, but where words of this sort are wanting I seldom say too much & sometimes not enough.

Monday 29 January [Halifax]

Cutting curl papers half an hour . . . Arranging & putting away my last year's letters. Looked over & burnt several very old ones from indifferent people . . . *Burnt* . . . *Mr Montagu's farewell verses that no trace of any man's admiration may remain. It is not meet for me. I love, & only love, the fairer sex & thus beloved by them in turn, my heart revolts from any other love than theirs.*

Thursday 8 February [Halifax]

Came upstairs at 11 a.m. *Spent my time from then till 3, writing to M— very affectionately, more so than I remember to have done for long . . . Wrote the following crypt, 'I can live upon hope, forget that we grow older, & love you as warmly as ever. Yes, Mary, you cannot doubt the love of one who has waited for you so long & patiently. You can give me all of happiness I care for &, prest to the heart which I believe my own, caressed & treasured there, I will indeed be constant & never, from that moment, feel a wish or thought for any other than my wife. You shall have every smile &*

every breath of tenderness. "One shall our union & our interests be"
& every wish that love inspires & every kiss & every dear feeling of
delight shall only make me more securely & entirely yours.' Then,
after hoping to see her in York next winter & at Steph's[2] before the
end of the summer, I further wrote in crypt as follows, 'I do not like
to be too long estranged from you sometimes, for, Mary, there is a
nameless tie in that soft intercourse which blends us into one &
makes me feel that you are mine. There is no feeling like it. There is
no pledge which gives such sweet possession.'

Monday 12 February [Halifax]

Letter . . . from Anne Belcombe (Petergate, York) . . . *nothing*
but news & concluded, 'from your ever sincere, affectionate, Anne
Belcombe.' The seal, Cupid in a boat guided by a star. 'Si je te perds,
je suis perdu.'[3] Such letters as these will keep up much love on my
part. I shall not think much about her but get out of the scrape as well
as I can, sorry & remorseful to have been in it at all. Heaven forgive
me, & may M— never know it.

Wednesday 14 February [Halifax]

From 1 to 3, read the first 100pp. vol. 3 *Leontine de Blondheim*[4] . . .
It is altogether a very interesting thing & I have read it with a
sort of melancholy feeling, the very germ of which I thought had
died for ever. *I cried a good deal over the second & more over the third*
this morning, & as soon as I was alone during supper. Arlhofe reminds
me of C—, Leontine of M—, & Wallerstein of myself. I find my
former feelings are too soon awakened & I have, still, more romance
than can let me bear the stimulus, the fearful rousing, of novel reading.
I must not indulge in it. I must keep to graver things & strongly occupy
myself with other thoughts & perpetual exertions. I am not happy. I get
into what I have been led with . . . Anne. Oh, that I were more virtu-
ous & quiet. Reflection distracts me & now I could cry like a child but
will not, must not give way.

Sunday 18 February [Halifax]

George took to the post office, this morning, my letter to Anne Belcombe (Petergate, York). There was the following observation on the 2nd page . . . 'You know I am not always happy; it is my misfortune to be singular in sentiment, & there lies the source of all that I lament in practice or in thought, & thence the deadly shaft that poisons my tranquillity. "But, mortal pleasure, what art thou in truth! The torrent's smoothness ere it dash below!"' *Mary, Mary, if thou wert with me, I think I should be happy.*

Tuesday 20 February [Halifax]

At 12, went down the new bank to Hope. Saw only Ellen, her mother & Mrs Waterhouse . . . Ellen never appeared more glad to see me. Spoke so kindly about the disappointment of not seeing me at Elvington [near York] that I felt quite sorry at having ever for a moment fancied she had taken it ill. *Conscience makes cowards of us all, & the feelings of not wishing to go made me fancy she might think so too. But she knows better & is glad enough to call such a one as myself, so well known at York, her friend. I believe she likes me, & certainly her mother likes me, at any rate.* From Hope, went to the library & staid about an hour reading . . . in the monthly magazine of July 1820 remarkable praise of the life & writings of the celebrated German philosopher & professor, Kant, born, I think, in 1723, died 1804.[5] Turned to the article again. I must know more about this extraordinary man & his works by & by.

Monday 26 February [Halifax]

I must think of some better plan of reading in future; for I feel that I have hitherto wandered over too many books with too little thought, & have always read too cursorily to do ½ the good that ought to be done.

Sunday 4 March [Halifax]

In the morning, looking over the abridgement of Spence's *Polymetis . . . that was Isabella's . . . Gave me the idea of writing a work on antiquities. I shall think about it. I must write something & it is time to choose my subject.*

Wednesday 7 March [Halifax]

In the afternoon, Charles Howarth came about making a book-case for the library passage . . . In the evening, measuring & planning about the bookcase. *My uncle gave me five pounds.*

Thursday 8 March [Halifax]

Just after breakfast Charles Howarth came, thinking to measure about the bookcase. Obliged to send him away again for my uncle sat like a post & absolutely would not say a word either he would have it or not. I never saw such a specimen of his temper before & a more stupid or unamiable-looking one needs not be. My aunt was ready to cry & he knew that very well. While she was out of the room, I sat & never uttered & talked of the fine day & going to Lightcliffe this afternoon. It is not for me to feel out of temper or vexed. I care nothing about it. But heaven defend me from ever shewing this sort of temper, & grant that I may so behave to those around me as to make them more comfortable as such humours as this of my uncle's could do. I should hardly have thought it of him.

Friday 9 March [Halifax]

I felt very low this morning & have been inclined to it all the day on account of this being the fifth anniversary of M——'s marriage, but I have driven off the remembrance as well as I could by constant occupation. Just before tea I talked to my uncle & aunt & walked about in the drawing-room. Indeed, I began dancing when by myself & got into a heat.

Thursday 15 March [Halifax]

Just before tea, Graydon brought me a pair of shoes he had soled. I said he had made the toes narrower. He would have it he had not. He will always, on these occasions, say black is white & I shall employ him no more. He saw I was not pleased & said he did not wish to make for those he did not satisfy, to which I gave no answer but walked off. I proved I was right & thus said too much to him. Fewer words & more peremptory shall do for such people in future.

Friday 16 March [Halifax]

My right eye has been so weak this morning I have read with considerable difficulty, frequently changing my [position?] & alternatively sitting & standing to see if it would do any good. I have the sensation of a cold air blowing into my eye &, as I read, the eyelids gradually close till they are almost shut & I am obliged to rest. I felt this more than usual yesterday morning, tho' not so much as today, & for the last 3 or 4 times I have been out, I have found the air too cold for my eye, & the lids a little swollen & nearly closed when I came in. This, however, gradually went off. Tho' I have a fire in my room & it fronts the south & is a warm one, I have a constant sensation of a cold air at my knees and arms & the back of my neck, & to remedy the latter, have sat with my dressing gown (thick dimity, the sleeves lined with calico) over my other things, which I have found very comfortable. In addition, I can very well bear the plaid doubled up & laid across my knees.

Friday 23 March [Halifax]

In the afternoon, at 4½, down the new bank ... to the Saltmarshes' . . . Found Emma Saltmarshe looking much better than I expected. *She talked at a famous rate, saying she had been so long without seeing anybody, it was quite a treat to her. She seemed to me, by these means, more vulgar than I remembered to have seen her before.*

Saturday 24 March [Halifax]

Before breakfast, from 7¾ to 9¼, & from 10¾ to 2½ (including an interruption of 20 minutes) read from v.1304 to 1527, end of *Philoctetes* of Sophocles, & afterwards from p.288 to 296, end of vol. 2, Adams's translation of the 7 remaining plays of Sophocles . . . I feel myself improved & only hope to continue going on prosperously. It is about 2 years since my first beginning Sophocles (*vid.* Friday, 13 March 1818) but I have had long & many interruptions during this time. Besides, I had then a bad plan of doing many things at once, mixing Latin, Greek, Hebrew & French all in one mess on one day. When at Croft Rectory[6] (near Darlington) about this time 12 months ago, Mr James Dalton suggested the attending to one thing at once. I stuck to Juvenal exclusively & found it answered & will now stick to Greek till I have mastered it, let this cost me what time & pains it may. Mrs C. Saltmarshe sent her servants this morning (which occasioned my 20 minutes interruption between 11 & 12) with a leg of Welsh mutton which, a part of the loin being cut off with it, weighs 5lbs. We were talking of Welsh mutton yesterday & her sending me this leg is particularly kind & attentive.

Sunday 25 March [Halifax]

I have lately sat, in a morning, with my feet on the hearth to keep them from being so deadly cold, but the fire & the light at that distance from the window do not suit my eyes, & I have made a change in the arrangement of my room. Got the higher frame belonging to my writing desk; shall raise my seat & try what I can do with my feet a foot from the ground. I know not how it is, I feel as if I was going to have an illness.

I have perpetually the sensation of cold airs blowing about me, particularly about all my joints, the nape of my neck & the small of my arms. My head seems heavy, as if it was too full & that this occasions a pressure over my eyes which makes them not bear reading. I am not right by any means. In the afternoon, my aunt & I read aloud the prayers.

Tuesday 27 March [Halifax]

All dined together at 4¼ on the leg of mutton Emma Saltmarshe sent on Saturday, & had tea at 7½.

Friday 30 March [Halifax]

To the Saltmarshes' to tea. Staid till 8.35 . . . *Mr Saltmarshe sat with us all the time after tea. Long talk about what books were improper & what not. They mentioned Lallah Rookh & their not finding it out. I said I thought it as much so as Little's poems, or even the two first cantos of Don Juan*[7] *. . . I don't know how it is, I thought Emma a little under restraint on this subject before her husband & that he might be a little so, before his wife. I have often thought married people the best company when separated. I never knew a woman so pleasant when her husband was by. I came away feeling unsatisfied, tho' they were both very civil & friendly. I would rather sit an hour with Emma & not stay tea. The evening is dullish.*

Thursday 26 April [Halifax]

Put on my summer things, my velvet spencer & my cotton socks.

Monday 7 May [Halifax]

Foolish fancying about Caroline Greenwood, meeting her on Skircoat Moor, taking her into a shed there is there & being connected with her. Supposing myself in men's clothes & having a penis, tho' nothing more. All this is very bad. Let me try to make a great exertion & get the better of this lazyness [sic] in a morning – the root of all evil . . . Now I will try & turn over a new leaf & waste no more time in bed or any way else that I can help. May God's help attend this resolution.

Monday 14 May [Halifax]

Went straight by North Parade to Mrs Stansfield Rawson's. Found them sitting down to tea . . . *Talked away famously about one thing or other, society, etc, without reserve. I fancy they thought me amusing & agreeable. At least, they were as civil as possible.* They asked me about my studies. Said how I had neglected them for several years &, in fact, had only begun to read regularly about 2 or 3 years ago, much the greater part of which time I had wasted in bad management by gaping after too many things at once e.g. mathematics before breakfast, French, Hebrew, Latin & Greek during the rest of the morning . . . Expressed my particular wish that all this should not be mentioned for that I should not like to have it known & should not have told it at all had not she, Mrs Rawson, asked me so particularly. *I do not think Catherine will make much out as a scholar. She seems better suited to be made a beauty of. With good manners & fashionable accompaniments, she might have been much admired. These would have served her better, I think, than Latin & Greek.*

Tuesday 22 May [Halifax]

Sat near an hour with Mrs Waterhouse. Very civil & very glad to see me & *a thoroughly good woman, but I am out of my element here & must have other society in days to come.*

Sunday 27 May [Halifax]

All went to the old church . . . *Noticed Miss Alexander, Dr Gervase's eldest daughter, at church. Paris seems to have improved her exceedingly. She appeared a fine-looking girl. I stared upwards* towards her so often that I think she observed it; in coming out of church, too & I thought of her all the while. I could soon admire her, I fancy, from seeing her this morning, but it would be great imprudence to think of such a thing. She is, or ought to be, quite out of my reach.

Thursday 7 June [Halifax]

Till very near four, trying on different things to see what would do & be wanted for my going to Newcastle.[8] *I seem to have scarce anything fit to wear, have little or no money & altogether, I felt despairing & unhappy. Resolved to go out to the Saltmarshes' & thus divert my thoughts.* In the afternoon at 4¾, down the old bank to the Saltmarshes'. Both gone out in the gig. Thence to Wellhead – came away because they had a party. Had not got much beyond the new church when 1 of the children (Ann) called me back. Could do no other than return . . . *Had a good dinner of sweetbreads, white & Italian cream, in the common sitting-room & Miss Rawson sat with me all the while, twenty minutes. It was she would have me sent for & she certainly seems very fond of me. Had one cup of coffee. Except the pale Miss Luthwaite, they looked rather a second-hand party. Mrs Stansfield appeared well but, on talking to her, on a par with the rest. However, I agreeablized, talked a little to all & was amused.*

Tuesday 12 June [Halifax]

At 10¾, Miss Rawson (Catherine) & Miss Crackenthorpe . . . called & staid ½ hour, Miss Rawson to say that, as it was Whitsuntide week, her father & mother did not like her to be out & hoped we should excuse her coming this evening . . . In the afternoon, at 5¼, walked along the new road & got past Pump when Miss Ann Walker of Crownest[9] overtook me, having run herself almost out of breath. Walked with her as far as the Lidget entrance to their own grounds & got home at

6.40. *Made myself, as I fancied, very agreeable & was particularly civil & attentive in my manner. I really think the girl is flattered by it & likes me. She wished me to drink tea with them. I hoped for another walk to Giles House & the readiness she expressed shewed that my proposition was by no means unwelcome. She has certainly no aversion to my conversation & company. After parting I could not help smiling to myself & saying the flirting with this girl has done me good. It is heavy work to live without women's society & I would far rather while away an hour with this girl, who has nothing in the world to boast but good humour, than not flirt at all. If I had M— I should be very different. She has my heart & I should want no more than her, but now I am solitary and dull.*

Wednesday 13 June [Halifax]

Finished my letter to M— . . . *I have not exactly given her a promise in a set form of words but I have done nearly, in fact, the same thing, so that I cannot now retract with honour. Well, I am satisfied to have done. I love her & her heart is mine in return. Liberty & wavering made us both wretched & why throw away our happiness so foolishly? She is my wife in honour & in love & why not acknowledge her such openly & at once? I am satisfied to have her mind, & my own, at ease. The chain is golden & shared with M—. I love it better than any liberty.*

Saturday 16 June [Halifax]

Between 3 & 4, a note & parcel from Mrs C. Saltmarshe *with my drawers that I lent her for a pattern several weeks ago.*

Tuesday 19 June [Halifax]

In the afternoon, at 3.50 . . . straight to the library . . . Mr *Browne came in just before 5 with one of the Dragoon officers of the Queen's Bays. The former spoke to me, I thought in too familiar a tone. I scarce looked up & answered coolly. He is a thoroughly vulgar fellow.* 2 troops of the Second Dragoon Guards or Queen's Bays came into the town a few days ago – to remain here some time.

Friday 22 June [Halifax]

I owe a good deal to this journal. By unburdening my mind on paper I feel, as it were, in some degree to get rid of it; it seems made over to a friend that hears it patiently, keeps it faithfully, and by never forgetting anything, is always ready to compare the past & present & thus to cheer & edify the future. In the afternoon, at 4.40, walked with my aunt to Butters' to choose stuff for curtains for my bed.

Saturday 23 June [Halifax]

A letter from Isabella Norcliffe . . . she gives a long account of a kick-up they have had at Langton among the servants. Hazelwood proved to have been a man of bad character & to have led astray Bessy, the dairy maid & Thomas, the footman.

Sunday 24 June [Halifax]

My uncle & aunt went to the old church & I to the new[10] . . . Called for Emma Saltmarshe as I went, sat with her, went home with her, & staid about ¾ hour . . . I feel as if I begin to speak too inconsiderately at the Saltmarshes'. Emma does not understand me, but takes for quizzing or satire what is really the innocent, careless buoyancy of uncontrouled [*sic*] cheerfulness, with no other feeling than of perfect good . . . I seem to have forgotten that Emma's society is merely the best substitute to be had here for what would suit me better & that, good-hearted as she may be, it is foolish to throw off reserve too much. I must try to hit upon a happier medium. She often thinks I mean ten times more than ever entered my head, & fancies smiles & looks & *double entendres* I never dreamt of.

Sunday 1 July [Halifax]

Till eight & a half, mending my chemise & white petticoat . . . Settled my accounts for the last month. *Find I have a penny too much, how I cannot tell for I think I have not missed setting anything down. Surely the mistake must have been committed I know not how long ago* . . . *My aunt gave me ten shillings for I told her, the other day, I must give the men a footing for leading the earth to the foot of the wall. We talked it over on Thursday evening & I said half a crown. I shall not tell her I promised them five shillings, for she has little idea of these things.*

Monday 2 July [Halifax]

Down the old bank to the Saltmarshes'. Got there at 5½ . . . Spent the evening with them & got home, in 20 minutes, at 9.40 . . . *Led into talking about myself after Mr Saltmarshe left the room. About my figure, manner of walking & my voice; their singularity, etc. Said I daresay Emma had sometimes wondered how I knew so much as I did but that many odd things had happened to me* . . . *Brought on the subject of my own oddities of which Emma seems aware but to which she does not appear to object. In fact, she thinks me agreeable & likes me. So does her husband. She looked pretty this evening & once or twice as if conscious of a peculiar feeling when I looked at her. I told her there was no house to which I could go with so much comfort. Said I thought Mr Saltmarshe the most gentlemanly man we had & I liked him for the best. At all events, I think I can please the wife.*

Tuesday 3 July [Halifax]

Foolish enough, but spent an hour & a half writing a prettily turned note to Emma, of which I have kept a copy . . . In the afternoon, at 4¾, went to the new road to speak to Jackman & thence down the old bank to the library . . . *Gave Jackman five shillings for himself & the leaders & fillers, for putting the earth at the foot of the wall in front of us, & gave the librarian his half yearly five, also, for letting me have what books I like.* From the library to the Saltmarshes to look at their bed to see how the curtains are made, as we have got new ones for my bed ... Went to Northgate & met there my father & Marian just arrived from the Low Grange, near Market Weighton, by this evening's mail ... *Shocked to see them both look vulgar. The first sight of them always makes me low & I feel it now, near nine, exceedingly. My father & aunt are gone out & I have left Marian to be by myself in my own room. I feel as if my heart was sick & my spirits frozen.*

Monday 9 July [Halifax]

At 6¾ down the old bank ... Walked with Mrs Rawson to Well-head. Mrs Waterhouse had a mantua-maker in the house; met me in the passage; very honestly but civilly & properly said she could not conveniently receive company & I came away without going beyond the door ... My father seemed satisfied about the road. I think it will turn out well & I shall continue to look after it & see about the planting, etc.

Wednesday 11 July [Halifax]

Bought a couple of single cotton night-caps this morning of Richards, an itinerant hosier from Nottingham, for 1/4 – i.e. 8d. each. Cheap enough.

Sunday 15 July [Halifax]

From church walked up to the Saltmarshes' ... *Emma in a particular way & always ill at these times. Mending my stockings, etc., & trying on some old white waists & contriving to make them do instead of handkerchiefs to wear under an evening waist ... Preparing clean stays, & dirty ones for the wash.*

Monday 16 July [Halifax]

In the evening, Lowe the taylor [sic] having just made George an undress suit of livery very well, came to take orders for a dress suit, & is also to make for my uncle himself, in future.

Tuesday 17 July [Halifax]

Came upstairs at 10.35. *From this to near three, planning about afternoon handkerchiefs, etc. I am sick of all this & wish I had anyone to do it for me, but all things have an end & surely I shall, by & by, get a style of dress that suits me without further trouble.*

Thursday 19 July [Halifax]

Trying loops to my stockings & garters from my stays, but I don't like the feel of them . . . Today being the coronation of George 4,[11] all the haymakers (10 of them, including our 3 farming men) have had a shilling apiece & a good additional quantity of beer to drink the king's health. The 7 men employed about the new road have had a shilling apiece, ditto the 5 men employed at the stone quarry. Our house servants likewise a shilling each & in addition, a bowl of strong punch of which the 3 farming men are to come in & partake & sup on roast beef. The allowance of punch is a pint for each person that, as the women will not drink their share, the men will have a tolerable portion. Fine day. Good hay day. Very warm.

Anne was due to pay a visit to M—'s brother and his wife at Newcastle, Staffordshire, where she & M— were to act as sponsors at the christening of Stephen (Steph) Belcombe's baby daughter. Steph Belcombe (M—'s brother) was a doctor in practice at Newcastle. It was during this visit that a new and very serious complication entered the lives of

Anne and M—. M— had, for a few days, been complaining of certain venereal symptoms. Anne developed the same symptoms. The two women concluded that they had contracted a venereal disease which M—'s husband had transmitted to her as a consequence of his extra-marital affairs, about which he apparently made no secret. M— in turn passed on the infection to Anne. The disease was to dominate Anne's life and her journal becomes a record of its progress until she begins to feel she has it under control, assuming that the lessening, or non-appearance, of the symptoms indicates freedom from infection.

Friday 20 July [Newcastle, Staffs.]

Awakened about 4 by the most violent beating of hail I ever remember to have heard in my life, accompanied with a little thunder & repeated flashes of vivid lightning. Nearly fair as I walked to Halifax. The mail did not set off till 8 or 10 minutes before 7 . . . Went as far as Sowerby Bridge in the inside. It being fair, went the rest of the way on the box . . . *Steph met me coming from the inn. Very glad to see me. Ditto Harriet* [his wife] . . . Note from M— to say they can't come till Sunday . . . M— *nervous about seeing me & wishes our meeting over* . . . Put by my things & settled my accounts & wrote this of today. *Had to dust out the drawers & shelves of the wardrobe. They are not used to have* [sic] *people so particular as I am. However, I feel comfortable & settled now.*

Sunday 22 July [Newcastle, Staffs.]

Had given up expecting M— when she arrived at 4½ in the carriage. Looking well, much improved in appearance since I saw her last in York 1½ years ago . . . M—*'s coming made me rather nervous & I therefore took two glasses of wine after dinner. She & I sat up talking . . . I am thoroughly convinced of M—'s*

attachment & devotion to me & have said all to comfort & reconcile
her to our situation.

Monday 23 July [Newcastle, Staffs.]

We talked all last night & only closed our eyes to dose [sic] about
half-hour, just before getting up. Went to M— but somehow did not
manage a good kiss. Refused to promise till I had really felt that she
was my wife. Went to her a second time. Succeeded better & then
bound ourselves to each other by an irrevocable promise for ever, in
pledge of which, turned on her finger the gold ring I gave her several
years ago & also her wedding ring which had not been moved off her
finger since her marriage. She seems devoted to me & I can & shall
trust her now . . . It has occurred to me – can C— have given her a
venereal disease? . . . About 1½, Mr & Mrs Meeke (she Harriet's
sister) arrived for the Xtening [sic] from the Broomes', near
Stone. At 2, we all went to the parish church . . . Mr Goldsmid,
& M— & myself being the sponsors for the little Mariana Percy
Belcombe, called at my request after M—. The child behaved
remarkably well. Just before dinner, had my hair cut by Mr
Williams who did it very nicely. M— & I made our little god-
daughter a joint present of a silver knife & fork & spoon in a
case and a little silver drinking cup. *Altogether, five pounds. M—*
bought them the other day at Liverpool.

Saturday 28 July [Newcastle, Staffs.]

M— & I talked matters over. We have agreed to solemnize our
promise of mutual faith by taking the sacrament together when next
we meet at Shibden, not thinking it proper to use any more still bind-
ing ceremony during C—'s life. Talked matters thoroughly over
during our walk. I should live with my aunt. If Marian does not
marry she must have a home with us & I thought I could eventually
make up fifteen hundred a year. C— will probably make up M—'s
income [to] eight.

Sunday 29 July [Newcastle, Staffs.]

About 6, the carriage came for M— from Lawton & she left us about 8. *She was very low. In consoling, I said we might perhaps get together sooner than we expected. She replied that there might be a rowe [sic] & a quarrel & a parting any day & that with little opportunity & importunity, I might bring it about whenever I chose . . . I see & believe she is entirely devoted to me. I have given her my promise & my faith forever. I love & trust her & shall henceforth only hope that we shall one day be happy together. From what Watson says, C— has been unwell & in a bad humour all the week.*

Anne remains at Newcastle for a few days after M—'s departure. In her discovery of certain symptoms, she turns to M—'s brother Steph, in his capacity as a doctor, for help, whilst carefully concealing her own case.

Friday 3 August [Newcastle, Staffs.]

In the morning, begged of Steph, & thus rescued from the <u>most ignoble of purposes</u>, the number of the Critical Review for July, 1774 . . . *Feel a queer, hottish, itching sensation tonight, about the pudendum.*

Saturday 4 August [Newcastle, Staffs.]

A few minutes conversation with Steph before breakfast. Mention M— & my suspicion of venereal. He said he was treating her as for this & suspected it, tho' there were certainly some symptoms against it. I hinted that some latent principle of the disease might have broken out in C—. He answered no, but it might or must be some late imprudence. Said I knew someone in the same situation. A young married woman, poor, who had tried much advice without relief & therefore asked Steph for the prescription he gave M—, which he promised. I begin to look at home, for the heat & itching I felt last night have been considerable today & I am persuaded of being touched with the complaint.

Monday 6 August [Manchester]

Talked to Steph a little before Harriet came down. He scarce knows what to think of M—. C— looked so innocent the other day, he hardly thinks him guilty. However, he has met with men in his practice, & who bear very good characters, who have played their wives this trick. Talked of old times. I said how gross C— used to be; that he complained to her father of M—'s coldness & he answered she required more dalliance. Said I accidentally saw a passage in one of C—'s letters when M— was last in York in which he said she could not expect him to be quite correct during so long an absence . . . M— came about 11. I believe her heart is wholly mine & I am quite satisfied. Told her she had certainly given me a venereal taint & that I had felt very bad yesterday. Said how I had got Steph's prescription & should begin to use it as soon as I got home. We neither of us seemed to care much about the thing . . . M— left us about 1 & I got into the Cobourg coach about 2 & arrived at Manchester about 7¼ . . . Dined at 8½ on mock turtle, veal cutlets, potatoes & tart, and afterwards, biscuits & cherries . . . Feel very comfortable here. *The heat & itching have not been near so bad today.*

Tuesday 7 August [Halifax]

Nice clean bed & slept very comfortably. The people very attentive & civil, nor do I think their charges high. Dinner, 3/6; dessert, 1/–; bed, 2/–; & breakfast, 1/9; my sitting room not charged. In fact, I have every reason to be satisfied & shall go to the Bridgewater in future. The mail left Manchester so punctually at 9, that it obliged me to bring away a crust of roll & leave my breakfast untouched. Had an inside place but came the whole way on the box with the coachman ... The man offered me the reins 2 or 3 miles on this side of Rochdale, gave me some good instructions & I drove 2 or 3 miles ... Got into Halifax at 20 minutes before 2.

Wednesday 8 August [Halifax]

My own room very comfortable. The new bed & window curtains put up & as soon as I am settled here, got all my letters written, etc., I shall resume my studies & enjoy myself.

Thursday 9 August [Halifax]

I felt so little inconvenience in my jurney [sic] home &, till this mornmg, I was in the hope this venereal taint would give me little or no trouble; that cold water would be enough & indeed, not take the cubebs[12] or use the wash, but the discharge is so much increased tonight, I shall begin with the medicine as soon as I can. It is an awkward business, tho' I hope I shall be well in a little while.

Friday 10 August [Halifax]

Called at Whiteley's & got vol. 1 Rousseau's *Confessions*[13] ... *Ordered Suter to make me up Steph's prescription for venereal & what I copied from Mr Duffin long ago for an injection. A scruple of calomel gradually mixed in a marble mortar with an ounce of sweet oil ... Two or three drops to be injected two or three times a day after making water generally cure in two or three days. Asked Suter if he had ever made up Steph's prescription before. 'Yes,' said he, 'very frequently.' I have felt the discharge a good deal today & as if my linen, rubbing against my thighs, made them feel hot & irritated. There can be no doubt, surely, of its being venereal ... Came upstairs at 11. From twelve until the time of getting into bed, trying to use my two ivory syringes that were Eliza Raine's. Let the common one fall & broke off the top of the piston but afterwards got to manage very well with the uterine syringe.*

Saturday 11 August [Halifax]

Just before dinner, George brought me the medicine from Suter's. The liniment for the injection, according to Mr Duffin; fifteen of his pills & Steph's cubeb powders & lotions. That is, an ounce of cubebs – pulvis cubebs – in twelve equal powders, one to be taken three times a day, & for the lotion, ten grains of hyd. oximur, that is, corosive [sic] sublimate, with two drams of tincture of opium mixed in a quart of water. Just after tea, poured about a tablespoonful of this lotion into a cup & used it with a bit of sponge. It did not feel sharp & I think will do me good.

Tuesday 12 August [Halifax]

I have told my uncle & aunt I am set wrong & shall take physic. She constantly inquires after me. How little she dreams what is the matter. How lucky that I happened to be rather out of sorts before I went, which makes my present condition easier to pass off.

The journal continues to relate day-by-day reports on Anne's attempts to cure herself of the infection she contracted from M—. The daily treatment of injections, washes, the taking of pills and powders continued unabated for a considerable length of time. M— supplied Anne with regular bulletins of her own state of health and Anne advised her of any new medication which she thought would better the condition. Once Anne ceased having sexual relations with M—, she eventually became free of infection.

Wednesday 15 August [Halifax]

Martha Ingham came to pay her church-pew rent . . . (She) mentioned a famous kind of man at Manchester who cures most inveterate rheumatisms, etc., by literally <u>sweating</u> people in a sort of stove. He watches them while they are in it, &

knows when they have been long [enough] by a particular vein in the head.

Friday 17 August [Halifax]

My aunt had a letter from Marian this morning announcing their having sent off 2 hedgehogs which have just arrived safe (about 12) by the mail coach, packed in straw in a basket. We have put them under a hot bed frame in the back room where they are to be kept a day or two, before being turned out into the garden to clear it of snails & other vermin, with which it is at present exceedingly infested . . . Went down to the hedgehogs for 10 minutes, took them a plate of gooseberries & watched 1 of them drinking the milk set for them.

Saturday 18 August [Halifax]

Mending my stocking tops for an hour . . . Just before I went out this afternoon, George took the hedgehogs from the back room & put them loose under the great yew tree.

Monday 20 August [Halifax]

George having to go for the lotion tomorrow, my aunt asked so many questions she almost posed me. I said it was to soften my hands. I believe she suspects something, for she said, 'Well, you're a queer one & I'll ask no more.'

Sunday 9 September [Halifax]

Sauntering about the back of the house & on the terrace till after 1, when the rain drove me in. Afterwards, in the bottom chamber, upper kitchen ditto, etc., planning alterations. To make a passage thro' the upper kitchen & buttery to a new *on-vous-savez*.[14] A back door thro' the near parlour window & a passage forwards to the back room turned into a store room. The bottom chamber to be a servant's room & the upper kitchen

181

chamber entered by the Blue Room (my room) stairs. Fireplaces in the ale-parlour & North Room to be opposite the windows. Did not mention these plans except casually, to my aunt.

Tuesday 10 September [Halifax]

Wrote 3pp ... & sent them off to M— (Lawton) at 1½ ... Settled that M— & I are, every morning at 10¾, to read a chapter in the new testament & asked her to begin next Monday. She first proposed at Newcastle our reading something, the same thing & at the same hour every day – & we have agreed on the new testament & the hour above named.

Saturday 15 September [Halifax]

Asked Fourniss for what he would make a first-rate set of gig-harness with covered buckles. These last would make it a few shillings dearer than with plated buckles, but he would make it for 7 guineas.

Wednesday 19 September [Halifax]

Went & sat ¾ hour at Well-head. Their maidservant ill in a rheumatic fever & the other servants tired with sitting up with her *that I went inconveniently, which she told me of in her usual awkward sort of way, saying they had no cold meat, no servant & no fire to cook any, etc., etc., at tiresome length. That she was the only one who told me honestly & she always would. Others received me when it was inconvenient & would not say a word. I wonder if she meant Emma? I said I really had not intended staying &, at last, she pressed me to stay [for] tea & said perhaps there might be some cold beef found. She means well & so does he, but I am sick to death of their vulgarity & shall not run the risk of going inconveniently often.*

On Tuesday 25 September 1821, Anne left Shibden to pay an extended visit to York in order to purchase a horse and gig for herself. While there she made short excursions to Market Weighton to sort out her father's financial affairs; to Elvington to visit Ellen Empson; and to Langton to stay with the Norcliffe family for a couple of days. She saw quite a lot of M— and Isabella who both visited Anne in York while she was staying with the Duffins and then later with the Belcombes.

Tuesday 25 September [York]

Mrs Duffin came to the door to meet me. Not so Mr Duffin. He went almost immediately to a small party at Mrs Crosby's . . . The Duffins seemed glad to see me but somehow there is a sort of dictatorialness or, I know not what, expecting of deference & attention about Mr Duffin that makes me never much like being here. Everything upstairs in my room is more comfortable than before. The whole chest of drawers & a foot-pot. I have the room over Mr & Mrs Duffin's, looking on to the wall.

Wednesday 26 September [York]

I went out at 12½ & went to 2 or 3 shops. Bean, in Stonegate, would cover my umbrella (with silk) for 25 or 26s., & Mr Metcalf, in Spurriergate, for 22s. or 23s. The former valued the old frame at 3s., the latter at 5, & advised a new thing altogether, for covering old sticks did not always answer . . . After staying about an hour at the Belcombes' . . . Mr Duffin called for me about 2½. We went to Morley's, the coach makers. Saw some very neat gigs and one, a Dennett, which I liked very much. They will let me have it, quite complete, with very good harness with covered buckles (which, the man said, made it a little cheaper) at £44. Lamps would be £2 additional. A Tilbury would be £50 or rather guineas. Surely the man at Leeds did not understand the difference between this & a Dennett. There is a difference in the springs, the former having a cross spring, or more springs in some way or other. Their lancer shafts are more bent at the ends & the box part under the seat is smaller than in a Dennett. Morley was not in the way, but the man said they would make a very good travelling-chaise for £180.

Saturday 29 September [York]

Before breakfast, wrote 2pp. to Marian . . . & bade her ask the price of Mr Inman's old gig . . . Asked Marian to ask my father what I should give for a gig horse, or if he had one he could lend me till February, when I could send it back by M— on her way here from Lawton . . . From the Belcombes' went & sat 20 minutes with Miss Hall *to shew myself in one of Mrs Milne's frills stuck on over my cravat, for she told me I should look better with one. Thanked her for being thus interested about me. Said what a bad figure I had & explained a little my difficulty in dressing myself to look at all well. Told her that, for this reason, I always wore black. She certainly likes me & I am indeed very attentive to her.*

Monday 1 October [York]

A young man from Morley, the coachmaker, came during breakfast with some drawings of gigs. Dennetts gone out of fashion, & Stanhopes, which would carry as much luggage in the same sort of way, superior to Tilburys and all the fashion at present. A very neat Stanhope with harness and lamps & quite complete, £47. Would build a capital chariot for £180 . . . Between dinner & tea, we [Mr Duffin & Anne] walked as far as the 2nd milestone on the Boroughbridge road. *Speaking of M—, was led into telling him that C— & I were not on speaking terms & why. Mentioned his intrigue with the housemaid, Sarah; that he did not like my firmness of conduct on this occasion, & afterwards, opened M—'s writing-case, took out one of my letters, & said what sort of consolatory sentence had caused the blow-up.*

Mr Duffin does not think well of him, but I said how he was now improved.

Wednesday 3 October [York]

Letter from my aunt (Shibden), mentioning the failure of her teeth & desiring me to speak to Horner & engage rooms for her at the George Inn, Coney Street.

Thursday 4 October [York]

Small parcel from Marian (Low Grange, Market Weighton). Might have Mr Inman's gig for £10 but it will cost £10 repairing & he will not sell the harness, which would be altogether about £30 for what, from Marian's account, is a Dennett & 'small & old-fashioned'. My father will lend us his mare till we can [get] a horse to suit us better, or let us keep her for always . . . Wrote 3pp. to thank Marian & say I should give up the thought of Mr Inman's gig.

Thursday 11 October [York]

The idea of publishing at some time or other has often come across me & I have mused on what subject to fix; it occurred to me, when getting up this morning, that people very often talk of things they don't understand & that, with tolerable management, one might give a few useful essays on these matters, such, for instance, as politics, religion, etc., & each essay containing a sort of digest of its subject.

Friday 12 October [York]

I begin to feel that want of freedom here that always annoys me sooner or later with Mr Duffin. He is unintentionally roughish & unpolished in his manners & I am tired of being here. He often contradicts on subjects I feel to understand better than he does.

Tuesday 16 October [York]

Found a note from Mrs Best [Isabella Norcliffe's widowed sister] asking me to dine with her at 6 . . . Went, had a very good dinner . . . *After dinner, Mary [Best] made a flourishing story of my going upstairs with loaded pistols & turning out a man. I therefore told the story as it was. He, Mr V., was one of Kit Saltmarshe's bride's groomsmen & had a jobation [sic] for ogling the girls at one of their parties. I alluded to it & did not much like his manner of acknowledging it. In fact, I never will refer to anything at Halifax, for it always ends in giving rise to disagreeable sentiments.*

Thursday 18 October [York]

Went over the bridge at 11¼. Went shopping with my aunt . . . Walked with my aunt round the castle yard (she wanted some knitted nightcaps of the debtors) . . . *I am glad the day is over. My aunt wants a little furbishing up & I shall be heartily glad when she is safe at home again. She is to dine at the Belcombes' on Sunday & talks of going that night by the mail* . . . Came upstairs at 10.35. Wrote the above of today. *Mending my stockings & gloves.*

Friday 19 October [York]

Called on my aunt at Horner's. Went to the Belcombes' to excuse her dining there on Sunday on account of her being able to go home tomorrow . . . *It was a great relief to me to know my aunt would go tomorrow. Sunday morning would have [been] an exhibition & a drag.*

Saturday 20 October [York]

Went to Whiskers for an eye-glass for my aunt, tho' none would suit, & got to the George at 5. At 5½ sat down to a goodish brown soup & good veal cutlets . . . had coffee at 9 & I did not come away till a few minutes before 10. *She got a gauze hand-*

kerchief she had bought, pinned upon a satin foundation, into a turban cap, at Miss Gledhill's. Gave me ten shillings to pay for it & a pound note besides, offering me more if I wanted it, saying she could spare a little more.

Monday 22 October [York]

Went to Breary's to look at the 2nd hand gig with a top to it. Afterwards, took Dr Belcombe & Anne to see it & I think I have determined to take it . . . *Told Anne this morning she had set me all wrong, unnerved me for the day, at which she seemed nothing displeased. I did feel slightly, but am really much altered in these matters since my more thorough engagement to M— . . .* Played 4 games at chess with Mr Duffin, of which he won the 1st 3. Then lost a game to Miss Marsh. My thoughts were not on chess.

Wednesday 24 October [York]

Went . . . to the Macleans' to play chess with Miss Breadalbin Maclean. Played 1 game – won it in an hour. Miss Crosby then came in & Mrs & Miss Fletcher of *bas bleu* celebrity. Staid them out & thought them neither very genteel, nor very profound, but probably *bas bleus* – learned ladies – in the most usual sense of the words – especially the young lady looked rather a figure & plebeian . . . Got home at 3½. *Can do nothing from dinner at 4 to tea at seven because we have no candles. Have once or twice written by my bed-candle but it seemed yesterday that Mr Duffin does not like it. His sort of temper is not pleasant to me & I am tired of being here. I cannot feel comfortable because far from independent.*

Thursday 25 October [York]

Isabella Norcliffe came a little before 9 & staid till 10, when I walked after her chair & slept with her at the Black Swan.

Friday 26 October [York]

A kiss of Tib, both last night & this morning . . . but she cannot give me much pleasure & I think we are both equally calm in our feelings on these occasions . . . For my own part, my heart is M—'s & I can only feel real pleasure with her. I hope Tib will not have caught any infection from me. At the moment of my offering to sleep with her, I forgot this, & afterwards there was no retracting . . . Set off with Isabella in the gig . . . Went to several shops. Ordered the gig at Breary's. Handsome brass harness (evidently only used 3 or 4 times) & lamps to the gig. All together, £48.

Tuesday 30 October [York]

Letter from M— (Lawton) . . . to say she was a good deal better . . . Francis, the footman, discovered to be a thief. Letter, also, from Isabella, (Langton). John Coates, the head groom, strongly advises me not to have the yellow gig, but the green one, which will cost £15 more. At 2, went to Breary's to look at it again & intend to follow John's advice. Soon after 3, Parsons came to cut & dress my hair.

Wednesday 31 October [York]

Went to the Belcombes' & staid some time, *sporting my false ringlets pinned on each side of my hat.* Eliza Belcombe . . . went with me to Breary's where I ordered the green gig with lamps & harness & all complete.

> From Friday 2 November until Monday 3 December, Anne left York to pay visits to friends and relatives at Darlington, Elvington and Market Weighton. She returned to York for one night during that period, but did not return again until 3 December. In the meantime, M— had arrived in York to

pay a visit to her parents and return with Anne to Shibden
for a few days.

Monday 3 December [York]

Got into York at 12. Left the coach at the end of the pavement
& walked to Dr Belcombe's . . . Isabella Norcliffe & Charlotte
here . . . *I rowed Isabella just before dinner for kissing & seizing hold
of M—, especially before the housemaid who was passing through,
& Tib seemed out of sorts the whole evening. M— very kind and
affectionate.*

Tuesday 4 December [York]

Fine evening or, rather, fine night when the Norcliffes went at
11.20 . . . *M— & I sat up talking till 1.50. Told her of the bad cooking here; that I could get nothing to eat here or, sometimes, even at
Shibden. We agreed we would have things nice sometime, our tastes suit
& we are very thoroughly happy together. We cosed very comfortably.*

Tuesday 11 December [York]

In the evening, at 8¾, M— & I went to a small party at the
Crosby's . . . Cold fowl, & sweets & hot port wine negus for
supper. Got home at 11¼.

Friday 14 December [York]

Mrs Belcombe & Mrs Milne & M— went before 7 to the Manor
school concert & exhibition – to shew of the music, dancing,
specimens of work, etc., of the schoolgirls. *Vulgar girls, Lady
Johnstone & a few others, & the rag, tag & bobtail there. I would not
go myself & did not like M—'s going, but could not well help it.*

Sunday 16 December [York]

Mrs Milne went to the Minster. Damp, disagreeable morning &
all the rest staid at home . . . Mrs Belcombe read to us, 1¼ hour,

the morning service & then some moral essays on sickness, gratitude, etc . . . *In the afternoon, Mrs Belcombe chancing to ask if I intended going to the Belfrey[15], I happened to say I should go if M— went, but if she staid at home, I should. Mrs Belcombe said, 'What! Does your religion depend on others? How foolish! How very silly you are!' with some allusion both to my being both at present and formerly very silly about M—. I made some reply about the injustice of this remark & shewed that I was annoyed. In truth, I felt so. This was always a tender point to attack me in, particularly now, when I have taken such pains to give them no reason to find fault & when I have seen that Charlotte & Harriet might steal the horse while M— & I might not open the stable door. To mend the matter, M— & Eli went to the Minster & I volunteered walking with Mrs Milne . . . I could not help thinking of all this all the time I was at the Minster. My pride was roused & hurt that I should be thus suffering myself to appear foolish & silly, & I absolutely felt as if I could not stand it. At dinner, I scarce spoke. I did not think of being observed but Mrs Belcombe electrified me by asking to hear the sound of my voice. I turned it off by pretending sleepiness from the heat of the fire at my back & came upstairs immediately after dinner to change my boots. M— came & talked to me & I promised to talk & so well feign nothing was the matter that none could find it out. When we came up to bed M— acknowledged that I had kept my word & done so well as would even have cheated her.*

Monday 17 December [York]

Could not get all this business out of my head last night & woke this morning with it full in my mind. Felt as if I would give the world to sit & never open my lips. Musing upon getting away as fast & well as I could, & upon giving them as few opportunities as possible, in future, of thinking me foolish & silly. Writing the above has done me more good than anything . . . At 9½, M— & Eli & I went to the rooms, the 1st winter assembly. A very good one . . . altogether a genteel, well-dressed assemblage. Lady Dundas & Mrs Lawley Thompson of Eskington in diamonds . . . Miss Fairfax very handsome, but shockingly disfigured with out-of-curl ringlets literally almost ½yd long, & an awkward dancer with elbows like skewered pinions. Got home at 1½. Sat up talking all over with Eli downstairs & having supper & wine & water.

Tuesday 18 December [York]

Miss Naylor came again to fit a lining on my new stays. Letter by a private conveyance from Isabella Norcliffe (Langton). They are well but the typhus fever is in the village & Harrison, the taylor, very ill with it. Mrs Norcliffe has sent a hare & brace of partridges to Shibden.

Wednesday 19 December [Market Weighton]

Got ready for setting off to Low Grange [Market Weighton, to attend to her father's business affairs]. Had the new gig from Breary's, & George & I drove from Dr Belcombe's door at 11½. The mare a little awkward at 1st, & I had not driven over a hundred yards before I ran against the wheel of a cart. However, we came along very well afterwards. I drove the whole way & we got here (Low Grange) in 3¼ hours, 19 miles . . . Wrote 3pp. to M— to say I should not be back till Friday.

Thursday 20 December [Market Weighton]

My father & I set off at 9½ in the gig to Selby, distance from here, 16 miles & from Market Weighton, 18 miles . . . Very bad roads . . . My father drove there in 3¼ hours. Stopt at the Inn close to the church – a very good Inn & surely not dear. George's dinner & the 2 horses' corn & hay, and our own lunch (cold beef, cold ham, goose-pie, tarts & bread & butter & ale) charged only 6/6 . . . I drove home in 3½ hours & got back at 6¼ . . . the 2 men met us at our own gate – one with a lanthorn, which in fact did no good but only made the darkness visible. A drop on one side & a moderately deep one on the other, neither very discernible. 1 of the men led the gig horse the latter part of the ½ mile thro' the fields & I was well pleased to get safe back.

Friday 21 December [York]

The mare stiffish & rather knocked up with her journey yesterday, & I could not get off from Low Grange till 11 . . . Drove off . . . in the midst of wind & rain which were just come on. Tried the mare with a pint of warm ale at Simpson's but she would not touch, nor did she eat well this morning or yesterday. Never saw an animal so idle & sluggish withal. She took more whipping even than yesterday &, a little beyond Barby Moor new inn, seemed determined to go no further. Went back to the house to get a poster. The man at the inn said it would break a pair. His horses were much worked by the coaches, etc., & civilly but positively said he really could not let me have a horse. Gave the mare a little warm water & made George drive forwards to York. The mare stopt 2 or 3 times & would turn in at 2 or 3 public houses by the way, & by dint of hard whipping, brought us here at last (Dr Belcombe's, Petergate) in 4 hours . . . So sleepy with being so much out in the air, & so harassed one way or other that I could scarce keep my eyes open & was obliged to come upstairs to bed directly after tea.

Monday 24 December [York]

M— & I went out together at 2. Went to Breary's. I ordered lamps to my gig & paid him for the gig & all its appurtenances, £65 2s.

Sunday 25 December [York]

M— & I went to speak to Mrs Small in College Street, who keeps the most respectable register office for servants in York.

We then went to the Minster in time for the anthem, & walked about the aisles till service was over. What a magnificent building. How striking the effect of its being lighted up throughout! Which it is every Sunday & was today . . . After dinner, all danced & made merry with the children, & I, while they played commerce [?] with them, came upstairs & finished the journal of yesterday & wrote this of today.

Thursday 27 December [Halifax]

We got to Halifax a little before 6, having been 2 hours all but 5 minutes in coming from Bradford, so bad were the roads . . . My uncle & aunt well & very glad to see us. Dinner soon after 7. M— rather tired. Came upstairs a few minutes before 11.

Saturday 29 December [Halifax]

At 1, M— & I set off in the gig to Halifax . . . *In driving up the main street, ran against a cart-wheel & in backing the gig, was as near as possible upset. We were just down on the left side but the crowd of men about righted & saved us. M— was shockingly nervous. I felt cool & composed. The horse behaved most marvellously well. My aunt Lister's servant, Thomas Greenwood, was one of those who prevented our overturning by lifting us up before we fell to the ground & he afterwards walked by the side & mostly led the horse thro' the town & went with us a little way up the bank till George came* . . . In our return from Halifax, M— got out & walked down the Cunnery Lane. In the evening, M— & my uncle played whist against my aunt & me . . . Rainy day, came upstairs at 10.35.

1822

Thursday 3 January [Halifax]

M— & I sat all the morning in the hall, writing letters . . . I wrote . . . to Isabella Norcliffe (Langton) to thank her mother, in my uncle & aunt's name, for a hare & brace of partridges received yesterday week – to announce my safe arrival here – say we should be glad to see her . . . Came upstairs at 10½. Sat up talking till after 1. M— *teaching me to do my front hair & we laughed heartily at my awkwardness. We are very fond of each other & perfectly happy together.*

Sunday 6 January [Halifax]

M— *very low tonight. We sat up talking & consoling each other & latterly in playful dalliance & gentle excitement. Our hearts are mutually & entirely attached. We never loved & trusted each other so well & have promised ourselves to be together in six years from this time. Heaven grant it may be so.*

Monday 7 January [Halifax]

The carriage at the door at 9.10 . . . Went with M— as far as a couple of miles beyond Ripponden, where they drove us in 40 minutes, then, meeting the Highflier coach, left M—, got into it & reached Halifax in an hour . . . M— *& I had parted tolerably but the sight of my room was melancholy. I sighed & said to* myself, 'She is gone & it is as tho' she has never been.' I was getting very low & therefore sat down to write my journal . . . Then obliged to while away my time talking to my aunt & doing nothing. How dull without M—, my wife & all I love . . . Felt very low & dull. Oh, that M— & I were together. Had a fire at night contrary to my usual custom. It cheered the room a little but everything looked, & I felt, desolate.

Sunday 20 January [Halifax]

My aunt & I read the morning service. *Before & during dinner detected the two little errors in my summary which have caused me a good deal of trouble, tho' I never in my life before was so quick & correctly ready at adding up. My expenses last year were £70 & three-halfpence, & on the first day of this year I had a balance in hand of one hundred and thirteen pounds, seven shillings & seven-pence farthing. Thank God that I am in so prosperous a way.*

Monday 21 January [Halifax]

Walked to Halifax. Was there just before the mail arrived &, after waiting some time for a chaise at the Union Cross, brought Isabella with me & we got in at 5½. She is looking well but has got a bad cold . . . Came upstairs at 11. *Melancholy enough at the thought of going to bed with Tib. I cannot even affect any warmth towards her.*

Tuesday 22 January [Halifax]

One of the Mr Taylors (the young man) came at 7 this morning to destroy the old mare, Diamond. He stabbed her thro' the heart & she was dead in less than 5 minutes & buried immediately . . . At 12, off in the gig to Halifax. Called at Isabella's washerwoman, then drove a little up Pellon Lane, then thro' the town . . . Got home between 2 & 3 . . . *Tib drove from Halifax to Lightcliffe this morning. I really think I am as good, tho' not quite so stylish a driver as she. She ran us with the top against the wool sacks on a cart at the bottom of the Cunnery Lane & if all the horses had not been steady it might have been awkward. In spite of her not allowing herself to be ever frightened at anything, she was rather nervous after it.*

Monday 28 January [Halifax]

Did nothing in the afternoon & evening, till 9, when I came upstairs ... *Talking of my sleeping with Eliza Belcombe, said I should not like it, & that I was much altered of late in all these matters. Tib laughed, looked incredulous, bade me not say so, & added, 'It would be unnatural in you not to like sleeping with a pretty girl.' I thought of M——, as I do perpetually & that for her I could & would do anything. Tib is affectionate, seems happy here & is quieter than she used to be. She appears to have no suspicion of my living [with] & loving seriously, any other than herself. Poor soul, I know how she will take it when the truth comes out.*

Anne paid a short visit to York to deal with her father's affairs.

Saturday 2 February [Leeds]

George & I off in the gig at 3½. The wind & rain so boisterous at the top of the bank we could scarcely weather it. However, Percy [her new horse] brought us here (the White Horse, Boar Lane, Leeds), 19 miles in 2¾ hours, tho' it blew hard & ... I was obliged to hold my hat on, tho' Isabella lent me her beaver ... Got in at 6 ... ordered dinner, boiled haddock, veal cutlets, tarts, jelly & preserved winesours and a pint of port wine ... This is a very comfortable inn. The wind seems even a good deal higher & it is a stormy, boisterous night ... Not being able to have the top up as we came, the rain beat in about the cushions. The seat part was wet & I was, on this account, obliged to change all my clothes as soon as I got in.

Sunday 3 February [Leeds]

Very comfortable bed . . . Had a great deal to do this morning to get Isabella's hat to look decent after its soaking yesterday afternoon . . . At 10, off to York & Percy brought us in 3 hours, 20 minutes so that we arrived at the Belcombes at 1.24. Sent George & the gig & horse to the Black Swan because he told me as we came along that he thought the people at the George were not very attentive to servants, & besides, they put him into a damp bed.

Anne returned to Halifax after attending to the business of taking a property agent around her father's estate. It had been agreed that the only way for Captain Lister to become solvent was to sell off his property and settle himself and Marian either abroad or in Northgate House, Halifax. Isabella Norcliffe was still at Shibden Hall when Anne arrived back on Friday 8 February.

Friday 15 February [Halifax]

After dinner, long & rather sparring conversation with Tib about M—, of whom she is perpetually jealous. She says I am not to think she has ever been gulled. She thinks M— is almost tired of C— & wants to have me. I fought off, saying I should not like another man's leavings. Tib owns M— might marry almost anybody if she was at liberty. Talked to Tib of the impossibility of Tib & I living together because she must be with Charlotte, but hinted that I should get someone & hoped Tib would come & see me. She would if she might sleep but never otherwise, but I might go & see her if I did not take my companion with me.

Saturday 9 March [Halifax]

Called at Whitley's. Saw there the *Leeds Mercury* & my father's estate advertised in it. Went to the library for a little while then went back to Northgate & met my uncle there. Isabella had walked to the library newsroom & came to Northgate just after I had got in . . . She had bought some smelts, & I brought them home as fast as I could to be in time for dinner . . . Got Isabella 1oz (1/6) Macouba snuff, said to be made by M., a Frenchman in the island of Martinique but, as Suter observed, it is most likely made in London. It is the most expensive kind of snuff.

Friday 15 March [Halifax]

Mr Edward Priestley called between 10 & 11 to give Isabella some melon seed . . . At 12½, Isabella & I set off in the gig. Went to her washer woman in Pellon Lane . . . Then proceeded along the moor to King Cross & then to Haugh-end, where we arrived at 2¼. Dined & spent the day there . . . Isabella gave imitations of Mad[eline?], Duchesnois of the *Théâtre français*,[1] & Talma, & Mrs Siddons, and of the Roman Catholic priests at high mass abroad, & made herself very agreeable. We staid till 9½. Had the lamps lighted, drove home very leisurely & got in at 10.40 after having spent a pleasant day.

> Whilst Anne had been away from home attending to her father's financial affairs, her Aunt Lister, who had lived at Northgate for many years, died and the property became vacant. When Anne began to discuss the possibility of letting the property with Isabella, it became the cause of a row between the two women, during which it became clear that Isabella must give up any idea of sharing her life fully with Anne. Anne was relieved that the issue had been resolved in view of her strengthened commitment to M—.

Sunday 17 March [Halifax]

Told my uncle as soon as I came in that Mrs Walker had said Mrs Rawdon Briggs had asked her if Northgate would be let &

that Mrs Walker knew of several people who would be glad to take it. After dinner, Isabella came upstairs & told me my uncle had asked her if she did not think the whole town would be up if my father did not live at Northgate, to which she replied 'Yes!', she thought it would. I unluckily & thoughtlessly said, 'How different M— would have judged.' *Tib took this in desperate dudgeon. Nothing I could say would appease her. She saw through me – she saw what I was – I had been guilty of the utmost grossness – she wished I had M— with me &, for her own part, it was well she was going so soon & she would never trouble me anymore – she had come for the last time. I did all I could to pacify & asked her to give me a kiss. She said she did not want one. I then said, 'Ask for one when you do,' & then went downstairs. She was out of sorts all the afternoon & evening, tho' downstairs almost all the time. She said nothing when we came to bed. I waited a minute or two to give her an opportunity & then went to undress.*

Monday 18 March [Halifax]

Got up without saying a word. Told Tib at a quarter past nine it was time to get up & I should order the gig to be ready for her a quarter before twelve. She merely asked if I should not go. I said I thought not, I was very bilious, & she just said she was sorry. I took little notice of her at breakfast but told them all I was bilious. She followed me upstairs & asked what made me so cross? I saw she was coming round & I told her I thought she behaved very ill & that it was for her to ask for a kiss if she wanted one. First she wished I had M—, then she was sorry for what she had done, would not do so any more, etc. Could not bear to think she did not suit me. Loved me better than anything in the world. It would be my fault if we did not live together. I quietly told her we never should & persisted that she did not suit & it was best to be candid at once. She cried a little & said she was very unhappy. I bade her cheer up & said there was no reason why we should not always be very good friends. She could not bear me to talk so. However, I gave her a kiss or two & we got the time over till twelve. At a few minutes before twelve, Isabella set off in the gig.

Tuesday 19 March [Halifax]

Tib & I parted without any nervousness. She said she would come again next year. I hope not. I am much happier not to have her & am glad enough that she is gone; that I have got my room comfortably to myself. She does not suit me at all.

Friday 29 March [Halifax]

Letter (notewise ½ sheet of paper) from Isabella (Langton), to say she had sent my aunt a graft of the 2nd year of the white moss-rose.

Sunday 14 April [Halifax]

Went downstairs a very little after 9 so as to have ½ hour before church for reading 2 or 3 old papers my uncle gave me last night. He & my aunt staid at home (it looked likely to rain) but I went to the old church . . . Home at 2¼. Staid out so long chiefly on account of my right eye, which felt very weak after being exceedingly incommoded by the draughts of air at church, admitted thro' the interstices cut at the bottom of the pew to admit hot air when the church is heated. I was obliged to keep my eyes shut, leaning on one hand, both while sitting & standing, almost the whole of the service time. These draughts of air are also very cold about one's legs & I was starved, tho' the morning has been so fine & pleasantly warm. Began Dr Johnson's tour to the Hebrides, *A Journey to the Western Islands of Scotland* . . . My aunt & I read aloud the evening service . . . *Staid down to supper & had a plate of hasty pudding & an old coffee cup full of treacle by way of physic, my bowels having been confined for several days. My aunt also took a little, with the same view . . . Near half-hour mending things & airing them.*

Anne was now thirty-one and felt it was time to take stock of her life. Her venereal disease gave her cause to reflect seriously before taking up new liaisons. Her relationship with Isabella had become platonic and M— was still far from being free to join her life with Anne's. On the social front the usual round of visiting at Halifax and York was beginning to lose its interest. Anne had always been a social climber and tended to want to increase her circle of influential acquaintances at the expense of her more homely companions. In her heart, she had never counted the Belcombes, the Duffins, or Miss Marsh her social equals and it was only her love for M— that kept her in touch with them. Indeed, one Halifax friend, Ellen Empson, took up the issue of Anne's disdain towards people from her own town.

Saturday 20 April [Halifax]

At 1.40, down the new bank to Halifax. Called at a shop or 2, & at Miss Kitson's. Went for ½ hour to the library till the Saltmarshes had done dinner. Read a few pp. of a translation of Cicero's treatise on old age. Went to the Saltmarshes' at 3 & got home at 5.40. Staid with them in the dining-room after dinner about an hour, then, going into the drawing-room, happened to mention the letter Mrs Empson wrote to me last autumn at Croft. [Darlington, where Anne was paying a visit to Isabella's relations.] One thing led to another till she & I (or rather, she) talked the matter entirely over. She seemed exceedingly warm & gave me little opportunity of saying much. She had written what she thought & felt & with reason. I had been a month in York without writing a word of inquiry, not even after her mother who liked me next to her own family, & had always been particularly kind & attentive to me. I had met Mr Empson in the street (at York) & only asked if Mrs Rawson was arrived, not if Ellen had got her confinement over. She heard of me being at every party, etc. I should not have treated any of my other friends so. I could not find even a day to go over & call, tho' I knew I might any time have the carriage or gig. I was always attentive in inquiring after & going to see her here . . . I attempted to take the thing civilly & said if she had merely told me in her letter, as she did now, that she was hurt, I should have understood it & been sorry, but that, even now, I should be happy to be convinced that she had the better cause of the 2. However, she was so <u>warm</u> & energetic in her manner, I scarce knew what to make of it. She said my conduct had been quite inconsistent with my professions. In reply to this, to the charge of calling on her here, I merely said calling on her here was in my way. I could not so call when in York & certainly could not *suppose* they would send twice 16 miles for me to make a call – for they must send into York 8 miles, take me to Elvington 8 miles, then back again 8 miles, then the carriage would return home 8 miles, so that the servant & carriage must have gone 32 miles on this occasion. Absurd! I told Ellen she was very warm & I very cool. She said she did not like these indifferent people. She '<u>liked a good fellow who would out with his mind & have done with it</u>!'[2] Vulgarity is a bad concern with me. It was no still small voice that saluted my ear, & I felt sorry for myself that a good fellow-liking lady should take occasion to call my sincerity & consistency in question. Perhaps the insinuation that I could call upon & be civil to her here tho' not in York, was not the most pleasing part of the story. When at first I said I was sorry (when she told me she had been hurt) and would write another time, she replied she begged I would not, for <u>it would be as bitter a pill to her to read as to me to write</u>, then spoke of the regard she <u>did</u> feel. I told her I had noticed the tense in which she spoke.

However, on my coming away, she would shake hands – said she should never think of it again – begged I would not 'ruminate' up the bank, for that I had her 'forgiveness'. I merely smiled & said I thought it was not for her to talk of forgiveness . . . *Such is the folly of getting into a sort of connections at home with people one is afterwards rather ashamed of. Besides, she merely suited me a little to flirt with her, before she was married. Tho' I really did, & do, think her amiable &, as such, should esteem her, but any great friendship is out of the question. She is too vulgar. I must manage as well as I can in future.*

Wednesday 8 May [Halifax]

Called at the Saltmarshes'. All out. Rejoined my aunt, called with her on Mrs Veitch – not at home. We then called on Mrs William Rawson – she particularly engaged & we did not see her. At this moment, Mrs Rawson, Mrs Empson & Emma came to call at Mrs Stansfield Rawson's. Spoke to them. Said I had been calling. Asked if they would be at home after dinner. Finding they were going out, said I would send a note to Mrs Rawson . . . We all looked rather like <u>shy-cats</u> but seemed to carry it off as well as we could . . . Then went to Holden's, the booksellers . . . on going out of the shop, as nearly as possible run over by a gig going at a great rate & very suddenly turning the corner.

Wednesday 22 May [Halifax]

On the bridge, met the Saltmarshes in the gig on the road to Harrogate. Fine-looking horse that could go 9 miles an hour, but they mean to drive him at the rate of 6, & will get to Harrogate about 5 in the afternoon. They had no servants. Emma had a shawl on, an imitation Kashmeer [sic] & they looked rather like mercantile people . . . Wrote to Walker, the glover, to order 8 pairs of his best French kid white long gloves for M—.

Thursday 30 May [Halifax]

Wrote 2pp. to Mr Duffin . . . [to] say we had just got a very pretty four-year-old, useful mare, fit for anything, & Mr Greenwood had met with a handsome 3 year-old bay colt that we mean to buy to match the horse . . . Having dated my letter tomorrow, I have mentioned the mare as arrived from Bradford as the last night, price £30, 'to be called Vienne, from a little circumstance relative to Vienne in Dauphiny.[3] The bay colt to be called Hotspur to match Percy.[4] Hotspur, I hope, £25. His owner is what Thomas calls "an innocent farmer" who might have a hundred guineas for the horse easily enough 2 years hence . . .' A minute or 2 before 12, Thomas (Greenwood) arrived from Bradford with the mare which, after giving his owner, a butcher, 4 glasses of gin & water, he managed to buy for £27 . . . She is a very pretty mare & very cheap. Thomas came into the room to us & staid till 11. To come early in the morning to try the mare in the gig. *He had a glass of gin & water & gooseberry tart in the room.*

Friday 31 May [Halifax]

Out at 7¾, looking after the mare. We had her in the gig & Thomas & I set off at 8.10. Led her through the hall-green & ½ way up Cunnery Lane. Then got in & Thomas drove as far as a little way beyond Haley-hill & then I drove to the railing beyond Boothtown. She is a very nice mare & likely to turn out all we want but she never had a curb bit in her mouth till yesterday & she must be put into the bridles a little, directly. *In attempting to turn her, she having no mouth & knowing nothing about it, she backed almost over the low side. We both jumped out & led her, then Thomas got in & drove & I led her, for he could drive her no better than I could. In fact, I think I am the better whip of the two.*

Saturday 1 June [Halifax]

My uncle brought down his will that he has written &, I think, has taken it with him to Halifax to give to Mr Wrigglesworth. I read it over . . . He makes out that my aunt will have rather more than four hundred a year, exclusive of Northgate, & I shall have about a hundred & forty-five. He never mentioned the turnpike money. But everything is secured to me except the navigation money, which will be at my aunt's disposal.

Friday 7 June [Halifax]

My aunt mentioned yesterday that Mrs Veitch told her that Mrs Kelly (Miss Brown that was) was expected at Halifax & is now probably with her father & mother at Westfield. *I made no remark. It has once or twice occurred to me whether to call or not, but I think I shall let it alone. She cannot call here. I have no reason for keeping up the acquaintance & have, in fact, thought little or nothing about it. Perhaps she may be at the old church on Sunday but if it is very hot I shall not see her for I shall not go.*

Sunday 9 June [Halifax]

In going into church, looked for Mrs Kelly &, in coming out, turned round in the aisle & used my glass, but did not see her. She could not be there or I should have seen her. The Greenwoods saw me look. I should have gone up & spoken & walked out of church with her if she had been there & asked when she would be at home that I might call. Vide my journal of last Friday, I will not neglect her. She might be hurt. It might be the town's plan, & they shall not have such glorious opportunity of haranguing about my caprice, etc. I now think of sending George to inquire when she is expected. I felt a little nervous, shall I call it, at the thought of seeing her. I wonder if she is improved or not . . . Just before supper, took a few turns on the flags without hat.

Monday 10 June [Halifax]

At 5¾, set off in the gig . . . Went forward to Crownest. Mr & Mrs Stocks (Michael, the justice of Catherine Slack) got out of their chaise just before me. I therefore sent in to inquire after Mr Walker & the rest. Mrs Walker came to the door & I would not alight for fear of stumbling on their choice company.

Tuesday 11 June [Halifax]

Before breakfast, wrote 3pp. of my letter to Isabel Dalton . . . mentioned also my aunt & I taking a fortnight's tour in Wales, & wished they knew anyone acquainted with Lady Eleanor Butler & Miss Ponsonby.

Sunday 16 June [Halifax]

Down the old bank, thro' the old church yard direct to the new church. Rang at the Saltmarshes' door. No one answered, all gone to church. Mrs Rawson (Mrs Christopher) drove up in her carriage. Offered to set me down at the new church. Of course, I refused, tho' as civilly as I could. Strange that she should not know better than to ask me . . . In passing Mrs Ralph's gate in returning this afternoon, saw Mrs James Stansfield there, (who seemed to hold out her hand very cordially) & the Misses Sarah & Emma Rawson, to whom I spoke *en passant. Shook hands with the former, of course it was her doing, but not with the others.*

Tuesday 18 June [Halifax]

Dined at 5¼, and at 6¼ off in the gig to Crownest, to take a walk with Miss Ann Walker, having talked of it ever since my walk with her last year. Only her sister & herself at home. They could not both leave the house & Miss Ann Walker & I were tête-à-tête . . . *Very civil, etc, but she is a stupid vulgar girl. Indeed, I scarce know which of the party is the least vulgar & I have no*

intention of taking more walks, or letting the acquaintance go one jot
further. I asked her to come to Shibden & walk in our valley & here
I hope the thing will end.

Sunday 23 June [Halifax]

We all set off twice to go to church & turned back on account of
rain. My aunt then staid at home & my uncle & I went. Mr
Knight (the vicar) preached 34 minutes (stupidly enough) from
2 Corinthians.ii.29, on behalf of the distressed Irish peasantry.
My uncle gave a pound note & I half a crown . . . Called at Jagger's
on my return to desire him to have light harness ready for Vienne
to go tandem . . . Got home at 1½. Went downstairs at 4.20. *In*
the meanwhile, mending my silk tops &, for about an hour, scaling my
teeth with a penknife. I have really got them pretty clear of tartar.

Thursday 27 June [Halifax]

Talking, after supper, to my uncle & aunt about M—. One thing led
to another till I said plainly, in substance, that she would not have
married if she or I had had good independent fortunes. That her
having C— was as much my doing as hers & that I hoped she would
one day be in the Blue Room, that is, live with me. I said we both of
us knew we could not live on air. Besides, I did not like her being
in Petergate [York] & had rather have her at Lawton than there. My
uncle, as usual, said little or nothing but seemed well enough satis-
fied. My aunt talked, appearing not at all surprised, saying she always
thought it a match of convenience.

Friday 28 June [Halifax]

Looking over M—'s letters of 1820, fancying it was then she &
Lou took their 2 little tours in Wales. Found, however, that it
was in June, 1817. Took out her 2 letters descriptive & mean to
take these with us when we go. Just before breakfast, 3pp. & the
ends & one side crossed, from M— (Lawton) . . . M— advises

drab for George instead of either black or green and says, 'Why not have, for undress, a white short jacket without either black collar or cuffs. Mrs Langley's undress is this, altho' her livery is blue & yellow & I have heard her give as a reason that it was less trouble to keep clean, & in travelling did not spoil by the dust' . . . Wrote 3pp. & one of the ends to M— (Lawton) & sent them this afternoon at 3.20 in the hope of its going by this afternoon's mail. Asked several questions what she gave the gardener for shewing Lady Eleanor Butler's & Miss Ponsonby's grounds at Llangollen, etc. *Asked also about George's coat &, on this account, want an early answer because it is time the thing was ordered.*

Sunday 30 June [Halifax]

At 2.25, set off with my aunt in the gig for Sowerby Bridge church. Drove there in 36 minutes. Left the gig & horses at the Inn. Mrs Dyson (of Willowfield) having seen us, sent her oldest son to beg we would sit with her, which we did, in the east end of the north gallery. Very civil in her. She asked us also to go back with her to tea, which we, of course, declined. Mr Franks preached 27 minutes, drawlingly & stupidly . . . Turned on to Skircoat Moor at King Cross. A ranter's meeting there & a great many people about what seemed like 2 hustings . . . *During supper, mending my nightcap.*

Monday 1 July [Halifax]

Letter from Isabella Dalton (Croft Rectory, Darlington). Her father says no introduction [to Lady Eleanor Butler and Miss Ponsonby] will be necessary. 'Any literary person especially calling on them would be taken as a compliment.' . . . Dawdled away all the morning . . . scratching my head & arrant dawdling. From 1¼ to 2¼, looking over my accounts & calculating our probable travelling expenses per day for my aunt &

myself & a manservant & 2 horses. For George & the horses I allow 15/– a day; & for ourselves (including a pint of wine a day) I allow 20/–; and the turnpikes I average at a penny a mile. In the afternoon, at 3¼, set off in the gig . . . sent George to inquire at Westfield if Mrs Kelly was come or expected. She had been come a fortnight. Drove up to the door for a minute or two & told her I could not possibly get out then, but would call some other time. She was looking very well, improved in looks *but her black gown was too much trimmed & her hands & nails not clean. I had my old pelisse on & was, in fact, too great a figure to get out. If I had taken no notice of her, she might have felt it & it might have been a town's talk. The sight of her looking so well made me feel that sort of interest I always do for women I at all admire. She seemed not grown more ladylike, but I shall call soon. My admiration of her is a sort of toy. I felt towards [her] as if I felt she had been an old flirt of mine & shall be glad enough to talk to her a little, tho' I shall, of course, notice her in future as may chance to suit my inclination & circumstances . . . My aunt told me this evening my uncle meant to allow me fifty pounds a year & she was to make out the rest. He will give me twenty-five at midsummer. He means it to be an agreeable surprise to me.*

Tuesday 2 July [Halifax]

Came upstairs at 11.50. About 12½, the dog barked. The cook got up to look out of the back kitchen window & there was a great tall fellow sitting on the stone bench by the door. I asked him gruffly what he was doing there but, not seeing him, he must have made off immediately on finding we were up. *I charged the pistol with ball.*

Wednesday 3 July [Halifax]

At 3.50, took George in the gig & drove in ½ hour direct to Westfield . . . Sat 50 minutes with Mrs Kelly . . . [She] *was evidently nervous at first but I rallied her about one thing or other & turned it off. Said I knew she had hardly expected my calling. She owned it. She thought I might have forgotten her. I told her she had not the faith that would remove mountains . . . She now & then rather coloured when I looked & spoke to her. Was glad to hear she was so happy. Said there was a great difference between a married woman & an inexperienced young lady. She looked pretty, I think, & rather improved in manner than otherwise. I know my manner might strike her as having all or much of its former peculiarity & I wondered what she thought & felt . . . My whole manner was a compliment. I think she felt it so & surely most women would.*

Friday 5 July [Halifax]

Before breakfast, writing out a rather altered & shorter Welsh tour, finding my aunt & I cannot be absent more than 14 or 15 days. *She talks of only affording twenty pounds but, my uncle says, is to take thirty if she brings the rest back.*

Saturday 6 July [Halifax]

My father & Marian arrived at 2 from Skelfler (Market Weighton) having come from York by the Highflier. They are both looking very well . . . *My uncle told me at breakfast this morning that he would give me twenty-five pounds now & regularly allow me fifty a year. I said how much I was obliged to him. I hope this & some small certainty from my aunt will make me comfortable in future.*

On Thursday 11 July, Anne and her aunt set off for a tour of North Wales. They were away from home until 27 July. The two high spots of the holiday, for Anne, were her meeting with M—, whom she arranged to meet for one night in Chester, and a visit to the Ladies of Llangollen.

Thursday 11 July [Manchester]

Breakfasted very comfortably, & my aunt & I off in the gig on our way to Manchester at 6½ . . . We reached here at 1.15 by the Manchester clocks. We had scarcely got into the gig before it began to rain a little & continued, more or less, till about 3 miles from here. We had the top put up in time & did not get at all wet, tho' the rain met us almost directly . . . The rain seemed so set in for the afternoon & evening that we have made ourselves comfortable for dinner at 5 & mean to go to bed *very* early that we may be off at 5 in the morning. We immediately sent for the coach-maker Mr Lacey employs & at his, Mr Lacey's, recommendation, are going to have the new front springs on a different principle which will raise the gig 1 or 1½ inch, to which, on the plea of the spring leather being likely to last longer & be safer, my aunt at once consented. The hack-horse had carried George very well. For this, & for his new riding coat & waistcoat, he had to wait last night at Halifax & did not get back till more than 10½. 'Tis now 4¼. It rains incessantly & I am ½ asleep . . . Dinner at 5¼. 2 very nice souls [*sic*], veal-cutlets, potatoes, peas, tarts & cheese. We did not have more than a glass of our pint of port . . . Came upstairs to bed at 8¾. The bill for the horses; hay 3/–, corn 2/8 . . . We got the waiter to give us sovereigns for some of our Rochdale & Halifax notes, for which we paid a penny each note.[5]

Friday 12 July [Northwich]

Very comfortable bed & slept all the while I was in it. We were not off till 5¾ . . . In turning at the bottom of Market St into Deansgate (a sharp turning from a narrow street) a heavy coach had nearly run over us. Percy & the leaders came in contact. Poor Percy trembled & was a good deal frightened, but stood still & behaved beautifully while the coachman pulled up &

waited a 2nd till we could get past. 'Hallo, you driving a gig there on that side,' said the coachman. We were on the left side & quite right. I called out I would go on the other side. 'You go to Hell,' said he, surlily. However, we got well off. At the 1st turnpike there was a caution pasted up to keep on the left side. The road was shockingly bad for 2 or 3 miles, full of great holes & pools of water . . . We got into Chester at 4.10. M— out . . . I was shockingly fidgetty. M— had left no. 4 *Retrospective Review* on her table . . . At last, M— came at 6, after I had waited 2 hours. *I had got into a sad agitation & fidgettiness.* Tried to make the best of the hours we had lost. M— had been sending the servants to inquire at the coach offices & watched the arrival of the last Manchester coach till after 6. Meant to have gone to bed very early but, after 9, M— asked me to go to see Madame Tussaud's waxwork figures . . . We were there some time. Did not go upstairs till a little past 10 & were not in bed till 12. Sat up talking. *Delighted to see each other, yet somehow I felt very low, but fought it off as well as I could.*

Saturday 13 July [Llangollen]

Two kisses last night, one almost immediately after the other, before we went to sleep . . . Felt better, but was so shockingly low last night I cried bitterly but smothered it so that M— scarcely knew of it. At any rate, she took no notice, wisely enough . . . M— told me of the gentlemanliness & agreeableness of Mr Powis who, it seems, might interest M— more than duly had her heart no object but C—, with whom she has had no connection these four months. Not down to breakfast till 11 . . . then, perhaps luckily for us, all in a bustle & M— off at 2¼. We were off in ½ hour.

Got here, the King's Head, New Hotel, Llangollen, patronized by Lady Eleanor Butler & Miss Ponsonby, in 4½ hours . . . Beautiful drive from Chester to Wrexham. It was market day & the town seemed very busy. Beautiful drive, also, from

Wrexham here but I was perhaps disappointed with the first couple of miles of the vale of Llangollen. The hills naked of wood & the white limestone quarries on our left certainly not picturesque. About 3 miles from Llangollen, when Castle Dinas Bran came in sight, we were satisfied of the beauties of the valley but the sun was setting on the castle & so dazzled our eyes we could scarce look that way. The inn, kept by Elizabeth Davies, is close to the bridge & washed by the river Dee. We are much taken with our hostess & with the place. Have had an excellent roast leg of mutton, & trout, & very fine port wine, with every possible attention . . . We sat down to dinner at 8½, having previously strolled thro' the town to Lady Eleanor Butler's & Miss Ponsonby's place. There is a public road close to the house, thro' the grounds, & along this we passed & repassed standing to look at the house, cottage, which is really very pretty. A great many of the people touched their hats to us on passing & we are much struck with their universal civility. A little [girl], seeing us apparently standing to consider our way, shewed us the road to Plâs Newyd (Lady Eleanor Butler's & Miss Ponsonby's), followed & answered our several questions very civilly. A little boy then came & we gave each of them all our halfpence, 2d. each.

After dinner (the people of the house took it at 10), wrote the following note, 'To the Right Honourable Lady Eleanor Butler & Miss Ponsonby, Plâs Newyd. Mrs & Miss Lister take the liberty of presenting their compliments to Lady Eleanor Butler & Miss Ponsonby, & of asking permission to see their grounds at Plâs Newyd in the course of tomorrow morning. Miss Lister, at the suggestion of Mr Banks, had intended herself the honour of calling on her ladyship & Miss Ponsonby, & hopes she may be allowed to express her very great regret at hearing of her ladyship's indisposition. King's Head Hotel. Saturday evening. 13 July.' The message returned was that we should see the grounds at 12 tomorrow. This will prevent our going to church, which begins at 11 & will not be over till after 1. The sevice is principally in Welsh except the lesson & sermon every 2nd Sunday & tomorrow is the English day. Lady Eleanor Butler has been couched. She ventured out too soon & caught cold. Her medical man (Mr Lloyd [or Ewyd] Jones of [indecipherable]) positively refuses her seeing anyone. Her cousin, Lady Mary Ponsonby, passed thro' not long ago & did not see her.

Sunday 14 July [Corwen]

At 11¾, my aunt & I, accompanied by Boots to introduce us, walked to Plâs Newyd. The gardener in waiting. We talked to him a good deal. He seemed a good sort of intelligent man, much attached to his mistresses after having lived with them 30 years. He had walked about the country with them many miles when they were young. They were about 20 when they 1st came there & had now been there 43 years. They kept no horses but milked 6 cows. Said I, 'Can they use the milk of 6 cows?' 'Oh, they never mind the milk. It is the cream.' He said Lady Eleanor Butler was a good deal better. He remembered Mr Banks – has been there 4 or 5 times. I told him I had longed to see the place for the last dozen years, & we have expressed our great admiration of the place. In St Gothams (for I know not how else to spell it & which we most particularly admired) was a little bookcase of 30 or 40 little volumes, chiefly poetry, Spenser, Chaucer, Pope, Cowper, Homer, Shakespeare, etc. I quite agree with M— (*vide* her letter), the place 'is a beautiful little bijou', shewing excellent taste – much to the credit of the ladies who have done it entirely themselves. The gardener said, 'they were always reading.' The dairy is very pretty, close to the house, & particularly the pump, Gothic iron-work from Shrewsbury (Colebrookdale perhaps, originally). The well, 7 yds deep. It is an interesting place. My expectations were more than realized & it excited in me, for a variety of circumstances, a sort of peculiar interest tinged with melancholy. I could have mused for hours, dreampt dreams of happiness, conjured up many a vision of . . . hope. In our return we strolled thro' the church yard. I shall copy the epitaph to Lady Eleanor Butler's & Miss Ponsonby's favourite old servant, Mrs Mary Clark, who died in 1809, when we go back . . . I wonder what success I shall have about Lady Eleanor Butler & Miss Ponsonby. Mrs Davies thought they would be pleased with my note, but I can't write more now than that we have had delightful weather today & have travelled on most comfortably. I am more than ½ asleep & must make the best of my way to bed. 'Tis now 11½ . . . I have heard the wind whistle here 2 or 3 times. What a dreary place it must be in winter!

Wednesday 17 July [Aber]

Went to see the castle about 10¼ . . . *Gave the man two shillings for shewing the castle. I think one would have done. The art of travelling requires an apprenticeship. Surely I shall improve in time. I have given many a sixpence that might have been spare. Always take in your hand what you mean to give before you go* . . . Conway seems a poor town of 2 or 3 streets. We have been comfortable here. Good, clean beds, tho' very small rooms. No window-curtains, no wash-stand. The pitcher & basin on the toilet table. Good breakfast & great attention. The people seem clean, tho' the house looks dirtyish & second-rate because, perhaps, it is old & not easily made look clean or kept clean. But, on going out here, it is evidently not the first-rate house. The White Lion, a few doors a little lower down the street appears a neat, new building &, as we passed, a gentleman's landau with his own post-boy & horses was at the door. *We do not cut a figure in travelling equal to our expenses. My aunt is shabbily dressed & does not quite understand the thorough manners of a gentlewoman. For instance, taking the man's arm so readily to Snowdon, etc. Indescribable! George, too, is a clown of a servant, too simple in the manners of the world. But we are not known. I wlll try to learn & improve in travelling matters &, by thought & observation, may turn all this to future advantage. But I feel very low. Somehow or other, seeing M— has been no comfort to me. When I asked her how long she thought it might be before we got together, & she seemed to fight off answering, on pressing further she said she felt some delicacy on this subject & did not like to talk openly of it even to ourselves, for, tho' she did not love him, yet kindness & obligation made her feel a wish to avoid calculating the time or thinking of [it] except in general terms. I promised not to press her on the subject again. All this has made a great impression on me &, I know not how it is, I cannot shake it off. She never did so before but talked as coolly on so many, five or ten, for instance, years as I did. She seemed as fond of me as ever, yet all the night when I was almost convulsed with smothering my sobs, she took no notice, nor was affected at all apparently. The next morning her eyes filled at parting. I know not how it is but she, as it were, deceived me once & I feel that it is miserable to doubt. My aunt observed that she did not seem so fond of me as I was of her. I wish I did not think so much of all this but, alas, I cannot help it. Surely I shall be better by & by. I feel miserably low. I remember, too, what she said of Mr Powis, that if her heart was not engaged as it is to me, she might be in danger of very undesirable & uncomfortable feelings of interest towards him. I might have written her a few lines but feel as if I had not resolution. Were I fit for another world, how gladly would I go there . . .*

Thursday 18 July [Bangor]

At 8¼, my aunt & I set off (a cunning little girl our guide, picked her up in the village) to see the cataract, Rhiader Maur . . . We had had breakfast. The milk in the house all sour.

Desired the waiter to get some elsewhere. Nobody kept any cows or even goats & no milk to be had. Sent for the mistress (Mrs Lewis). She was very civil. Said it was a shame to live in the country & have no milk & she sent somewhere, borrowed a pint & I had, at last, coffee *au lait* as usual, & a good breakfast. In paying the bill they gave me, in change, 2 Irish tenpennys, but valued them at only 9d. I gave the waiter one of them & 2d. & the chamber [maid] the other (i.e. 9d.) not giving her anything for my bed because the sheets were certainly not clean, of which I took care to tell both her & her mistress . . . Left Aber at 11.10 . . . Got out at the Castle Inn Bangor (at the back of the cathedral) at 6 . . . It is the best inn in the place, but bad enough & dirty enough.

Friday 19 July [Caernarvon]

Beautiful drive from Bangor here . . . We have a sitting-room, 11 yds by 6, lighted by 3 large sashes. I should think it about 14ft high or more. Have had a good breakfast & are very comfortable . . . Dinner at 6¼. Salmon & a roasted leg of mutton, 7 or 8lbs & very good. It was, the waiter said, the common size. He mentioned Mr Roberts, the harper, who won the silver medal (a small silver harp) at the Eisteddfod in 1821 at Wrexham. We asked what we should give him. The waiter said people seldom gave him less than ½ crown, & if he made a charge, he would charge ½ crown an hour, for he was not a common harper but a sort of teacher & master bard among them. He came at 9 & played 1 hour 5 minutes in our room, for which we gave him 3/–. He seemed satisfied – played us several Welsh airs, Handel's 2nd concerto, etc. He is certainly a fine performer with great execution & taste. He had no unnecessary quavering with his hands but held them steadily parallel with the strings . . . He went to the party in the next room & we still had the benefit of him.

Monday 22 July [Bala]

Just before leaving Dolgella, for 20 minutes walked round the town. Certainly a poor place according to English ideas. The cottages miserable, tho' apparently of the better sort for North Wales. Mud floors. The smell of the peat fires is strong & disagreeable to those not accustomed to it. Square large masses of the dark mountain stone used for building, the unevenness of them in all but the better kind of houses, filled up with lesser fragments, give the buildings an unusually dark, rude appearance which, with broken windows, completes the shabby look of the cottages in N. Wales. But the fine blue roofing slate, very commonly used, is remarkably neat & seems oddly contrasted with the rest . . .

Bala. White Lion Inn . . . Got here at 5.50. The landlady is a very nice woman. Everything seems very clean & comfortable &, so far, I should certainly recommend the house. My aunt rather had a little mutton broth with a boiled steak or 2 in it. I had a small loin of mutton (very good), roasted, good peas & potatoes, & a very good bilberry tart. No wine, only cold water. Walked a little, into the town before dinner (sat down to table about 7) & also afterwards . . . Great deal of hay to get in North Wales & a good deal to cut. The grass <u>very</u> thin & short, not at all equal to one of our middling pastures. Little corn to be seen anywhere & then only thin, short oats & barley. I have somewhere seen a little rye but do not remember any wheat in North Wales. Very few cattle & those only the small black breed & occasionally a few brindled red. Sheep up & down the mountains, but not so small as I expected. I have only seen 1 goat, a little tame thing at Caernarvon. I had an idea of pretty grey Welsh ponys [*sic*] but have seen nothing of the sort. I would not have known the horses I have seen from English . . . Sat up hunting for a frill & adding up my accounts. Find one pound short. In taking out my purse at Tain y Bwlch, I let fall some sovereigns & surely did not pick them all up.

Tuesday 23 July [Llangollen]

A drop or 2 of rain just after setting off & a shower for about the 3rd mile from Llangollen. Heavy rain just after we got in. Mrs Davis received us at the door & came into our rooms to answer our inquiries after Lady Eleanor Butler. Mrs Davis was called up at one last night, & they thought her ladyship would have died. She was, however, rather better this morning. The physician does not seem to apprehend danger but Mrs Davis is alarmed & spoke of it in tears. Miss Ponsonby, too, is alarmed & ill herself, on this account. Pain in her side. 'She is a lady,' said Mrs Davis, 'of very strong ideas; but this would grieve her, too.' Mrs Davis had only known them 13 or 14 years, during which time she had lived at this house but she had always seen them 'so attached, so amiable together', no two people ever lived more happily. They like all the people about them, are beloved by all & do a great deal of good. Lady Eleanor has the remains of beauty. Miss Ponsonby was a very fine woman. Lady Eleanor Butler about 80. Miss Ponsonby 10 or 12 years younger. The damp this bad account cast upon my spirits I cannot describe. I am interested about these 2 ladies very much. There is a something in their story & in all I have heard about them here that, added to other circumstances, makes a deep impression. Sat musing on the sopha [sic], wotting what to do, inconsolate & moody, *thinking of M—. Low about her. I cannot shake off the impression of what she said at Chester about delicacy in calculating C—'s life, Mr Powis, etc. I know not how it is, I am shockingly low altogether.* Mrs Davis being going to inquire after Lady Eleanor Butler, my aunt & I walked with her to wait for her giving an answer to our inquiries. The physician there. Strolled about for 10 minutes &, he not being gone & it threatening to rain, returned & only just got in before a tremendously heavy shower. Then sat down & wrote the above of today. I feel better for this writing. In fact, come what may, writing my journals – thus, as it were, throwing my mind on paper – always does me good. Mrs Davis just returned. Brought a good account of her ladyship & a message of thanks for our inquiries from Miss Ponsonby, who will be glad to see me this evening to thank me in person. Shall [go] about 6½ or 7, just after dinner. *This is more than I expected. I wonder how I work my way & what she will think of me. Mrs Davis wishes me to give all the comfort, all I can, & not to mention that I know of her having been called up last night.* Dinner at 6. *Before dinner, about two hours upstairs washing & cutting my toenails, putting clean things on.* At 7, went to Plasnewydd & got back at 8. Just an hour away & surely the walking there & back did not take more than 20 minutes. Shewn into the room next the library, the breakfast room, waited a minute or 2, & then came Miss Ponsonby. A large woman so as to waddle in walking but, tho', not taller than myself. In a blue, shortish-waisted cloth habit, the jacket unbuttoned shewing a plain plaited frilled habit shirt – a thick white cravat, rather loosely put on – hair powdered, parted, I think, down the middle in front, cut a moderate length all round & hanging straight, tolerably thick. The remains of a very fine face. Coarsish white cotton stockings. Ladies slipper shoes cut low down, the foot hanging a little over. Altogether a very odd figure. Yet she had no sooner entered into conversation than I forgot all this & my attention was wholly taken by her manners & conversation. The former, perfectly easy, peculiarly attentive & well, & bespeaking a person accustomed to a great deal of good society. Mild & gentle, certainly not masculine, & yet there was a *je-ne-sais-quoi* striking. Her conversation shewing a personal acquaintance with most of the literary characters of the day & their works. She seemed sanguine about Lady Eleanor's recovery. Poor soul! My heart ached to think how small the chance. She told me her ladyship had undergone an operation 3 times – the sight of one eye restored – couching by absorption. I said I believed it was neither a painful nor dangerous operation. She seemed to think it both the one & the other. Mentioned the beauty of the place – the books I had noticed in the rustic library. She said Lady Eleanor read French, Spanish & Italian – had great knowledge of ancient manners & customs, understood the obsolete manners & phrases of Tasso remarkably well. Had written elucidatory notes on the 1st 2 (or 4, I think) books of Tasso, but had given away the only copy she ever had. Contrived to ask if they were classical. 'No,' said she. 'Thank God from Latin & Greek I am free.' Speaking of translations, she mentioned La Cerda's, I think it was, as the best according to some [bishop?] friend of hers, of Virgil, & Cary's as being most excellent of Tasso, literal & excellent for a beginner & which she should recommend to anyone wanting assistance. She somehow mentioned Lucretius, but it was 'a bad book & she was afraid of reading it'. I asked why. He was a deistical writer. I mentioned Dr John Mason Hood's [Good's?] translation, adding that I believed he, Dr Good, was not a high church man. 'No!' She knew he was heterodox. I observed that she might think all the classics objectionable. Yes! They wanted pruning, but the Delphin Editions were very good. As people got older, she said, they were more particular. She was almost afraid of reading *Cain*, tho' Lord Byron had been very good in sending them several of his works. I asked if she had read *Don Juan*. She was ashamed to say she had read the 1st canto. She said I had named Mr Bankes & asked if it was Mr Bankes Cleava. I thought not. Did not know him, but he was the most particular friend of a friend of mine. It was Mr Bankes, the great Grecian, said to be now the best in England since Mr Parsons' death. She did not think he had ever been there, did not know, did not remember him. She asked if I would walk out. Shewed me the kitchen garden.

Walked round the shrubbery with me. She said she owned to their having been 42 years there. They landed first in South Wales, but it did not answer the accounts they had heard of it. They then travelled in North Wales &, taken with the beauty of this place, took the cottage for 31 years – but it was a false lease & they had had a great deal of trouble & expense. It was only 4 years since they had bought the place. Dared say I had a much nicer place at home. Mentioned its situation, great age, long time in the family, etc. She wished to know where to find an account of it. Said it had been their humble endeavour to make the place as old as they could. Spoke like a woman of the world about my liking the place where I was born, etc. Said I was not born there. My father was a younger brother but that I had the expectation of succeeding my uncle. 'Ah, yes,' said she, 'you will soon be the master & there will be an end of romance.' 'Never! Never!' said I. I envied their place & the happiness they had had there. Asked if, dared say, they had never quarrelled. 'No!' They had never had a quarrel. Little differences of opinion sometimes. Life could not go on without it, but only about the planting of a tree, and, when they differed in opinion, they took care to let no one see it. At parting, shook hands with her and she gave me a rose. I said I should keep it for the sake of the place where it grew. She had before said she should be happy to introduce me some time to Lady Eleanor. I had given my aunt's compliments & inquiries. Said she would have called with me but feared to intrude & was not quite well this evening. She, Miss Ponsonby, gave me a sprig of geranium for my aunt with her compliments & thanks for her inquiries. Lady Eleanor was asleep while I was there. Miss Ponsonby had been reading to her *Adam Blair*,[6] the little book recommended to me by M— at Chester. I had told Miss Ponsonby I had first seen an account of them in *La Belle Assemblée* a dozen years ago, & had longed to see the place ever since. She said some people had been very impertinent, particularly Dr Mavor, who had in some way displeased (laughed at, or something) the old housekeeper to whose memory they had erected a monument in the church yard & it seems the ladies had a particular objection to Dr M—, but Miss Ponsonby appears to have lost her teeth & occasionally mumbles a little that, as a stranger, I did not always perhaps quite understand her. It seems 2 of the Cromptons & their brother (of Esholt) were lately sketching the place. The ladies sent them chairs – went out to speak to them (for they were retiring, fearing they had offended the ladies) – formed an acquaintance &, wanting to know something about the Derwentwater family, which the Cromptons could get to know, there has been a correspondence. Miss Ponsonby said she has not answered their last letter but meant to do it. Lady Eleanor Butler & Miss Ponsonby seem great pedigree people. Antiquarians, topography, etc. I came away much pleased with Miss Ponsonby & sincerely hoping Lady Eleanor will recover to enjoy a few more years in this world. I know not how it is, I felt low after coming away. A thousand moody reflections occurred, but again, writing has done me good . . . I mean to dry & keep the rose Miss Ponsonby gave me. 'Tis now 10¼. Sat talking to my aunt. Came upstairs at 11.10.

Wednesday 24 July [Denbigh]

Came downstairs at 9.20 . . . Have seen Mrs Davis. Lady Eleanor has had a good night . . . Left Llangollen at 11¼. Did not get here [Ruthin] till 3.05 . . . It seems a nice, neat town but I have felt too unwell ever since getting up this morning to stir out. The acid apple tart I had yesterday disagreed with me. A *lax early this morning before I could get washed.* There is a woman, by the way, squalling in the house in a very improper way & I would not come here again . . . Just before breakfast this morning, sent George with compliments to Miss Ponsonby, to inquire after Lady Eleanor. The former much obliged to us for sending. The latter has had a good night & was better. Went into Mrs Davis' room & begged her to write me a few lines in about 10 days, to say how Lady Eleanor was. Said I was going abroad & should feel anxious to hear. Begged her not to name this to Miss Ponsonby. Gave my address & I have no doubt Mrs Davis will write. Spoke, too, to the waiter about sending us Welsh mutton. ½ a sheep will travel better than a less portion on account of less of the meat being exposed to the air. The surface of the chine-bone protecting the meat. It will be 5d. a lb & 1½d. a lb carriage, exclusive of one yd of cloth wrapper that will cost a shilling. It will arrive at Halifax in 3 days . . . Left Ruthin at 5 & got here (The Bull Inn, Denbigh) at 6.30 . . . Market day & the streets pretty full tho' a small market because it was the fair last week . . . The waiter at Llangollen recommended us to the Crown Inn, but the look of it determined me to see the Bull &, the latter having much the better appearance of the 2, here we are. An old house. Narrow oak staircases that have a dirty look, but very civil, attentive people & we are certainly come to the right house. Ordered dinner in an hour & sat down at 7½. My aunt's bowels being still far from well, & myself very bilious, we had minced veal (white) & a light batter pudding with a lump of preserved apricot on the top. All very good &, quite contrary to expectation, I had some enjoyment of my dinner . . . We have a comfortable sitting-room upstairs. A *double-bedded room adjoining & I have my wash-stand. Dress & undress here in the sitting room.* Got a little out of our way in leaving Ruthin & passed the White Lion Inn – a very nice, largish-looking house – certainly the place we ought to have gone. George tells me the other was not respectable. The <u>man</u>, landlord, was a horse-dealer, & the squalling came from his daughter whom some man was laying hold of. Both my aunt & I felt too unwell to stir out again after dinner. 'Tis now 10p.m. when I have just finished writing the latter half of today. *At ten, discovered a neighbouring double-bedded room at liberty. Had all moved there & glad to get a place to myself.*

Thursday 25 July [Chester]

Went to a glove shop on the same side as the inn, a little higher up (Denbigh being celebrated for gloves). The shop shut up (only one shop of note) & the gloves in the window damaged & of very inferior make & appearance. Mrs Salisbury sent to the glover's house. He was in his hay field & had taken the key of his shop. His wife, who came to us, was sorry we could not wait. Off immediately at 10¾ . . . Stopt here, at Willoughby's, the Royal Hotel, Chester, at 7½ . . . Were shewn into the sitting room which we had a fortnight ago. Asked to have the same lodging rooms & have got them. *My aunt went upstairs. I sat musing on M——, thinking I wasted my life in vain expectation, hoping for a time which she is too delicate to like to calculate. Somehow I cannot get over this.* Sat down to dinner at 8½. Giblet soup. Excellent veal cutlets. Potatoes, peas, currant tart, & a bottle of port wine. My aunt better & I felt as usual again today & have enjoyed my dinner. I have just settled with George & written the last 20 lines of today & it is now 10.40 . . . Came upstairs at 11.20.

Friday 26 July [Manchester]

Slept very well last night for the bedrooms were comfortable & I had taken seven glasses of wine, which helped me to sleep in spite of the thought of M——. I mused but for a short while. 'I was unhappy,' said I, 'the last time I was here. I cannot be worse now.' This delicacy of M——'s, about C—— I cannot forget. Perhaps I think more of it than it deserves. Perhaps I am too fond of her. Did not lie long awake this morning. My aunt's bowels unwell in the night. Breakfasted at 10 . . . Did not get off from Chester till 1.35 . . . Stopt here at the Nag's Head Inn [Warrington], evidently the best in town but very busy & bustling. 'Tis now 6.30, not an hour since we arrived & 8 coaches have changed horses or stopt at the door during this time. Surely 5 or 6 of them have changed horses.

Bridgewater Arms, Manchester, 12p.m. I had scarcely written the above at Warrington when it struck me we ought to have something to eat. I had utterly forgot it before. Ordered coffee & my aunt & I strolled down the street to make out the road to Manchester. Returned in 20 minutes. Hurried over our coffee & off from Warrington at 5. The street all about the Nag's Head was, & had been since our arrival, full of people, apparently to watch the coaches. 1 or 2 new ones within the last few days or weeks. On inquiry found 14 coaches were daily horsed at this inn. I think in the space of the 1st 2 miles from Warrington, we passed more than a hundred carts coming towards Manchester . . . Very handsome approach to Manchester as far as the light permitted us to judge . . . Out of the gig in our sitting-room here in 2 hours 40 minutes, that is, arrived at 9.40. The house full. Obliged to be in the bar-parlour & I to sleep aloft, a mile from my aunt.

Saturday 27 July [Halifax]

Slept very well. Everything very comfortable . . . When we had been about an hour at Rochdale I left my aunt & went to Mr R—'s. The servant said Mrs R— was ill but on mentioning my name & my desiring him to ask if his mistress had anything to send to Halifax, Mr R— came out & ushered me into the dining-room where he & his wife's sister & 2 cousins, the Misses Martha & Anne Holdsworth, were sitting over their wine after dinner, at not more than 1¾p.m. by the Rochdale clocks. A more thoroughly vulgar party I never beheld. I thought it right to stay ¼ hour & then returned to the inn absolutely sick of my visit. Out of sorts & uncomfortable & did not get right again for at least an hour. I always do these civilities with a good grace, but none surely can imagine the sort of feel, the sort of dissatisfaction I invariably experience after things of this kind. In fact, I promised myself the indulgence of never calling again unless something very particular should change my mind. Left Rochdale at 2.25. Got here [Halifax] exactly at 6, I mean all along by my watch which is 8 minutes later than the church clock at Halifax & 20 minutes later than our kitchen clock. 3 hours & 35 minutes in coming here i.e. 17 miles. Percy very much tired . . . The hack horse, too, a little tired & we shall, therefore, not send him home till tomorrow morning. Found all well here. 5 letters for me . . . *M—'s letter has done me good for it is very affectionate. She meant not, I am sure, to say anything to give me uneasiness. She asks if our meeting gave me as much pleasure as it did [her], as if she suspected it did not* . . . I shall answer all these letters soon & then notice their contents in my journal. Now I have no time to spare. Veal cutlets & cold duck, potatoes & currant-tart & strawberries & cream – but did not relish anything but the tart & strawberries. Came upstairs for an hour, between 8 & 9, musing over my letters.

Monday 29 July [Halifax]

Crossed the 1st page of the 1st sheet written to M— yesterday. Determined to send it this morning, that she may have an account of our arrival at home . . . the ends of my paper contain the following . . . 'Charmed as I am with the landscape & loveliness of the country [of Wales], I do not envy it for home. I should not like to live in Wales – but, if it must be so, and I could choose the spot, it should be Plasnewydd at Llangollen, which is already endeared even to me by the association of ideas. Well, therefore, may it be on this account invaluable to its present possessors. My paper is exhausted; it has worn out my subject perhaps sufficiently. I am again seated quietly in my own room at Shibden where the happiest hours of my life have been spent with you & whence I shall always feel a peculiar satisfaction in assuring you that I am now & for ever, Mary, faithfully & affectionately yours.'

Anne described her meeting with Miss Ponsonby to a friend in York, Miss Sibbella MacLean, with whom she frequently corresponded.

Saturday 3 August [Halifax]

'. . . If any of your friends are going to Llangollen, pray recommend them to the King's Head or New Hotel, kept by Mrs Davis. A very comfortable house. Everything good & Welsh mutton in greater perfection than we had it anywhere else. Never ate anything so excellent. Lady Eleanor Butler was seriously ill. An inflammatory complaint. She had been couched. 3 operations by absorption. The sight of one eye nearly restored. Caught cold by going out too soon & staying out too long, and late, in the evening. On our return she was rather better. Miss Ponsonby, by especial favour, admitted me & I spent an hour with her most agreeably. She had been alarmed, but was returning to good spirits, about the recovery of her friend. There was a freshness of intellect – a verdure of amusing talent which, with heart & thorough good breeding, made her conversation more time beguiling than I could have imagined. She told me they had been 42 years there. 'Tis the prettiest little spot I ever saw – a silken cord on which the pearls of taste are strung. I could be happy here, I said to myself, where hope fulfilled might still "with bright ray in smiling contrast gild the vital day." You know, Miss Ponsonby is very large & her appearance singular. I had soon forgotten all this. Do not, said I, give me that rose, 'twill spoil the beauty of the plant. "No! No! It may spoil its beauty for the present, but 'tis only to do it good afterwards." There was a something in the manner of this little simple

228

circumstance that struck me exceedingly . . .' Foolscap sheet from M— . . . She seems much interested about Lady Eleanor Butler & Miss Ponsonby and I am agreeably surprised (never dreaming of such a thing) at her observation, 'The account of your visit is the prettiest narrative I have read. You have at once excited & gratified my curiosity. *Tell me if you think their regard has always been platonic & if you ever believed pure friendship could be so exalted. If you do, I shall think there are brighter amongst mortals than I ever believed there were.'* . . . *I cannot help thinking that surely it was not platonic. Heaven forgive me, but I look within myself & doubt. I feel the infirmity of our nature & hesitate to pronounce such attachments uncemented by something more tender still than friendship. But much, or all, depends upon the story of their former lives, the period passed before they lived together, that feverish dream called youth.*

Wednesday 7 August [Halifax]

Mended my skirt & gloves . . . At 4.10, down the new bank (walked) to Halifax to make some shoppings, order about a trunk, etc. Saw a handsome rosewood, perhaps about 16 ins square, writing box handsomely mounted with brass (at Adams' shop) £2 8s. Large portmanteau trunk at Furniss's (apparently a very good one, 45/–). I should like to have it but I can do without it, & this is reason enough for me not to think of it. At Butter's shop, no real Welsh flannel – nothing but Lancashire, now made so like it, none but judges can tell the difference . . . Got home at 5.50. Miss Kitson told me the English lino was not like the French. My trunk would cost 11/– entirely covering. They would make a new one like it for 18 or 20, judging from what the man said about other trunks. I remember it cost a guinea. In the evening, at 8, went into the garden; ate gooseberries (only the 3rd or 4th time I have eaten them this year except in pies), then walked on the terrace till 9.

Thursday 8 August [Halifax]

All the morning, from 11¼ to 3½, rummaging out my canteen & taking an inventory of the things, books, etc., in it. At 4¼, took George in the gig & drove to Kebroyde. Took 1 cup of coffee with Mrs Priestley & sat with her till near 6, talking over the changes of times ... In going, met Mr & Mrs P. of White Windows ... Should not have stopt to speak to them but mistook them for Mr & Mrs Henry P. Met them again in returning home & just bowed. In going, ordered Furniss to make Marian a black leather trunk, outside dimensions 2ft 3½ ins and 1 ft deep. 2 grooves to be made in each side of the trunk midway & quarter to admit a loose slide which Marian may move as suits her best.

Saturday 10 August [Halifax]

Mrs Saltmarshe drove, in their gig, her sister, Mrs Waterhouse, to call here. They came at 1 & staid rather more than ½ hour. Mentioned my having seen Miss Ponsonby ... Not a little to my surprise, Emma launched forth most fluently in dispraise of the place. A little baby house & baby grounds. Bits of painted glass stuck in all the windows. Beautifully morocco-bound books laid about in all the arbours, etc., evidently for shew, perhaps stiff if you touched them & never opened. Tasso, etc., etc. Everything evidently done for effect. She thought they must be 2 romantic girls &, as I walked with her to see her off, she said she had thought it was a pity they were not married; it would do them a great deal of good. Mrs Saltmarshe was less pleased [displeased?] with the place than she was – but when she came to get back to the inn, she agreed it was not worth going to see. Little bits of antiques set up here & there. They themselves were genuine antiques – 80 or 90! She hoped I should not despise her taste. I merely replied most civilly, 'No!' I was delighted to hear her account by way of contrast to what I had thought myself . . . Note from Mary Priestley – a very proper one – very attentive in her to write to me so soon. She will be glad to see me any time & hopes I will spend a long day with her . . . I have several times said to my aunt that, of all the people here, I liked Mary Priestley & Emma Saltmarshe the best, but doubted between the 2. Emma's remarks this morning & Mary's note this afternoon have made up my mind on this point in favour of the latter, as, I think *pour toujours*.

Anne received letters from both M— and Isabella who were both spending some time at Buxton in separate parties, although attending the same social functions. The rivalry between the two women for Anne's affections is evident.

Sunday 11 August [Halifax]

A letter from Isabella (Buxton) enclosed with ½ sheet (2pp.) & the envelope written by M— . . . M— *very affectionate. She thinks Isabel would not suit me: '. . . looks fat & gross She danced on Wednesday & looked almost vulgar. I could not keep my eyes off her or my mind from you.' They had a squabble on Friday evening, just before M— began to write . . . 'Oh, how I hate squabbles. They make me low & nervous & my mind always turns to you & the prospect of having, by & by, a safe mooring from all strife & con- tention, with a sort of anxiety which makes me sometimes very impatient of delay . . .' This does not correspond with the delicacy she felt on the subject at Chester. I shall not advert to it. I believe she loves me. Surely our fortunes are now bound together. I will not dwell on what has given me so much pain* . . . Isabella tells me it was reported that Lady Eleanor Butler was dead . . . Isabella just mentioned the bishop of Clogher that so much is said about in the paper – caught with a private of the Guards in an improper situation.

Tuesday 13 August [Halifax]

Went to the Saltmarshes'. Sat with them 1½ hour. Mr Christopher Rawson came in soon after me & staid the whole while. Unsatisfactory sort of visit. All <u>very</u> civil, but Mr C.R. is flattering, vulgar & therefore a bore & I felt unsatisfied altogether as I generally do in our Halifax society.

Thursday 15 August [Halifax]

Before breakfast, from 7 till 8½, planning a dressing box, getting out all the things required, trying what space they would take ... In passing thro' the town, called at Furniss's about a leather cover for my writing desk ... Great deal of talk with Major P— about horses ... He strongly advised getting Hotspur broken at the Dragoon Barracks at York, which might be done thro' the favour of the commanding officer, & paying the government allowance for the horse's keep. I am very strongly inclined to do my utmost to try this plan. The dragoons never whip the horses in breaking now. They are several of them turned loose in the manger. Those that have done well are patted & have a little corn, & those that are sulky & ill tempered are taken no notice of.

Friday 16 August [Halifax]

Letter from Isabella (Buxton), acknowledging the receipt of the gooseberries ... 'She (M—) brought Mr Lawton [C—] with her the other day, & he is certainly better looking than I expected, & is certainly very gentlemanly in his manners, but his figure is dreadful. He pressed us very much to go to Lawton but I fear we shall not be able to accomplish it. Just before he took his leave, he said that he never saw anything so extraordinary as my likeness to you; upon which M— exclaimed with a very silly face, that it was paying me a very great compliment; on any other

occasion I should have said the same thing, but I was so astonished at hearing him mention your name, that I was (as we say
in Yorkshire) perfectly dumbfounded.'

Monday 19 August [Halifax]

Off at 6 in the gig . . . to call at Crownest & Cliff-hill . . . Met
Mrs Walker at Cliff-hill. Only the 2 young ladies at home at
Crownest & deadly stupid this evening. Of course, I talked for
them all, but such almost threw me into the vapours. Foolishly
took a glass of ginger wine at Cliff-hill which has rather disagreed with me.

Saturday 24 August [Halifax]

2½ hours copying out from 13 July up to today of the index to
this volume . . . The looking over & filling up my journal to my
mind always gives me pleasure. I seem to live my life over again.
If I have been unhappy, it rejoices me to have escaped it; if
happy, it does me good to remember it.

Sunday 25 August [Halifax]

All went to church. Mr Franks junior preached 42 minutes from
Psalm cxxii.6 and following vv. Good language & a good sermon
but as much to put us in love with our political as religious constitution &, perhaps, more apt against radicalism than for the
society for the promotion of Xtian knowledge, in behalf of which
there was a collection after the service. He seemed as if he
scarcely knew how or when to conclude. To me his voice is so
feminine as to be distressing – the more striking because his
appearance is not [at] all so; bald & a very sufficient black beard.
But he is clever & his style & manner gentlemanly in the
pulpit . . . My father & Marian went to bed at 11, my aunt at 11¼
& my uncle & I stood talking by the fire half hour in the kitchen
about my father's affairs. His being without a home; going to France,

etc. Also of Marian's character. How much she is like my mother &
my uncle would not trust her further than he could [throw?] her. I said
she could never throw away the estate for I should only leave it her for
life, that whether she married or not, Listers in Wales would get it. My
uncle made no remark on this but it seemed to satisfy him & he said
soon afterwards, 'Your uncle Joseph used to say he could not depend
upon any of them & you know, there are too many women that one
really cannot depend [on],' to which I exprest, [sic] & felt, consent.

Monday 26 August [Halifax]

Letter from Mrs Davies, 'Llangollen. August 24 1822.' It gave
me heartfelt pleasure & really exhilarated me to find Lady
Eleanor Butler 'quite recovered & her eyes are improving daily;
she is able to distinguish almost anything without the use of her
glass; which she has not been able to do for many years before.
I would have written sooner only I was prevented by her
Ladyship, to wait till she was sufficiently strong to take a prom-
enade as usual thro' her delightful shrubbery which she fancied
confirmed her recovery.' The following thanks very properly
exprest for my promise to recommend their hotel. Altogether a
very proper letter. The sentence about 'prevented by her
Ladyship' must surely mean that her ladyship knew of Mrs
Davis's writing &, consequently that Mrs Davis must have told
them I had asked her to write to me. I thought she would mention this tho' at the time I particularly begged her not. I do
indeed feel anxious & interested that these ladies should live at
least a few years longer. I should like to see them both together
& should like M— to be with me. Will this ever be or not? . . .
Sewing a little . . . Above half-hour putting cotton wool into stays &
sewing in the steel . . . Making a bag for my syringe & another for
buttons. Siding my work-box. Putting all my bits & scraps into the
gig imperial, all which jobs took me all the day & all the evening.

On Friday 30 August, Anne left Shibden to go to France with her father and her sister, Marian, in an attempt to sort out her father's tangled financial affairs. He was constantly in debt due to his bad management. Anne was extremely irritated by the fact that she was expected, or dutifully took it upon herself, to sort out his affairs. She certainly did not want him living either with her or near her, as she saw him as a social embarrassment. To this end, she conceived a plan whereby his estate in Market Weighton was to be sold, his debts paid, and he and Marian were to find a residence abroad where they could live cheaply off the remaining capital.

Before Anne left Shibden Hall, she made out her will in M—'s favour.

Thursday 29 August [Halifax]

Went downstairs & staid with my uncle & aunt till near 9. They both witnessed my will in favour of M—. My aunt very low. My uncle carried it off better than I expected but I fear they will be dull & somewhat desolate at first. I made the best of it but the thought of my father's affairs & one thing or other made me sick enough at heart ... Got off from Shibden at 9.20. The moon obscured. Too dark for me to see & George drove me here (Northgate House) in the gig ... 'Tis now 11 at Shibden, 10.50 here. I feel as if it was all more like a dream than reality. Here I am in the dining-room to the front at Northgate ... writing on the eve of going to France for I know not how long, to be with my father & Marian. How strange! My thoughts are unsettled. I shall go upstairs & lie down & try to sleep a couple of hours. Good-night, Mary. You are in my heart & mind ... Writing my journal always does me good. I feel better now. I shall strap up my writing desk & be in bed, or on it, in 10 minutes.

The next day the party set off for France, travelling by road to Selby, then by steam packet from Selby to London, and then to Dover to embark for Calais. Anne was grimly determined to make the best she could of the whole unwelcome episode. As usual, her journal is her greatest source of comfort to her.

Friday 30 August [Hull]

Had a couple of cups of coffee & a glass of cold water & cold bread & butter & made a tolerable breakfast ... The mail unusually late ... It was very hot inside ... I had my eyes shut but did not sleep – musing on one thing or other. The pewter bottle I had cast for my writing-desk I was obliged to leave. Just in time (at 9 last night), discovered the ink oozing out of a small flaw in the casting. I am determined to make neither difficulties nor disappointments. I shall put ink in one of the glass bottles in my dressing box. Musing of home & M— ... Stopt at the Petre Arms, Selby at 9. On board the steam-packet, *Favourite*, at 9.25 & weighed at 9.40. Ordered breakfast & 9 of us sat down to it at 10. Bad butter. Bread & muffins tolerable. No coffee on board. It might have been got for me, if I had spoken before we sailed. 1/3 each, the charge ... The cabin is very comfortable & I am writing pretty much at ease ... Eleven of the passengers have just dined close to my elbow & are paying 1/9 each for dinner & 9d. per bottle of porter and 1d. per biscuit. They are giving the woman waiter 2d. each ... 2 hot roast-fowls, done by steam of course, at top, 2 ducks done at the bottom, a large cold ham & piece of cold roast beef at the bottom, potatoes & some sort of vegetable. Strong smell of onions ... How nicely I have got on with my journal & my letters ... Landed at 7. Immediately came here [Shakespeare Tavern, Humber St. Hull], took our rooms ... a very secondary sort of house.

Saturday 31 August [London]

Landed at Tower Stairs at 6 & got to Webb's Hotel[7] (220, the number has been altered, instead of 234) at about 7. Sat down to dinner a little before 8. Giblet soup, cold roast beef for my father, & ½ a calf's face, boiled. Bottle of Vidonia. Very fair wine. Got my journal book out about 9, but too sleepy to write & determined to go to bed . . . Between Woolwich & Greenwich, close to the river on our left, opposite to Blackwall, 3 gibbets standing at a little distance from each other, the 1st shewing remains of one man – the others the remains of 2 men each. They were Malays (sailors) executed perhaps 8 or 10 years ago for murdering their captain.

Monday 2 September [London]

Nearly worried last night with bugs. All my throat, my right eye almost swelled up & my left hand bit & my arms a little, but Mrs Webb so sorry & civil about it, I don't mind the thing. I believe they take all possible precautions but, if there be a bug in the house, it is sure to find me. Neither my father nor Marian bit at all . . . Ordered dinner at 5½ . . . A minute or two before 5, we all set off to the horse guards, thence into the Birdcage Walk . . . did [not] get back to sit down to dinner till 5.50. Gravy soup. Cold roast beef for my father. Large piece of excellent hot boiled beef & a good boiled bread pudding. At 7, all set off again. Walked along what they call the new buildings to the end of Portland Place, now terminated by what they call Park Crescent opening upon the Regent's Park. All this done since June 1819. I was perfectly astonished. Surely there is not so fine a street in Europe – so long, so spacious, so consisting entirely of beautiful buildings. Houses like palaces, noble shops. How poor Paris will appear! The Haymarket is so improved I should not have known it again. We were out an hour & got back at 8 . . . *All this put me in better heart. I was low before. My father is so desperately vulgar. He speaks loud of what he used to see & do long since. Points at everything & spits every now & then. Surely this is the last journey I shall ever take with my father & Marian both together. But seeing this fine street made me think, Well, perhaps I am repaid, for nobody knows me* ... I think the watchman is just crying half-past-eleven. I began writing about 9 ... Extracting some memoranda from a little red morocco pocket case with asses' skin leaves that was Eliza Raine's[8], previous to rubbing out all the writing & using the case in common for memoranda & notes made on the spot for my journal. This plan will save me much trouble & I shall always be sure, as I travel along, that my observations when made at the instant, are correct, at least as far as they can be so. Did not shut up my writing box & go to my room till 11.

Tuesday 3 September [London]

Set out at 10.40. The middle of the street of the upper part of the Haymarket full of waggons laden with hay. Literally a hay-market ... Walked over Waterloo Bridge & back again, for which we paid 1d. each [to] the man at the turnpike ... Took a coach & set us down in Pall Mall for 1/6 & a penny [for] the man who opened the door. Got out at Carlton Palace. My father a little impatient about what sort of money he was to get from Hammersley's,[9] but I always say to myself, temper, temper, temper, i.e. keep your temper & I think I managed pretty well. Hammersley asked if we had succeeded in getting our passport. I was merely giving an answer in the affirmative, when my father began explaining all about it ... I saw Hammersley or rather the gentleman we saw 1st yesterday look, & my heart died within me, as well it might all things considered. *Heaven grant this to be my last journey with my father. I am shocked to death at his vulgarity of speech & manner ... I am perpetually in dread of meeting* anyone I know. I am wretchedly ashamed &, for a moment now & then, till I rouse myself, feel low & mortified & unhappy, wishing myself out of the scrape, but all things have but a time & I will profit what I can. Catch me who can another time. From Hammersley's strolled along to Westminster Abbey . . . & got back to dinner precisely at the hour fixed, 5½ . . . I think we must have walked altogether 12 or 13 miles today . . . Marian does not complain much of being tired, nor my father, nor am I tired at all. But I was worried with bugs last night as well as the night before. My other, that is, my left eye, was made up this morning. I was not fit to go out, but what could I do. My father has no idea of these things. I have about thirty bites on my left hand & arm, several on my right & on my face & arms & body, & my throat is covered.

Wednesday 4 September [Dover]

Did not sleep comfortably last night for pain of the bites & the great itching & heat, & fancying the dirty animals perpetually at me . . . At 7.10, off for Dover . . . and at 6½ were set down at the London Hotel close upon the harbour & custom-house. Ordered our rooms & dinner in private. A little to my silent amusement, a gentleman who had come on the outside of our coach & breakfasted with us at Dartford . . . came into our room as tho' he had a right. 'Twas evident, however, it was merely on account of not knowing better &, being a civil, respectable sort of man, booked like ourselves for Paris, we let him join us. Sat down to dinner at 7½. Gravy soup, soles & beefsteaks, tart & cheese, & a bottle of sherry for my father & Marian & myself, of which, however, our friend took 2 or 3 glasses besides his brandy & water.

Thursday 5 September [Calais]

On board the Dasher steam-packet at 11¼. Began to move out of the harbour immediately & landed on the pier at Calais in

[2 hours] 55 minutes, at 2.10. Came here, to Oakeshott's, the White Lion (Lion d'Argent, Rue Neuve). Handsome looking hotel. We have a very good sitting room opening into two good lodgings rooms, which my father & Marian have & I have a view-room not far off . . . Very rough sea. Our vessel . . . pitched a good deal & almost every passenger on board sick. I, some 8 times. Marian tolerable. My father had not been sick. It would have been better perhaps if he had. He is very unwell now (8p.m.) with a bowel complaint . . . He has a great deal of pain & talks of being dead in 2 or 3 days if he isn't better – but I do not think his spirits ever buoyant when he is at all ill. However, all this makes one uneasy. I have no hope of his being able to go forwards tomorrow morning at 9. Marian & I . . . dined at the *table d'hote*. 14 of us sat down exclusive of Mr Oakshot [*sic*]. An L table. On our part, 3 roast fowls at the top before Mr Oakshot, which had succeeded gravy soup & a handsome head & piece of salmon from London. Soles at the bottom next to the fowls (all down the middle). Very large cauliflower fricassee. Sweetbreads done white. Both these very good. Stewed pigeons. Boiled potatoes. Boiled leg of veal, or rather, a large knuckle &, afterwards, snipes, tart, sweet omlet [*sic*] etc. Then cheese, Gruyère (Swiss, white, & something like Cheshire). Then a dessert of green grapes from Fontainebleau, most excellent pears, beautiful looking apples, walnuts, nuts, etc. Altogether an excellent dinner. We 3 had 2 bottles of *vin du pays* amongst us. Came upstairs again as soon as we had done dessert . . . My father's being unwell is a sad business but I hope he will be better soon & that we all get on well.

Friday 6 September [Calais]

My father better this morning but not well enough to go forwards . . . Only 7 of us, including Mr Oakeshott sat down to dinner today . . . Vermicelli soup, saltish cod & soles, leg of roast merino mutton at the top, looked small & excellent. Fricasseed fowl. 3 or 4 other substantial dishes. Partridges, 2nd course. Excellent sweet omlet [*sic*]. Grapes, pears, etc. Very good dinner. Everything well cooked.

Monday 9 September [Calais]

My father a great deal better today. Ate an egg at breakfast & another at tea & had cold chicken. He is a great advocate for eating as soon & as much as he can. *He is sometimes very impatient. I felt quite low when sauntering about with him this morning. I feel solitary & forlorn. Marian, poor girl, is no society for me & I am thoroughly ashamed of my father's vulgarity. I do indeed wish I was out of the scrape & at home. Yet never despair. I will make the best of it & improve myself as much as I can. I could hardly make myself understood at the library today & felt forlorn altogether, but my wine at dinner has made me better this evening.*

Tuesday 10 September [Calais]

Reading a few pp. of my Paris guide in French, for the sake of reading French & it being the only book I get. Breakfast at 10 . . . At 12.40, set out walking with my father & Marian. Along the quay, on the north sands, then the pier . . . *This is dull work. I shall walk before breakfast tomorrow & then, if I can, stay at home & read* . . . They are good sands to walk upon but the sun is baking. Dined on gravy soup, stewed eel, a hot *fricandeau de veau*, & a little hashed hare, both very good. Fritters, dropt thro' a spoon with a round hole an inch in diameter at the bottom of it, light & excellent. Swiss cheese Gruyère (3 francs a lb) & pears. A bottle of common wine of which I had only about 3 glasses . . . Sent a few things to be washed yesterday, which the woman brought back this evening. Her charge higher than I should have paid in York.

Wednesday 11 September [Calais]

Walked close to the water & on the sands an hour. Then walked on the pier to the end of it & walked back & got home at 2.20. My father had returned ½ hour before feeling tired. But he looks & is much better today, tho' still complaining of pain on the right side of his stomach. Went out again & bought him ½ lb of raisins . . . I do not think he much likes France hitherto. He told me this morning he thought we should all go back together for he is sure Marian is tired already. I think my father is, whatever she may be. He is constantly saying Frenchmen are what they were 50 years ago i.e. what he knew them in Canada & he seems neither to admire them or anything about them. What his plans are in case of speedy return, Heaven knows. I can't have an idea of them. *He says he can travel about till the money is done & we shall be tired before then. What can he mean to do? He cannot be long at Shibden nor afford to live at Northgate. The prospect seems darksome but he appears to take it very quietly. He must order for himself & I shall fidget myself not more than I can help.*

The Listers stayed in Paris until Saturday 28 September, when they began the return journey to England. Captain Lister had decided that living in Paris, or any part of France, was not to his taste. On Monday 30 September, they landed in England much to the relief of all concerned. A few days were spent in London and they returned to Halifax on 8 October.

Tuesday 1 October [London (Webb's Hotel)]

Slept very comfortably & very well last night on the sopha . . . Walked 1st to no. 17, Albermarle St, Miss Harvey, M—'s dressmaker. Staid a long while there & liked her very much.

Explained about my bad figure, etc. That I always wore black. Wished to leave all to her choice. Had a limited allowance, could not afford more than one gown a year. Hoped she would charge me as little as she could, which she promised to do, & ordered a velvet spencer & black velvet hat, to be sent to Shibden. Somehow told her of spending all my money in books & I think she understands me to be a character. She evidently took me for a gentlewoman. I can make my way well enough when left to myself. To have my father or even Marian would have spoilt it & I managed well ... From Miss Harvey's walked forward to Buckley's, 7, Upper Grosvenor St. Ordered a black pelisse to be sent to Miss Harvey to be sent by the waggon. In returning, strolled up Burlington. Went into 2 or 3 shops to see if I could get a hat but unsuccessfully. *I went out in one of Mrs Webb's bonnets, black leghorn, & looked very decent in it, but so unlike myself Mrs Webb almost smiled* ... After all this, got home at 1 ... Marian, too, bought a leghorn bonnet, pair of stays, pair of shoes, & may at last begin to shift a little for herself. *I had told her of a leghorn bonnet nine shillings dearer, but, more than that, neater, in Burlington, but of course have said nothing but of approbation of her choice, tho' I certainly would not have advised so city-like a concern. It is too gaping & staring now when little bonnets are beginning to be worn.*

Wednesday 9 October [Halifax]

From 11¼ to 2.40, watching Chas. Howarth put up the bookshelves in my closet, & then arranging my books in there – bringing some from the library passage. From 2¾ to 4.05, writing the account of the journey.

Saturday 12 October [Halifax]

Mr Green brought me a box from London, dated 5 October ... by waggon from the Bull & Mouth & a letter from Miss Harvey. *Gown & velvet spencer from Miss Harvey & pelisse from Buckley.*

*Till twelve trying them all on & going down to shew my aunt. They
all fit beautifully. From twelve till two thinking how to put them
away (gown & spencer in the gig imperial, I want more room, another
drawer) & trying how the leather girdle I got in Paris will do with my
old pelisse. Miss Harvey's bill eleven pounds, eighteen & twopence.
My pelisse will be eight pounds, as many shillings being discount
allowed for ready money . . . I must manage my dress as well as I
can. All my pelisses from Buckley (7, Upper Grosvenor St) &
something yearly from Miss Harvey (17, Abemarle St). If my aunt
will give me thirty a year in addition to my uncle's fifty, I can do &
have a book or two into the bargain. I should like to save fifty more
so as to have a good five pounds a year but I know not what I can do
towards it. This year I have already spent sixty-three pounds, three
& ninepence, & books, etc., & the twenty I have to pay in town will
make it above ninety before the year's end. But I shall want very little
dress for some time to come. 'Tis enough to frighten one who has
never had so much to spend before. But I see my yearly expenses get
more & more & I must take care, but I have always had more than
I have spent & I will try to manage so, always. At all events, I keep
good accounts.*

Monday 14 October [Halifax]

From the post-office to Whitley's . . . Speaking of paying ready
money, said I never paid postage when I sent a bill for ready
money. No, said he, nor I, when the bill is not under £2.
Thought I to myself, I have come at the knowledge I wanted.
I was right not to pay the postage to Miss Harvey, nor will I
ever pay it to any tradesperson when the bill is not under
£2 . . . *Told my uncle the amount of the bill. He had asked my aunt
& I thought it best to tell at once. He seemed rather startled at the
amount. Said it is to them both, Miss Harvey & Buckley. I have
spent almost all my aunt's legacy. 'Yes,' he replied, 'It soon goes.' I
must be very cautious how I seem to spend money & must make a*

great appearance of carefulness. Not a word about all these addi-
tional books.

Thursday 24 October [Halifax]

Letter from Mr Duffin, (York). No York news. A dead time just now. He had mistaken Hotspur for Percy. 'You do not surely mean to have him trained for your own riding, & why send him to the barracks?' ... but I have settled the business with Major Middleton who is the present commander at the barracks, who says, 'You shall have every care taken of the horse; that he shall stand in his own barracks, & fed by the contractor the same as the troop horses, & that the use of the riding-house, under the eye of the riding sergeant who is a careful man, shall be afforded him.'

Saturday 26 October [Halifax]

Wrote 3pp. & the ends to explain to Mr Duffin about Hotspur ... Hotspur is the colt we bought last spring & perhaps it will be soon enough to put him in bridles next February or March, when we can send him over or, if I should happen to be going to York about that time, he can run alongside the gig-horse.

Sunday 27 October [Halifax]

Out at 7½. Went immediately into the stables. Set John (Booth) to sweep & wash it. Latterly had William Green to help & staid with them 1 hour 10 minutes to see they did it properly – but not having time to have it done as thoroughly as I wish, desired them to be here by 7 tomorrow morning & we will have it as clean as hands can make it. I am determined to look after the stable thoroughly & try if I cannot manage it as it should be.

Sunday 3 November [Halifax]

3pp. & the ends from M——. They were at Birmingham on Friday & got back at 1 on Saturday morning. The night had been fine & this led M— to muse on 'the past, present & to come'. The whole of her letter bears the stamp of this . . . 'but hope still occupies the heart of your friend, & the state of my mind was, on the whole, favourable to our mutual happiness . . . If some we know could glance over what I have written, they would say I had turned methodist.' It seems as if Miss Ellen Pattison, who had been staying with her, had given rise to much seriousness.

Monday 4 November [Halifax]

Speaking of the Staveleys (Mrs Staveley, too), said no talent could make up for such bad manners. Bold, boisterous, vulgar, & Mrs Staveley slatternly, strangely singular . . . Met her walking one day in the town with her hands under her petticoat & she pulled out 2 great muffins.

Wednesday 13 November [Halifax]

Harriet Baxter, our new housemaid from Whitchurch, sent by Davis's mother, arrived about 6 yesterday evening. *My aunt does not like the look of her; large & grinning & up-shouldered and awkward. My aunt sick at the sight. I have only had a glimpse but think my aunt rather too hard upon her. She may turn out very well.*

Thursday 14 November [Halifax]

George does not like to be both groom & footman – does not like to bring breakfast in.

Saturday 16 November [Halifax]

Letter from Isabella Norcliffe (Langton) . . . 'The new Dean has already given great offence by not remaining there above one day & only staying ten minutes in the Minster. His great desire was to know everything about the fines & releases. I hear his health is so bad that he is obliged to reside ½ the year in

Devonshire & that his wife is very high & mighty. He has 3 or 4 sons.' So much for Dr Cockburn & his wife, the sister of Mr secretary Peel.

Tuesday 19 November [Halifax]

Shockingly late. Out at 7.55. Detained ten minutes or quarter hour giving Davis my dirty stays to be washed, taking the cotton wool out, etc. At 9, down the old bank to the vicarage to speak to Mr Knight about 1 of my uncle's library tickets being so made over to my father that he might be allowed the use of it. Staid at the vicarage (found them all at breakfast) 12 minutes. Returned in ¼ hour & got home at 9.40. Always go into the stables both before & after my walk . . . At 11¼, off in the gig. Drove my aunt thro' the town . . . then drove down to Messrs Jones & Ashforth's in Horton Street, to Mrs Taylor, the miniature painter. I agreed to go again in an hour to sit for a 2 guinea water colour sketch . . . Surprised at Mrs Taylor's saying she thought I had no recollection of her. Certainly I had none, but soon remembered her when she told me she had been at school (Mrs Haigue's & Mrs Chettle's, Low Anne's Gate) with me at Ripon . . . I was only just 7 the month before I went to Ripon . . . It seems I was a singular child & 'singularly drest, but genteel looking, very quick & independent & quite above telling an untruth.' Whistled very well. A great favourite with Mrs Chettle.

Wednesday 20 November [Halifax]

At 12.40, took George in the gig & drove to Mrs Taylor's. Sat for my likeness perhaps 1¼ hour. Very well satisfied with the sketch. There is something so very characteristic in the figure. Paid for it, 2 guineas . . . Neither Mrs Rawson nor Catherine thought it a good likeness. Found great fault with the mouth &, at first, with almost every part of the whole thing.

Thursday 21 November [Halifax]

Before breakfast, out at 8¼. Down the old bank to Mr Stansfield Rawson's. Breakfasted there . . . thence to the Saltmarshes'. Shewed them my picture. They did not like it at all. Thought it very silly looking. The mouth, a little open, was frightful. Not at all like me. What was meant to be mouth seemed like the tongue hanging out . . . Mr Stansfield Rawson . . . thought [it] a very strong but very unpleasant & disagreeable likeness . . . Went to Mrs Taylor . . . sat nearly an hour during which she closed the mouth, improved the picture exceedingly & made it an admirable likeness . . . Got home at 2.25. The likeness struck me as so strong I could not help laughing. My aunt came up & laughed too, agreeing that the likeness was capital. Ditto my uncle. We are all satisfied, let others say what they may. *Settled with Davies about what she had to sew for me & set down what I spent this morning &, except cutting open my book, spent all the rest of the afternoon looking at my pictures, thinking how pleased Mary would be.*

Towards the end of November, Anne went to Langton Hall to pay a visit to the Norcliffes; the stay highlighted her disillusionment with them. She made it plain to Isabella that she had no plans to include her in a longterm domestic relationship and though they might carry on an intermittent sexual liaison, Isabella was to understand there would always be someone to whom Anne would be closer. This might or might not be M—, depending upon future developments. Anne also obtained medical advice whilst at Langton on the treatment of venereal disease.

Sunday 24 November [Langton]

Off from Northgate in the new mail at about 1½. Terribly stormy over Clayton Heights. Got to Leeds about a little before

4. Stopt there almost an hour. I sat by myself in the mail at the door of the Golden Cross. *Opened the coach door & sat down, or squatted, in the bottom & made water, so that it ran out* . . . Got into York at 7.40 . . . the chaise took me up at 9¾ & I got out here, at Langton, at 12½.

Monday 25 November [Langton]

Better kiss last night than Tib has given me for long. Uncomfortable in dressing with Tib in bed. She taxed me with using a squirt, as she called it. I denied, but won't use the syringe again, however gently, when she is in the room. Cut my finger with the broken handle of the foot-pot. Sad, careful, economical or stingy work. Dawdling & did not come down till ten & a half. Tib soon followed. A little bit of butter at breakfast, but saw it would not do to ask for more. Two saddish, old-made buns, & it will take some time to reconcile me. I shall be glad to get home again.

Tuesday 26 November [Langton]

Out with Isabella about planting laurel & spruce firs near the house . . . *In the morning & evening talking about housekeeping. Mrs Norcliffe has twenty-one hundred a year. All her taxes, one hundred & fifty. Uses not quite three bushels of wheat, & nine & a half stones of all sorts of Shambles[10] meat, per week. Veal, 7d. & beef & mutton, 5d. per lb.*

Wednesday 27 November [Langton]

Walked around the garden & looked at the laurels & the newly planted shrubs . . . Isabella & I sat up talking in my room till 12.20. *She takes much less wine now, for economy's sake. Only four glasses a day . . . Told her how much she was improved. We talked about M—. She likes her as much as ever. Nothing can ever make her dislike her again. If she lived with me, Tib would come & see us &, tho' M— slept with me, Tib would not dislike her.*

Tuesday 10 December [Langton]

At 2¼, set off to Malton in the gig with Isabella & got back at 4. In passing, Isabella set me down at Dr Simpson's & took me up as she returned. *Consulted the doctor about my complaint & the consequent discharge. Said I had caught it from a married friend whose husband was a dissipated character. I had gone to the cabinet water-closet just after her. Mentioned the state she was in & my fears. Said I had taken cubebs & used a wash of corrosive sublimate & opium &, latterly, alum lotion. He would consider the case & wished me to call again tomorrow.*

Wednesday 11 December [Langton]

John Exley, the groom, drove me to & from Malton. First set me down at Dr Simpson's for ½ hour . . . *He said . . . such habits of cleanliness like mine would have worn out whites, or even nature herself might have done it. The disease might be merely local but by continuing so long, it might be absorbed into the habit. He could give me a wash for the present & some pills, not intended for my present cure but merely to guard against any future inconvenience. With these pills, which will be mercurial, I am to avoid evening & the early morning air, & to take no acids. The water I wash with is to have the cold taken off. His prescription will be ready for me tomorrow. Said how old I was, that is, thirty-one, but that it was my family constitution to give up my 'cousin' early, & I should be glad to do it while I had strength of constitution to get over it & would, therefore, never take forcing medicines to bring it on again. He said I was right & that I should leave nature to herself . . . Gave the doctor a guinea.* I liked Doctor Simpson's manner of conversation & had deemed him a man of talent & shall adopt & follow his prescriptions implicitly . . . *Burnett told me this morning that, tho' we have soup every day, there are only six pounds a week of gravy beef, the shin bone included in this weight. Mrs*

Fisher is surprised at the smallness of the quantity, for there used to be three pounds a week merely for gravies.

Saturday 14 December [Langton]

I had a very good kiss last night. Tib had not a very good one . . . I have been perpetually in horrors for fear of infecting Tib. I wonder whether the discharge is at all venereal or not?

Sunday 15 December [Langton]

The following paragraph, apparently cut out from a newspaper, but without date or reference, has been lent me by Mrs Norcliffe. 'Old maids. A sprightly writer expresses his opinion of old maids in the following manner: – I am inclined to believe that many of the satirical aspersions cast upon old maids tell more to their credit than is generally imagined. Is a woman remarkably neat in her person? "She will certainly die an old maid." Is she particularly reserved towards the other sex? "She has the squeamishness of an old maid." Is she frugal in her expenses & exact in her domestic concerns? "She is cut out for an old maid." And, if she is kindly humane to the animals about her, nothing can save her from the appellation of an "old maid". In short, I have always found that neatness, modesty, economy, & humanity, are the never-failing characteristics of that terrible creature, an "old maid".' Burnett brought into Mrs N—'s room, this morning, some black bombasine, a petticoat, she had had washed for her. It had not run up much, if at all. Had kept its colour. Looked very well. It had been washed with beast's gall – a lather made of it by pouring it gently into the water & stirring it & thus making the lather with the hands all the while. Get the beast's gall in a bladder! To have washed the bombasine with soap would have made it shrink & look white.

Monday 16 December [Langton]

Letter from my aunt (at Shibden), to bid me make no further inquiries about a housemaid. Things going on rather better in the kitchen at home, & resolved to go on as we do at present, at least till the winter is over. *I am glad enough to have no more trouble & I shall care no more about it . . .* At 3, went into the village & then, after taking a pencil sketch of Mrs Norcliffe's entrance gate, past Etty's to the turn up to Malton. Isabella asked me, on Saturday, to ask at Todd's what would be the price of a translation of Pliny's *Natural History* & Plato's works. Musing on this as I walked along. *Thought I myself would fit myself to translate Pliny & also that I would write an account of my acquaintance with M—, surely in a series of letters to a friend. Think of calling myself, 'Constant Durer', from the verb dure, to endure.* In the evening, wrote the whole of this page. Mrs Norcliffe had just shewed a most excellent composition candle. Outside, wax. Inside, tallow. Wick waxed. Excellent light, very steady, from Brecknall & Turner, Tallow Chandlers, 6, Charles St., Covent Garden, London. 2/9d. per lb.

Tuesday 17 December [York]

Packing. Not down to breakfast till 11.50 . . . *Mrs Norcliffe had exprest [sic] her obligation for my going there & seemed as sorry to lose me as Tib did, who bore my going without the smallest pretence at a tear & this made me care little or nothing about it. However, I spent my time pleasantly enough at Langton. The Duffins glad to see me.*

Wednesday 18 December [York]

In the evening, dressed & we all went to the Belcombes', I in a chair, at 7½ & we got back at 12 . . . Miss Bell Fenton & Miss Jane Smith met us in the evening. The latter a friend of Eli's.

Not popular in York. Thought rather forward. She is like a Bath-girl . . . had speaking black eyes & had plenty to say for herself. Towards the close of the evening I talked to her ½ hour. Rather agreeablized & I think she liked it. She prefers the society of gentlemen to that of ladies & would rather make a friend of the former. I could flirt with her if I liked. Miss Fenton would gladly attract Colonel Spearman. *She is about forty. Large & fat & ready to marry almost anyone. She is fruit that would fall without shaking.*

Anne was back in Halifax on Christmas Eve.

Tuesday 31 December [Halifax]

The end of another year! God grant that I may go on improving in virtue, in happiness & in knowledge.

1823

Friday 10 January [Halifax]

At 11, my aunt & I were off in the gig to Pye Nest . . . Sat ½ hour with Mrs E. & her daughter, Delia & sons, Charles, Henry and Thomas. *A sad, vulgar set. I said nothing but my aunt exclaimed about it as soon as we were out of the house. I thought she would. The servant came in with his linen jacket & apron on.*

Wednesday 29 January [Halifax]

Went to Northgate. My father gone since 12 to an assessed taxes meeting. Sat with Marian till 3.50 . . . *She thinks the housekeeping will only be about eight pounds a month now, instead of ten as at first. Mainly advised her getting my father to give her ten shillings a week for pocket money when he settles the week's accounts. This will be twenty-six pounds a year, with which she thinks she can do.*

Thursday 30 January [Halifax]

Called at the Saltmarshes'. Sat 40 minutes with Emma Saltmarshe. She had a headache & was not well, but she told me of the splendid ball & supper the other night at the Moores' at Northowram Hall. The company were obliged to walk up & down the hill. The horses could not keep their feet. Many hair's breadth escapes. Mrs Pollard staid all night. Durst not return. About 60 persons there. Magnificent supper. Everything from

Liverpool, even the pastry. So handsome an entertainment never given here. Yet was outdone by the ball & supper at Mr James Rawdon's of Underbank last Monday. 20 different sorts of wines. All sorts of fruit, French, Portuguese, etc. None of the visitors ever saw anything so splendid. 85 persons there. 42 staid all night. 2 ladies to each bed. The gents in 1 room (a warehouse) as Emma called it, 'the dormitory'. Very comfortable. The floor covered with small mattresses, 1 for each gentleman, & plenty of covering or bedclothes. 45 sat down to breakfast next morning. Great betting & gambling. No long whist – nothing but shorts & loo plaid [sic] all night & till ten the next morning.

Saturday 15 February [Halifax]

Letter from M— (Lawton) . . . *I know not how it is. I am beginning (to have) not sufficient interest in her letters. Perhaps I am best satisfied to think little upon the subject & certainly she is not constantly in my mind. How will this all end? Were I to meet with anyone who thoroughly suited me, I believe I should regret being at all tied . . . Oh, that this were not so. How will it all end?*

During the month of February, Anne met a new friend, Miss Pickford, who was staying with her sister, Mrs Wilcock, and with whom she struck up a strong, platonic friendship. The two women's intellects were well-matched as were their natures. As they became more friendly, Miss Pickford began to confide in Anne, telling her about her relationship with a Miss Threlfall. Anne began to suspect that the involvement was that of lover and loved, as was hers with M—. The town was again on the alert to Anne's new friendship.

Sunday 16 February [Halifax]

Called at the Saltmarshes' . . . I spoke chiefly in favour of Miss Pickford. *They think her blue & masculine. She is called Frank*

Pickford. She frightens Emma & seems to enjoy doing so. Miss Pickford is certainly like a gentlewoman & clever, to neither of which can Emma, or the people here, lay claim. Miss Pickford's friend, Miss Threlfall, has West India property. It was 5 or 6, or about 5 hundred a year, but has fallen to almost nothing.

Monday 17 February [Halifax]

Got to the lecture room at 12.10 by the old church . . . Sat next to Miss Pickford as usual . . . *How I can still run after the ladies! She seems sensible & in my present dearth of people to speak [with], I should well enough like to know more of her. I talk a little to her just before & after the lecture &, if she were young & pretty, should certainly scrape acquaintance but, all things considered, I must be cautious. I have no house to ask her to. I must hope for some society in days to come.*

Wednesday 19 February [Halifax]

Miss Pickford came up to me in the lecture room . . . I said I should be most happy to call upon her but it was quite out of my power to shew her any civility or attention under present circumstances &, not visiting her sister, there was a delicacy & awkwardness in the thing, but was glad to have met her at the lectures & should always be happy when any casualty gave me the pleasure of seeing her. She said she had often thought I should be congenial with herself. Had moved to me & tried all ways to renew our acquaintance 1st formed 9 or 10 years ago (in 1813) at Bath, but she found it would not do. Thought I had quite forgotten her, did not know her, & she had given up the hope of succeeding. I said I had been asked 2 or 3 times to meet her & had always refused, not wishing to increase my acquaintances at present, but I was glad I had not known what I had lost . . .

Asked Miss Pickford if she should return in a chair. No.

Offered to walk back with her. Left her a moment to order the gig, which was waiting for me, to follow. On its beginning to rain a little, said I should ask her to take a seat with me in the gig but I had a young horse, only in the 2nd time. She said she had no fear & we both drove off. Among other things, I noticed Mr W—'s having called the air 'she'. Miss Pickford spoke of the moon being made masculine by some nations, for instance, by the Germans. I smiled & said the moon had tried both sexes, like old Tiresias,[1] but that one could not make such an observation to every one. Of course she remembered the story? She said yes. I am not quite certain, tho', whether she did or not. 'Tis not everyone who would (*vid.* Ovid *Metamorphoses*). This led us to talk of saying just what came uppermost, sure that one's meaning would always be properly taken. She held out her hand to shake hands. I set her down at Mrs Wilcock's gate & we parted very good friends.

Wednesday 26 February [Halifax]

Changed my dress & got ready to drive to Halifax to call on Miss Pickford. Off at 11¼, drove the black mare . . . Sat with Miss Pickford from 11.55 to 12.35. Found her very pleasant & agreeable. She went to ask Mrs Wilcock to come in, but Mrs Wilcock was *very* busy writing & could not appear. *I think she did not choose it &, in fact, we were just as well without her. I talked very unreservedly & we seemed to suit & like each other very well. I played with scissors or anything that was on the table & seemed much at my ease. Said I generally formed my judgement of people in a minute. Was much pleased with her for saying at once she had been reading Madame Marcet's Conversations on Chemistry & Natural Philosophy when I asked if she was prepared on these subjects. Yet, on coming away, I felt as if I might have comported myself better & [am] not satisfied with myself.*

Thursday 27 February [Halifax]

Told Miss Pickford I was going about a servant to Willowfield & would walk with her as far as Savile-Hill . . . She is certainly pleasant & agreeable & seems by no means displeased with my attentions . . . After parting with her, walked forwards to speak to Mary Noble [a girl whom Anne wished to employ as a servant at Shibden Hall] . . . She looked pale & pretty & interesting. Had been rather unwell. I staid ¾ hour, telling her I would call sometimes to see her, at which she appeared much pleased. *I mused as I returned. Thought of giving her something. What should it be? Thought of making up to her. She is pretty. If it were safe to venture, fancied I might visit her occasionally &, if I could contrive to have the house clear, might manage matters* . . . Got home at 5.10. Found my father & Marian here. They had come up in high glee with the *Leeds Intelligencer*. Marian delighted to tell us ministers had taken 50 per cent off the window, horse & carriage taxes . . . Did nothing in the evening. Harriet Baxter left us this afternoon & went to live with the Prestons of Greenroyde. Elizabeth Wilkes Cordingley (our old servant) came in the evening to assist us.

Friday 28 February [Halifax]

Went with [Miss Pickford] thro' the market-place . . . We are certainly very gracious. She will be here again in the summer & will bring down her sister, Mrs Alexander, *who is very particular. Wants Miss Pickford to wear a bonnet, etc., which she therefore does sometimes when she is teased into it. She cares nothing about dress; never notices it. Speaking of her liking another tour abroad, I said I should like a tour with her. We should not tease each other about wearing bonnets. She is a regular oddity with, apparently, a good heart. Talking of quarrels, she always forgot them. She could not support the dignity of a quarrel. As to not noticing dress, etc., she*

supposes me like herself. How she is mistaken! She loves her habit &
hat. She is better informed than some ladies & a godsend of a com-
panion in my present scarcity, but I am not an admirer of learned
ladies. They are not the sweet, interesting creatures I should love. I
take hold of her arm & give her the outside & suit her humour.

Saturday 1 March [Halifax]

Set off to Halifax at 12 . . . Got to the lecture room in 20 minutes . . . Followed Miss Pickford into the room. Talked a few
minutes. She thought Lord Byron the best poet of the day.
Always got up languid from the perusal of Moore, & prefers
Milton to all other poets . . . Miss Pickford asked if I had anything particular to do. No! I had got into the habit of walking
home with her, it was an agreeable habit & I should be happy
to keep it up today. We called at 2 or 3 shops (I shook hands
with our vicar at Whitley's) . . . & I left her at Mrs Wilcock's
gate. She had told me that by pronouncing some words properly, e.g. satellites (in 4 syllables), giving plants their botanical
names, etc., she had been called ridiculous. Had made some
foolish enough to be afraid of her. I said I could bear witness to
some instances of the latter which, had I known her sooner, I
should certainly have mentioned to her. I always made a point
of considering with whom I was, whether they were literary or
not & that, according to this, I always regulated my conversation & therefore avoided, I believed, the imputation either of
pedantry or conceit. Strongly advised her pursuing the same
course. Said I had thrown off all reserve in my conversation
with her. Talked of learned ladies having no medium in their
agreeableness in general. Literature was anything but desirable
if it interfered with any of the kindred charities of domestic life.
She took my arm today. Seemed to do it naturally & never think of
offering hers. She certainly likes me & perhaps I shall soften her a
little, by & by . . . She afterwards alluded to the loss of her oldest

sister, *who had taken great care of her, who was a delightful companion & with whom she could never have been dull anywhere. She owned she was sometimes vapourish & often, in very cold weather, so rheumatic she could not stir* . . . Went into the stable for a minute or two on returning from Halifax . . . Went down to dinner at 6.20, rather later on account of continuing to have it by candle-light.

Wednesday 5 March [Halifax]

Miss Pickford & her niece, Miss Wilcock (about 9 or 10) called at 11.55 & staid till 12¾. My aunt was just setting off to walk to Halifax but came into the room for ¼ hour or 20 minutes & seemed to like Miss Pickford very well. She had very good-humouredly brought me a very nice pair of cloth (Kerseyman) gloves to drive in . . . Walked with them to Halifax . . . The air, or something, seemed to have particularly exhilarated my spirits as I walked along, & I told Miss Pickford I was in my highest spirits & rattled away as much as I ever can do. Reminded her of several little things she had said. Hinted my suspicion that few had passed thro' life without having known the force of early attachment . . . Got home at 5½. Dawdled with my aunt in the stable. Down to dinner at 6½ . . . *My aunt & I had been talking about my being not well. She fished hard. I did not tell her it was any venereal [matter] but my manner might have struck one more experienced. I ended by saying I had been unlucky & she said she believed M— was the cause of my illness. How, thought I to myself as I carelessly said, 'Oh, no,' there is many a true word spoken in joke. Mentioned going to Langton this autumn. If, after taking his medicines, mercury, this spring, I was not better, said perhaps Paris might do me good & my aunt said this should be managed if I thought so. My uncle went out for a few minutes. My aunt said we were but few of us, & spoke as if all hung, as it were, on me. Speaking of uneasiness, I said I had had more about M— than any other cause & never was so wretched in my life as in January, 1815. She thought it would have got the better [of me]. I said so did I, too, but I had got over it & things were different now. I could never feel so much again.*

Friday 7 March [Halifax]

[Walked] home with Miss Pickford . . . I wish she would care a little more about dress. At least not wear such an old-fashioned, short-waisted, fright of a brown habit with yellow metal buttons as she had on this morning. Were she twenty years younger I could not endure it at all. Walked home with her & called to speak to Mrs Wilcock about a servant. This turned out all a humour, but I saw Mrs Wilcock & she was uncommonly civil. Said she should be most happy to see me & assured me she did not say what she did not think. *The cloth laid, she a fat, dirty, vulgar, good sort of looking woman.*

Monday 10 March [Halifax]

Went to the bank to draw my ½ year's dividend but, finding they had placed it to my account, I left it so to remain there. Went to the Saltmarshes' to ask about a servant that should have come up yesterday. She does not intend to go to place again. Staid about ½ hour. *I am not satisfied with Emma. She is not as she used to be. I have long observed she [never] asks me to have a meal & never seems to wish me to prolong my visit. Is there any nonsense about Mrs Empson? 'Tis not unlikely. I shall take no notice but manage according to circumstance. I will gradually shorten & rarify my visits.*

Wednesday 12 March [Halifax]

Wrote a note to Miss Pickford . . . to say I would call about 11 to walk with her . . . and set off myself at 10.40 . . . to Mrs Wilcock's. Waited some time. *Miss Pickford had lost her pelisse.*

She put this & her gayters [sic] on in the sitting-room. I found fault with the latter, but she does not like boots. We talked about her sister . . . She spoke of Mr Wilcock as a great simpleton. I told her [her] sister's vulgarity astonished me when I called. Our conversation all in the confidential style, but it begins to strike me that were there not such a dearth of companions here I should not care much for the society of Miss Pickford. I would rather have a pretty girl to flirt with. She is clever for a lady, but her style of manner & character do not naturally suit me. She is not lovable. Flattery, well-managed, will go down with her as well as others & she is open to it on the score of mentalities. My attentions have pleased her & she is taken with me . . . We walked back all along the high road to the White Lion to wait for the Manchester mail by which the sister of Mrs Wilcock's governess was expected . . . We sauntered up & down the town . . . & then received the lady & another ½ sort of lady who appeared to be with her. Both, I think, shook hands with Miss Pickford. I had before observed it was very amiable in Miss Pickford thus to wait for the mail, saying how many there were who would have sent a servant. Miss Pickford thought I should have done as she did. I answered certainly – I <u>hoped</u> I should. I neither meant nor thought of insincerity at the moment but certainly I should have done no such thing. *I do not quite admire all this. I had before told her that tho' we had known each other but a short while, we had seen much of each other & [she] saw me as she would have seen me had she known me these seven years. She would never see me different & I hoped we should always continue equally good friends. Spoke of her coming to see me, etc. I begin to think a little of these things. I do not greatly admire Miss Pickford, nor have I ever behaved to her as if I did . . . I feel that I have jumped too soon to conclusions with Miss Pickford, but 'tis no matter. Time will set all right. She has not dignity enough for me. Till I get M— or someone else, I do believe I shall never know how to conduct myself to ladies. I am always getting into some scrape with them.*

Saturday 15 March [Halifax]

Miss Pickford called at 1.05 . . . *My aunt seems to like her & I begin to like her better than I thought . . . I rattled away to her. Said how much I would like to see Miss Threlfall. Five minutes would do. She owned I had made some good hits about [her]. Wanted to know exactly what I thought. This I would not tell for fear of being wrong, for I would not make a mistake in such a case for sixpence. Talking in such a manner that if there is anything particular between them, Miss Pickford might possibly suppose I had it in mind. Miss Pickford thought gentlemen, in general, pleasanter than ladies. I said my feelings with the one & the other were quite different. I felt it more incumbent to talk sense & felt more independent with gentlemen, but there was a peculiar tenderness in my intercourse with ladies & if I was going to take a walk, I should infinitely prefer a pleasant girl to any gentleman.*

Wednesday 19 March [Halifax]

Sat with Mrs Wilcock & Miss Pickford ¼ hour or 20 minutes . . . she goes by the mail at 7 tomorrow morning . . . Went to the baths at 12.40. Left Miss Pickford for 55 minutes while she took a hot bath, heated to 96°, in which she continued 30 minutes. She sometimes stays in 40 minutes, advised by 2 physicians for rheumatism. *She has nothing on in the bath . . . Rattled on as usual . . . in a style which, if she has much nous on the subject, might let her into my real character towards ladies, but perhaps she does not understand these things.*

Wednesday 26 March [Halifax]

Bridget Whitehead, our new housemaid, (aged 19) from Hopton, near Mirfield, came about 4½ this afternoon. Her father, a respectable-looking farmer, brought her on horseback behind him.

Thursday 27 March [Halifax]

A note from Mr Duffin [York] . . . The officers of this regiment (2nd Dragoon Guards) are to give a breakfast at the race stand with races afterwards, on the 9th, & a ball in the evening & Mr Duffin wishes me to be there in time for these gaieties . . . Stood musing over my own fire about going to York sooner than I had intended.

Sunday 30 March [Halifax]

Having gone to the new church, did not stay the sacrament either today or Friday. *I doubted whether to stay today. Felt remorse at not having fulfilled this sacrament & afterwards, in bed at night, prayed to be pardoned in this thing.*

Monday 31 March [Halifax]

Went to Haugh-end. Sat an hour with Major & Mrs Priestley . . . Mrs H. Priestley allows her woman 1½ guinea per annum for tea, therefore Mrs Priestley of White Windows[2] allows 2 guineas. At White Windows they give their menservants 2 complete suits, 2 hats, aprons, linen jackets, & the groom, a stable dress & the footman, a morning jacket extra, and 20 guineas a year, & the footman wanted more wages because he had so much to do, & because Mrs Pollard's & Mrs Wilcock's servant had more, & the Priestleys gave him more. The H.P.'s boy (they took him entirely to teach) was to have 7 guineas the 1st year & what clothes they thought he required, (he has had one complete suit) & 10 guineas the 2nd year & perhaps more clothes. The lad complains, tho' they pay for his washing, which costs them *very* nearly 3 pounds.

On Thursday 3 April 1823, Anne paid a visit to York. The main purpose of her visit was the stabling of her horse,

Hotspur, at the army barracks in York, for him to be broken in so that she could ride him.

Friday 4 April [York]

At 10.40, set off to call on the Belcombes', Charlotte Norcliffe, & to arrange with Miss Milner about a dress for the ball on Wednesday . . . Mrs Norcliffe & Charlotte Norcliffe went with me to Miss Milner & then to Day's in Ousegate & chose me a striped black gauze . . . Mr Duffin & I pursued our way to the barracks. Saw the groom & rough rider. Very good account of Hotspur . . . I mentioned my wish to ride Hotspur as soon as I could & to have a lesson or 2 from the rough rider, to which the colonel very handsomely consented. Returning from the barracks, we sauntered about in Rigg's gardens. The weeping ash not compelled to weep by artificial construct, but a different species from the common ash, & weeping naturally.

Saturday 5 April [York]

Called on Mrs Willey to ask if she would go to the stand to see the races. No! that I cannot go with her. Miss Willey laid upon the sopha having sprained her knee.

Sunday 6 April [York]

Called on Miss Yorke to ask if she was going to the stand to see the races on Wednesday. She was undetermined but would let me know. *Offered to join her at the pair of horses. Her mother, having been very unwell, I never thought of her going & it just strikes me I was so bearish as never to inquire whether she would or not, but addressed my whole question on the subject to Miss Yorke.*

Monday 7 April [York]

Called & sat some time with Mrs Gilbert Crompton to ask her if she could give me a seat to the stand on Wednesday but she

& her husband & Miss Robinson of Thorpe Green³ would fill the carriage. *Yet she would have taken Miss Willey had she been well enough to go. She mentioned Mrs Best, for me to go with her, for she had a carriage & we were both two independent people. I thanked her for mentioning [it], observing I had not thought of it, but it was unpleasant to be with a person on such bad terms with many people. Thought I to myself, 'What means your blarney? You will not try much to oblige me.'*

Tuesday 8 April [York]

Sat with Mrs Milne till 3½ . . . *Very flirting style of manner & conversation & some double entendre. Bad enough. She likes it. I feel no esteem for her & flirt & make a fool of her, & perhaps myself, too, for doing it.* I had given up all thought of going to the stand but it struck me at dinner to ask Mrs Willey for her carriage. After dinner, at 6, went to ask Mrs Willey if she would lend me her carriage. She was very civil about it. Would do it with great pleasure.

Wednesday 9 April [York]

Out at 7¾. At the Belcombes' before 8 to ask Mrs Milne to go with me in Mrs Willey's carriage to the race-stand. *Sat on the bed near half-hour, she hiding her face, shocked at having me before she was up. Did not know who it was or would not have let me in* . . . Letter from my aunt at Shibden *containing my black silk apron* . . . Ready for the stand at 1. Mrs Milne came in Mrs Copley's carriage with Miss Copley & Miss, & Miss Eliza, Belcombe. Got out here & joined me in Mrs Willey's carriage. We took up William Milne near the mount & drove to the stand. *The instant Mrs Milne got out of the carriage she had Miss Copley on one side & Eli on the other, & left me to Anne. I therefore left them all. Talked first to one, then another, but chiefly to the Cromptons & none would suppose me not of their party. I found fault with Mrs Milne for leaving me but she said Miss Copley would not let her do otherwise & I was too happy, for I do not much like being with any of them in public.* Norcliffe brought me a letter from Miss Marsh (Langton) & drove Mrs Best in his gig to the stand. *I was not more with her than I could well avoid for she is rather out. Norcliffe, Mrs Milne afterwards observed, is much gone off & looks vulgar. Not perhaps exactly vulgar but certainly not particularly gentlemanlike.* Subscribed a shilling to a lottery with Mrs Best. Lost, & lost a shilling bet to Miss Crompton, & won a shilling & lost 2 to Miss Henrietta Crompton. Altogether a very pleasant race. Got there first, before they began, but came away about an hour before they were over . . . The stand was very well & very numerously attended. I saw Mr & Mrs Empson in the room at the stand. Bowed to the latter. The former sitting at too great a distance to make it necessary for me to take any notice. She seemed sitting aloof, knowing nobody, unless she took someone with her. Parsons came to dress my hair at 7. *My dyed satin made into a slip. A striped black gauze over it, prettily trimmed round the bottom. Blond round the top. I looked very well. The chair took me at a quarter before ten.* Mr Duffin & I together all the evening. Walked about & sat at the top of the room, chiefly with some of the Cromptons. The ball numerously attended but by no means very select. Very few county people there . . . Bowed to Mrs Empson, sitting as if unknowing & unknown . . . The Cromptons (Miss Margaret) pointed out Mrs Pollard & Miss Greenwood [from Halifax] & quizzed me about having such countrywomen. Surely one had never seen such objects in a ballroom. They were the amusement of the whole room. Dancing all the night, quadrilles & waltzes. I just spoke to Mrs Pollard but was glad to be off thinking such a thing to Miss Greenwood, & passed her close several times without taking the smallest notice. She had a long, round, pink-tipped feather in her head dangling as low as her elbow, & an apron bordered round with roses. Mrs Pollard's white gown a mass of crimson sheneel [*sic*] up to the knees & the waist of gold tinsel or something so thick & shiny & metallic she was said to be in armour. Tea, coffee & ices. Supper at one. It did not do much credit to Mrs Barber of the Black Swan. No shew of plate. Neither the ball nor the supper to be compared with what was given 2 years ago by the 4th Dragoons. Mr Duffin & I just took a turn or 2 in the great room after supper & then came away & got home at 2.20. *Mr Duffin could not get a rubber. I did not think he would like my leaving him. Was, therefore, tagged to him the whole night & never found a ball more stupid. What a difference between this officers' ball & the last. How I do abominate being tied to anyone. I am beginning to be tired of being here, tho' not so much as I have often felt before. He took me up to speak to Mrs Sympson. She has a party on Monday & Mr Duffin will be there, yet she never asked me. The last time, I think it was, I was at the Belcombes', she saw me there, yet never asked me to her party tho' they were going. Is it rather odd? Nor does she ever call on me. I have neither curled tonight or last. Parsons' dressing was stiff enough.*

Friday 11 April [York]

Mr Duffin went out riding a little after 11 . . . Went to the Cromptons' to pay the 3 shilling bets I forgot to pay yesterday. *They meant to be very civil but I thought of [what] Mrs Milne said yesterday, that they were vulgar. They are not remarkably the contrary.* Miss Mary played on the harp, Miss Margaret on the piano (a duet), tolerable. Then called at the Yorkes'. They were seen to advantage. They seemed well-bred. Miss Yorke shewed some sketches, very good copies from Claude Lorraine. Mr Duffin came back. We called together at the Willeys', then went over the bridge. I paid my bill at Day's & at Miss Gledhill's.

Saturday 12 April [York]

At 10.35, Mr Duffin & I set off walking along the fields by the river towards Poppleton. Turned & went by the new walk to the barracks & got there at 12.10. Hotspur going on very well. I may ride him the latter end of next week. Spoke to the veterinary surgeon. He thinks him a very fine colt. Any dealer would be glad to give 50 guineas for him now. If he is lucky, he will be worth 200 guineas, at 6 years old, for a chariot. A dealer would match him & sell the pair for 400 guineas. Mr Woodman (the veterinary surgeon) approved my plan of letting the horse lie out from May to September, taking him from 10 to 6 during the day, & riding him 7 or 8 miles a day . . . Mr Duffin & I walked over the bridge. He called at Lady Crawford's. I ordered boots at Hornby's . . . Crossed the water & went behind the walls to Micklegate & the bar, then down behind Mrs Price's to the ferry & then returned & got home at 2¾.

Sunday 13 April [York]

Went to the Cromptons'. Met them coming to me. Miss Crompton (i.e. Elizabeth), Mary, & Henrietta. Met Miss Yorke just out of the bar. She turned back with us & we all walked to the turnpike house beyond Dring-houses. The party rather too large for me. I should have preferred a tête-à-tête with any one of them. *Henrietta talks the most. 'Tis flip, fancy & nonsense & attempt at wit. I like her the best, except Margaret, & have not determined whether to prefer Mrs Crompton or Mary. They are not very genteel – not elegant enough for me. Mary, it seems, is shy & rather afraid of me. Perhaps she likes me. She asked how many hearts I had rent. My penchant was for her on Tuesday evening. Is it talent or what that gives me a general sort of ascendancy, in spite of other opposing circumstances? For I find both the Cromptons &*

Miss Yorke *rather to wait for my paying them attention than vice-versa. I have fancied Mrs Sympson neglected me & that I was not sufficiently called upon & made much of, but I see I have probably no reason to be dissatisfied. If left at liberty, I could get on well enough.* I am to go to the Cromptons' on Tuesday morning to have a little music . . . Returned home & went the back way to see Jameson, the poor invalid woman Miss Marsh & many other ladies patronize so much . . . We all went to Trinity Church. Mr Lund did all the duty. Preached stupidly 28 minutes from some verse of Acts XXIV.

Tuesday 15 April [York]

In the evening, played 4 games at chess with Mr Duffin. Lost the 1st 3, made the last a drawn game . . . Miss Willey came just after breakfast. She was going to walk a little out of the bar . . . Perhaps she thought of my offering to walk with her. *So I would but I knew Mr Duffin would not like it & alas, I am anything but at liberty here. Surely I shall not always have to buy a little society so dearly.*

Wednesday 16 April [York]

At 12¼, went to call on the Miss Cromptons'. Miss Henrietta Crompton shewed me one of her own letters . . . from a lady giving an account of a visit to Sir Walter Scott – his partiality for dogs & cats, his 'silly little' wife, his vain admiration, loving daughter, Miss Scott; & Miss Breadalbine Maclean's letter, dated 27 February, in which she speaks of a lady, 'not 30' & single, going to see her sister, Sibbella, in a gig with only a servant. Calls it a 'daft-like project'. *I explained & laughed, for they knew it alluded to me* . . . Miss Mary Crompton played on the harp, an accompaniment to Miss Margaret on the piano. Staid luncheon (did not eat anything) . . . & then a little after 2, set off to walk with all the 4 Misses Crompton. Met Miss Willey, who walked just beyond the bar. We then walked as far as the 2nd milestone (beyond Dringhouses) & when we got back, it was just 4. *Mr Duffin scarcely seemed quite pleased. What shocking thraldom! I feel it is an abomination to me but, for the present, I must not be in York at all or take it quietly. Henrietta talks incessantly. The rest are stupidish & all are vulgarish & occasionally rather provincial, especially Miss Crompton. I told them I preferred one of them to the rest but would keep it secret which it was. They are to call for me to walk some other day. Met Mrs Milne & Anne in the bar just as we returned. They looked significantly to see me with the Cromptons.*

Thursday 17 April [York]

Went out at 12.55. *Passed Mr Christopher Rawson & Mrs Empson near the bridge but their backs were turned & I took no notice. It made me feel a little queerish but I walked quickly . . .* Went to Breary, the coachmaker, to inquire about a pony-carriage. Could not make a handsome one (such as he should like to turn out of his hands) with 4 wheels under £40. With 2 wheels, about £25 . . . *Mr Christopher Rawson, Mrs Empson & Eliza Belcombe on the other side of the street, nearly opposite the Belcombes' passage. Mrs Empson went into a shop. The others turned their backs. I took no notice. Lucky, thought I, to be near-sighted . . .* Saw, at Breary's, a new yellow travelling chaise, just finished, about £200, which Mr Christopher Rawson is to take home tomorrow.

Saturday 19 April [York]

At 11, Mr Duffin & I walked to the barracks. About an hour in the riding school. The riding master there, the 1st time we had seen him. Hotspur carried me & behaved remarkably well. The 1st time I had mounted him. The riding master gave me a lesson & will ride out with me on Monday.

Monday 21 April [York]

Miss Yorke called at 2¼ for me to walk. We went to Rigg's garden, bought geraniums, then sauntered to the white house out of the bar, & I came in just before it struck 4 . . . Came upstairs at 10½ . . . 'Tis high time to go to bed. I have been musing this hour past, & it is just one. There is one thing that I wish for. There is one thing without which my happiness in this world seems impossible. *I was not born to live alone. I must have the object with me & in loving & being loved, I could be happy.*

Thursday 24 April [York]

In the evening at 6¾, Mr Duffin & I walked to the theatre. *Kenilworth* the play, *Family Jars* the farce, bespoke by the officers (of the 2nd or Queen's Dragoon Guards). *Not luckily seated. Felt stupid & thought plays dull things – ranting nonsense & childish pageantry. The occasional music, military band, making me melancholy. Mr Duffin on my left. Miss Preston, neither young nor pretty, on my [right]* . . . Miss Henrietta Crompton changed places with Miss Preston. We talked during the rest of the play. Knew little about the farce, & agreeablized almost entirely to each other. *Talked of Esholt. She never said they should be glad to see me there & this put me a little out of love with her, but this did not appear for she thanked me for being so entertaining.*

Sunday 27 April [York]

Fixed Monday 12 May, for the horse to return, on which day he will have completed the 7th week of his being at the barracks . . . *Just before, told Mr Duffin I had fixed 12 May for going, saying then the horse would have been seven [weeks] . . . He seemed rather cross, saying, 'You would not have come but for the horse.' I answered that I certainly could not but I was glad of the excuse & what could I do? I was not quite at liberty. My uncle & aunt liked to*

have me at home & I must, at all events, oblige them. I think Mr
Duffin likes my company but he has a touchy temper & seems rather
jealous of my having made a convenience of him. However, I
thanked him for all his kindness, which I could never forget . . . &
this seemed to set him right. I believe he would like my coming over,
now & then. I must think of this, tho' I am always under restraint
here & generally sick of it & yet I get society & I will try to manage
a visit here sometimes.

Tuesday 29 April [York]

At 8.40, Mr Duffin & I went to a select party at the Cromptons'.
Walked there & back. Got home 2 or 3 minutes before 11. *No
fan. A pocket handkerchief in my hand all the evening. My long-sleeved
silk gown on. Did my hair myself therefore felt not well enough dressed
& awkward. Talked chiefly to Henrietta & Margaret Crompton.
Vexed I had not thought of sitting by & talking a little to Miss Yorke.
Came away dissatisfied with myself, with my manners altogether this
evening, saying to myself, 'This has not pleased me. Let me forget it.'*

Thursday 1 May [York]

George arrived & brought me a letter from my aunt (Shibden)
at 7. All well. Desired him to be in readiness to set off with
Hotspur on Monday week & left him to do as he liked till then.

Friday 2 May [York]

In the evening, at 7½, Mr Duffin & I walked to the Belcombes'.
A large rout party for the time of the year. 2 whist tables & a loo
table. A quadrille in the breakfast room. Mrs Milne playing on
the piano accompanied by Eli on the harp. Pleasant evening.

Monday 12 May [York]

Went out at 12½ . . . to Barber & Whitwell's, Jackson's &
Cattell's, to see for a silver tankard for Mr Dyer [the riding-master

at the barracks]. Saw Colonel Kearney in the street. He mentioned this for me to give. The tankards too high in price. Fixed upon a pair of salt-cellars, gilt inside, very handsomely chased, very handsome. Second-hand, tho' it could not be guessed, or I could not have had them for three pounds nine . . . Called at the Cromptons' about 1¾. Miss Henrietta gave me a pink & blue riband purse she made for me while she was at Thorpe Green last week. *She likes me & supposes herself my favourite & her sisters evidently allow her claim & don't interfere with it. Yet they are all rather vulgarish. I do not admire them much & I must not go too far but I begin really to think Henrietta the best. She certainly sketches well.*

Tuesday 13 May [York]

Mr Dyer called at 10.40 . . . Presented [him] with the pair of salt-cellars, for which he seemed much obliged. *He rose from the ranks. As far as himself was concerned I might safely have given him money, but being now an officer he must be made a gentleman of, & the regiment would not let him take money.*

Saturday 17 May [York]

At 12½, the Misses Mary & Henrietta Crompton called for me to walk. We went to Bacchus's garden . . . Went down Tanner Row directly to the river & crossed the Lendal Ferry. The Cromptons & I had met the Wynyards. They were to have a musical party tonight. Mrs Wynyard said she should be glad to see me, if I would condescend to go. I said I was much obliged. The Cromptons were in hope I would & wished it. *I said of course I should not go as Mrs Wynyard had not called on me. I thought to myself, I wondered at her talking of condescension . . .* After crossing the ferry, went to call on the Salmonds in the Minster Yard. Met Miss Maria Salmonds at the gate & walked back with her as far as St Martin's Lane on her way to the

Hotham's. *We walked side by side till half thro' Coney Street. I then asked if she ever took anyone's arm & she immediately took mine. She would not have offered but waited for my doing so. After all, I generally meet with a sort of deference I can scarce know what to attribute. Do they think me so clever that they shew it to me?*

Sunday 18 May [York]

Down to breakfast at 9¼. At 9¾, set off to the Minster to hear the dean preach. Overtook the Misses Mary & Henrietta Crompton. *Wished to have passed them but they called me. I had purposely gone on the other side of the street.* We all went together. Got seats just under the pulpit. The chaunting beautiful. The dean preached 25 minutes, from John XIV.25, 26. A most excellent sermon, appropriate to the day & very finely delivered. Walked home with the Cromptons. Left my prayer book at Miss Marsh's & went to the Cromptons' to wait for them, to go to see Hardman's (the druggist's) show of tulips in his garden at Bishophill. Staid there with the Cromptons some time . . . & then went over the bridge to the Belcombes' . . . & Miss Marsh & I walked home together . . . *Miss Marsh observed Anne was rather huffy to me. I rallied [her] about it. She said she acted from principle. My Micklegate friends spoilt me – puffed me up with vanity. In fact, Anne is jealous & I am not [at] all attentive to her.*

Monday 19 May [York]

Called on Mrs Willey to ask her to let me have her carriage . . . Went to offer Mrs Best a seat in the carriage. Went to her in bed. She gladly accepted. Then went to the Belcombes' to take leave of Mrs Belcombe & Anne, going to Scarbro' tomorrow . . . *Anne is certainly a little jealous. Says she knows me well enough. I never talk to her when I can get anything prettier or better. Both she & Eli seemed to think I had not been much there, tho' Eli has really been very good-humoured to me* . . . Crossed the water . . . Found Mrs

G. Crompton ½ hour dressing for the race-stand. Mrs Best, Miss Marsh & I set off at 1.40. Several ladies there. Lady Milne & her family; Mrs Wynyard & ditto ... Talked chiefly to the Misses Henrietta & Mary. Lost 2 shilling bets to each of them & one shilling in a lottery. Mr Gilbert Crompton's horse, Barefoot, (entered in Mr Watson's name) won the last race. Miss Mary Crompton asked for my profile ... Henrietta said ... *I had an odd trick of looking at people when I spoke to them, & looked her out of countenance. In fact, she is flattered by my attention & likes me. Surely, when I look round, I do not see all people pleasanter companions than myself* ... We saw the last race & got home at 5¼ ... In the evening Mr Duffin & Miss Marsh played écarté & I dozed. Fine day but no sun. Coldish on the stand.

Wednesday 21 May [York]

At 11.30, Mr Duffin & I went over the bridge to Barr, the sadler's, to look at my saddle ... Paid for my saddle at Barr's (£6 6s.) & bought 2 pairs long white French kid gloves. *Sent them ... to Mary & Henrietta because they said they forgot & would not take two shilling bets I lost on Monday* ... Got a pot of cocoa-paste & gave it to Jameson as we returned.

Thursday 22 May [Halifax]

My father met me at the inn at Halifax ... George gone to Atherton fair with the black mare ... *Musing, as I came along, about the Cromptons. William was at the inn with the cart & my father. 'What a shockingly vulgar concern,' said I to myself. My heart almost sickened. How, thought I, can I think of the Cromptons? Am I not foolish to have begun an intimacy with people so near me, within twelve miles? But yet I am glad to be at home again. I am at liberty at all events. There is no ill-twined Mr Duffin to snub & control me. Surely, in due season, I may have all things better. But God's will be done.*

Friday 23 May [Halifax]

At 3.50, it having been fair for the last hour, set off riding . . . Hotspur carried me very well, tho' I found it was time I should ride him again myself. George must have whipped him when he stumbled, from his darting forward when he stumbled, as if afraid. The saddle was so unsteady I left it in passing (as I returned) at Furniss's, to get more stuffing put into it. Got home at 5.30 (having walked from Halifax) & stood by, while George dressed Hotspur, three-quarters of an hour.

Tuesday 27 May [Halifax]

Wrote a note of inquiry after Miss Pickford, begging her to give my condolences & compliments to Mrs Wilcock on the death of her husband, who died this day week & was buried this morning.

Thursday 29 May [Halifax]

Went down to dinner at 6. My father & Marian had been here an hour. They staid tea & till a little after 8. *They are a forlorn looking pair & none of us scarce know what to say to either of them.*

Sunday 1 June [Halifax]

Note from Miss Pickford (Savile-hill, Halifax) excusing herself for not having answered mine sooner. Meant to have sent a servant over. Obliged, at last, to put it into the post office. Mrs Wilcock paricularly wishes her not to be seen at either of the Halifax churches, or at Sowerby Bridge, lest any acquaintances should call. Therefore, she is to go to Southowram. Says, 'I fear it may yet be some time ere I have the pleasure to see you, unless you ever chance to go to Southowram church. Mrs Wilcock 'better than she was last week & more composed.' Perhaps she will not like Miss Pickford's going to

Southowram church. If so, Miss Pickford had better have staid quietly at home. It would have been better to have done so, at all rates ... At 5.50, a loud rap & who should come in but Miss Pickford. She had been at Southowram church in the morning ... She staid about 10 minutes. *She certainly likes me & pays me a sort of deference. Odd enough from someone so much older than myself. Neat gros de Naples silk mourning & bonnet & she looked better, more feminine than in her habit.*

Tuesday 3 June [Halifax]

At 11, took George in the gig & drove the black mare to Lightcliffe. Very glad I went. Sat an hour with Mrs W. Priestley. Her friend, Miss Grisdale, in bed with a little cold ... *Miss Grisdale has only one hundred a year. Makes it do by living on her friends that Mrs Priestley will not send her off. It is a sort of charity to keep her & she stands on no ceremony with her.*

Wednesday 4 June [Halifax]

A ½ sheet note from Miss Pickford ... 'Did I see you upon the moor, where occasionally, by day, I breathe the fresh air, notwithstanding the respect to etiquette, I should venture to walk up & speak to you, perchance observe your horse, & comment thereon. The desire to see which, & the rider perchance might make me so informal as to breathe mountain air when I might be most likely to have a sight of you – could I guess the likeliest time for such rencontre! ...' Miss Pickford called at 7.50. Took her into the stables to see Hotspur ... *I daresay knowing me is a godsend to Miss Pickford. She can be more companionable than anyone here, but she is too masculine & if she runs after me too much, I shall tire. Her manners are singular. Sometimes she seems a little swing-about. She is all openness to me about her sister.*

Thursday 5 June [Halifax]

At 8.25, mounted Hotspur. Rode him down the calf-croft an hour. Rode in my greatcoat, the first time, instead of my habit . . . Down the old bank, up Horton St. to Crossley's, *to leave him my false curls to do up.*

Sunday 22 June [Halifax]

From 1 to 2¼, walked on the terrass [sic]. My aunt sauntered with me ½ hour, *vexed that I was so by the new roadside not being limed far enough. It would only be a few years & then I would have all as I liked. She is very good to me. Will give me more money after the rent day. I daily, more & more, see my importance at home* . . . About 5½, Mr Wiglesworth came & staid tea. He was at Ilkley the Saturday after we were – left his little granddaughter there for the benefit of her eyes. The spouting them, as they call it, with the waters had an astonishingly good effect even the 3rd day. The child is boarded with the people who rent the well & live 2 or 3 hundred yards from the church.

Tuesday 24 June [Halifax]

At 10.40, off to Halifax on Hotspur. Rode thro' the shews, etc, to the post office. George put in my letter to Isabella . . . then rode thro' the horse-fair in Harrison-lane & thence to Savile hill (Mrs Wilcock's) to call on Miss Pickford. Had the horses walked about & sat an hour with her. Presently came Mrs Wilcock to us (in the drawing-room). Then came the 2 Misses Preston of Greenroyde. I came away almost immediately after them. (Mrs Wilcock looked rather more like a gentlewoman, or less like the contrary, than I have ever seen her before. She was quiet, tho' very civil & her weeds became her) . . . Rode thro' the horse-fair again. Nothing there worth looking at.

Thursday 26 June [Halifax]

At 10½, mounted Hotspur . . . & got to Haugh-end at 11¾ . . . The Astleys expected next Thursday. I declined dining there the following day because Mrs Priestley of White Windows would be there. Promised to dine there the week following, but declined to call on Lady Astley because it was not in my power to shew her any civility at Shibden, & because my calling would oblige her to return the call, & our road was so bad, etc. I thought it best to explain the matter to Lady Astley, to make my speech & there let it rest. Mrs Priestley agreed, but I think she had thought of them coming here. She said it was a nice old place. Sir John would like to see it. Regretted they could not have much company to meet them. There was nobody to ask – engaged one way or other.

Friday 27 June [Halifax]

Went into the stable immediately. Gave Hotspur & Percy their corn, & the mare a little to keep her quiet. In ¼ hour turned them both, the 2 first, into the field & came upstairs again at 6.10. In the stable at 7. George had turned out the black mare. Ordered her to be brought up again to go in the gig after breakfast. *I had told Cordingley last night to tell him to leave the key of the corn bin with the door key. He told her he should be up as soon as I should, & he did not leave it. I told him this morning to do as he was desired another time* . . . At breakfast at 9.40. At 10½, set off with the black mare in the gig. Drove my aunt to Halifax. Set her down at Miss Ibbetson's shop & took up George (who had walked by the side) . . . then drove to the moor, ¾ hour there driving about, teaching the mare to turn to the right. On returning from the moor, drove to Lowe, the taylor's, to have George measured for a new suit of livery. Then drove to the Saltmarshes' & sent George with the gig to wait at Northgate.

Sat ¼ hour with Mrs Saltmarshe & her mother, Mrs Rawson. Mrs Saltmarshe looks well. The child (a little girl, born Thursday 12 June) a fine, large one. Hot cordial brought in coffee cups, & plum cake sugared like bride-cake, & biscuits & dry toast . . . On going to Northgate, persuaded my aunt, & my father joined us, to go & look at some of the shews. Walked past them all & went to the theatre (admittance, 2/– each) to see the panorama of the coronation of George 4, & of the Battle of Trafalgar & death of Lord Nelson. This kept us above an hour – well enough worth seeing.

Tuesday 1 July [Halifax]

Turned the horses out immediately. At 7¼, set off to walk, after having been ¼ hour in the cowhouse & about . . . Called at Lightcliffe to speak to Mrs W. Priestley about some grey cloth to cover the hall floor. Sat ¼ hour with them (during their break-fast). Mrs W. Priestley walked back with me as far as Whitehall. I turned with her, & she again with me, as far as German house . . . *Miss Grisdale wondered what we could find to talk about. I think she may possibly be a little jealous.* Got home at 10. Breakfasted at 11.

Thursday 3 July [Halifax]

Sent for Chas. Howarth to speak to him about repairing the new stables. He is to come on Monday. My errand to Northowram this morning was to desire Mrs Wood, the leech-woman, to come this evening at 6 & bring a dozen leeches to apply to my back . . . Came upstairs at 6 to prepare for the bleeding . . . In bed at 7.40. The leechwoman, Jane Rotheroe (daughter to Mrs Wood, who is from home) came upstairs immediately & put 12 leeches on my back, from the bottom to 5 or 6 inches upwards. It was 1¾ hour (9½) before the last leech was taken off & I was <u>very</u> much tired of lying so long in one position. The blood drawn by the midway leeches (one in particular on the left side) was <u>very</u> black & thick, the woman said. The blood of the topmost leeches was the best. The places bled very much after the leeches fell off, which was, from 1st to last, ½ hour, that those which had been on the shortest while, had been on 1¼ hour. After they were all off, had an oatmeal poultice (hot) applied & kept on 20 minutes. Then felt tired & weakened. Dozed myself into rather disturbed sleep about 11.

Friday 4 July [Halifax]

Bled a good deal in the night. Felt weak & languid . . . Down to breakfast at 12. Attempted a turn or 2 on the terrace but soon came in & upstairs at 1½ . . . In the evening, my father & Marian came. Would not say I had been bled. But said I was *very* sleepy &, after staying with them about 5 or 10 minutes, came up to bed at 7.50.

Saturday 5 July [Halifax]

I could not walk . . . on account [of] fridging [*sic*] the leech-bites, which itched exceedingly all the while I was downstairs, the minute I was unemployed . . . Sent for a blister today, at Suter's.

Sunday 6 July [Halifax]

The blister had doubled up this morning & had only blistered one side. Very uncomfortable. Had it unfolded, respread & put on again. Sat up to breakfast & afterwards all the day, in my dressing gown & greatcoat . . . My blister had run thro' greatcoat & everything. Very uncomfortable . . . Went to bed a little after 5. Had my blister dressed at 6. Put on my greatcoat & went down to dinner at 6½.

Monday 7 July [Halifax]

My back very sore but would have no more dressing with ointment. Sponged it well with cold water. Put a dry piece of linen next it & dressed . . . In the evening . . . *bathed my back with urine with my hand, having first sponged it with cold water, & put a little tallow on.*

Wednesday 9 July [Halifax]

In the gig to set off to Haugh-end at 11.50 . . . Mrs H. Priestley & her sister, Lady Astley, Sir John, the son & daughter & Major Priestley being all gone to call at Thorpe, I drove after them, sent George back to Haugh-end with the gig, & walked back myself with the party . . . All went into the breakfast room to luncheon. Sir John & I seemed to talk for them all. He acknowledged keeping a journal. So did I, & we promised not to note down anything against each other. Made bleeding & blistering an excuse for only taking a morning dress. Sat down to dinner at 6 instead of 5½. George waited in his new livery that came home on Saturday . . . Coffee at 8. Came away at 9¼ & got home at 10.20 . . . Sir John Astley is a large, good-tempered, good-countenanced, talkative man, rather aping humour, gentlemanly enough but nothing particular. Likes to talk of his contested election for the county of Wiltshire, and of his seat in Parliament, & of the House of Commons in general. Said he liked everybody & everything he saw here . . . laid aside all his hauteur here. He quizzed & teased his daughter a little too much about putting an oyster shell down her back & played up the word <u>sauce</u> she made use of at dinner, saying he had <u>too much of it</u> (too much of her sauce) already. We had just been talking of Paris & French cookery, & I could not help observing that, 'Sir John is *piquante*; 'tis French sauce, not English.' I think he made no attempt at wit of this sort afterwards . . . Lady Astley is quiet & by this means escapes vulgarity. She told me of my being 'so clever'. The Knight-of-the-Shireship had evidently not brought them into society in London as yet. She told me all the gents of the House of Commons knew each other quite well, but that did not at all apply to their wives. She thought it ought. Sir John was present. I talked of the caprices of society, admitting some & not others. All depends on our début – whether we happened to take with them, etc. He agreed & seemed to speak from some home-felt experience. I do not think his wife & daughter will ever shine much. Lady Astley told me that the honourable Mrs Wandsford, wife to the lieutenant-colonel commanding the Wiltshire militia (the regiment in which Sir John was captain & is still major) was a great disadvantage to them. Jealous because they could return civilities & she could not – prevented people calling on them. Said they were shy & did not wish for company. I smiled in [my] sleeve to hear Sir John tell Major Priestley he would not like to leave his regiment (the 2nd West York) even if it was called out again into action. He 'would not like to lose his rank'. Militia rank! Young Astley, Frank (Francis) aged 17, 6ft one inch, is a fine looking gentlemanly young man, far the best of the party, but Lady Astley regretted that he had been unlucky in his schools. Told me a long history about them. He had laid aside Greek & knew little of Latin, but he had a private tutor & is going to Christ Church, Oxford. Miss Astley, older than her brother, say 18, seems a good-humoured girl. Rather littlish; not thin. Neither pretty nor much like a gentlewoman. Says 'Ma'am' almost every time she answers a lady. Her face a little broke out. The Astleys were in mourning. *Perhaps* they looked the better for it . . . What a dose of the Astleys!

Thursday 10 July [Halifax]

Got home at 1.50. Found Mr & Mrs Stansfield Rawson here. Came in Mr William Rawson's gig with perpendicular wheels, looking very ill from behind.

Friday 11 July [Halifax]

Miss Pickford came at 6¾ . . . staid with us till about 9 . . . *I talked rather more nonsensically last night. She owned to growing a little romantic now & then. Surprised me by hinting that Miss Threlfall would, perhaps, be jealous of me &, altogether, it absolutely occurred to me that, if I chose it, I could even make a fool of Miss Pickford. My aunt observes she looks at me as if she was very fond of me. She certainly softens down a little with me & flatters me both in word & action in every way she can.*

Saturday 12 July [Halifax]

Could not sleep last night. Dozing, hot & disturbed . . . *a violent longing for a female companion came over me. Never remember feeling it so painfully before . . . It was absolute pain to me.*

Monday 14 July [Halifax]

Letter from Miss Marsh (Micklegate, York) . . . wants me to subscribe 5/– for a book of poems written by a young woman reduced from affluence to great poverty for whom Mr Marsh [Miss Marsh's brother] is much interested. He corrects the press . . . Called on Miss Pickford (for a dress she had lent my aunt to look at) . . . She told me the manner in which I had spoken of Miss Threlfall on Friday evening had rather bothered her. *I think, from her manner, she had something in her head about my alluding to a particular connection between [them], which she seemed to wish to contradict. I said she took my meaning too far, but I would be more careful in future. I certainly did allude to this but so covertly, I can talk it off.*

Tuesday 15 July [Halifax]

Got home about 1. Found Miss Grisdale (from Lightcliffe) here . . . [She] had had one glass of wine & I easily persuaded her to take another.

Thursday 17 July [Halifax]

At 11, set off to Halifax in the gig . . . Called at Shepherd's, the breech-maker's, in Southgate & ordered a pair of leather knee-caps to keep my knees warm when I am reading & save me the trouble of having the plaid to lay over them . . . Went into the stables. The plasterer (William Eden & his young man) had just finished putting the 1st coat of underdrawing & plaster on the stable. Went for a few minutes into the hay field. Saw the 2nd & last load of hay brought in. Came in at 6. Mr Wriglesworth drank tea here. My father & Marian came up after tea & all went away at 8½. Came upstairs at 9.05. Played the flute, by note, till 9¾.

Friday 18 July [Halifax]

½ hour in the stables, (looking after the horses, giving Hotspur oatcake) & just walked a little down the lane to see that the hay-makers were at work. At breakfast from 9½. From 10 to 11.10, sauntered with my aunt into the Allancar to see the hay-makers there, & weeded the quick-wood hedge planted in the winter. Making dye & blacking for the gig after M—'s receipt . . . *Curled my hair. Had it pinched, ready for the evening.* Note from Miss Pickford, a line or 2 to say her nephew, Sir Joseph Radcliffe, was come to Savile Hill & she could not walk with me this afternoon. Sent the servant back with my compliments, no answer required. Mean to write her a little note, relative to her question when she last drank tea here, about the funeral rites of the Scythians . . . At 5¾, down the old bank to Well-head. Got there at 6 by the church. Only the family, Mr & Mrs Waterhouse & their 3 oldest daughters. Speaking of parliamentary elections, said there was no subject on which I felt more warmly. Wished for another contested election & that we might be able to bring in 2 ministerial members. Mr Wortley [the present MP representing Halifax] was likely to have a seat with the peers. Whom should we get in his place? Lord Harwood had not a son fit for it. We did not know whom to mention, but, so far from 2 blue members, Mr Waterhouse feared we should not have one . . . Sat up talking to my uncle & aunt till 11.50, *spiriting up my uncle about the pride of the family, about Shibden, etc . . . After coming upstairs, began thinking of a contested election & a plan for bringing two blue members. Thought of writing an anonymous [letter] from Bradford (but to be directed to me here) to ask the Chancellor of the Exchequer whom we should choose if Wortley is made a peer. Began building castles about the result of my success, the notoriety it would gain me. An introduction to court. Perhaps a barony, etc. A glass of hot red wine, negus, taken with Mr W. (I never take any) heated me. I thought to myself, how slight the partition between sanity & not. The blood seemed in my head. I was not likely to sleep. I tried to compose myself by thinking [of] that Almighty Being who had created me. I had already said my prayers fervently &, on getting into bed, began repeating the Lord's Prayer aloud, again & again & for ten minutes, till the tears trickled down my face &, a little after it struck one, fell asleep.*

Saturday 19 July [Halifax]

The near front gig-spring broken. Sent George off with the gig to Halifax to get it mended . . . at Furniss's. 2/6 mending. A new one would be 10/6 or 11/6. A set of new harness, like ours, would be £10. A pair of new reins would be 10/6 . . . Went into the barn a minute or two. Rather frightened about the hay now. It smells of burning & smokes a good deal. Came upstairs at 2.55. *Put my hair in twelve curls. In getting up this morning I should have mused again of my electioneering scheme, but I was luckily too busy.*

Sunday 20 July [Halifax]

Walked 20 minutes on the terras [sic], when a slight shower sent me upstairs. I was musing on having had no letter from M——. I fear she is ill – perhaps in bed with a bilious attack, but she must know my anxiety . . . Could she not have written one line; or could not Lou have written for her? As I returned from the library on Thursday, & afterwards during dinner (the rest were in the drawing room), I was musing on the good things I had to enjoy. The independence, easy circumstances, & domestic importance, etc., & felt a feeling of happiness that the thought of M— did not break in upon to disturb. On Friday, too, while driving out & as I walked to Well-head in the evening, the same sort of happy feeling made my spirits light. Yesterday, my time was broken into. I had had no letter. I tried to chase away the thought. I dozed in the evening, for my spirit was heavy. Today I am uneasy; I disquiet myself perhaps in vain; my fancy & my thoughts are sick. M— is uppermost in my mind & she has taught me to live without her, yet not without regret. *The want of a thousand little delicate notices in her letters, of what I have written & of what she might know I have felt, often makes me fear she has not that fineness, that romantic elegance of feeling that I admire & that she scarcely understands me well enough to make me so happy as perhaps I once too fondly thought.* Perhaps I require too much. It must be an elegant mind joint with a heart distilling tenderness at every pore that can alone make me happy. But away! away! ye moody thoughts that crowd on me; for 'painful thinking wears our clay'. I shall turn for a while to Urquhart's commentaries on classical learning. O books! books! I owe you much. Ye are my spirit's oil without which, its own friction against itself would wear it out.

Tuesday 22 July [Halifax]

Letter from M— (Lawton) dated yesterday . . . *Wishes me to be circumspect* [about the nature of their relationship] . . . '*I have a feeling on the subject which no earthly power can remove &, great as the misery which it would entail upon myself might be, I would endure it all rather than the nature of our connection should be known to any human being . . .'* At 10¾, in spite of the perpetual showers . . . set off to Halifax . . . to ask Miss Pickford if she would allow me to drive her to Haugh-end. (George rode Percy.) The Priestleys & Astleys, 2 Miss Butlers, staying in the house, & Mr John Edwards, of Pye Nest, all assembled in the drawing room soon after our arrival . . . Gave Mrs H. Priestley Mr Marsh's letter [concerning the subscriptions to the poems of the young woman who had fallen on hard times] to read & she instantly & handsomely gave me her name as a subscriber to Miss King's poems. Lady Astley would have done the same but Sir John, on reading the letter, thought there was a particular etiquette to be attended to in these sort of applications. That he, as Member for the county of Wiltshire, ought to have been applied to at home (at Everley). The printed names of the sub-scribers he knew well. Knew many of the people mentioned intimately. If Mr Marsh applied to him, he would be happy to put his name down. Would be happy to do anything to oblige. I might hint this when I wrote . . . The recent but worthy baronet took some pains to assure me there was a certain eti-quette in these matters, as Member for the county, necessary to be attended to. He knew I was aware of this, etc. At this moment (5p.m.) I am <u>smiling quietly</u> at all this importance. It might be a subscription for raising a Wiltshire corps of volun-teers, or for some great concern of vital consequence to the interests of the county & its members, instead of a 5 shilling subscription to a small volume of poems, published for the ben-efit of a poor girl & her family, reduced to indigence by agricultural speculations! 'Tis but a trait, but how biograph of Sir John . . . The 2 Miss Butlers are vulgar looking girls. Miss Astley seemed much at home with them. Appearances made no *very* individual distinction between them. I suppose his con-tested election cost Sir John £70,000[4], and he has 12 or 14 thousands a year. Lady Astley said to me when I dined there, 'Sir John is of a very old family. They were barons in the time of tilts & tournaments.' Does not the present importance of the house of Everley rest less upon the manners than the money of the family? Perhaps their county is yet but young. But they are very civil to me, & little ween this ink shed of my pen.

Thursday 24 July [Halifax]

Went into the hayfield to look after the men. Just changed my dress while they went to their dinner & with them, & saunter-ing about till 6.10. Went into the Trough-of-Bolland wood to see what trees were pulled, what left to stand. My aunt walked with me to Charles Howarth to order about some jobs to be done tomorrow at the new stable. Then sauntered with my aunt along the new road & then returned to the haymakers, saw the Pearson Ing cleared. I had, in the 1st instance, helped James Smith off with some of the hay from the still smoking mow. Found it not quite so bad as I expected. Got a thorough heat-ing. The gardener having come today, begged him of my aunt & sent him into the hayfield . . . With the gardener & George, we had 15 men & boys at work. *All this ordering & work & exercise seemed to excite my manly feelings. I saw a pretty young girl go up the lane & desire rather came over me*. In the evening, at 8, my father & Marian came. Staid a little while with them & then went into the garden. Ate some cherries & strawberries & wished them all goodnight in the sitting-room. Came upstairs at 8.50.

Friday 25 July [Halifax]

In the evening, read in the European magazine for last month, an additional memoir on the life of Napoleon . . . Napoleon preferred Corneille to all dramatists. If he had lived in his time, he would have made him a prince. Madame de Staël[5] rather too tender to Napoleon. One day, to get quit of her visit, he sent to say he was not quite dressed. She replied, it mattered not, 'Genius is of no sex.'

Saturday 26 luly [Halifax]

At 10¼, went into the stables. The plasterer there (Wm. Eden) painting a darkish drab – quite a wrong colour. Did not sufficiently fill up the worm-eaten holes in the wood. Staid there painting these parts over again myself till 12.40, then called in because Miss Pickford had called . . . *She rather fought off on the subject of Miss Threlfall, then allowed, or rather, encouraged it a little, that I told her she coquetted on this subject, & she did not deny that perhaps she did do so; that my remark was not unjust. We had been talking about being whimmy. I said I believed the people here thought me so. She had heard this, & that I did not go to the Saltmarshes' so often as I used to do. I excused myself that I really had not time. I said I was more whimmy in speech & appearance than reality. We agreed there were some subjects one could not be whimmy upon. Not, for instance, in early-formed close connections. The tie was strong. Said Miss Pickford, 'I could not be so, for I know I could break [Miss] Threlfall's heart.' I took no notice of this but thought to myself, more than ever, what the connection between them must be. Miss Pickford has read the Sixth Satyr [sic] of Juvenal.*[6] *She understands these matters well enough.*

Monday 28 July [Halifax]

Called . . . at Northgate to speak to Thomas Greenwood about a black gig horse, price 50 guineas, to be bought of Illingworth of the Anchor public house. The horse to come here at 4 this afternoon. *Thomas had heard from several, Sugden, the horse breaker said he used to see George galloping & lashing the horse thro' the town & on the moor last winter & people said we must have a very bad groom at Shibden Hall. Thomas did not wish to injure any* poor man, any servant, but our horse had looked like [it] all the year. I said I should not bring his name into the business . . . My aunt & I sauntered down the lane into the hayfields. I told her the black mare had gone lame this morning . . . (George rode her yesterday to Huddersfield to see his friends at Lascelles Hall). She never went lame before. Did not hint at what I had heard but said, as I have often said before, I was dissatisfied with George as a groom & much wished my uncle would let me hire one myself & have him entirely of my own ordering, then perhaps we might have our horses as we ought to have.

Thursday 31 July [Halifax]

Took Miss Pickford into the stable. She thinks the alterations very good. At 8.40, set off to walk with her . . . *Got on to the subject of Miss Threlfall. Went on & on. Talked of the classics, the scope of her reading, etc. & what I suspected, apologizing & wrapping up my surmise very neatly till at last she owned the fact, adding, 'You may change your mind if you please,' meaning give up her acquaintance or change my opinion of her if I felt inclined to do so after the acknowledgement she had made. 'Ah,' said [I], 'That is very unlike me. I am too philosophical. We were sent on this world to be happy. I do not see why we should not make ourselves as much so as we can in our own way.' Perhaps I am more liberal or lax than she expected & she merely replied 'My way cannot be that of many other people's.' Soon after this we parted. I mused on the result of our walk, wondering she let me go so far, & still more that she should confide the secret to me so readily. I told her it would not be safe to own it to anyone else, or suffer anyone to talk to her as I had done. I think she suspects me but I fought off, perhaps successfully, declaring I was, on some subjects, quite cold-blooded, quite a frog. She denied this but I persisted in that sort of way that perhaps she believed it. I shall always pursue this plan. I would not trust her as she does me for a great deal. It will be a famous subject for us & she owns she* does not dislike it. I never met with such a woman before. I looked at her & felt oddish, but yet I did not dislike her. It was too dark to analyse each other's countenances & mine would have betrayed nothing. She will amuse me. I will treat her in her own way, that is, as I should treat a gentleman & this will suit her. She rather looks down, I think, on women in general. This is a foible I can manage well enough.

Friday 1 August [Halifax]

At 4, had the black horse, Caradoc, in the gig & drove to Skircoat Moor. Had not been there more than ¼ hour when a car-man said a lady in black had just been inquiring which way I went & she was gone down by the free-school. I followed & soon overtook Miss Pickford. Took her into the gig & made George walk . . . *Our subject, both driving & walking, was Miss Threlfall. I said I knew she could not have made the confession if she had not supposed I understood the thing thoroughly. She answered, 'No, certainly.' I dilated on my knowing it from reading & specula-tion but nothing further. She was mistaken. 'No, no,' said she, 'It is not all theory.' I told her her inference was natural enough but not correct. Asked if she had heard any reports about me. I said I had only two very particular friends. Miss Norcliffe was out of the ques-tion from her manners, habit, etc., & the other, M—, was married which, of course, contradicted the thing altogether. Asked her which of them it could be of whom the report could be circulated. At last she said it was M—. I said I knew the report & should not have cared about it had it not annoyed M—. For my own part I denied it, tho' Miss Pickford might not believe me. Yet, in fact, I had no objection to her doubting me for, had I had the inclination for such a thing, I should have pleased myself by trying &, could I have succeeded, I should have thought myself very clever & ingenious & that I must be very agreeable, but I must [say], really, Miss Pickford, it seemed, could make herself more agreeable than I could. I wished I had her* secret. I dwelt a good deal on having had no opportunity, & the frog-gishness of my blood. She told me I said a great many things she did not at all believe. Whether she credits my denial of all practical knowledge, I cannot yet make out. However, I told her I admired the conduct of her confession & liked her ten thousand times more for having told me. She was the character I had long wished to meet with, to clear up my doubts whether such a one really existed nowa-days. Said she was very agreeable. I just felt towards her as if she were a gentleman, & treated her as such. This seemed to suit very well.

Saturday 2 August [Halifax]

In the stable immediately. Stood by while George whisped Caradoc an hour, tho' he said he had dressed him an hour already. Set John to clean the gig, William to clean the knives & shoes, & George to do his plate that he might go out with me after breakfast . . . I had previously desired John to be ready to dress the horse immediately while George got ready for dinner. Stood over John while he dressed the horse for 40 minutes. Then saw him fed & the stable swept. Before I got back, I had taught Caradoc to bear the whip playing about him in all direc-tions. Walked him gently up the hills. He went very well, so much improved from yesterday I am quite sanguine about his turning out well.

Monday 4 August [Halifax]

Gave John my old, black cloth mantle with a pocket in it that I used to go to Mr Knight in from North Bridge . . . Wrote . . . 4pp. & the one p. of a ½ sheet envelope to Miss Marsh . . . Told Miss Marsh I had asked Mrs Norcliffe for a bed [during the coming music festival at York in the autumn] on hearing she, Miss Marsh, would have her brother with her &, as the Duffins' house would be full, she might wish to give ½ her bed to Miss

Maria Duffin [niece of Mr Duffin who was coming over from Ireland for the festival].

Tuesday 5 August [Halifax]

At 11, took George in the gig & set off to Haugh-end . . . All the girls at home with the addition of 'Captain' Butler, a very good sort of vulgar, quondam captain of an Indiaman. The young people did not appear till luncheon. Sir John Astley franked my letters . . . & they went in the Haugh-end letter bag in time for yesterday's post. Nothing particular in conversation . . . Sir John is evidently looked up to as an oracle by them all tho' his responses will never set the Thames on fire by their wisdom. He complimented his wife exceedingly. In fact, she is pretty enough, stylish enough, sensible enough, everything enough, for him. Speaking of the place of family, she observed she always thought the Astleys were an envied family in Wiltshire. 'My dear,' said she, 'They envy me for having got you.' It is plain enough to me from their manners, etc., that they are not exactly *comme il faut* with the Wiltshire county society. They have their house in London that Sir Jacob Astley had had & many calls were therefore made upon them by mistake. They returned some – were admitted at one house, the manners of the lady shewed they were not expected & the Astleys took their leave. A party was soon afterwards given by the family & they (the Astleys) were not asked. They do not get on in London society nor, as yet, perhaps, are they likely to do, nor will Miss Astley even after 'she has been presented' at court. Lady Astley has not worldly nous enough to keep all these things to herself . . . Staid till about 3.

Called at Saville Hill to ask Miss Pickford whether, when she called with me at Haugh-end, she meant to call on Lady Astley or not. Not . . . We then walked to Halifax . . . *Our chief conversation about Miss Threlfall . . . I said I considered her connection* with her friend a marriage of souls & something more. That if they were on a visit & their friend provided them separate rooms, it would be unnecessary & they would presently defeat this arrangement by being together. Under other circumstances it would have been a wonder that, with beauty, fortune, etc., Miss Threlfall did not marry, but now it was no wonder at all. Asked Miss Pickford if she now understood me thoroughly. She said yes. I said many would censure unqualifiedly but I did not. If it had been done from books & not from nature, the thing would have been different. Or if there had been any inconsistency, first on one side of the question, or the other, but, as it was, nature was the guide & I had nothing to say. There was no parallel between a case like this & the Sixth Satire of Juvenal. The one was artificial & inconsistent, the other was the effect of nature & always consistent with itself. 'At all events,' said I, 'you remember an early chapter of Genesis & it is infinitely better than the thing alluded to there, meaning onanism. This is surely comparatively unpardonable. There is no mutual affection to excuse it.' Miss Pickford did not say much but seemed satisfied. 'Now,' said I, 'the difference between you & me is, mine is theory, yours practice. I am taught by books, you by nature. I am very warm in friendship, perhaps few or none more so. My manners might mislead you but I don't, in reality, go beyond the utmost verge of friendship. Here my feelings stop. If they did not, you see from my whole manner & sentiments, I should not care to own it. Now do you believe me?' 'Yes,' said she, 'I do.' Alas, thought I to myself, you are at last deceived completely. My conscience almost smote me but I thought of M—. It is for her sake that I first thought of being, & that I am, so deceitful to poor Pic, who trusts me so implicitly . . . We parted mutually satisfied, I, musing on what had passed. I am now let into her secret & she forever barred from mine. Are there more Miss Pickfords in the world than I have ever before thought of?

Came into dinner a little before 7. Had ordered George to have the gig ready a little before 9 in the morning to go to

Huddersfield to speak to Ponty about coming over to plan our new road to the house, but finding my uncle against it, contrary to my expectations (I had always thought all he said against it in joke), immediately countermanded the order, quietly determining never to mention the thing again, nor to mention planting, or otherwise improving the place. I told my uncle very quietly I certainly would not tease him any more on the subject, & I shall indeed change my mind if I do. The thing absolutely did not annoy me at all. I immediately thought to myself, perhaps it is best as it is. I incur no responsibility. *Perhaps I may save my money in future instead of laying it out on the place, & leave things as they are.*

Saturday 9 August [Halifax]

At 4.50, off down the old bank to the library. Found Miss Pickford there, in spite of finding a note from her on my return home this morning to say she could not go there on account of walking with the children to Horley Green wood to botanize. Walked with them ½ way up the new bank ... *Told her how untidy the children were. She is sadly plagued with them & they are a disagreeable, vulgar set. She owned this very feelingly. I told her she did not enough keep up her dignity. Spoilt everybody about her, her sister &, as I begin to learn, Miss Threlfall too, who has some traits she knows I should not admire. She is whimmy.*

Tuesday 12 August [Halifax]

Got to Haugh-end at 12¼. After luncheon, we all walked to Mill House ... Lady Astley must surely have taken a fancy to me. She told me she talked to me as if I was a neighbour of theirs ... *In the evening, Lady Astley asked me 3 times to go to Everley. Begged I would go any time ... Sir John was joking about his having to go to Bath to buy linen or they would have no sheets ... Lady Astley ... turning to me, said, 'I assure [you] we shall always have a pair of sheets for you.'* . . . [She] mentioned the Warnefords again (Lieutenant-Colonel of the Wiltshire Militia, of Warneford House, 31 miles from Everley, which latter is 33 miles from Bath). They had only 2 daughters, the oldest 31, the youngest, 24 or 25, very large. Would have £20,000 each. Spoke highly of the oldest. *She is determined not to marry but to live like her maiden aunt Caroline; single & in good style, like hers. Would this Miss Warneford suit me? It struck me instantly & I would go to Everley if I had any chance of, seeing her there* . . . Sat down to dinner at 6. Coffee at 8. Played (& lost) a hit at backgammon with Miss Astley after dinner. She played a little to me on the piano before dinner. Poor girl! She has not much in her, like the Miss Butlers. Likes dancing at Halifax quadrilles.

Thursday 14 August [Halifax]

Letter from M— (Lawton). Proposes leaving home on Monday or Tuesday. Can go no further than Manchester the 1st day on account of some private reasons of Lou's, & must be in York the 2nd evening, & proceed immediately to Scarbro', 'for I have much health to seek & little time to do it in. For the last ten days I have been as bad as ever & very hysterical. I feel quite unequal to any exertion.' . . . Wishes me to spend the last fortnight with her at Scarbro'.[7] She is to be there a month . . . 'Meet me there' – at Halifax – 'if you can, tho' it will be but a glimpse of each other.' She would rather have had me in Micklegate . . . Wrote 2½ hurried pp. to M—. Told [her] I should make no remark upon her health save to bid her not be dispirited & that perhaps I was in better hope about it than while reading with fearful doubtfulness the wonder-working effects of blisters, etc. . . . *I cannot endure the thoughts of her being ill. My affection returns. I first thought of seeing her at Manchester.* I felt a little headache to say nothing of heartache on reading this letter.

298

Friday 15 August [Halifax]

Dined at 5. At 6.35, put Percy in the gig & drove to Lightcliffe.
Mr W. Pearson not at home. Spent a pleasant evening . . . *Very
confidential sort of conversation. Speaking of my father as if I had
never taken a meal at Northgate since he lived there – that he shone
very provincially, & my manner shewed that I thought him vulgar.
Speaking of our using a metal teapot, she said ours was the last house
where she would have expected this sort of thing. She always fancied
we had everything quite proper. I said my aunt would keep a house
of mine very differently from one of my uncle's. He was very amiable
but sometimes a little nattering & required some management. 'Ah,'
said she, 'how little one knows people.'*

Saturday 16 August [Halifax]

Called for Miss Pickford to return with me for breakfast . . . We
came upstairs into my room while they laid the cloth for breakfast . . . *When I at first said I had heard of Miss Threlfall, Pic said
she knew there had been several reports . . . but that some of them
were quite false. I asked if they affected her reception in society. She
said no . . . Pic's oldest sister did not smoke the nature of the connection . . . I always insist on its being all theory on my part & she
says she believes it & I constantly observe that my manner & conversation would mislead her if she did not know me so well, to which
she agrees. I said to her, 'I am more commonplace than you are. The
world is of one order; you of another; & I neither of them, but the
connecting link between the two.'*

On Tuesday 19 August 1823, M— set off from Lawton Hall,
to begin her journey to Scarborough. Anne was to meet her
in Halifax and join her on her journey, stay with her for one
night in York and then return to Halifax while M— went on
to Scarborough. Anne was to join her there later.

Anne's enthusiasm at the thought of meeting M— again was such that she could not contain her impatience long enough to remain in Halifax and wait for the stage-coach to bring M— and her sister Lou, and perhaps a friend of M—'s, Miss Helen Pattison, into the town. Instead, she set off to walk over the moors to meet the coach on its way from Lancashire. This impulsive decision was to have fateful consequences for the relationship between the two women. Anne's bizarre and wild appearance in the middle of nowhere, as it appeared to the more conventional M—, provoked her to respond in a way which Anne never forgave, and their love affair never really recovered from the emotional trauma into which Anne was plunged. The story is told in Anne's journal entry for Tuesday 19 August which she wrote once the party of women had reached York.

Tuesday 19 August [York]

Having swallowed a draught of water & taking 3 small biscuits to eat as I walked along, set off to Halifax hoping (our clock being ¾ too soon) to be in time for the Manchester mail, to meet M— on whatever part of the road she might be . . . I had just got out of the town when I turned back, took my coat & green bag to Furniss, the sadler's, thinking them not quite safe undirected in the Traveller's at a 2nd rate inn, & at 7.50, set off again to walk till I met the carriage. Turned down Pye Nest lane but, having got ½ way down, the possibility of their missing me made me retrace my steps to the high road. Thought perhaps the coach might overtake me [the coach from Halifax] & I might get a lift if I felt inclined. A mile on this side of Ripponden a few drizzling drops of rain made me push on, meaning to wait at the turnpike. However, tho' this threatening continued, it did not become worse & having houses (shelter) all along, I continued walking forward till I came to the 8th milestone & the turnpike 8 miles from Halifax & the same distance from Rochdale, & 4 from Littlebrough. Only one house (& that 2 miles off), the inn[8] at the top of Blackstone Edge, looking down on Littlebrough & Rochdale. The drizzling went off, the prospect cleared & I walked forward, enjoying the clear mountain air. Between the 9th & 10th milestone, passed the division stone between the counties of York & Lancaster. A dreary mountain moor-scene, the river but a small stream murmuring on my left; the lake-like reservoir of the Rochdale canal on my right. A dreary prospect. A countryman observed in passing, 'It's but a wildish place, this.' The inn soon came in view. Perhaps it is 200 yds from the 10th milestone (from Halifax).

I had just determined to go in & order a little boiled milk, was turning towards the door, when I spied the carriage winding up the hill. It was a nameless thrill that banished every thought but of M—, & every feeling but of fearful hope. It was just 11.50 as I reached the carriage, having walked about 10½ miles in 3 hours, 10 minutes, i.e. at the rate of a mile in 18 minutes to the very top of Blackstone Edge. Unconscious of any sensation but pleasure at the sight of M— who, with Lou, had been dozing, one in each corner of the carriage, the astonished, staring eyes of the man & maid behind & of the post-boys walking by the horses were lost to me &, in too hastily taking each step of the carriage & stretching over the pile of dressing-boxes, etc., that should have stopped such eager ingress, I unluckily seemed to M— to have taken 3 steps at once. I had still more unluckily exclaimed, while the petrified people were bungling about the steps, that I had walked all the way from Shibden. What with exclamation & with stride, the shock so completely wrapt round M—'s heart it left no avenue to any other feeling than joy that her friend, Miss Pattison, was not there! *She would have been astonished & M— horror-struck. Why did I say I had*

walked from Shibden? Never saw John's eyes so round with astonishment; the postboys, too; & how fast I talked! Thought to have met
me at Halifax. Why did I come so far? Why walk? Why not come in
the gig? I did talk fast. My words flew from me as tho' disdaining
to touch on utterance. I expected them an hour earlier. Must
either walk forwards or stop at an alehouse or a cottage, when
the suspense & anxiety of waiting would have been insupport-
able. The gig horse was taking diuretics. *But the poisoned arrow
had struck my heart & M—'s words of meeting welcome had fallen
like some huge iceberg on my breast.* In vain the assurance of my
talking slower when agitation had gone by. In vain the endeavour to excuse myself; to say I was neither really become
ungentle in my manners, nor at all changed since she had seen
me last. *In vain the gentle reproach that she was unused to me &
had forgotten me & that this sort of reception was, at the best unwelcome. I had only just ceased to remember what she had said to me
when we met last year at Chester & that when we met four years ago
at Manchester. The agitation of my inmost soul was met, not with
any female weakness of sympathy but with the stronger mien of
shocked astonishment; the awkwardness of the cut & curl of my hair.
M— began to excuse herself. Told Lou the fright I was at the time
alluded to & would prove it was all her affection for me that made
her so alive to my appearance. Said she was taken by surprise. In
fact, she saw she had gone too far. 'I shall take five minutes,' said
I, 'to get right again. Let me lean back & sleep a little.' I felt – yes –
unutterable things. Roused again. We sparred a little. I pretended to
laugh it off, say I was a little put out of temper. She offered to give me
five minutes to recover in. I leaned back again. I scarce knew what
my feelings were. They were in tumult. 'Shame, shame,' said I to
myself, 'to be so overcome.' I talked as well as I could. Yet it was
evident, as M— said, that <u>I was not right</u>. She said something to
me about Scarbro'. 'We will talk about it another time. Write to me
about it. I meant to have gone with you . . . but now perhaps . . .'*

'Now,' said she, 'you are going to vex me. Hold your tongue.' How little she knows me. I uttered not for a minute or two, then turned to indifferent subjects, Miss Pickford, Miss Pattison ... <u>Miss Warneford</u>, place Wiltshire, granddaughter of the late Viscount Ashbrook, aged thirty, twenty thousand pounds. Will just suit me, etc. M— began to look low. My heart relented. Paid her two or three affectionate compliments. Lou owned I had had a trial of temper. I laughed & said I was getting over it & by the time we had reached King Cross I felt myself more easily under my own control ... We were now all quite right & merry. Alas! I had not forgotten. The heart has a memory of its own, but I had ceased to appear to remember save in occasional joking allusions to '<u>the three steps</u>'. I soon found my mind had been stronger than my body. I began to feel my headache accompanied by strong bilious symptoms & before we drove down upon Kirkstall Abbey, I had lost all power of expressing what I intended, yet joked it off, laughing at the blunders I had made. Just beginning to speak better when we alighted at the White Horse, Leeds, at 3p.m. Slank away into a lodging room. ¼ hour retying my neck hand-kerchief after the heat I had had in walking. Could not change my things. In driving so quickly past the White Lion, I had left my green bag at Furniss's. It did not appear that M— had thought of looking for me but on entering the room, 'Bless me,' said she, 'where have you been? I could not tell where you were.' In fact, I had felt very unwell but of course said nothing of this & merely asked for a little dry toast & boiled milk (having had no breakfast) while M— & Lou had sandwiches & soda water. Ate 2 or 3 small bits of toast & drank 1½ basins of milk. Off from Leeds in about ¾ hour. 4 or 5 miles off began to feel very sick. M— blamed the milk. It was not that. I laughed & said it was the shock of 'the three steps'. *Ridentum dicere verum quid vetat?*[9] The truth was told with impunity. I do not think M— noticed it. A 3-fold relief to my stomach made me

303

feel considerably better when we reached Tadcaster. Here, to prevent the bustle of dining in Petergate (York), M— ordered beefsteak, a roast chicken & vegetables, all very nicely done, in about ½ hour. I ate a little bit of beefsteak & 2 large pickled cucumbers to coax it down. There being an organ & plenty of music, Lou played & accompanied me in 3 or 4 songs till a minute or two before dinner, when M— & I went upstairs . . . *Surprised to find me so unwell . . . She knew I had more discharge than she had & of my consulting Dr Simpson. It was she advised my being bled & blistered tho' she never once remembered to – forgot to – inquire whether I had followed her advice, or whether it had answered or not. She said she was sorry but the expression of her sorrow, on this occasion, was tame indeed compared with the expression of her surprise on our meetmg this morning. I proposed sleeping in Petergate. She thought I had better not. She was afraid of doing harm. I promised to put this out of the question.*

Wednesday 20 August [Halifax]

Soon began on the erotics last night. Her warmth encouraging . . . Both awoke at five in the morning & talked till seven. Asked if this was not better than my sleeping in Micklegate [at the Duffins']. Yes, but it was prudence on her part. She had a feeling she could not describe. Would make any sacrifice rather than have our connection suspected. She seemed very affectionate & fond of me. Said I was her only comfort. She should be miserable without me . . . [I said] 'This is adultery to all intents & purposes.' 'No, no,' said she. 'Oh, yes, M—. No casuistry can disguise it.' 'Not this then, but the other.' 'Well,' said I, choosing to let the thing turn her own way. 'I always considered your marriage legal prostitution. We were both wrong. You to do it & I to consent to it. And, when I think of blaming others, I always remember nothing can at all excuse us but our prior connection.' I did not pursue the subject, nor did M— seem to think much of it. The fear of discovery is strong. It rather increases, I think,

but her conscience seems seared so long as concealment is secure . . .
Told her she need not fear my conduct letting out our secret. I could
deceive anyone. Then told her how completely I had deceived Miss
Pickford & that the success of such deceit almost smote me, but I had
done it all for her, M—'s, sake. 'Why should it smite you? It is deceit
that does none any harm.' I made no reply but mused how sophistry
might reign within the breast where none suspected it. How might the
argument be stretched from one deceit to another. Mary, you have
passion like the rest but your caution cheats the world out of its scandal, & your courage is weak rather than your principal [sic] strong.
Yet, is it I who writes this? She is true to me, yes, but she has not that
magnanimity of truth that satisfies a haughty spirit like mine. She is
too tamely worldly & worldliness is her strength & weakness, her
foible & her virtue. She loves me, I do believe her, as well as she is
capable of loving, yet her marriage was worldly; her whole conduct is
worldly to the farthest verge that craven love can bear. How often has
it struck me that, years ago when once talking to Lou about this marriage & the powerful circumstances that almost compelled it, 'Well,'
said she, 'you do not know M—. She is worldly.' And the match was
worldly altogether. This did indeed strike me at the time but it never
struck me as it does at this moment (Thursday 21 August, 3.55
p.m., 1823). It now opens upon me as the key of all, that all I have
never yet been able to comprehend in her character. I have doubted
her love. I have doubted her sincerity. How often, with an almost
bursting heart, have I laid aside my papers & my musings because I
dared not pursue inconsistencies I could not unravel. I could not
deem the dial true, I would not deem it false. The time, the manner
of her marriage. To sink January, 1815, in oblivion![10] Oh, how it
broke the magic of my faith forever. How, spite of love, it burst the
spell that bound my very reason. Suppliant at her feet, I loathed
consent but loathed the asking more. I would have given the 'Yes' she
sought tho' it had rent my heart into a hundred thousand shivers. It
was enough to ask. It was a coward love that dared not brave the

storm &, in desperate despair, my proud, indignant spirit watched it sculk [sic] away. How few the higher feelings we then could have in common! The chivalry of heart was gone. Hope's brightest hues were brushed away. Yet still one melancholy point of union remained. She was unhappy. So was I. Love scorned to leave the ruin desolate; & Time & he have shaded it so sweetly, my heart still lingers in its old abiding place, thoughtless of its broken bowers, save when some sudden gust blows thro', & screeching memory is disturbed. But oh! no more. 'The heart knows its own bitterness' & it is enough. 'Je sens mon coeur, et je connais les hommes. Je ne suis fait comme aucun de ceux que j'ai vus; j'ose croire n'être fait comme aucun de ceux qui existent.'[11] *Rousseau's Confessions, volume & page, first. She loves me, tho' it is neither exactly as I wished nor as I too fondly persuaded myself ere years had taught me to weigh human nature in the balance, or unlock the loveliest of bosoms with the key of worldliness. Yes, she loves me. My own feelings shall descend to hers. They have done so, in part. How I could have adored her had she been more of that angelic being my fancy formed her. No thought, no word, no look had wandered then. Surely my every sentiment toward her had had less of earth in it than heaven.* 'How like the visions of romantic youth.' I know she might have realized them. 'Je sens mon coeur.' But no more, no more. I seem unable to return to the dry detail of a journal. . . . Went downstairs at 8½. Breakfasted . . . took leave & off from the Belcombes . . . *I never uttered all the way. Wrapt in musing. Thought of M— & the 'three steps' business. Then about my manners & appearance. Building castles about their improvement; elegance; engagingness, etc.; the good society I hope to get into.*

Thursday 21 August [Halifax]

From 11¼ to 6, writing 2½ letter-paper pp., very small & close, of rough draft of the remainder of my journal book. I only meant to have written a few lines of rough draft but thoughtlessly got into the midst of the thing & <u>could not</u>, did not like to, stop till I had done it, for if I once break the thread of my ideas I can never get on so well afterwards. *Just before breakfast I thought of M— till the tears stood in my eyes. Alas! said I, she has everything to hope from my regard & everything to fear from my reflection.* I feel better tonight. Writing my journal has composed & done me good; so it always does.

Friday 22 August [Halifax]

A letter this morning from M— . . . [She] will go to Scarbro' . . . on Saturday. Would like me to go next Wednesday week. *'I have settled with my mother to give her three guineas a week & she will find all except wine.'* Only this sum for us all, herself & me & the servants. It is little enough. M— has the following, beginning at the fifth line of her first page, relative to our meeting on Tuesday. *'You know, my Fred, I love you very dearly; too dearly for either time or circumstances to make any change & tho' the tongue may sometimes, at unawares, speak unpalatable truths, this heart never wrongs you. Do you not believe this? I was really distressed on reflection at what I had said on our first meeting, but absolutely I feel jealous for you of everyone's good opinion & I would not have you excite wonder, even in a postboy.'* 'Really distressed on reflection!' I wonder if she & Lou had any conversation on the subject. *Lou owned I had had a trial of temper . . . Perhaps she might give M— some useful hint that sharpened up reflection. It was a luckless moment for the tongue to have the mastery of the heart. (Second Kings. ten: fifteen)* – 'Was thine heart right, as mine heart was with thy heart.' Then thy heart had been king, & no subservient member has had power to rebel. It is 'at unawares' the door of thought is best thrown open; it is 'at unawares' that thoughts peep out in their own natural order, & outermost & uppermost come 1st to view. 'Jealous for you of everyone's good opinion!' Is she herself deceived? And does this web of sophistry ensnare its weaver? O world, I know thee well! Thou art a subtle creature full of thine own littleness; fawning in our prosperity, faithless in our adversity; braggart in victory, dastard in defeat! Thou pointest thy finger at the speck affection's beam would melt away; thou makest the heart turn coward to itself & shrink, at thy capricious nod, with shame from that it loves! Thou sorcerer! Thou dealer in false words! 'Jealous for you of everyone's good opinion!' Nay! <u>Speak the 'unpalatable truth'</u> out plainly. Teach her the import of her own feelings and bid her say, ashamed for you of the fear of everyone's disparagement. Mary! Your friend had other things to think of than a postboy's wonder; & is surely, in the esteem of others, neither so poor as to need, nor so niggard as to desire your jealousy of the good opinion of anyone.

Saturday 23 August [Halifax]

This '3 steps' business haunts me like a spectre. I cannot throw it off my mind; it is my 1st thought in a morning & last at night. *It teems with reflections that discomfort me. Alas, it was not a trial of temper. That I could have borne. It was one of heart. My love was plaintiff & reason mourned to give high damages that neither time, nor she that did them, can repay. 'I was really distressed.' There is a mock kindness in this that sickens me. Has she deceived herself? Perhaps she understood not her own motives. Nay, might start to hear they were the mere paltry selfishness of coward fear, & <u>shame</u> that prouder circumstances did not attend me. Fear lest such unschooled nature should betray us. Had I driven up in my own chaise & four, I might have stepped with impunity, heedless of the world's opinion or the postboy's wonder. But she is worldly, therefore she is selfish. <u>She had a feeling she could not describe</u>. She is worldly. It is the generic character of 'us poor humans'. Oh, visit it not too harshly. Excuse & pity & forgive . . .* Wrote a page to Dr Belcombe . . . to say I had sent him a brace of moorgame (killed on the 20th) by today's mail. (Mr Wriglesworth sent my uncle a leash of birds last night.) Went down to breakfast at 9.35. William, having to go a 2nd time to Halifax, sent by him my letter to Dr Belcombe (Petergate, York) to the post office, & the birds, packed in a box with a little hop under each wing, to go by the afternoon's mail . . . Came upstairs immediately. Wrote the following to Mr Radford, 188, Fleet St London. 'Sir, if you turn to your day-book of Wednesday 2nd October, 1822, you will find an anonymous entry of a lady's measure for a greatcoat. I wish you to make me a fashionable one, according to that measure, of good strong materials, sufficiently wide in the sleeves to be easy over my pelisse & not cramp my arms in driving. I understand the charge to be 5 guineas. I will pay you immediately on receiving the coat, which I particularly wish to be sent off not later than this day-week, or tomorrow-week, by one of the coaches, directed to Miss Lister, Shibden Hall, Halifax, Yorkshire . . .' Promised to meet Miss Pickford at Whitley's at 5. *Almost all the way, this morning & yesterday, & perpetually besides, talking of my uncle's being bothered; not able to save much; how poor we are & always have been; our ideas above our means. My aunt, nervous tears starting in her eyes. Who that sees me could guess all this. Alas. Who dreams that such pecuniary troubles thus beset me. How little even M— divines the difficulties that beset me. Surely time will mend with me, by & by.*

Monday 25 August [Halifax]

From 9.35 to 11, writing 2¼ widish[12] pp. to M—. So long about it because musing how to express myself. Labouring with the feeling of constraint. After all, if she knew me (but she does not), the style of my letter would be enough . . . In spite of all I have written in my journal, I have not unburdened my heart enough. I am still vapourish, still sick of thought. M— *has not the way, I see, to lull me into sweet forgetfulness. Should we be happy together? I dare not doubt it. Can I believe it?*

Thursday 26 August [Halifax]

Talked this evening to my uncle & aunt of going to Manchester to consult Mr Simmons. They both of them seem to approve & wish it. My aunt proposed my going in the gig on Thursday. *She seems as if she knew more about my complaint. Asked if she had spoken to Cordingley but she would not tell me. Fancy she may know of my linen being stained but can't make out. Never spoke before in this way of my not being well to my uncle. Said it was now two years since I began. He did not seem strange to it & says he will give me five napoleons, that is, sovereigns, to go with. My aunt thinks I must owe M— a great deal. I fight off. How little my aunt guesses the truth & that I would not be obliged to M— in money matters on any account, if I could help it, which, thank God, I have done hitherto.*

Wednesday 27 August [Halifax]

During dinner, told my aunt about my complaint, that I thought it venereal. She guessed I had got it at the Duffins'. Then at Croft. This I denied but did [not] say how or where I had got it, tho' I said I knew very well. My aunt took it all quite well. Luckily, thinks the complaint very easily taken by going to the necessary, drinking out of the same glass, etc. & it is lucky enough she does think so. I am just going to tell my uncle. I told Pic I was going to Manchester. She asked what for. I would not tell at first, but did afterwards, talking about having sprained my back in such a way that Pic might have smoked if she had been as knowing as I am. She has not read all Juvenal, perhaps only the Sixth Satyr [sic], nor Martial, nor Petronius. Said there were few classical works of this sort I had not read . . . Just before I had set off to Halifax . . . my uncle gave me five sovereigns to go to Manchester with & seemed satisfied at my going. My aunt had fancied there was some impostume forming on my back, or that I was scrophulous [sic] or some such dire concern. *Venereal had occurred to her from my manner, but she durst not name it for fear, if she was wrong, I should laugh & never let her hear the last of it.*

Thursday 28 August [Manchester]

Got into Manchester. Stopt at the Bridgwater Arms at 3.50 . . . *Mrs Lacy did, or I fancied she did, look a little surprised at my walking alone. The gig could not get to the door for a carriage & four, but she was very civil. Yet I have a very small room on the third floor, & the bar parlour.* Ordered dinner at 6. Washed & made myself comfortable. It was 4.40 before I set off to Mr Simmons, George St, having previously written a note to leave if he was not at home. It was 5.55 when I left him, that I must have been a full hour with him. A plain-appearing, plain-mannered man . . . *He talked of organic disease. I was anxious to know that the complaint did not go beyond the vagina. He hoped not. Asked if I had had many children. From the impulse of the moment I said, 'Lord bless you, no. I was never married,' but my life was of too much consequence to my family for me to hesitate to do anything likely to be of service. He then proposed an examination. I said I should not think it right to refuse to submit . . . The handling hurt me & I felt it quarter or half-hour afterwards but otherwise I did not mind it much. These things are chiefly in idea for, strictly speaking, there is no real indelicacy in submitting to a thing of this kind when so necessary.* Dinner not ready till 6.40. Then sat down to boiled salmon, mutton chops, boiled potatoes, plum tart, a pint of very tolerable port, & biscuits. Enjoyed my dinner. Came upstairs at 10¼ having paid my bill, determining to be off before breakfast at 7 in the morning.

Frtday 29 August [Halifax]

Very comfortable bed & slept well . . . Sat down to breakfast (boiled milk & hot rolls) at 8½. It just then occurred to me that the last time I was in this room (the ground-floor parlour on the left entering the Bridgewater) was with M— on the night of 9 March 1816.[13] A host of reflections crowded on me. *I felt the tears starting & my heart grow sick. 'How foolish,' said I. Then sank into the thought that my knowing her had perhaps been the ruin of my health & happiness. She has not the heart to suit me. Perhaps I should not be happy with [her], yet almost feel I should not be so without. I had almost said, 'Oh, that I had not a heart' but God be merciful to me a sinner & enable me to fix it where alone true joys are to be found. How very little M— guesses what passes within me. I do not blame her. Heaven has not given her that sweet sensibility of the soul after which my spirit panteth like the hart after the water brook, than which nothing less can satisfy a romantic, enthusiastic mind like mine. To M—, if I shewed myself more openly, I should be an enigma she could not understand. We have not much fellowship in feeling, yet am I attached to her. Alas, I see, more & more plainly, too deeply for my own happiness, were I to tell her the effect of this 'three step' business, she could not comprehend it. She would think it perhaps unforgivingness of temper rather than that wound at heart which festers unseen. It has taught me that, tho' she loves me, it is without that beautiful romance of sentiment that all my soul desires. But mine are not affections to be returned in this world. Oh, that I could turn them with virtuous enthusiasm to that Being who gave them. Oh Mary! You have enticed me with a glimpse of happiness & my heart has pursued the 'ignis fatuus'[14] till retreat is impossible or vain. But no more . . .* Got home in 3¾ hours, at 5¾, i.e. just before it struck 6 by the kitchen clock . . . Told my uncle & aunt Mr Simmons thought he could cure me but could answer for it better if I was in Manchester under his own eye for 2 or 3 weeks. My aunt wanted me to give up going to Scarbro' & York & go to Manchester immediately. This, I of course declined, saying I may perhaps be able to do without going to Manchester at all.

Saturday 30 August [Halifax]

Wrote a few lines on ½ sheet of paper (which William took to the P.O. before breakfast) to 'Mrs Cook, Straw-hat maker, Coney St. York,' to desire her to have black chip in readiness to make me a hat in a day if possible. I should be in York on Wednesday or Thursday . . . A long while in the stables & did not come in upstairs till 2¼. From then till 4½, looking out my clothes, what wanted mending, etc., for my journey to Scarbro' & York . . . Then walked down the new bank to Halifax to meet Miss Pickford at Whitley's . . . She turned back with me to go to several shops . . . Asked what Mr Simmons said. *Wished much to see his prescription. Had thought much about me. I would not shew it her or tell what he had said. She asked me with more apparent anxiety or curiosity than usual. She would understand the whole thing, I laughed & . . . Shewed her Steph's prescription of two years ago, cubebs, etc, passing it off for Mr Simmons's. She said it was an odd one. In walking home with her, laughed & talked nineteen to the dozen. Would make her tell what she thought & screwed it out by piecemeal. She said could that be Mr Simmons's, it would do no good. At last I made her own mercury was the only thing. My whole manner convinced her I was in the venereal. Said Mr Simmons wanted me to go to Manchester for a fortnight or three weeks. Could not yet tell whether, after getting better, I might have any relapse or not. Owned that was [not] his prescription. I had consulted four or five . . . She said she knew something was the matter. Whatever it was, I looked ill. She seems at home about the venereal disease. I tried to find out if she had had a touch of it. She said nothing to contradict, or yet exactly to own it. I was rattling on. Asked if she knew what lady-sick was. Said I could tell her something for which she would box my ears. She wanted me sadly to say it. I declined for the present (I meant I might sometime pretend I had gulled her, all I had said was a joke). 'Is this,' said she, 'your philosophy? Does your conscience*

313

never smite you?', perhaps alluding to my having before so strongly denied the thing. 'No,' said I, 'It does not. But I mean to amend at five & thirty & retire with credit. I shall have a good fling before then. Four years. And in the meantime shall make my avenae communes, my wild oats common. I shall domiciliate then. She laughed . . . Said one of my friends said if I had not my talent, I should be abominable. Pic thought I should not find fault with others. She had before told me of her putting on regimentals & flirting with a lady under the assumed name of Captain Cowper. It did not seem that the lady ever found it out but thought the captain the most agreeable of men. Just before we parted, 'Now,' said I, 'do you like the philosophy or the vivication? Do you think me less agreeable?' 'No,' was the answer. 'Do you think me more so?' 'Yes, I do.' She will breakfast here on Monday for I talk of going by that night's mail.

Sunday 31 August [Halifax]

We all went to church. Mr Franks preached 39 minutes. Good sermon but too long. From Luke xv. 7. 'There is joy in heaven over one sinner that repenteth,' made applicable to the occasion of collecting for the national schools – his majesty's letter desiring church collections to be made throughout the kingdom was read last Sunday.

Monday 1 September [Halifax]

I walked with Miss Pickford . . . *I had chiefly talked off the worst of what I had said on Saturday &, questioning her very closely whether she thought I ever had a friend on the same terms as Miss Threlfall, she said no, she did not think I ever had; that she seemed persuaded I never had any criminal connection with any of them. She seemed wanting to fight off this herself. Said I thought worse of her than she deserved; carried her meaning too far, but this I denied & maintained & she could not be off but said, very oddly, when I talked of a marriage of souls & hinted at bodies too, mentioning connections*

314

of *les esprits âmes et corps*, that it was all *esprit* on her side, insinuating that it was *les corps* on Miss Threlfall's part only. I looked surprised. 'Then,' said I, 'there is only one alternative. Do you know it? No, of course you did not say.' In my mind thought of her using a phallus to her friend. She was sure I thought worse of her ... Speaking of what they said of me, one lady who pretended to know me well (somehow I could not help suspecting Miss Waterhouse), 'It was melancholy that I had so little sense of religion.' Pic thought quite the contrary. Has a high opinion of me in all things. Thinks me most consistent with myself, most refined in sentiment ... 'When,' said I, 'Shall I see you again?' 'Perhaps never,' she quickly answered. Altogether the last half hour did not please me & I parted from her sensible of her abruptness, her want of gentleness or tenderness of feeling & acknowledging to myself that I wished I had not staid so long with her. Yet I stood in the old bank watching the last of her as she turned up Horton Street. Watching, I scarce knew why, as if I had not felt towards her as if I thought her so gentlemanlike as I had said. I stood watching her so long the people might stare at me. It has before struck me she likes me more than I might expect. It is very odd, but if I tried, would it be possible to make her melt at all?

Tuesday 2 September [Halifax]

My new greatcoat from Radford's (27, Piccadilly) came this morning. Merely wrapped in paper which was rubbed thro' in one place. A mercy the coat had not suffered. Bad cloth. The inside under the collar not lined. Not at all well done, tho' the cut looks fashionable enough. Only 1 real cape & 1 false one. Left the coat with Lowe to be lined with silk. Determined never to trouble Radford or any such advertising cheap person again.

On Friday 12 September, Anne joined M— and her two sisters, Louisa and Elizabeth, in Scarborough. She had not yet recovered from the psychological shock of M—'s horrified reaction to her wild appearance on the Blackstone Edge moors.

Friday 12 September [Scarborough]

Got to Scarbro' at 7. Eli received me. M— & Lou out walking. Eli & I went out to meet them just the cliff end of the street (Long Room St), *the 'three steps' business so in my mind, I seemed coolish, I daresay, & formal. Spoke very low & little. Said I was sleepy. Went upstairs at ten. M— came & talked to me.*

Saturday 13 September [Scarborough]

Did not come to breakfast till 10. Read M— some of my journal. Dawdled away the morning, talking to 1 or other, till 3 when we dined. Much too early for me, but convement to have little cooking & have the servants dine after us. In the afternoon, read aloud the first 30pp. *Glenarvon*,[15] vol. 2. Miss Goodricke called & sat a little while with us. The girls introduced me. She thanked me for the book I had brought for Miss Morritt from Miss Emily Cholmley . . . Thoroughly rainy day. None of us able to stir out at all, not choosing, like Miss Morritt, to brave the rain in a great plaid.

Sunday 14 September [Scarborough]

M— & I went out at 4 & sauntered on the sands to the Spa & beyond it till near 5. Met the girls coming to say dinner was ready. Sat down to dinner at 5. In the evening, from 6¾ to 8, M— & Lou & little Charles Milne & I sauntered along the North sands as far as Scorby Mill. Darkish when we got back. Meaning to go to bed soon, came up to my dressing room at 9.50 . . . Perhaps about 12½, every door & window in the house seemed to rattle, which disturbed us exceedingly. At 1st, we thought someone [was] breaking into the house but the continuance of the noises & the pattering of rain soon ushered in a tremendous thunder storm. Very vivid, fast-succeeding flashes of lightning enlightened the whole room. After some time came 1 or 2 tremendous peals of thunder & the heaviest rain I almost ever heard. *In the midst of all this, we drew close together, made love & had one of the most delightfully long, tender kisses we have ever had. Said she, in the midst of it, 'Oh, don't leave me yet.' This renewed & redoubled my feelings & we slept in each other's arms.*

Monday 15 September [Scarborough]

M— & I called on Miss & Miss Margaret Crompton, of Esholt, staying with their aunt Crompton (from Woodend) on the cliff. *The Cromptons very civil to me . . . observed it was very good in me to call on them first. They had seen me walk past on Sunday. I had then my cloth pelisse on & all the people stared at me. M— owned afterwards she had observed it & felt uncomfortable. This morning I wore my velvet spencer & a net frill over my cravat. I must manage my appearance & figure differently. Must get a silk pelisse, perhaps from Miss Harvey. When I have more money & a good establishment I can do better. In the meanwhile, I will not be much in M—'s way. When I can give her éclat it will be very well. At present I cannot. She owns this sort of thing makes her feel uncomfortable. Is she ever conscious that she is at all ashamed of me? I could & ought to excuse & forgive it. I do do so, but my proud spirit whispers the consolation that it shall not always be so. It excites my emulation & ambition & may the day come when, even in outward circumstances, my friendship may do some honour to those who have it. When even the Misses Morritt & Goodric of their day may think it worth their while to pay me some civility.* Eli had mentioned it & Miss Crompton laughed & asked if it was true, that I had walked to the top of Blackstone Edge. Eli & Lou called for us at the door & from the Cromptons' we sauntered round along the sands to the Lighthouse, meaning to have gone on board a revenue-cutter lying in the harbour. Fortunately, it was 2 instead of 1 o'clock. The midshipman was not there & we came away. From the look of the thing altogether, I should not have fancied going on board. There was a ball given on its deck the other night. The party was asked, by some means or other, & Eli had even hesitated to refuse! The ladies danced quadrilles . . . Sat down to dinner at 3. A note from Miss Goodricke to M— or Lou to ask '<u>one</u> or <u>two</u>' to go there in the evening. *Would not ask all because they knew they had friends with them. Miss Goodric was introduced to me on Saturday & thanked me for the book I brought them . . . They passed us, too, this morning. It is quite evident they particularly mean to avoid shewing any civility to me. Miss Fountaine of Bath told them, in 1814, that I was masculine & said what they have never forgotten. Before this, they wanted to know me but ever since, they have lost no opportunity of shewing more than once, at the expence [sics] of common civility, that they are determined not to know me. Before, & at the time M— married, we both resented this & all but cut them. Now she & they are good friends again. I make no remark. I care nothing about it. I excuse them all &, tho' the thing mortified me, I said not a word to betray this but soon acknowledged to myself that perhaps I was obliged to Miss Morritt & Miss Goodric. I am so little used to this sort of thing, perhaps it is a wholesome lesson to my vanity. I have no feeling now but the wish to live to shew myself to them in happier circumstances of society & general reputation. I should like to stand above them & have it in my power to throw them some civility from higher ground from that on which they stood. But I have some curiosity to know what they think of me. The very fault they find with me – is it in my self, my manner, or my situation in life? . . .* In the evening from about 6¾ to near 8, walked towards Oliver's Mount, then towards the Spa, & driven back from both routes by the high wind. Sauntered up & down the terrass leading up from the sands. A beautiful moonlight night. Sat down to tea at 8.

Tuesday 16 September [Scarborough]

Wrote the whole of the journals of yesterday & Sunday & so far of today, all which took me till 3½. M— having come in from walking ¼ hour before dinner (came in at 3) sat talking to me . . . I have left them to dine without me. Shall have a little cold meat at tea-time. Still very biliously inclined, but writing my journal has amused & done me good. I seemed to have opened my heart to an old friend. I can tell my journal what I can tell none else. *I am satisfied with M— yet unhappy here. I seem to have no proper dress. The people stare at me. My figure is striking. I am tired of being here. Even if I looked like other people I should soon be weary of sauntering on the sands. I dawdle away my time & have no pleasure in it . . . M—* came up to me for a few minutes before dinner . . . *We touched on the subject of my figure. The people staring so on Sunday had made her then feel quite low. I expressed my sorrow & consideration for her. She knew well enough that I had staid in the house to avoid her being seen with me. 'Yet,' said I, 'taking me altogether, would you have me changed?' 'Yes,' said she. 'To give you a feminine figure.' 'I would be contented with intellectuals & could you be contented with these, M—?' 'Yes,' said she. 'I could. It would make no difference to me.' She had just before observed that I was getting mustaches [sic] & that when she first saw this it made her sick. If I had a dark complexion it would be quite shocking. I took no further notice than to say I would do anything I could that she wished* . . . Sat down to a slice or 2 of cold boiled beef at 8. Had a glass of madeira, & then took tea with the rest. Felt much better for having fasted so long. Talked away the evening. Agreed that Lady Caroline Lambe's novel, *Glenarvon*, is very talented but a very dangerous sort of book. Long conversation on religious subjects. Eli a little Calvinistically or evangelically, or pietistically given, or whatever else it may be proper to call it.

Wednesday 17 September [Scarborough]

Talked a little after we got into bed. Told M— I would not be with her again in strange places till I had an establishment of my own & that degree of importance which would carry me thro', for that she, & she owned it, had not consequence enough to, as it were, pass me off. If she were a Lady Mary it would be very different, but I knew her feelings & excused them. I felt for, & had a great deal of consideration for her, more than she was aware. I was going to offer never to be with her again till we could be together entirely, but I stopt short, tho' not before she guessed that I meant offering to be off altogether. This seemed to affect her. I said I had stopt short, doubting whether it would be right to make such an offer, for things had perhaps gone too far. It was necessary for people to meet sometimes & I had no right to propose what might weaken the tie between us. For the intellectuals might not be enough for me. She said I did not know her feeling; the objection, the horror she had to anything unnatural. I shewed her I understood her & then observed upon my conduct & feelings being surely natural to me inasmuch as they were not taught, not fictitious, but instinctive. Said from my heart, I could make any sacrifice for her, tho' she could not for me. I could have braved anything. Yes, I have often felt I could have rushed on ruin. She said it was lucky for us both her feelings were cooler. They tempered mine. I said this was not necessary. I had met with those who could feel in unison with me . . . My feelings now began to overpower me. I thought of the devotion with which I had loved her, & of all I had suffered. I contrasted these with all the little deceits she has put upon me & with those cooler feelings with which she thought it so lucky to have tempered mine. I thought of these things & my heart was almost agonized to bursting. The tears ran down my cheeks. I stifled my sobs but at last my agitation could not be concealed. M— bade me not try to hide it & it must have been about half past four before I could at all compose myself & drop to sleep quite exhausted.

My head much swollen in the morning, yet I got up & cold water made me decent enough to appear at breakfast. M— cried a little last night & several times asked, 'Can I say nothing to console you?' 'No, my love,' said I, 'nothing human can just now or I am sure you could.' It was with great difficulty I could contain myself all the morning . . . I have been twice to the place with a bowel complaint & feel far from well. Surely both Lou & Eli must wonder what is the matter. Lou must have thought me in bad spirits yesterday, much more than today. M— has been sitting with me this last half-hour. I have been telling her she is not to blame. She could not make the sacrifice for me I could for her but I do not, ought not, to blame her for this. It is her nature & perhaps a wise dispensation of providence for us both. I have mentioned that Miss Morritt & Miss Goodricke's conduct is so pointed they must have some especial reason for it. It cannot be merely my relative situation in life or my manners or my appearance. There must be something affecting character more than we know of. Explained that their civility was of no importance to me but such a pointed way of appearing to shew that they did not think me fit society for them would be striking from any persons. Said I only cared on M—'s account. Said more on the subject of acquiring more importance & then I could do with impunity what I could not do now. The day might come when I should be very differently off & then whatever éclat I had, I should be glad to shed it on M—. This did move her. She just said, 'Fred, I do not deserve you,' & burst into tears. She was rather convulsed, apparently unable to listen to me. I therefore sat by her in silence. She said she too had a bowel complaint. Had been gone into the garden half-hour ago & I have not seen her since. Lou has been here. Is just going out walking & I have desired her to take M— with her. I shall go & inquire after her. 'Tis now just 5½ . . . M— did not go out. I found her crying in her own room. Staid a little, then left her for an hour to compose herself. Then we had a long conversation. She said I had done her good & seemed sensible of the truth of my remarks. She thought I should be *happier without her. She was always giving me pain. I could do better without her than she without me. I behaved affectionately. She said she would have more energy of character. She would suit me better, for she loved me with all her heart & as well as she was capable of loving. I said this business might make us understand each other better & do us both good. We were mutually affectionate & kind & I hope we shall go on well together in future.* The girls came home to tea. Cheerful chit-chat in the evening.

On Sunday 21 September, the company left Scarborough. Anne went to stay with the Norcliffes at Langton until 17 October and then joined M— at York until 22 October, when she returned to Shibden, taking M— with her. M— returned to Lawton Hall on 1 November.

Whilst at Malton and York, they attended the Music Festival (which ran for three days and evenings in York Minster), the theatre and went to a ball. M— went to stay at Langton for a couple of days in October.

Anne, while content enough to have M—'s company for this long period of time, still continued to analyse the events of the summer and autumn and found it hard to reconcile herself to M—'s evident feeling of shame at being seen in public with her. However loving they were when they were alone together, Anne recognised that something irreplaceable had gone from the relationship and it would never be the same again. Anne was now thirty-two years old. She considered herself no longer young, and, in addition, had suffered some severe psychological shocks due to M—'s behaviour and the dawning realisation that people such as the Miss Morritts and Miss Goodrickes of this world studiously avoided being seen in her company because of her 'masculinity'. Anne's youthful exuberance and romanticism were slowly giving way to a rather cynical worldliness. The ownership of property, travel, social aspiration, and her desire for a life-partner who would enhance her own status – all became desirable goals. Some of these ambitions were achieved in her lifetime; others were to bring her further humiliations as the years unfolded.

Sunday 21 September [Langton]

All off from Scarbro', Watson & I on the barouche box behind, at 11.55 . . . I got out at Malton at 3.20. Mrs Norcliffe had sent John Coates to meet me & he drove me in the gig to Langton. *Mrs Norcliffe very glad to see me.*

Monday 22 September [Langton]

Down to breakfast at 10. Slept in Isabella's room last night. Most comfortable. At 11¾, Mrs Norcliffe & Burnett & I off in the carriage to York . . . Miss Marsh here to meet us. All went out immediately about tickets for the ball on Wednesday. Then went to see the balloon ascend from behind the house of correction. Mr Sadler was to have ascended at 4 but the day was very unfavourable, rainy & windy. The silk burst once or twice & it was 5 before he was off. He then struck against the walls & we all thought he had been kicked out. However, he got clear off &, we have heard tonight, landed at Selby & came here immediately in a chaise. It was said Captain Basil Hall R.N. had given a hundred pounds to ascend with him but I think he changed his mind, seeing the state of things so adverse. Mrs Norcliffe & Charlotte & I contrived to stand in the tread-mill & were thus sheltered from the rain. Got home to dinner at 5½ & sat down to dinner at 6. Charlotte Norcliffe & I walked back. Mrs Norcliffe had a chair from Miss Marsh's. At 7, Isabella & I went to the theatre to see MacReady in *Virginius*. A very full house. MacReady's act <u>very</u> fine. I sat between M— & Isabella. Lou behind us . . . Came up to bed at 11½. Put by all my things. Wrote the journal of Friday, Saturday & yesterday. Found a letter this morning waiting for me from my aunt (Shibden), to say she had sent 2 brace of moorgame which we ought to receive tomorrow morning.

Tuesday 23 September [York]

At 10¼, Isabella & Charlotte & I were seated in the nave of the Minster about midway between the 2nd & 3rd pillar from the orchestra. We had 1¾ hour to wait but had we been later we could not have got good seats. The Minster very full . . . 400 performers formed an excellent orchestra, the stands so arranged as to make the whole thing have a very fine effect opposite the gallery. Madame Catalani seemed tired & not well & her singing, tho' wonderful, did not quite equal my expectations. Mrs Salmon sang most beautifully. Surely she is one of the best singers of Handel's music. Pickpockets in the gallery. Dr Blonberg told us this evening at the concert it was true he had had his pocket picked in the gallery of £20. It is said 2 or 3 suspicious people have been taken up. Came away from the Minster just before the performance was over. Dashed thro' the people & the rain & . . . got home at 4.35 & immediately sat down to Parsons to have my hair dressed. Then dined & dressed & the whole 7 of us went to the concert at 7.05, only just in time to get seats on the 3rd & 4th benches from the orchestra. Madam Catalani sang beautifully, particularly 'Rule, Britannia!' at the end. Beautiful violoncello solo from Lindley, & beautiful solo from Nicholson of Liverpool on the flute, <u>wonderfully</u> well played. A sad rowe [sic] about chairs. Mrs Norcliffe & I, after standing on the wet flags of the portico a considerable time, came home in 1 chair & the rest of our party followed as they could in chairs, very fortunate to have got them at all so soon.

Wednesday 24 September [York]

M— came & breakfasted with us. She did not go to the Minster today. Isabella, Charlotte, the 3 Daltons & I went at 10, just before the doors were opened. A desperate crowd. Pushed thro' with difficulty & by dint of perseverance & management, got into the nave, the 5th bench from the orchestra . . . Our seats were excellent – much better than yesterday. The music & singing capital. The *Messiah*. Madame Catalani sang 'I know that my Redeemer liveth' better than 'Comfort ye'. Mrs Salmon sang perfectly well. Never in better voice. The 'Hallelujah Chorus' transcendentally fine. Cramer, the leader, says there will never be such a thing again during the life of this genera-tion. The Minster cannot be had again during the present dean's lifetime. About 5,000 people in the Minster. Called for ¼ hour *en passant* at the Belcombes'. Parsons dressed my hair today as yesterday, before dinner. M— dined with us. I persuaded her to go with Mrs Norcliffe, Marianne & Esther Dalton, to the ball instead of the play. After dinner, dressed & wrote 3pp. & an end to my aunt, acknowledgement of the birds & account of the festival. Got to the rooms at 10¾. Found them full. A great squeeze to get in. Paced up & down & got home at 1.20. The Marchioness of Londonderry a blaze of diamonds – most beau-tiful large bouquet of diamonds. The Marquis, too, wore his star. A splendid ball & a very pleasant one. 16,000 [1600?] people in the room. Had a little red wine & water & came upstairs at 1¾. Wrote the above of today & had just done at 2.25. Lord Grantham is said to have offered twenty guineas this morning for a gallery ticket & could not get one. Five guineas offered in vain for a centre, or even side aisle, ticket.

Thursday 25 September [York]

Anne Belcombe called about tickets for the Minster at 8.20. Went out with her & got them. Only just in time for gallery tickets . . . M— got her own breakfast & then came to make us ours. She & I set off to the Minster at 9¾. The rest soon fol-lowed, & after a tremendous crowding & pushing, we all got

well in, 7 from here [the Norcliffes' house in Petergate, York] &
7 from the Belcombes', partly on the 1st, 2nd & 3rd benches
from the orchestra. We fancied ourselves rather too near, but
perhaps we were not. Catalani sang with rather more spirit this
morning & much better. Mrs Salmon excellent as before. Miss
Travis, Mrs Salmon & Catalani were each encored this morning at the desire of the archbishop. No! It was the dean who
hoisted the white handkerchief signal of encore! This made us
late, & tho' we came away just before it was over, it was 4.55
when Mrs Norcliffe & I got home. At 7, we all went to the concert. Every seat full. By dint of management we had 2 benches
brought & put before all the others that we were quite close to
the orchestra. The encoring made us late home tonight. Mrs
Norcliffe & Charlotte & Marianne returned in chairs. We would
not wait & ran off home. A more crowded room than last night
& capital music. Got home at 12.20.

Friday 26 September [York]

Out at 8¾ & went to the Belcombes' to ask them to invite
Catalani for Sunday, as she is to dine with them one day . . .
Came home to breakfast at 9.35. It was ten before we set off
to the Minster. A great crowd in getting in but not so bad as
Wednesday. Too late & obliged to sit on a side bench
between the 2nd & 3rd pillars from the orchestra . . . The
Minster seemed very full, but could not be so full as on
Wednesday because several tickets were unsold . . . Catalani
sang Luther's hymn, which was encored & Miss Stevens sang
'Pious Orgies' instead of the song printed, & was encored.
Mrs Salmon sang 'Let the Bright Seraphim' <u>perfectly</u> well.
She had determined to sing well at this festival. She walks
before breakfast. She & Mr Sapio were on the walls this
morning at 7. She drinks hard they say & is kept by the
editor of *The Times* . . . Did not get home to dine till 6. Found

Isabella gone to dine at the Belcombes'. All the rest but I went to the play at 7½.

Sunday 28 September [York]

Out at 8¼ & went to the Belcombes'. Sat by M—'s bedside till 9¼, then went home, breakfasted & went with Mrs Norcliffe to the Minster at 9¾ ... At 1, went over the bridge. Intended crossing the water but found no boat ... It was 3 before I met Mrs Norcliffe at Mrs Best's ... Mrs Norcliffe soon left me at Mrs Best's & I staid by her bedside (she was unwell – knocked up with the gaieties) till 4 ... Dined at 4 & at 4.50 went to take leave of the Belcombes. Madame Catalani went to dine there at 5 instead of 6, & nobody being ready, I staid & had a little tête-à-tête with her till Mrs Belcombe came & then M— & Mrs Milne. Madame Catalani is certainly a very handsome, elegantly mannered & fascinating woman. I stammered on in French very tolerably. Saw M— merely for a moment. *Somehow I relapse too often into a feeling of imperfect satisfaction with her ... she wants tenderness in her manner towards me. She is too commonplace. Her sensibility seems rather weakness of nerve than the strength of affection. She thinks a good deal of her appearance & dress & has not had time to think much of taking care of mine yet. She is subject to a feeling of shame about me, such as at Scarbro'. I fancy she would sometimes rather be without me. She too much makes me feel the necessity of cutting a good figure in society & that, if I was in the background, she would not be the one to help me forward. She is not exactly the woman of all hours for me. She suits me best at night. In bed she is excellent.*

Monday 6 October [Langton]

From 3½ to 4.50, walked with Charlotte Norcliffe to the wold. *Confidential, cordial sort of conversation, altogether gently flattering to her. Mention my wanting a new friend as a constant companion*

& to keep house for me, sit at the head of my table, etc. Just before tea . . . read from p. 126 to 168, *Collections & Recollections*. The last article a pretty well done account of Lady Eleanor Butler & Miss Ponsonby. Near ½ hour's tête-à-tête with Charlotte Norcliffe. *Talk of wanting a new friend . . . If M— & Tib were together, I would shew the latter the precedence in my attentions. Would not say which I liked best. Declared they never did, or ever could, interfere with each other. Both kept their own places.*

Sunday 12 October [Langton]

Mrs Norcliffe & I went to church at 10.40. The girls followed. Mr Simpson preached ½ hour . . . Dullish sermon. We all staid the sacrament . . . From 3 to 4½, Charlotte Norcliffe & I walked on the wold & took a turn in the garden. In the evening, in 38 minutes, read aloud sermon 3, Dr Young, on the predestination of St Paul, which is proved to be very different from that of Calvin.

Monday 13 October [Langton]

Down to breakfast at 10¼. Mrs Norcliffe having had a letter from M— this morning to propose her coming here tomorrow . . . I concluded Mr Charles Lawton fixed not to go to Scarbro'. Wrote 3pp. to my aunt (Shibden) to thank her for my letter . . . & say I hoped to be able to fix the day for my return after I had seen M— here. Sent off this letter to my aunt by John, who went to Malton at 1 to order post horses . . . From 3¾ to 4.20, walked to the wold, round the race-stand & back. After dinner, borrowed the butler's (Mr Hill's) flute and played on it a little. Played also, on the piano, his copy of Knapton's arrangement of church psalms.

Tuesday 14 October [Langton]

Isabella went to bed at 9 this evening feeling unwell with difficulty of breathing. John Coates shaved her head this morning with the view of making her hair grow black & thick. Perhaps the pressure of her wig, being uncomfortable at first, might give her a little headache. In the evening . . . playing a little on Hill's flute & psalm tunes on the piano . . . Very fine day yet did not stir out. I must have less bed & more exercise when I return home.

Wednesday 15 October [Langton]

At 4, went to dress for dinner. At 5¼, Mrs Norcliffe & Charlotte Norcliffe & M— & Lou arrived from York, *& Watson & John, M—'s servants. I felt oddish when they came & did not go downstairs quite immediately. This Blackstone Edge & Scarbro' business so clings to my memory I can't shake it off. They must have all thought my manners coldish.* After dinner, played 4 hits at backgammon with M—, of which she won 3 . . . I came up to bed at 11. The rest followed in about ¼ hour. *M— came to my room & we managed to have a little tête-à-tête. Hurt at my manners. Afraid I shall never forget Blackstone Edge, etc. . . . In fact, I felt low & unhappy & could have cried, with pleasure, all the evening. I told M— I was put out of sorts a little but bade her not mind. She said she could not help it. I saw she was getting unhappy. This melted me. I promised to return with her* [to York and then eventually to Shibden] *& we both got a little better. I believe she loves me but oh, I agreed with her when she said she would give anything to efface the last three months. Alas, they have altered me. How they have revolutionized my feelings of love & confidence towards her.*

Thursday 16 October [Langton]

At 12.20, I slank off to my room & wrote the whole of the journal of yesterday, a rainy morning keeping us all in the house. *M— is evidently wishing to bring me round & is more attentive to me than I to her. For the life of me I cannot forget &, what is worse, I cannot cease to remember. Told M— honestly I could get over the*

Blackstone Edge business. It was the Scarbro' concern that was the worst, the being ashamed of my figure, etc. If she was in London & I there too, or in any strange place, I felt that I should get out of her way as far as possible. 'Never mind,' said I, 'I shall get right by & by.' 'But not, I fear,' she said, 'while I am with you & then I shall not know that you are right & I shall fret.' She has just been to beg I will go downstairs or she shall be low too. She cannot talk without me so I must go . . . In the evening, played backgammon with Mrs Norcliffe. Won a game & lost 2 hits. All went upstairs at 11.20 & came into my room where we all sat telling stories & being very merry till about one.

Friday 17 October [York]

From 11¾ to 12¾ packed all my things. Took leave of the Norcliffes & M— & Lou & I off at 1.50. M— & I got out to see the church. About 10 minutes looking at the new painted window given by the Norcliffes. Arrived at Petergate at 4.50.

Sunday 19 October [York]

At 12.40, M— & I came upstairs, she to settle her accounts & I to write my journal . . . *Began talking of one sort of thing or other . . . She said I had mistaken [her] speech at Scarbro', but she would not undeceive me, for it was a subject on which a sort of pride had all along made her wish to conceal her feelings, even from me. She had shrunk from me knowing that she had so much passion in her composition. She had meant that if I had a feminine figure she should be satisfied with intellectuals, that is, she should think I had enough of these, but insinuated she did not intend to say she should wish for nothing more. I think it would have been impossible for me to guess this from her speech & manner at the time, but I did not press the point but congratulated her on having casually discovered what made me feel much better satisfied than before; what reconciled me more than anything else could to the Blackstone Edge & Scarbro' business*

& would, I hoped, make us much happier in the future. She persuaded me I had often done her injustice; often thought her careless of me & cold & worldly, when she was neither one nor the other. We talked on & were very affectionate & mutually satisfied with each other. She could do anything for me. Share poverty with me, or live together in a coal-hole.

Monday 20 October [York]

At 10.40, went out with M—, first to Barnett's in College Street to have M— taught by him to paint on glass & burn in the colours. 1 hour & 35 minutes there. Saw the whole process of laying on the colours & burning them in, as well as could be done, by laying the glass on a plate of iron in the fire. It would have taken too much time to regularly heat & use the man's furnace. M— must have an enamelling furnace. May get a small one from the potteries. All the colours used are metallic. Those used as paints are mixed up with fat turpentine; those used as stains, with water, which, being driven off by the fire, leaves the colouring powder, having imparted its stain, to be rubbed off by the finger. Red is the only stain that requires being laid on both sides of the glass. Green is made by burning in blue paint on the one side & then burning in the yellow stain on the other. All the colours are mixed up with a flux of glass; & the moment these colours flux, that is, assume a shining appearance on the glass, it is time to gradually cool down the heat of the furnace. Manganese forms black, silver, pink or orange, according to the heat employed; gold forms purple, etc. The colours that require least heat should be put on last. Orange requires least heat of all. Each colour should be burned in separately, so that 1 piece of glass should have as many burnings as there are different colours employed. The glass that is coloured *en masse*, that is, that has the colour ground down & fused with it *ab origine* in the furnace, is called potglass, from the circumstance of its being all melted down together in the same pot or crucible. Left Mr Barnett at 1.20 & went about shopping with M— for about ½ hour.

Wednesday 22 October [Halifax]

Had my hair cut. Parsons came at 8.35 & kept me till after 9. Hurried breakfast & off at 9½. *In high favour at Petergate. Asked when I would go again. If I could not have a whole bed, I should have half or, if not that, a third with Dr & Mrs Belcombe . . .* M— impatient to be off. She & I drove from the door at 12 & got to the White Horse Inn, Leeds, in 2½ hours. Changed horses at the Sun Inn, Bradford & the Union Cross, Halifax & got to Shibden at 6. My uncle & aunt quite well & very glad to see us.

M— stayed at Shibden until Saturday 1 November. Most of the time was taken up with discussion and letters to and from Dr Belcombe on ways and means of getting C— to insure his life in M—'s favour in order to give her a little security should she be left widowed. In the absence of M— producing an heir, which seemed increasingly unlikely as time went on, the Lawton estate devolved upon C—'s family alone and M— would have no claim whatsoever unless C— provided an annuity for her. C— appeared not at all willing to make this provision for M— and, as she had relinquished her claim to any of the Belcombe estate in favour of her unmarried sisters, her future prospects looked bleak indeed. She began to make tentative arrangements to insure Anne's life in her favour as an additional safeguard.

Saturday 25 October [Halifax]

At 11½ (down to breakfast at 10.05) M— & I off in the gig . . . & called at Pye Nest & sat with Mrs Edwards 20 minutes. She had us upstairs in her room, being brought to bed three weeks of her 10th child, to be called Harriet. They have eight now living. In returning, meant to have taken a drive round the moor but, having the hounds, we soon retraced our steps to the turnpike & high rd & got home a few minutes past one. M— & I tête-à-tête in the drawing-[room] almost all the time. Brought down Dr Ash's little book, *Institute of English Grammar*, trying to give M— some instruction & lent her the book . . . Dinner at 4. Tea at 7.50. Afterwards, my aunt & I lost a bumper to M— & my uncle, & then won a rubber of 3 points of them.

Tuesday 28 October [Halifax]

Sat up talking over M—'s affairs; C—'s insuring his life, etc. *She at last proposed insuring my life at twenty pounds a year for eight hundred at my death. This seemed to satisfy her as providing for the only contingency that can leave her destitute. She is, she says, sure of a home if I live, but life is uncertain & she would provide against my death. We got ourselves into a grave humour, unfit for a kiss.*

Thursday 30 October [Halifax]

M— had a kind letter from C— to say he would meet her at Manchester on Saturday . . . M— had just finished her 2 letters, one to C— & one to her father & we set off to walk to Halifax to put them into the post office at 2¼. Met the mail in Northgate. Gave the guard the letter to Dr Belcombe & a shilling to see it delivered to Dr Belcombe tonight, which he promised . . . Went to several shops for M— to buy gowns as presents to her servants . . . Got home at 4.10. Sat down to dinner at 4¼ & dressed afterwards . . . Wrote the journal of yesterday & so far of today & went down to tea at 7¾ . . . M— seemed to have got a little cold & had some warm wine & water just before getting into bed.

Saturday 1 November [Halifax]

M— off from here at 10.40. We stopt at the Cross to put on an additional pair of horses. I went with her tête-à-tête in the carriage about ½ mile beyond Ripponden (nearly 7 miles from Halifax) then left her at 12.10 & walked back to the library in 2 hours. Staid there about 2 hours . . . Got home about 4½. Staid talking to my uncle & aunt till 5½, then went into my [room]. My heart died within me as I entered it. *Oh, that we were together.* I mused, I scarce know what, after leaving her this morning, & went to the library *pour passer le temps*, & delay my return to the place she had left.

Sunday 2 November [Halifax]

Down to breakfast at 9¾. We all went to church. Mr Knight preached 33 minutes . . . The church was heated the first time this season. I must give up going & go to the new church again. George brought back a basket of game from Langton – a brace of partridges & a wild duck; my boots from Rutter's & a letter from Isabella Norcliffe 3pp. Poor soul! She has 'been very unwell for the last few days' & seeming rather alarmed & low about herself. *'I have been unwell since last Friday & it has turned to the fluor albus* [i.e. leucorrhoea or 'the whites'] *& most violent. Cobb was sent for & he says it is owing to relaxation & says I must sleep in a room without a fire & take regular but moderate exercise. It has made me feel very weak but certainly better today & I trust in God will soon go off.'* All this has struck me like a thunderbolt. My heart sank within me as I thought of the injury I was so unsuspected of having done her. I am not to name the thing to anyone. She would not like it to be known. Remorse struck me deeply. Oh, M—, M—. What have you done? Surely, said I, I am more sorry for poor Isabella than you were for me. Sat down to write to Isabella . . . Tried to cheer her up & inspirit her. Wrote affectionately. Gave my uncle & aunt's love & that we should all be delighted to see her here in January. *The complaint was not at all considered a dangerous one. If it roused her into a better system of management it might prolong, instead of shorten, her life.*

What strange beings we are! I felt relieved by writing & even smiled at the thing. But oh! It is, or was, a bitter smile. I have promised to tell no one. I will not tell M——. It could do no good & might make her uneasy. She might dread its leading to some discovery. It is a sad business & poor Tib little knows the trouble & tediousness of it. We may none of us get better for years. M—— now seems satisfied that it must wear itself out. This proves that whites are surely more infectious than may be generally known.

For the remainder of 1823, Anne's life was uneventful. She spent her time riding and attending to her horses, Caradoc and Hotspur. She resumed her studies, of Greek mainly, and continued with her usual programme of intellectual pursuits. She went to church, undertook a little social visiting, attended to one or two alterations on the Shibden estate, and advised her father and Marian on their financial affairs. Her correspondence with M——, Isabella, and one or two other friends, took up a great deal of her time.

Saturday 8 November [Halifax]

In the stable 20 minutes … At 10½ (in spite of the damp & small rain) off on Hotspur to Halifax … Called at Lowe, the tailor's. (He punched buckle holes in a pair of new garters) and at Furniss's. Got the bridle, all new but the steel bits … Got home at 12.35. Gave Hotspur beer & oatmeal & water.

Sunday 9 November [Halifax]

From about 2¼ to 4¼, wrote 3pp. & the ends, very small & close, & under the seal, to Mrs Norcliffe in answer to her letter … Not able to tell any news except the following Mrs Veitch told us on Saturday night. Speaking of Mr Henry Slingsby, 'He would not take his wife's fortune (it was very small) but, desiring it to be divided among her sisters, settled three thousand a year on her, & begged that from that time, one of those, her sisters, would consider his house her home & live with them always, and require nothing from her family. This offer was wisely accepted (I find the Atkinsons did not leave Manchester with much spice of Manchesterian riches) and Mrs Atkinson, the mother, was almost beside herself, they say, for joy at so great a match for one daughter & so good a home for another, where who knows what matrimonial prize-ticket may turn up. As to your friend, Sir William Ingleby, I am told by a lady who saw him in this costume & absolutely took fright at it, that this eccentric baronet walks about Ripley & Ripon too, in his dressing-gown, without smalls or neckcloth on. The absence of the former was luckily disguised by the wrap of the gown, & is alleged on hearsay; but the naked throat, shirt-collar displayed à la milord Byron, had a striking effect, & produced the scarecrow impression alluded to above. Milady, in a pink-striped gingham, rode one white punch-pony on the sands at Scarbro' & Sir William another.'

Friday 14 November [Halifax]

At 10½, off in the gig . . . Stopt a moment at the door to inquire after the Saltmarshes; took up a tremendously large parcel at Northgate, (drugget, or rather grey drab milled cloth to cover the hall floor). Got home at 1. Gave the horses oatmeal & beer . . . At four, read the letter I had this morning from Mrs Norcliffe (Langton) . . . very kind letter. 'What do you say of Captain Parry's match being broken off? The true reason is that the young lady formerly, when very young, it was thought, had a penchant for their groom, or coachman. But he was apprised of the fact by her uncle & being fond of her was willing to overlook it so long as it was not generally known. But on his return, finding it had been universally talked of, he declined the connexion. It is rather hard on the young lady, who has

336

behaved very well ever since they were contracted & had never deceived him. His sisters were always against the match. <u>Time</u>, <u>absence</u> & <u>friends</u> will work wonders, & I presume he will be reserved for some Lady Mary or Lady Betty who, if <u>no better</u> than poor Miss Brown, will have title & blood to hide any failings.' Mrs Norcliffe afterwards hints that the lady was 15 when she had this penchant for the groom. 'The errors of 15 might, I think, have been forgotten at, let us say, 25.' Had <u>I</u> loved the girl &, knowing the fact, given her my promise, I would have kept it, but I can't fancy myself doing either the one or the other, in such a case. The objections of the sisters & friends seem natural enough. I would do my utmost to screen a girl under those circumstances & to keep her in society, but there is a wide difference between this & marrying her.

Saturday 15 November [Halifax]

At 8.10, I set off to walk. Went to Bailiff Bridge to see the new road they are making from there to Brighouse & which, when finished, is to extend from Bradford to Huddersfield. It will not be done till next summer or autumn. Under the superintendence of Mr Platt of Bradford; appears from 42 to 45 ft wide . . . Saw one man at his work breaking stones for which he has 5/– a rood . . . After stopping to talk to the road-men & Jackman, got home at 11¼. The former say the stones break much better when they are not fresh got, when they have been got 6 months. Jackman was stopt by 3 young men between 11 & 12 last Saturday night at Boylane-end . . . & robbed of 2 pound notes & ½ crown. They had blue coats & trousers and good hats on. Never spoke when he begged them to spare his life (he was not much frightened), ran away towards Halifax, & were not Irishmen. A man was stopt about the same place some months since, but ran away. The same man had his horse's bridle reins cut about 3 weeks ago, but still rode off & escaped.

In the stable ¼ hour seeing John wash the stable, young James Smith bringing the water for him, not to hinder John from thrashing. They want 2 strikes more wheat to finish sowing the upper Cunnery field. Came in to breakfast at 11½. A basket of game had come from M—, (a pheasant, hare & brace of partridge), with a book (*Adam Blair*).

Wednesday 19 November [Halifax]

From 2.40 till 5, dawdling over 1 thing or other. Assorting my minerals got in Craven & Whitby. Oh, that I was comfortably settled down to my routine of employment! But still I want a day or two more for looking over my papers. Then surely I shall recommence something like study. I will have less trouble about my clothes, etc., in future. I will burn my letters except, perhaps, M—'s & Isabella's, as soon as answered & will be careful to accumulate no more papers but such as are worth keeping. 'Tis now 5.25 & I have just finished writing all the above of today.

Thursday 20 November [Halifax]

Looking over & arranging my box of oldest letters & papers. Burnt several letters . . . Perhaps if I had waited I should not have made up my mind to part with them. Time, with me, is such a sanctifier of everything. It is a noble effort thus to make room in my writing desk at present & resolve never to cram it in future. It is a prudent effort. Now that I have begun the good fight I hope I shall go on & destroy my letters as soon as answered.

The destruction of many reminders of her past life was, undoubtedly, a symbolic act. Never again was Anne to be as vulnerable to hurt as she had been in the past. She continued to receive many hurtful snubs at the hands of society, particularly as she began to move in higher circles at home and abroad, but she braced herself against the treatment handed out to her, confiding her hurt feelings to the ever-faithful pages of her journal.

From the autumn of 1823, Anne began to think more and more of living elsewhere than Shibden Hall, although she would not have dreamed of relinquishing the estate or letting it pass, by any other means, out of the Lister family hands.

Friday 21 November [Halifax]

This place does not agree with me. My gums are almost always soft-ish and whitish, as if a little ulcerated & would be more so if I did not take a glass of port wine every time they are not so. Elsewhere the house is old & cold & full of air in all directions & damp. The situation also. I will get away as soon as I can & either build some newer rooms or not live here. I should be rheumatic, like my aunt, if I did not sit in my greatcoat & wrap up so exceedingly.

Monday 24 November [Halifax]

At 7½, off to Northowram to tell Blamire to come take off Hotspur's shoe & bleed him in the toe, if necessary . . . It was one o'clock before I came in. Miss Hudson of Hipperholme then called (Mrs Wm Priestley having taken her in a carriage, called also). They staid ½ hour or perhaps more. Miss Hudson's call to me – I must return it some time. She laughed & grinned almost all the time. I certainly have no fancy towards her.

Thursday 27 November [Halifax]

At 10½, my aunt & I off in the gig. Stopt at Miss Ibbetson's for my aunt to buy a black veil. Saw several furs. A fur lining for the whole inside of a cloak (hamster fur) 28/–. Fitch fur, (*vid.* Encyclopaedia, 'Fitchet, a name given by some to the weasel').

Friday 28 November [Halifax]

Went into the stables to give the horses their oatmeal & water. George shewed me a swelling likely to suppurate on the right of Hotspur's withers . . . Poor Hotspur is very unlucky & George is not groom enough to see these things in the 1st instance. Surely he might have known on taking the saddle off whether the horse had been pressed on the withers or not. I must better & better understand, & more & more look after, these things myself. It is the old gentleman's saddle (not fit to put on any horse) that has done the mischief . . . At 4¾, read from p.91 to 188 *The Art of Employing Time*,[16] which, from p.134 to where I have left off, I am more particularly pleased. There are several hints for journal-keeping on which I shall think seriously. There is something highly novel in this work altogether, & withal, interesting.

Tuesday 2 December [Halifax]

Got home a few minutes before 1 . . . Found Mr Sunderland here by mistake instead of tomorrow. Had my tooth out (one of the right cuspids next to the molaris). It took a desperate pull & splintered the alveola in coming out, but I am glad to be rid of it. The decay, tho' as yet <u>very</u> little would have injured the neighbouring teeth . . . Just before Mr Sunderland went, rinsed my mouth with ½ teaspoonful of liquor opii (3 times as strong as laudanum) in ½ wineglass full of water.

Wednesday 3 December [Halifax]

Lay in bed on account of my tooth . . . My face a little swelled today & my gum rather painful, but not much.

Saturday 6 December [Halifax]

Mr Sunderland came to see Bridget [the housemaid]. Was of opinion she would be laid up in a rheumatic fever. Might be sent home today or perhaps tomorrow. My aunt came up to me. I advised the poor girl's being off in a chaise as immediately as possible. Went downstairs at 12½. Mr Sunderland said she was of an inflammatory habit & had probably been imprudent in clothing. He agreed with me, had she been bled & physicked last Monday when she felt the 1st symptoms of the complaint, she might have escaped. Took Mr Sunderland into the stables to see Hotspur. Stated the case. He did not think I had poulticed too long . . . Recommended a turnip poultice every night for 3 or 4 nights . . . He thought the best stopping was 2 parts clay and one part cow-dung well mixed up. He said Hotspur would make a valuable horse if properly taken care of . . .

Set off to Halifax at 3.20 . . . Called at the vicarage to inquire after Mr Knight, taken ill with an attack of the gallstones last week . . . *On returning, midway the new bank, up came a young man in very good black clothes & asked me how I did. I looked & said, 'I do not know you.' 'My name is Joseph Lister of Shelf.' 'But I know nothing about you.' 'But you might know if you inquired.' 'Which I should not choose to do.' 'Oh, very well, ma'am.' He hung back, dumbfounded. I walked forwards at a smart pace as before. I always feel annoyed at these ignorant impertinences, for I believe the fellows know no better. I never mention these things for impertinent letters have ceased for a long while. Surely they will not begin to come again* . . . Cordingley went home with Bridget (a mile from Mansfield) at 2½, (2 hours going, very bad road) & got back at 8½. Bridget apparently no worse for the journey.

Sunday 7 December [Halifax]

Awoke about 5 with a <u>very</u> bad headache. Got up about 8½. Went downstairs & into the stables for a moment or 2; then washed my teeth, etc & got into bed again as fast as I could (a very little before 9). Lay in bed the whole day, scarce able to move my head from the pillow, till 8.25. Then washed, put on my greatcoat & went downstairs till they made the bed & got into bed again at 9. At 1st, thought it must be a bilious headache, but from my not being sick & the pain continuing so long & so bad, I think I must have got cold in my gum yesterday. I felt it very cold to the side of my face & the hot room afterwards seemed to make my head ache a little.

Monday 8 December [Halifax]

My head rather better this morning but still very far from well . . . At breakfast at 9.50. I hardly spoke, feeling as if I had not resolution to open my lips. Came upstairs at 10½. Chilly & musing melancholily over the fire till 11. From then till 3.10, read the whole of (M— sent it to me Saturday 15 November) 'Some passages in the life of Mr Adam Blair, minister of the Gospel at Cross-Meikle. Wm Blackwood, Edinburgh; & T. Cadell, London 1822. Let him that thinketh he standeth take heed lest he fall. St Paul.' . . . It is a singularly interesting pathetic story, doubly so because told as truth & not improbable. It affords an appalling instance of the fall of a good man & an edifying example of the repentance . . . *I read & roared over this thing till my head ached, tho' not perhaps worse than it would otherwise have done, & my eyes were as red as ferret's. The night poor Adam fell, he was starved with his journey & with fatigue. Charlotte had made him take many a glass of wine. Perhaps this as well as the story of insults helped to do the deed* . . . Staid down talking to my aunt . . . *Told her I was poorly & low . . . & thought the grapes & pears of Paris did me more good than anything. 'Well,' said she, 'perhaps, if we live, you may go next year.'* She is really very good & anxious about me.

Wednesday 10 December [Halifax]

My head quite better this morning . . . At 11.20, walked with my aunt along the road to Lower Brea . . . In returning, went to

Dumb Mill to speak to Jackman, who is finishing some repairs there. Looked over the buildings inhabited by 2 families (all related). Very comfortable place, or may be when made neat all about, having a nice bit of garden. They pay for the whole building (it would easily make 4 good cottages) £7 a year.

Thursday 18 December [Halifax]

Having been talking about farming & rents, turned to my paper of memoranda. Added some fresh ones. Adding up & calculating till near twelve. My uncle must have now a clear income of nine hundred & above eighty pounds a year. By the time all centres in me, supposing my aunt to have fifty pounds a year Navigation stock, I can make thirteen hundred a year. It has just struck me, I will make the Cunnery cottages & barn into a farmstead & let off with it fifty out of the hundred & ten days work my uncle has in hands. This will give me another hundred per annum & I will fudge out one more, some way or other, so as to make an income of fifteen hundreds a year.

Monday 29 December [Halifax]

Ten minutes in the stable. I have to brush my pelisse & dress myself in a morning, now that Bridget is gone, which makes me longer in being ready to sit down to reading . . . At 10.40, set off to walk to Halifax. Called for a moment at Northgate. A Miss Plummer (a great, fat, vulgar-looking woman) there from Market Weighton. She & Marian sitting very quietly together at breakfast. Just gave Marian my aunt's message & hurried off . . . Got home (returned up the old bank) at 11¾ . . . ½ hour looking at my pistols, powder & ball in case they should be wanting, for highway robberies are taking place close to us perpetually.

Wednesday 31 December [Halifax]

A longish letter from [M—] (Lawton) . . . Praise of Miss Pattison. She & M— are to try botany together. M— in despair about painting on glass. All her glass breaks & the colours do not turn at the proper shade. I have told her it is the too sudden heating of her furnace & not the colours that are in fault . . . M— *means to give me my flannel waistcoats* . . . Chas. Howarth came just before breakfast (which interrupted me a little) to take measurements for the roof of the shed adjoining the barn-porch . . . At 3¾, set off to walk to Halifax . . . Went down the old bank. Put into the post office my letters . . . having 1st called at Mr Wiglesworth for a few minutes to ask him to come & talk to my uncle about stopping up the footpath behind our house.

1824

The year 1824 can be seen as the year in which Anne's life took on a different direction. The emotional ties between herself and her two greatest friends, Isabella Norcliffe and Mariana Lawton, had considerably weakened. In Isabella's case, her physical deterioration, her heavy drinking and unpredictable temper had all served to convince Anne that they were no longer compatible. Despite this, the two remained friends, occasional correspondents and visitors to each other's houses.

The emotional dependence between Anne and M—, because of its greater intensity, took longer to die. Anne had been severely shocked by M—'s reservations about Anne's appearance and also by M—'s antipathy to anyone knowing the true nature of her friendship with Anne. Added to this was the fact that M— was becoming, at least superficially, more settled in her married life. M— was making new friends, taking up new interests and generally arranging her life so that she was not so vulnerable to her husband's neglect and therefore not so needy of Anne's love and comfort. Anne began to feel that she need not take on quite so much responsibility for M—'s happiness, although she always retained a residue of love and affection for M—, as M— did for Anne.

At Shibden, as the health of her uncle and aunt began to decline, Anne began to take on more responsibility for running the estate and dealing with the finances.

During 1824, she also put into action her plan to travel and live abroad for fairly lengthy periods. On 24 August 1824, she left Halifax for Paris with only her maid, Cordingley, for company. They lived in Paris until 31 March of the following year, 1825, when they returned to Shibden. As business and travel added a veneer of sophistication to her intellectualism, Anne found herself becoming even more distanced from her former friends and acquaintances, particularly in the Halifax area. She came to view them as being rather provincial, apart from Isabella, who was a much travelled woman herself. The beginning of 1824 shows Anne in a quiet but busy period of her life, concerned with making improvements to the estate and laying plans for the future.

Tuesday 6 January [Halifax]

In the evening did nothing but talk to my uncle . . . He seemed satisfied with all I had said & done. Listens more patiently than ever to my little plans about a few improvements at home & appears to have confidence in my being able to manage things. *I think I shall, by & by, have all my own way. I certainly felt my own importance more than ever. The feeling of this, while at Yew Trees this morning seemed to invigorate me.*

This mood of optimism seemed to enable Anne to put behind her, so far as she was able, the miseries and humiliations of the last summer and autumn. Writing to a friend, Miss Henrietta Crompton, who was bemoaning the passing of the old year, Anne contradicted her, saying, 'I am not sure that I sympathize with you in taking leave of the old year with regret. Perhaps I have mourned as little as most people over departed hours. I am certainly happier now than formerly & would not like any part of my life over again, even were it in my choice. Secluded as I am, & must be for some time to come, yet I have never felt to have so many means & instruments of happiness within myself as at present.'[1]

Friday 9 January [Halifax]

Got a new watch-glass at Pearson's & asked him to let me see a clock taken in pieces. I am to call next Tuesday for this purpose. Then went to Furniss's the gunsmith. The main spring of the pistol was broken. George must have done it by main force of awkwardness, for the metal of the spring & the spring itself were <u>very</u> good. Paid the man 3/6. He always [charges] 9d. each pistol for cleaning. Prefers steel barrelled pistols to brass when the steel is left in its natural state & not polished for then, even if much used, it will be perhaps a 12 month without wanting cleaning. But brass is apt to be verdigrized & should be cleaned after every 4, 5, or 6 times using. He shewed me a very nice pair (would kill point blank at 40 yds' distance) of his own make, percussion lock, 8 guineas. If the touch hole be at all above the breach the gun or pistol will always rebound, put in what charge you will. A dram of powder & two drams of shot a proper charge for my brass horse-pistol. Prefers a percussion lock for pistols because safer. Throw them about as you will, the powder cannot escape from the pan, which is often the case with common locks. Prefers a secret trigger when he knows that it is made of good steel. If it is made of iron it is apt to wear soon & get out of order. He shewed a brace of nice small pistols, percussion locks but not secret triggers, price 2 guineas, that had carried a ball thro' a 3-inch deal at 20 yds distance. He will be making a brace of pistols the latter end of next week & will let me see him put them together.

Saturday 10 January [Halifax]

Washed & scaled my teeth with my penknife. Letter from M—
(Lawton) just before I went out . . . She is pretty well. Going to
the Pattisons' for a couple of days on Tuesday & to a masquerade
at Audsley, Sir John Stanley's, on Thursday. Means to go as a
housemaid or 'ballad-singer', but I think the latter. 'Can you
send me some good songs to sing . . . one of our party goes as a
bell-man. If you can rummage up any odd things for him to cry,
it would be a kindness to send them to me . . . If you can give me
any hints for the masquerade, do. Let me hear from you as soon
as possible.' . . . I must now . . . think what I can do for M—.
From 3¼ to 5.55, looking over my papers to look for 'Billy Vite'
& any other old ballads I might have that would do for M—.
Thought of writing her something for the occasion & wrote 3 or
4 stanzas of 4 lines each, to the tune of 'Brighthelmston camp',
that I used to hear & whistle when a child.

Sunday 11 January [Halifax]

Rubbed out, or very materially altered, the 3 or 4 stanzas written yesterday afternoon, & wrote 9 new ones. This took me till
after 9. At breakfast at 9.25. Left my aunt at the old church &
went to the new . . . I am shocked to say I was asleep all service
time . . . Got home at 1. Made a 10th stanza as I walked back &
2 more directly after coming upstairs & thus finished the ballad.

Monday 12 January [Halifax]

From 6.50 to 9¾, wrote a foolscap p. to M— by way of envelope
to the sheet containing the ballads & to make some observation on the manner of singing them. Containing also the 3
following for her friend who is to go as the bell-man. 1. 'This is
to give notice that I, Richard (Woodhead or another name),
commonly called Cockle Dick, will never more pay any debts

348

whatsoever of Sally, my lawful wife, commonly called Fish Sal, in regard that no law of the land repels a man to ruin by his wife.' 2. 'Lost; a new leather woman's pocket, between the hours of 8 & 9 of the night of the day of the last of this present month, that contained nothing in it only a few brass. Notice is hereby given that whoever will restore the same shall be hamperley rewarded.' 3. 'This is to give notice, last time of crying this 3rd market day, I, John Buck, shall lawfully 'liver up & sell Betty Buck at the Market Cross, my wife. No blemish – but we can't agree. To part we are resolved – so no less bid nor ½ a crown – 'livered in a halter – halter an'all.' . . . At 12.20, sent off by George my double letter (1½ foolscap sheets) to M— . . . 1. Cockle Dick is now living at Halifax. His wife used to drink & he sent the bell-man to give notice he would not pay her debts. He turned her out of his house, & being summoned before Dr Coulthurst to take her back, he declared he would not for she would be the ruin of him. 2. This crying a leather woman's pocket is a story of my uncle's; it happened in Halifax perhaps ½ a century ago. 3. John Anderson used to tell me long since of wives being cried 3 market days at the market cross & sold the last day & 'livered (delivered) in a halter. He said Phebe Buck, the leech-woman still living, I believe, at Market Weighton, was sold in this way & bought by Buck, the man she lived [with] ever after.

Wednesday 14 January [Halifax]

Went upstairs again at 10.40. From then to 11¾, copied the remaining 2pp. & the ends of my letter . . . At 12 had closed & directed my letter. To my surprise & great sorrow found, on taking my watch out of my pocket for my favourite seal (a pelican feeding her young with the blood from her breast), & which seal I have constantly used ever since I used a seal at all, that it had broken off from my seal-ring & was lost for ever. My mother gave me this seal when I was a child. The carnelian was picked up in Prussia by Count de Obzendorf & cut in Paris. I am very sorry to have lost this seal. Looked all round the room for it in vain.

Thursday 15 January [Halifax]

On making the bed this morning, they found my pelican seal . . . Letter from Isabella . . . to say she would be here by the afternoon mail. Game basket from Lawton containing a fine hare, a large spare-rib of pork, my aunt's cherry-coloured cloth winter gown from Birmingham, a very neat muslin habit-shirt of M—'s own making for me & a few lines for me to say, in a great hurry, she got my letter on Tuesday & that she thought the songs excellent. 'You are only too good to me, Fred.' They were going to ride to Westhouse, the Pattisons' . . . Came upstairs at 2¾. Putting things in their places ready for Isabella. Sent off George to meet her at Halifax & a little after 4, drove my father to Northgate (had Percy in the gig) & brought back Isabella. Looking very well, rather larger, I think, than when I saw her last in October. She & I dined at 6 . . . *Poor Tib! My heart aches & is indeed remorse-struck. She never expects to be well of this complaint & it inconveniences her very much. I said I would write to Mr Duffin for a syringe. I have not yet told M—. It is a bad business. Poor Tib. I will, at any time, make up for it all I can by double attention & kindness. If she knew the truth, what would she think?*

Tuesday 20 January [Halifax]

Called Isabella. Left her to breakfast without me & went down at 9.40 . . . Went out & staid with Jackman & his 2 sons & Mark Hepworth (one of the road-men, of Yew Trees Cottage) walling till 1 . . . The 4 men that are dressing the sets at Northowram quarry have long wanted something to drink.

William told my uncle some time ago & he said they were paid for their work, & gave them nothing. I, however, gave William ½ crown for them today, & they promise that the sets shall be capital. Nothing like something to drink. One seldom loses by giving them a shilling or 2 now & then.

Thursday 22 January [Halifax]

At 2¾, set off to walk with Isabella to Halifax. Went to Whitley's & the library. Left Isabella to return to Whitley's while I called & sat 6 minutes with Mr & Mrs C. Saltmarshe. The baby quite well again. *They were very civil but I don't like going there. She does not seem quite at home with me & is vulgar.*

Friday 23 January [Halifax]

Read my letter (by this morning's post) from M— (Lawton) . . . There was some mistake about the tickets to the masquerade at Sir John Stanley's (Alderley Hall) & after all, M— & her friend, Miss Helen Pattison did not go. A great disappointment. M— hears it went off very well. My notices for her friend, the bell-man, were useful. C—, fancying the ballad for the occasion her own, 'declared they were the best verses he had ever read. By George, he would have one & sing it himself . . . he tells everybody of what a capital song I wrote . . . I can't help smiling to think how prejudice carries us away. If I had told him they came from you, he would have thrown them away as trash, & rather rejoiced in the circumstance that had prevented their being sung.' Tho' M— had observed before, 'I verily believe his disappointment that I could not go was even greater than my own.'

Sunday 25 January [Halifax]

Isabella & I down at breakfast at 9.40. She & my aunt & I went to church . . . Mr Warburton did all the duty . . . I was asleep all the while . . . From 2¾ to near 4, began my book catalogue – to be a catalogue of all the books worth buying & by all means to be read, referred to by the different authors I read.

Saturday 31 January [Halifax]

Letter from M— (Lawton) . . . going to have the house full of company again. Has given up all thought of having a masquerade; that at Alderley 'does not seem to have given general satisfaction. Much party spirit appears to have prevailed, & the opportunity was taken to say many ill-natured things.'

Wednesday 4 February [Halifax]

The inquest that sat till 10p.m. yesterday on the young man found murdered at the top of Winding Lane on Saturday night, is adjourned to 10 o'clock tomorrow morning, the people examined gave such contradictory evidence. We have had a great many highway robberies this winter & some houses & several warehouses robbed, & seem to have a sad set about us.

Friday 6 February [Halifax]

Wrote 2 & two-third pp. to M—. Nothing particular. *Ask how her finances go on & say I particularly wish her to be beforehand by midsummer. The fact is, but I shall not tell her so, I begin to think I may get off to Paris in the autumn & then I shall want money* . . . At 1¼, went to Turner, the gunsmith's. We went into a field just above the gibbet[2] to try the gun. He fired the 1st time, & only once. Filled a brown paper about a foot square with shot at about 37 yds distance. Then I fired 3 times, but never hit the paper once. Yes! The last fire sent one shot completely thro' it. The gun recoils scarcely at all. When the touch-hole is not bored quite at the bottom of the pan, or if the barrel of a little larger bore near the back, be not a regularly cylindrical bore of equal calibre all throughout, the gun will recoil. 2 drams of powder & 1¾ oz. of shot no. 5, the proper charge. Went back to Turner's shop, took the gun in pieces myself & saw it cleaned, washed with cold water. Staid till 3. The gun itself, £2 15s. Powder & shot, cleaning apparatus, spring-screw, screw-driver, etc., came to £1.6. He shewed me a new handsome double-barrelled gun with percussion locks, weight 7lbs, he had just made for Mr (Rawdon, I suppose) Briggs, £24. The double barrel cost 8 guineas. The mahogany gun-case would be 2 guineas additional.

Obviously, in view of the robberies and the recent murder, people who could afford it were taking the precaution of carrying firearms, or at least having them available on the premises. The following extract from a letter to a family friend gives some indication of how Anne was spending her days in the early months of 1824.

Saturday 7 February [Halifax]

Nothing particular in my letter to Mrs James Dalton but the following account of my time; 'You ask me to tell you what I am doing & think about, & I ought not to talk about being so busy without giving some reason for it. My average hour of getting up in a morning is half-past five. Dressing & (keep the secret & do not laugh) going to look at my horse, takes me an hour and a half. From 7 to 9, I read a little Greek & a little French. From 9 to 10, looking after the workmen. From 10 to 11, breakfast. From 11 to 2, out of doors looking at 1 thing or other, workmen, etc. From 2 to 3¾, walk out Isabella. Should drive her out but our gig-horse is laid up for the present & I have turned out my own horse for a winter's run. From 4½ to 6, at dinner & sitting afterwards. From 6 to 6½, dawdle, trifle, call it what you please, with Isabella. From 6½ to 8, write letters or notes, or "<u>the book</u>", or take a <u>little</u> miscellaneous reading, & indeed, it is a little, for some days I never open an English book. At 8, go downstairs to coffee & we all spend a sociable evening together till 10. Isabella retires about ½ hour after me, & my uncle & aunt sit up till 11. Such is the model of my present day; such it must continue till we have done with workmen; & then I shall have about 4 hours a day more time; only just enough to keep one's mind in proper order.'

Wednesday 18 February [Halifax]

At 8½, set off to Lightcliffe. Walked there in just ½ hour. Spoke to Mr W. Priestley about Jonathan Mallinson's nephew wanting to take Yew Trees. Mr Priestley would not let him a farm; for he did not believe he was worth £15 besides the poor horse & the poor cart he had to lead coals with – and it was always reckoned in farming counties that a farm would require £10 an acre to stock it with. That at this rate, a tenant taking Yew Trees (48 days work, or about 32 acres) should have £320. As breakfast was just over at Lightcliffe, I would not take any. Sat talking a good while to Mrs Priestley. She shewed me their offices & about all her store-room. *It seems she keeps all herself. Gives out everything for consumption weekly or some trifles, eggs, etc., daily. Her method seems excellently adapted to the gentlewomanly management of their present income, five hundred a year. She does not like her own clothes to cost more than forty guineas a year, & these & her whims & everything, don't exceed one hundred. Mr Priestley does not spend so much, & her hundred is made up by a sort of secret purse of thirty pounds a year.*

Saturday 21 February [Halifax]

Called Isabella at 9, which took me 5 minutes . . . [She] *poisons me with her snuff. I can hardly bear [being] in the room. How heartily I wish she was gone. I already begin to count the days to the twenty-fourth of next month.*

Monday 23 February [Halifax]

Gave Hotspur oatmeal & water . . . From 8 to 10¼ wrote 3pp. & the ends to Miss Maclean[3] . . . told her I had written by candle-light before breakfast. In fact, I did do so. I kept the candle burning (my dressing-room, or the corner of it where I sit, is so dark) till 10. Went down to breakfast at 10.25.

Sunday 29 February [Halifax]

Isabella went down to read prayers this afternoon. *She drinks a bottle a day, all but two glasses that my uncle & aunt take. The latter leave the room at luncheon to let her take three or four glasses, but I am to be sure to take no notice of this. What a shame Tib should do so. She goes into the dining-room about seven in the evening to have a glass of wine & sends for George or Cordingley to get it. She shall not come here again soon if I can possibly help it.*

Tuesday 2 March [Halifax]

Walked with Mrs Priestley ½ way to Cliff-hill to meet Miss Walker with whom she was going in the carriage to make calls. They took me up & set me down at the top of our lane at 10¾. *When walking with Mrs Priestley, said she would believe I should never marry if she knew me better. I had been pretty well tried. I might have had, & perhaps might still have, rank, fortune & talent, a title & several thousand a year with thorough worth & amiability added to great learning. In my own mind alluded to Sir George Stainton. But I refused from principle. There was one feeling – I meant love – properly so-called, that was out of my way, & I did not think it right to marry without. I should have a good fortune & had no occasion. Not that I could live without a companion. I did not mean to say that. She said I should be too fastidious. There would be none I should choose. 'No,' said I, 'I have chosen already.' Mrs Priestley looked. 'One can but be happy,' said*

I. 'It is a lady & my mind has been made up these fifteen years.' I ought to have said a dozen for, of course, I meant M—, but said I never mentioned this to anyone but my uncle & aunt. 'You will see, in time. I am sure you will like my choice.' Here Mrs Walker's carriage came up & stopt our conversation. I wonder what Mrs Priestley thought. She will not forget &, I think, was rather taken by surprise.

Thursday 4 March [Halifax]

Went out to the workmen at 9.05. Came in to breakfast at 10. Both Jackman & his 2 sons & the gardener here this morning ... Wrote 3pp. to Burnett to thank her for a pot of marmalade & 13 buns she sent me ... Told [her] M—'s message to Charlotte Norcliffe about having Miss Wickham's spinning wheel valued, that M— might buy it if not too dear.

Thursday 11 March [Halifax]

Got to Lightcliffe to breakfast at 8.35. About 10, it began to snow & rain & turned out very stormy. This detained me & I sat talking to Mrs W. Priestley till 2. *Mutually confidential ... Talked over our own individual characters. Her sentiments republican – mine monarchical ... I talked very gently in a rather sentimental style of feeling, but I declared her less commonplace than I & more singular than Miss Pickford &, in reality, tho' without appearing so, the most singular person I ever met with. I twirled my watch about, conscious of occasionally bordering on a rather gentlemanly sort of style. She seems to feel but not quite understand this. She would prefer my society to that of any lady, perhaps scarce knowing why. She has pondered over my having chosen a lady for my future companion.* A child ill in the measles was given up. The measles were gone in & there was no chance for it. Mrs W. Priestley had the child fomented all over with flannels dipped in hot water, for 1½ hour, then put into a warm bed.

The child fell asleep. The measles appeared next morning & the child did well.

Friday 12 March [Halifax]

Called at the Saltmarshes'. Mrs Catherine Rawson there. Sat with Mrs Saltmarshe & her about 10 minutes, then took my leave fancying them not sorry. I have long perceived a reserve in Mrs Saltmarshe's manner to me. It strikes me more & more, & I less & less like calling. There seemed even something of the same in Mrs Catherine Rawson. Called, as I went, at the bank & desired them to make out my account. Called for it on leaving the Saltmarshes'. I have now got a banking book in which my account will be regularly settled ½ yearly. *The balance in my favour, including three half-year's interest, is sixteen pounds, nineteen shillings.*

Saturday 13 March [Halifax]

At 2.50, set off to Halifax with Isabella. Just called to ask Thomas Greenwood if he could get 2 blue cats from Norway. Yes, he could. A friend of his at Hull would get them. Got home again at 3.50. Dressed & sat down to dinner at 4¼. Went upstairs at 6 . . . & came down to coffee at 8.07. Snowing hard when I got up this morning. The ground covered with snow & several snow showers during the morning . . . Long argument with Isabella just before coming upstairs. She denied that 6 horses (to a carriage without a box) had ever been driven in England by 3 postilions. I said I believed it, seen it. The equipage of the late Mr Fox of Bramham Park many years ago, driving into Leeds.

Thursday 16 March [Halifax]

Came upstairs at 6.10. Talking to Isabella near ½ hour. *She was furious at my being so proud. Never knew anyone have so much pride. She could not bear it. She was not fit to be here. Would not* soon get herself into the scrape again. Did not suit my uncle & aunt. She saw it plainly. At last she came round & got right again. Oh, how glad I shall be when she has gone. Heaven be thanked, she is to be off tomorrow week. Can they really be so fond of having her at Croft? The time she is out of bed is chiefly spent in drinking wine & taking snuff, & my aunt says her hot temper would frighten her if she did not know her so well. Surely Tib cannot long be an acceptable visitor in people's houses. She is going the way to lose herself a little, by & by, & she takes very near a bottle a day of our hot sherry.

Wednesday 24 March [Halifax]

Wrote 1½ p. to M— to ask whether she would give 3½ guineas for Miss Wickham's spinning wheel (Autis's patent – now selling at 5 guineas). Took a <u>very</u> little milk & bread while Isabella got a hearty breakfast of coffee, & was off with her in the gig at 7¼. Saw her luggage put on & in the Alexander coach . . . saw Isabella safely in it, followed as far as Ambler Thorn turnpike, then turned back . . . & got home at 9½ . . . Sat down to breakfast at 9¾. Not much said about poor Isabel but we are to dine at 2 & relapse into our usual habits directly. I told Tib the other day, when she talked of coming next year, that my uncle was getting old. Liked his own hours & she had better only come once in two years. She took it very well . . . Poor soul, she does not suit my uncle & aunt . . . I really did feel a little dullish last night, thinking what a change there would be today & that, after all, I should miss my companion a little. At last, I said I was low & several times turned the conversation into this channel when we were alone. But poor Tib, as I even told her, had less sentiment than I had; she merely seemed to wish to get rid of the subject. Her feelings were never finely acute. Now they are blunted a good deal . . . Her memory is worse. She tells her stories much oftener over than she used to do, forgetting that she has told us the same again & again. She is growing gradually larger. About an ounce of fire-shovel, burnt, Irish-blackguard snuff & very

358

near a bottle of sherry per day, with nine or ten hours bed, would feed anyone . . . It does no good to talk about it. Had she been different in these matters, how I could have loved her. Yes, how adored her, had she had that temper & conduct which temperance & good sense might easily have secured. But alas, it has not been so. But yet, in spite of all, I feel a tenderness towards her I could not feel for such another & could forgive in her what I could not in anyone else. But let me leave this subject. It makes my heart ache. I dare not hope she will improve but may she be as happy as such a life can permit. Had Isabel been half she might have been, my affections never could have strayed to M— or to any other. But no more. God bless thee Tib. Our interests are separated forever, but still, when I forget myself, I almost love thee. No, I do not love thee but love thy happiness . . . 2.10p.m. I have just finished so far of this journal of today. They are clearing my room that I am sitting alone in the drawing-room . . . I feel rather low. I must turn my mind into another train of thought.

Once Isabella had gone, Anne began to resume her social round of visiting in the town. She realised that her attitude towards her erstwhile friends in Halifax was the subject of comment and it appears that she was anxious to find out exactly where the trouble lay and, if possible, to repair a few broken friendships.

Thursday 25 March [Halifax]

Went to Halifax to the Saltmarshes'. Mrs Rawson staying there. Mrs Kenny calling there & staying some time. Sat her out, apologized for so doing, saying that I really wished to ask Emma a rather singular question, but one I hoped she would at once answer candidly. A yes or no would be sufficient. I wished to know whether she had the same pleasure in seeing me now she used to have. No! she had not, was the honest answer. Everyone said I changed my friends or knew them here but not from home, & she had experienced it herself. She thought as if I wished not to know her at the festival (the first ball-night last September). There were several Halifax people there whom I took no notice of. It was the common quiz, 'Have you seen Miss Lister? Of course, she will be glad to see you,' meaning that I should not speak, but Miss Prescott said I had behaved very well to her, for I had spoken to her. Emma said I knew she was very modest and, therefore, when Mr Saltmarshe (Philip) had observed, 'Now here is someone you know', meaning me, she waited for me to speak, to see what sort of reception I should give her. Both she & her husband were struck with my coolness, and when I called on her on my return home, I brought my aunt with me & behaved very differently from formerly. Indeed, she had addressed her conversation much more to my aunt than to me. She meant to make a difference in her conduct but was only afraid she had not been able to shew it sufficiently. A friend of mine (she would not tell her name, I think it was Mrs Henry Priestley) said I never knew any of them from home – it would be her turn next. Now I had turned off Mrs Saltmarshe, but she did not care. She supposed I should know her again, by & by. Emma said she denied my having turned <u>her</u> off; for she would not be so <u>turned off</u> and wondered — would submit to it. She confessed she, (Emma), had been hurt about it. She used to delight in seeing me – in hearing the sound of my voice. Her husband had observed what pleasure they used to have in seeing me, but now it was all at an end. She wondered why I called at all, for I was so different from formerly. But her mother had always taken my part. I briefly explained. Said all imputed to me was certainly not intended. What motive could I have for cutting her? She was with her husband, and Mr Saltmarshe (Philip), a person deservedly held in high estimation in the York society. I had not intended to slight any Halifax person I ought to know. I had even, at the expense of much quizzing, made a point of speaking to Mr & Mrs Pollard ... The only person in the room I intended to cut was Miss Caroline Greenwood; and Emma had often heard me previously name my intention of doing so & the reasons for it. She owned that she herself & Mr Saltmarshe had cut the Greenwoods. As for changing my friends, there was only one person whom I never [meant] to call on again, Mrs James Stansfield, but she was married. This made a great difference. I should say more but for Mrs Rawson & Emma. She smiled & understood me to mean some dislike to Mr James Stansfield. I said I had long observed a change in Emma's manner towards [me]. Observed it before the festival, as my journal could testify. I had named it to my aunt & fancied it must be on Mrs Empson's account, as I had also observed to Miss Norcliffe, but I had continued calling at intervals of a fortnight or 3 weeks, because the change in her conduct had been so gradual I had not had reason to take notice of it & could not bear the thought of seeming fanciful. One thing that struck me was that frequently as she used formerly to ask me to stay dinner or tea, she had not done so for the last year past. I had once or twice staid till just past their dinner hour for the mere purpose of trying whether she would ask me or not. However, I was always candid & open. I would not be thought changeable unjustly, nor could I endure any change or any misunderstanding between us, without doing all I reasonably could to explain it away. I hope she did not think with Mrs Empson that my word might be doubted. No! Indeed she did not. I trusted, therefore, she would believe me on my word, that whatever appearances might have been, I had no intention to behave less kindly or attentively than I had formerly done, & that I only hoped she would be able to adjust the matter to our mutual satisfaction & think no more of it. I fancied there was a starting tear in Emma's eye as she mentioned the sorrow she had felt about it, & she would forget the business at York. She was expecting company to dinner at 2. I hastened away. Shook hands with her. Then turned back from the room door, shook hands again & saluted her. Then did the same to Mrs Rawson. The people say I am 'heartless'. I told Emma & Mrs Rawson surely that, at least, was untrue. From the Saltmarshes' went to the library. Mr Knight there. Asked him to dinner tomorrow. Chancing to say I had not seen him for long, but might have passed him a hundred times, to my surprise he seriously answered I had passed him, he did not know whether intentionally or not, but he supposed it was for some fault he had committed. Of course, I expressed my sorrow & truly said I had never knowingly passed him without speaking. But it might happen, I was near-sighted. I had passed my own father, who fancied it done on purpose. 'Then,' said Mr Knight, 'I may be excused for thinking so.' He did not seem to believe me near-sighted. From the library to Mrs Stansfield Rawson's. Sat there with Mrs Stansfield Rawson & Catherine about 1½ hour, very comfortably. Mentioned my adventure with Mr Knight saying I was quite shocked he should think me capable of so slighting my old master . . . Then went to the Waterhouses'. Sat with Mrs Waterhouse 1¼ hour. Slightly mentioned Mrs Saltmarshe's having thought me changed in my manner towards her & alluded to the common report of my knowing people but not from home, my fickleness, etc. Mrs Waterhouse laughed, said they said she turned off her friends & never went near them, but she never minded. Yet she thought me given to change my friends. Miss Pickford the reigning favourite now, but I had always been the same to her (Mrs Waterhouse). Told her what Mr Knight had said. She answered I often passed her without speaking. I 'turned my eyes inwards and saw nothing outwards'. They had all observed I had gone out of church oddly some time ago. Had taken no notice of any of them. She had bowed to me in a carriage one morning with —. The lady pointed me out. 'There is Miss Lister but she never knows me.' 'Well, but,' said Mrs Waterhouse, 'she will know me, or if she does not, she will the next time.' . . . We had over the story of my not visiting Mrs Christopher Rawson. She said I was as bad as an officer for taking offence. She cared nothing about these things. But it was my journal that frightened people. She had made up her mind not to open her lips before me. Mrs Rawson, at the Saltmarshes' had abused my poor journal – wished I would destroy it – it reminded me of a great deal I had better forget. Returned up the old bank; staid a few minutes with the workmen & came in at 6¼. Dressed & sat down to dinner at 6.35. Told my uncle about the adventures of today. Glad the thing had so ended with Emma. From 8 to 9.55, wrote all the above journal of today.

Tuesday 30 March [Halifax]

Dawdled over 1 thing or other & from 1¼ to 3.40, wrote 3pp. & the ends (pretty small & close) . . . to Mrs Norcliffe . . . I would send 17/– for Burnett to pay Rutter's for the strong leather boots Isabella brought me, & 3½ guineas on M—'s account to pay Miss Wickham 'for the spinning-wheel which she (M—) shall be glad to have, provided Miss Wickham will be good enough to take the trouble of seeing it properly packed & sent off' . . . Speaking of Isabella, 'The worst thing, the most injurious, is that lying in bed in a morning. The great degree of relaxation produced by this alone is too evident to be mistaken. I told her I should ask you to give Burnett orders to get her up regularly every morning at 9. I told her I should entreat to have the bedclothes taken away, to prevent the possibility of her getting in again and that, if she bolted the door, the bolt should be taken off. She exclaimed against all this. The childishness etc. I grieve over the necessity of the thing, but where life & health are so at stake, ought it not to be done?'

Thursday 1 April [Halifax]

Letter from Miss Henrietta Crompton (Micklegate, York) . . . chiefly an account of the public fancy-ball last Tuesday week in the rooms at York. 'Mr Fox (of Bramham Park) & Mr H. Fawkes, who have been at most of the splendid things in London, declared it was better managed than anything of the kind they ever saw. Mr Waterton (of Walton, nr Wakefield) who was a complete Indian chief – face stained and ear-rings & necklace of exquisite little birds, assured us it far surpassed Preston Guild! . . . Miss Charlotte Norcliffe I think looked very handsome as a Polish lady . . .' At 11.35, walked with my aunt to Northgate . . . We all 4 went to the Talbot great room to see the 2 Esquimaux [*sic*] Indians now exhibiting there. They are man & wife. Have had 1 child but it died. They mean to go back in about a year (having now been 14 months in England) to see their friends, but otherwise would have no wish to go back at all. Their only marriage ceremony a rude dance, or lifting up first 1 leg then the other, which they performed to us on a table, was so ridiculous I could not help laughing. The man got into his boat, threw a couple of darts to shew us how they caught their food, seals, etc. One of the dogs (they have but one here) drew them round the table in a little low sledge just large enough to hold one person. They seem quite happy & like the amusement of being shewn. They don't know what to do with themselves on a Sunday. The man was very ill about a fortnight ago & has still got a bad cough – now that they take so little exercise, raw meat does not agree with them so well – they take it about half done. They are shewn by a young man who, having been in the Hudson-bay fur company, speaks their language. He has taught them to read a little, for the new Testament has been lately translated in the Esquimaux language. They can speak a very few words of

English. There is shewn along with [them] a considerable collection of Esquimaux & Indian habiliments, arms, etc. The vicar & all his party were there.

Tuesday 6 April [Halifax]

I shall be rheumatic if I stay here very long. I begin to feel my knees cold again in spite of my leather knee-caps that I always sit in. I have just rubbed them with oil of almonds to soften & keep cold out. I often think I shall not stay here more than I can help. I will go abroad as soon as I can ... Had ¼ hour's nap from which I had just roused myself when Cordingley came up to say Mr Hudson wished to speak to me. My surprise was not small (he had just seen my uncle & was waiting for me in the hall) when he opened by saying he was going to take a great liberty with me. He wished to know in what he had offended me. I had shewn such marks of displeasure in my countenance towards him whenever I saw him, he thought he must have offended me. He had observed it of late – when he saw me at Mrs Stansfield Rawson's (the last time I called there), once when he had met me in York (last spring with the Cromptons walking in Petergate). He was a public character; might lose his influence by offending me – the influence he ought to have as a clergyman. I think that surely he must be rather besides himself. He begged me not to mention what he had just said. His daughter would be hurt to know he had taken such a liberty. Poor man! I told him truly I was quite unconscious of having shewn any displeasure towards him in look or any other way; that I was near-sighted & stopped long to speak to anyone by the way, but that I had perhaps oftener stopped to speak to him than anyone, as I generally stopt when I met him & could only beg he would believe no displeasure meant, for I had no reason for any, & never did anything without a reason. I hoped he would think no more of it. He said he must be satisfied with my word,

& went away not perhaps quite satisfied in his mind. Surely he must be in his dotage. I might have shaken hands with him & been what Isabella would call more <u>liant</u>, but I could not make up my mind to it. I will call on his daughter soon & take care to speak to him more smilingly in future.

Wednesday 7 April [Halifax]

Drove to West House (Mr Browne's). Mrs Kelly at home. Sat with her 40 minutes. *She seemed glad to see me but, as I told her, she was never quite at ease & right. The first [time] I saw her I knew she was always wondering whether I should call on her or not. She owned it. I said I would call again & sit an hour with her. Said I had now cut the Greenwoods & we none of us spoke. She asked why. I said I had always told her I should. Their so trifling about with the officers of the Sixth Foot, when here, was enough for me. Besides, there was no reason why I should know disagreeable people & I meant to get rid of them all. Ah, said she, I was a privileged person, but other people could not do these things. Emma had told me she was sometimes rather frightened of me . . .* Mrs Kelly looking very interesting & more than pretty. Very large. To be confined in August.

Friday 9 April [Halifax]

At 1.10, set off down the old bank to the post office . . . *In returning gave a shilling to the wife of the man in the old church yard who applied to me about three weeks [ago]. The town, I said, would inquire about him of Mr Knight. He was no impostor & I thought it right not to forget him. The woman looked ill. I felt pleased in giving her the money & only wish I had more to give.* A well-speaking woman with a long story of her husband having failed, etc. . . . I said, I always mean to say in these cases, I have resolved only to relieve those I know. I thought, at last, the woman slightly smelt of spirits.

Monday 19 April [Halifax]

No workmen here but Jackman & his 2 sons, who were to be off in the afternoon to see the balloon ascend at 3 . . . Set off to Halifax at about 1¾. The road crowded with people. Called for a few minutes at Northgate. My father & Marian did not go to the Piece Hall to see the balloon & I went to the Saltmarshes', having promised to go with them. We got there at 3. A great many people there but the place would have held 4 times as many, at least. After waiting 1½ hour, Mr Green at last ascended at 4½. Went up steadily & beautifully & remained in sight 20 minutes. Returned up the old bank & got home at 5½. Had no idea what a business it would be. I had to wind & push my way thro' one continuous crowd from the Talbot Inn to nearly the top of the old bank (to the lane leading to Bird-cage). The people were returning to the town from the hill, where they had assembled, some said, to the amount of fifty thousand to see the balloon. The High Sunderland range, Bairstow & Beacon Hill range were beautifully studded with spectators. The sight of them was as well worth seeing as that of the balloon. The day was remarkably favourable. People came from far & near & few who could leave home seemed left behind. Not a soul left in the house here but my uncle & aunt . . . Jenny Hatton & her daughter, from Lightcliffe, were here when I went downstairs the 1st thing this morning. Come to make the drugget for the hall. They are to stay, & stay all night till the thing is finished.

Tuesday 20 April [Halifax]

Drove to West House. Mrs Kelly at home but just going out . . . Mr Kelly there. I instantly went up & shook hands with him & said I was glad to see him. He looked better (more presentable) than I expected, really very fair. Said how glad he was to see me of whom he had heard his wife speak so often & seemed pleased at the manner in which I had met him. Did the thing make her a little nervous? I saw her blush deeply. Her mother was in the room when I entered but had glided out. *Drove off in good style at a quick trot as if I knew what I was about. My new hat & greatcoat on. An India handkerchief around my throat. My usual costume. I wonder what he thought of me. If it was good, she will tell me. He must have been struck one way or other.* Then drove to the Saltmarshes' & sat a full ½ hour with Emma. I told Mrs Rawson this morning I liked her (Emma) better than ever since the explanation business; and so I do. Her manners – who can expect to have the polish of courts? – but she has a kind & affectionate heart & this is everything to me. *Told her how I had received Mr Kelly. That she had blushed. How pretty she looked & I had looked round, in spite, to enjoy it. 'Ah,' said I, 'the people round here do not understand.' 'No,' said Emma. 'Indeed they do not.' Do not I wish them to do so? 'Only you know better in future &', be appearances what they may, believe nothing but what I myself say.'*

Wednesday 5 May [Halifax]

Washed & changed my pelisse & sat down to dinner a little after 5. My father & Marian here & drank tea with my uncle & aunt. Went out a little after 6 & talked a little while to Jackman & at 6.25, set off to walk to Yew-trees. Mark to go & see the state Sowden left it in. Nothing can be dirtier or in worse condition than the house, except the land, which is terribly run out. Saw Mark's wife, who looks fitter for the miserably small cottage in the yard, in which they have lived there 15 years, than for the farmhouse which seems so large to her (4 low rooms & 4 chambers over them) she is frightened to live in it by themselves & wanted a couple of cottagers for company . . . *I would not have let such a farm to Mark. My idea was, as I told my uncle, to keep the place in my own hand & let Mark farm it for me till I could let it to my mind . . .*

Monday 10 May [Halifax]

At 9, set off in the gig. Drove Caradoc to Ripponden turnpike &, in returning, got out at Westfield for a couple of hours, to call on Mrs Kelly . . . Caradoc made a piece of work in passing some caravans in going, and in returning . . . Mrs Kelly rather indisposed, a little squeamish, yet looked very pretty. *She is evidently flattered by my attention . . . On taking leave, I saluted her left cheek, which I believe I have not been in the habit of doing before & begged her to give my compliments to her mother & say I should be much obliged to her to stop me when she met me, as I should be glad to hear of Mrs Kelly. My manner was not quite so flirting this morning. I am well enough satisfied with it. We were talking of my dress. She said people thought I should look better in a bonnet. She contended I should not, & said my whole style of dress suited myself & my manners & was consistent & becoming to me. I walked differently from other people, more upright & better. I was more masculine, she said, She meant in understanding. I said I quite understood the thing & took it as she meant it. That I had tried all styles of dress but was left to do as I liked eight years ago. Had then adopted my present mode & meant to keep it. She asked how I employed myself. Said to keep up Latin & Greek would take a good deal of time. I spoke of Greek as my favourite language.* Mrs Kelly told me a brother-in-law of hers . . . was out of patience with people setting ladies up as so learned. They none of them knew more than a schoolboy (applying particularly to the classics). Speaking generally, I said I would agree with him. Ladies, in general, have neither time nor opportunity to compete with men of college or liberal education.

Tuesday 18 May [Halifax]

We called at Northgate. Saw Miss Ibbetson's fine shawls & silks she has just brought from London . . . At 3¼, set off down the fields to Lightcliffe. Found Mrs Paley & 3 of her children there, Mrs W. Priestley & her cousin & visitor, Miss Hodgson, from Carlisle. Strange to say, in introducing Miss Hodgson, Mrs W. Priestley also introduced her sister, Mrs Paley, forgetting at the moment how often she had heard me say I certainly cut her completely the 1st opportunity, & would not speak to her anywhere. (My aunt called on her in their new house some years ago, 2 or 3?, & she never returned the call.) I scarcely moved on being introduced & kept my word in taking no notice of her whatever. Laughed & talked to Mrs W. Priestley & Miss Hodgson as tho' nothing was the matter. Sat about an hour, took no notice of Mrs Paley or any of her children in coming away. I spoke to her daughter, aged about 17 or 18, on her entering the room, for I have seen her with Miss Pickford. Mrs W. Priestley came out with me to the gate. I just said the meeting was unlucky. Exprest my sorrow on her account, certainly none on my own.

Wednesday 19 May [Halifax]

Wrote 3pp. to Marian to ask her what my aunt should get to wear this summer; what sort of shawl, & what to wear in the gig. Said, rather than she should be hurried, I would 'for this time only, if it was necessary', allow her to delay her next letter a couple of days, i.e. I would wait patiently for it till next Monday. Said I felt rather bilious – that some of the *agréments* of her society would do me more good than anything. This, & other expressions, quite obscure to others. She will understand. . . . Isabella sent me, from Croft, *The Globe & Traveller* of last Friday, containing the account of the death of Lord Byron 'at Missolonghi, on 19 April, after an illness of ten days. A cold, attended with inflammation, was the cause of the fatal result'. The Greek account says his lordship died 'about 11 o'clock in the evening, in a consequence of a rheumatic, inflammatory fever, which had lasted for ten days'. 37 min. guns (he was in the 37th year of his age) were ordered to be fired, by sunrise, on 20 April, from the batteries of Missolonghi. All places of amusement, courts of justice, & shops (except provision & medicine shops) ordered to be shut for three days. A general mourning ordered for twenty-one days & funeral ceremonies to be performed in all the churches. The body will be brought to England. 'The Greeks have requested & obtained the heart of Lord Byron, which will be placed in a mausoleum in the country, the liberation of which was his last wish.' Came upstairs at 11.05. Who admired him as a man? Yet 'he is gone & forever!' The greatest poet of the age! And I am sorry.

Monday 31 May [Halifax]

Went to the Saltmarshes' again, having to thank Emma Saltmarshe for offering to get my aunt a sealskin shawl, but refusing the offer for the present. Sat about an hour. *Very good friends. She very civil, but oh, what a falling-off there was . . . Emma seemed sadly vulgar as she was shewing me her new pelisse from town that did not fit, & was telling of fashion, & my heart sighed after some better & higher bred companion that it could love. I felt thoroughly low as I walked along . . .* The time seemed but so many seconds so intently yet so moodily was I thinking. I sauntered up the bank . . . *intently thinking still & feeling desolate & unhappy. I cannot dress like the rest. I want someone whom I can respect & dote on, always at my elbow.* I mused a while – thought how we disquiet ourselves in vain – that happiness is impossible in this world. Sat down to my journal . . . 'Tis just before 6.05 as I am writing at this moment & in the last 2½ hours, I have gradually written myself from moody melancholy to contented cheerfulness. I am better than I have been since Wednesday. Surely my mind & heart will by & by recover their healthy tone, & I shall resume my usual occupations with energy &

interest & pleasure. What a comfort is this journal. I tell myself to myself & throw the burden on my book & feel relieved.

Saturday 12 June [Halifax]

The party [of magistrates and others who were visiting Shibden Hall concerning the stopping up of a public footpath near the house] were all assembled by 12 . . . All took a glass of wine & water & in about 10 minutes, left us, apparently hoping & thinking we should succeed [in getting the footpath stopped up]. *They would not eat anything. We had had a bustle about getting ready the luncheon tray & had only just finished when they returned; 'Oh,' thought I to myself, 'This would never do for me. I must have M—, or somebody that knows how to manage my house, & I must have servants that know what they are about.'* . . . From 8.05 to 9.40, sauntered with my aunt to the new footpath & then, near ¾ hour, both of us weeding the vetches in the paddock. Coffee at 9.40.

Tuesday 15 June [Halifax]

Ready at 3 to set off to Halifax . . . Called for Emma Saltmarshe . . . We sauntered out again immediately, talking of going to Mr Nicholson's sale at or near Ward's End, but when we got there saw a crowd of people. Emma recollected that her aunt Stansfield was very ill & she, Emma, ought not to be seen there . . . Had scarcely got back to the Saltmarshes' when it began to rain pretty heavily. Detained there till about 6¾. Mr Saltmarshe then ordered his gig for me & his servant drove me home. Came in at 7¼. The Saltmarshes very civil. Very civilly asked me to dine there – to have a mutton chop while they had their tea. This I positively refused, but took one cup of tea with them. Speaking of the Miss Wickhams as women of the world & fashion? or rather as having seen a great deal of the world & good society & being too high for this & that, perhaps I too truly observed I did not quite see the reason of this – that I remembered York society 15 years [ago] – remembered their mother selling laces for charity & being suspected of making a handsome profit. That she was quaintly called Mother Wickham & her daughters Nanny & Harriet . . . *I ought to have said nothing about . . . the Wickhams. I will better weigh my words in future. Somehow both Christopher & Emma struck me as vulgar & I felt uncomfortable amid all their civility. How different is Miss Maclean & good society.* Told the Saltmarshes I should not, probably none of us would, ever enter the new assembly rooms. I knew not what would tempt us. <u>Perhaps</u> Catalani might for one concert. They said how unpatriotic to our native town. I said the town is little to us. Merely one market & post town. Perhaps they guessed not what passed in my mind.

Friday 18 June [Halifax]

From 2 to 6, looking over volumes 2, 3, 4, & 5 as far as p. 111 of my Journal. *Volume three, that part containing the account of my intrigue with Anne Belcombe,*[4] *I read over attentively, exclaiming to myself, 'Oh, women, women!' I thought, too, of Miss Vallance who, by the way, is by no means worse than Anne, who took me on my own terms even more decidedly. The account, too, as merely noted in the index, of Miss Browne, amuses me. I am always taken up with some girl or other. When shall I amend? Yet my taste improves . . . I could trace much inconsistency & selfishness noted down against M——.*

Saturday 19 June [Halifax]

At 8¾, set off to Lightcliffe . . . Mrs W. Priestley had a bad headache & did not make her appearance of above ½ hour. All this while, tête-à-tête with Miss Hodgson who afterwards was obliged to leave the breakfast table to lie down on the sopha, she being in a very delicate state of health. Both seemed better

373

& wishful for me to stay & I did so till 2. *Talked of one thing or other. Rather complimentary, tho' properly so, enough to them both. In short, said & did nothing at all I repent of* . . . [Miss Hodgson] *evidently likes me, I think she has no objection to Mrs Priestley's leaving the room. I could make rather a fool of her, perhaps, if I liked, but she seems sensible enough & I have neither intention nor inclination to amuse myself at her expense, tho' I am very civil to her* . . . *Speaking of my oddity, Mrs Priestley said she always told people I was natural, but she thought nature was in an odd freak when she made me. I looked significantly & replied the remark was fair & just & true. After all, she herself is proud of being thought a friend of mine & I now have certainly made up my mind, I think forever, to like her better than anyone else here* . . . Walked leisurely home & got back at 2¾ . . . Sat reading & musing . . . feeling rather chilly, got up & absolutely put on my other greatcoat &, feeling utterly disinclined for reading, for writing out French or Greek, composed myself & dozed till about 4½ . . . Wrote all this journal of today, feeling not at all too hot in my pelisse, plaid wrapt fourfold round my loins, & 2 greatcoats put on over all, besides my leather knee-caps on & a thick dressing gown thrown across my knees over coats & everything. I sit close to the window, all things considered the only seat in the room that suits me. A large high green baize, fold screen on my right to exclude air from the door. The curtains drawn so as only just to admit light enough, to keep out air from the window. Yet, still, in spite of all this & my towel-horse with a large green baize thrown over it to keep the air from my legs next to the window, an air always does come thro' the very house-side, as it were, & makes me always sit, the hottest day we have had, in all the clothes I have on now, except the 2nd greatcoat. Always 2 thick blankets on my bed, & a great coat & plaid thrown over my knees. Without these precautions, I know not how it is, but I should be as rheumatic as my aunt . . . Went down to dinner at 6½. Mr Steel, of Belvidere, came a little before 8. Wanted to speak to me. Stood talking to him a considerable time in the hall. He proposed that . . . if my uncle would allow him to lead his coals along the cow-lane, as he called it, he himself would engage to pay one pound a year for the privilege & said he was sure that, if my uncle would agree to this, he, Mr Steel, could persuade 'Lewis & his son, Robert, too' not to oppose my uncle in stopping the footpath up our own courtyard. It would be much better for my uncle to agree; the footpath must be a great nuisance . . . Indeed, said I, it is a public good to stop up all unnecessary footpaths. Mr Steel thought so, too. 'There were far too many.' He, for his part, was for making a good road all along the common wood & stopping up the footpaths thro' all the fields . . . (but) he must say he remembered how old a foot-way it was. He had gone up & down it many a time with Dr Drake. 'It was a pack-horse road.' (My uncle declares it was no such thing . . . that there never was a pack-and-prime road at any time along any of those fields of his . . . he had heard that, very anciently, people on horseback had gone along the bed of the brook from Will-royde as far as Godley-bridge. But that was not our footpath.)

Saturday 3 July [Halifax]

From the library, went to the Saltmarshes'. Saw them both. Sat there just ½ hour. *Emma very civil & kind but always strikes me as being vulgar & somehow, whether her fault or mine, I do not feel there as I used to do. All is right again & quite made up but there certainly is not that constant cordial invitation to stay this meal or that, as in days of yore.* Mr & Mrs Saltmarshe expected at Mr William Rawson's & they are to spend a few days at the Saltmarshes' house . . . Said I should not call on them. It would be absurd as it was not in my power to shew them any civility. Emma said she did not expect it. I never had called on anyone staying with her. Said I never called on anyone's friends unless I had previously known them or unless something very particular made an exception, urging the reason alleged above.

Monday 5 July [Halifax]

Walked forward to Lightcliffe. Mrs W. Priestley & Miss Hodgson at dinner . . . Would call again in ½ hour. Did so, after loitering that time, reading the gravestones in the churchyard. The ladies were still in the dining-room. Said I would call another day, & returned. *No attempt to call me back. I marvelled. Most people, in such a case, would have had the servants prepared to shew me at least into the drawing-room, or Mrs Priestley might have come out to me herself. I do not feel quite pleased. Said I to myself, I shall not go of a week hence* . . . From 8.30 to 9.10, walked on the terrace, occasionally reading Young's *Night Thoughts*.[5] Coffee at 9.10.

Anne had, for some time, been turning over a plan to travel to Paris and stay there for a few months, mainly in order to recover her health. She wanted to consult medical men in Paris about the venereal disease she had contracted from M—, and believed that the fruit which she could obtain on the Continent would be beneficial. She also wanted to improve her mastery of the French language, broaden her experience of the world, and get away from the provincialism of Halifax. She outlined her plans in a letter to Isabella.

Tuesday 6 July [Halifax]

'Your mother would tell you I thought of going to Paris for a little while this autumn. I begged it might not be mentioned because something or other may prevent it. What with 1 thing or other, I am ½ stupefied to death &, if, of the many going to Paris, I can pick out an escort I like, I shall take Cordingley & be off, as I told your mother, any day after the 20th of next month, before which time it is impossible for me to leave home . . . You have often heard me speak of Madame de Boyve[6] – of her, and of Fontainebleau grapes & Normandy pears I have craved for the last, almost, 2 years. Mme de Boyve tells me she will do everything in the world she can to make my visit agreeable; & I make myself sure she will succeed. I know she is in good society . . . She can't speak one word of English; nor, except for Cordingley, do I expect to hear one word of it, during the few weeks of my stay. If I go, I shall be delighted, my dearest Isabel, to do anything I can for you, & any, & all of you. Only remember, I cannot bustle about as you can, I have not the tact at understanding shops & shopping, & I cannot smuggle.'

Anne was expecting a short visit from M—, on her way back to Cheshire from York, where she had been hastily summoned on account of the sudden serious illness of her father, Dr Belcombe.

Tuesday 20 July [Halifax]

A little after 6, awakened by a rap at my door. It was M—, who had arrived by the mail . . . *I certainly did not seem in extasies [sic] at seeing her but pretended I was half-asleep. She thought she should have found me at my studies. Did not take much persuading to get into bed & gave me one kiss immediately.* At 8¼, I got up, went downstairs & gave Hotspur his oatmeal & water. M— breakfasted in bed & I sat by her & had my breakfast between 9 & 10. My aunt came & sat with us a good while . . . At 5¾, took M— in the gig & drove to Haugh-end to inquire about their being able to receive Dr & Mrs Belcombe & Mrs Milne & Tatham, the next day . . . The Priestleys very glad to see us. Will be glad to receive the whole party. *I had kissed M— in the morning & behaved kindly to her, yet the business of last August was in all my thoughts & I did not feel right towards her at heart. In driving* her to Haugh-end, I began talking. How altered I was. Grown more selfish, more positive in my own ways. Could never again be led by the nose, etc. I saw she was getting low & I talked of common things. On returning, I renewed this subject, asking if she thought me improved. She said she would tell me tomorrow. At last, it came out, she thought me more selfish. She had been saying she should not like me to drive four horses. I had said, Well, but if I liked it, she ought to give up her wishes to mine, for I must have my own way. From little to more. I got her to confess it had struck her I was saying all this against myself because perhaps I wished to be off as well as I could . . . After a minute's hesitation, which evidently alarmed her, I denied what she fancied, but explained candidly the impression the Blackstone Edge & Scarbro' business had made on me. That I could not shake it off . . . She explained as well as she could . . . that I had taken it up too strongly. I said there was no accounting for feeling but, at all events, M— must manage me better. I could not stand it. She seemed low & did all she could to conciliate. I could not bear the thought of making her unhappy & reassured her that, with a little good management, she might bring me right again.

Wednesday 21 July [Halifax]

Tidied our room & made these memoranda of today. I had told M—, in the gig this morning, I was got quite right again . . . *Poor M—. I do believe she loves me with all her heart & I really think she will take some pains to manage me better in future.*

Thursday 22 July [Halifax]

Two last night. M— spoke in the very act. 'Ah,' said she, 'Can you ever love anyone else?' She knows how to heighten the pleasure of our intercourse. She often murmurs, 'Oh, how delicious,' just at the very moment. All her kisses are good ones . . . At 12, took M— in the gig & drove to Haugh-end. Major Priestley & Mrs Milne set off on horseback to call here. By some means or

other, we missed them altogether. Found Dr Belcombe looking better than I expected . . . Mrs Belcombe looking harassed
& ill. Mr John Edwards of Pye Nest & young Mr Dearden of
Hollins were calling at Haugh-end, 2 young men of whom it
was chiefly difficult to say which was the most vulgar. Got
home at 3.

Friday 23 July [Halifax]

M— at breakfast about 9¾ & I at 10. At 11.20, off in the gig to
Haugh-end & got there in about an hour. *Behaved very affectionately to M—. Bade her be happy. Said I was come quite right
again & that she had never before made me so happy. She seemed
satisfied . . . She had not been so happy these eight years. Was
rejoiced I was going to France. Thought it would do me good & she
never left me before in such good spirits. She felt that she should be
happy. I had all her heart.*

The two women were not to meet again for some time. Anne
and her aunt set out for a short tour of the Lake District the
day after M—'s departure and, shortly after returning from
the Lakes, Anne travelled to Paris, where she made an
extended stay into the spring of 1825. So, though on this
occasion Anne & M— parted on a happy note, the relationship, for Anne at least, had more or less run its course
and was never to reach its former intensity. The decline was
accelerated by Anne's increasing sophistication and interest
in cosmopolitan life.

Saturday 24 July [Skipton]

*Too busy all yesterday afternoon & night to think much of M—,
but what I did think was comfortable.* Cordingley awakened me
before 6 . . . My aunt & I breakfasted . . . Off at 8¼. 1 hour, 50
minutes, driving here (the Sun Inn, Bradford). Had a basin of

boiled milk with a very little bread in it . . . Got here (at the Devonshire Hotel, Skipton) at 6½. Ordered dinner in an hour & beds for the night. Washed & made myself comfortable & sat down to my journal . . . Dinner at 8. Good trout – bad mutton chops – <u>old</u> peas, new potatoes sent up in bad butter, bad gooseberry tart, not good bread, & vilely bad water. I could not drink it & had a large basin of boiled milk. My aunt complained of cold & shivering & had a glass of hot white-wine negus . . . Very much annoyed with dust all the day, but the plaid over my aunt, & my greatcoat and a large handkerchief round my throat, protected us pretty well . . . All the servants here have wages & give the mistress of the house all they have given to them. The young woman who waited on us at dinner has 12 guineas a year. She lived last year at the Golden Lion (Mr Hartley's), at Settle, but left there because the wages were too small. She had only 6 guineas a year & gave all the vails, as here, to her mistress.

Sunday 25 July [Settle]

Drove thro' Settle to Giggleswick (for my aunt to go to church). Annoyed to find the Black Horse, kept by Waller, a poor place, quite a common alehouse, adjoining the churchyard . . . but the people were clean & very civil, & gave us tea & good boiled milk & bread & butter & good cream, & we both got a good breakfast & were satisfied . . . but we were determined to return to Settle & rest there for the night . . . At 1½, off to Settle. Got here in a few minutes. Ordered dinner & beds. I sat down almost immediately . . . It is really so dull for my aunt to have me always writing, I shall write no more, save my journals & accounts . . . Dinner at 6.10. Soup, part of a boiled neck of mutton, a roasted chicken, peas & potatoes, potted trout & potted beef, & preserved gooseberry tarts. We both made a good dinner. At 7.20, set out sauntering about the town . . . Had a glass of hot, red wine negus just before getting into bed, which made me sleepy.

Monday 26 July [Kendal]

Off from Settle (the Golden Lion, now styled Hartley's Hotel) at 9.25 . . . Settle is a romantic or rather foreign-like looking town. The market place has something of the air of a *grande place* abroad. This morning was the fortnight fair & the market was full of sheep penned off in divisions; & there were a great many head of cattle . . . Kirby Lonsdale a picturesque sort of little town . . . Off to Kendal at 3¾ . . . The inn (King's Arms or Jackson's Hotel) cuts a poorish figure (an old, very odd but good house) compared with what it is. Sauntered out ¾ hour then at 7.40 sat down to dinner. Trout, roasted chicken, all excellent. Mutton steaks good. Excellent little sweet puddings. Currant tarts & custard. Enjoyed our dinner. Immediately afterwards, at 8.20, I took an old man to shew the way & went to the castle . . . Very fine cool day. A little dust now & then but not much. A beautiful day for travelling. Brought in the horses after travelling 31 miles with not a hair turned. They ate their food well on coming in, & seemed quite well & not at all tired.

Tuesday 27 July [Bowness]

Slept well last night. *Mended my petticoat, stockings, hair cap & gloves.* At breakfast at 9½. My aunt had tea as usual & I my boiled milk with bread in it. Settled the account . . . White Lion, John Ullock, at 4.10 . . . Very hilly road, tho' very good road from Kendal to Bowness, a neat little white-washed vlllage with a good church, white-washed, prettily situated on the edge of the lake (Windermere) . . . Much pleased with Bowness & the inn. Ordered dinner & beds. Had a boat & were on the lake at 4½. The man rowed us first to what is called the Station, a pretty sort of tower observatory commanding a fine view of the lake . . . A very pretty gravel walk up to it. 2 stories high. Painted glass in the upper. The blue makes the scenery look like winter – the green like spring – the yellow like summer, & the orange like autumn . . . Sat down to dinner at 7¼. Soup (with vegetables in it, _very_ good), a most excellent & beautifully dressed (boiled, & then a little fried or crisped) pike. A roasted fore-quarter of lamb, potatoes & peas, 2 little sweet puddings, a tart & jellies. All most excellent. We never enjoyed a dinner more. At 8¾, we went out to see the church . . . Sauntered about the village ¾ hour, listening to the village band playing on the lake . . . Sat with one door open (our very nice little parlour looks upon the lake, & a door opening upon some steps leads to the garden) listening to the band, clarionets, horns, great drum, etc. Very beautiful. Thought I will bring M— here some time. My aunt & I joked & said when M— married the Blue Room, we should make a little tour here.

Wednesday 28 July [Keswick]

Comfortable bed. Slept well last night. _Mended my black silk petticoat._ Off at 8½ . . . Large, handsome, well-furnished inn at Ambleside. Very civil people. I must bring M— here. Everything good at breakfast. The best breakfast I ever remember to have had at an inn. Tea cake & wig [kind of bun] with caraway seeds in it, & a small bread loaf with a little rye in it, and clap-cake, i.e. oat cake made very thin & without leaven. My boiled milk excellent. The Duke of Buccleugh & his tutor in the house. Had been 2 or 3 days. On coming away we, at their request, entered our names in the company book. Mrs & Miss Lister. Shibden Hall . . . Off from Ambleside at 2.05 . . . The lake & vale of Grasmere sweetly beautiful. The village & its neat white church _very_ prettily situated . . . Left the village a little on our left & went the direct road to Keswick . . . We had a tremendous descent to the town & stopt at the Royal Oak at 7½. Ordered dinner & beds. Made ourselves comfortable. Sat down to dinner at 8.05. A small salmon (1 of the size, they call them <u>gilts</u> here), ½ of it boiled, ½ fried. Veal cutlets, rather hard. Most excellent hind ¼ lamb, cold, potatoes & kidney beans, & tarts & jellies. Yet we did not enjoy our dinner quite as much as yesterday. Comfortable bedrooms. Very large, good sitting-room. But indifferent stabling & hay, tho' good corn . . . After dinner, wrote the whole of this journal of today.

Thursday 29 July [Keswick]

Breakfast at 9½ . . . Drove down to the lake (Derwentwater) & sent the gig to meet us at Lowdore. On the lake at 11.10 & landed at Lowdore . . . at 12¼ . . . Off from Lowdore at 12.50. I drove my aunt & Mr Hutton [a guide they had engaged] & George walked. At the Bowder House at 1¾. Mr Hutton can remember it 60 years (he is a wonderful old man, at least 80 . . .) . . . I knew there was a foot road from here to Wastwater. It struck me at the top of Bowder stone, I should like to explore. Mr Hutton would have persuaded me against it. It was a most fatiguing rough road over the mountains. The nearest place I could sleep at (Strands) was 14 miles off. Then I must go to Calder Bridge, 6 miles from Strands, & then 16 miles further from Calder Bridge to Scale Hill, where my aunt must meet me tomorrow, with the gig, & from which place we should easily see Crummock & Buttermere lakes. All this was not enough to deter me. Well then, we must go on to Rosthwaite & he would see if he could get anyone to go with me, but all the people were busy with the hay. Stopt at the Miner's Arms (kept by widow Coates) at Rosthwaite. The woman's son, James Coates, a shoe-maker, agreed to go with me, stay all night at the inn where I was to sleep & pay his own expenses there, for 12/–. At 3.40, we were off . . . the road much worse over the mountains than the ascent to Snowdon from Capel Curig. <u>Very</u> steep, as James Coates called it, 'very <u>brank</u>' . . . the path cut alongside the huge mountain covered with the very small fragments (the size of large gravel) that lie along the mountains, & so loose & slippery as to make the path doubly fatiguing . . . We came to Strands but, my guide being willing to go forwards to Calder (he seemed to have understood that to be his agreement) we unluckily left Strands a little on our right & kept the Ravenglass road, passed over Santon Bridge . . . & soon afterwards lost ourselves . . . Got to a farmhouse where, it being near 10, I would gladly have stopt & slept by the kitchen fireside for the people, a man & his wife, were very civil. The woman said she had some milk in the house, but they said there was a good inn at Gosforth & we had much better go to it. If we went to the end of the lane leading from the house, it was only ¼ mile & we should then come into the high road. Turn to the right, & after passing 3 houses, turn again to the right for about a hundred yards & we should be at the inn . . . We got to the inn at Gosforth. The kitchen was full of men drinking. The woman was just going to bed & said she was very much tired. I told her she must get me a bed ready & something to eat, for I had had nothing since breakfast, had walked at least 20 miles. Said where from and how we had been lost, & that I was almost famished. The woman looked astonished. I thought she was in no hurry to take us in. She said she had not a drop of milk in the house. 'Come, come,' said I, 'my good woman. I'll pay you what you like for your trouble, but you must get me this room (I had gone upstairs) ready & some milk if you can.' I left my guide & told him to shift for himself. The woman went out & borrowed some milk. The people were all gone to bed or she could have got plenty. She put so much bread in it, it was like a pudding. Had, or seemed to have, an odd taste & I could not touch it. I was parched to death with thirst. The cheese & bread the man brought me from Rosthwaite had been in his pocket all the way & I had hoped to sup at Calder bridge, & consequently neither ate nor drank since breakfast at 9½.

The woman had no meat in the house but ham – but she thought a ham rasher would make me more thirsty. Eggs I could not bear the name of. Tried bread & butter. Could not take it. What could I have to drink? I must not drink cold water. Not a dry thread upon me from fatigue, or rather exertion & anxiety at the thought of our being so lost at night, when we could not possibly see to set ourselves right & the people were gone, or going, to bed. The woman had ale & a treacle bun. Either would have sickened. Asked if she had any gin. Yes! She brought me about a pint in a decanter, and some loaf sugar. I drank 4 glasses of weak gin & water – nay, perhaps 6, for the gin seemed so strong, however small the quantity I took, that in filling up the glass again & again, I drank 4 pitchers full (perhaps at least from 3 to 4 pints) of hot water. The woman wished I could eat something. It was in vain. I could have drunk twice as much. Never was so thirsty in my life. The bed was ready & neat & clean. Borrowed the man's nightcap. The bed had not been slept of a fortnight, the woman owned. Put on my greatcoat over my pelisse & all my other clothes, merely taking off my boots & stockings, & jumped into bed at 11. Fell asleep almost immediately, till 2, then dozed afterwards till about 5, & got up at half past . . . We had walked very fast up the mountains & averaged 3 miles an hour the whole way. They all agreed we had walked above 20 miles . . . If left to myself I should not have so lost myself. I said repeatedly we must be wrong, but that my guide must know better than I did.

Friday 30 July [Keswick]

Got a towel & water & washed as well as I could. Breakfast at 6¼. A basin of boiled [milk], no bread in it, & a good teacake. The woman said the young man (aged 22, he told me) confessed I had tired him out. Asked the woman what I had to pay. 2/– for the guide. As for myself, what I had had was not much,

I must give her what I pleased. Asked her to calculate. Why, she thought a sup of gin & water was not much, & all I had had was not more than 6d. Gave her 4/6 for myself besides the 2/– for the guide, with which she seemed much pleased & told her she had been so civil (& so she really was) if I ever went that way again I would call & inquire after her. The guide & I were off (from the Lion & Lamb ... Gosforth) at 7.37. Walked to Calder bridge & stopt at the Stanley Arms, Christopher Birkett, at 8.20. Finding they had horses, sent back my guide (who had offered [to go] forwards with me to Scale Hill, thinking he could find his way by daylight) and agreed for a couple of horses for 10/–. Had a basin of boiled milk ... Off at 10.10. Mr Birkett said the mare had a bit of a limp. So she had & stumbled desperately ... Got to Scale Hill at 2¼ ... My aunt had been at Scale Hill above 2 hours ... Off to Crummock lake at 2.50. My aunt could only walk slowly. They called it ¾ mile, but we were 20 minutes walking it. In the boat on Crummock at 3.10 & landed at the Buttermere end at 4.05. The lake shut in by fine mountains but my aunt was at first so frightened she could not admire or enjoy it ... Only a few houses at Buttermere. The lake a very pretty small one ... Mary of Buttermere[7] married to a farmer who has forty pounds a year of estate & lives about 20 miles off, I forget where. 50 minutes seeing Buttermere & its lake. Back on Crummock at 5. Landed at 5.50 & got to our inn (Scale Hill) at 6¼ & sat down to dinner at 6.20. Roasted leg of mutton (good, but too fresh killed), peas & potatoes & gooseberry tart & cream. Off from Scale Hill at 7¼ ... we descended the hill upon Keswick about 9. Came up to bed at 9¾.

Sunday 1 August [Pooley Bridge]

Never had a better or more comfortable bed. Everything most comfortable in my bedroom. Slept very well from about 3 to 7.

Sided my things in the Imperial. At breakfast at 10. At church at 10½ . . . The church seemed full. A very respectable-looking congregation. We were in the seat belonging to our inn. Apparently an elderly clergyman. Read the prayers very fairly . . . The 1st part I did not well hear. Most of the rest, I was dozing. The Te Deum was chanted . . . Paid our bill & off from the Crown . . . 12.40 . . . Drove slowly, the lanes stony, & got to Pooley Bridge at 5¾. Ordered beds & dinner. A poor-looking place after the inn at Penrith. ½ the house on one side of the road & ½ on the other . . . Sat down to dinner at 7.10. Potatoes not ½ boiled. Peas too old. Veal cutlets tolerable but I waited till they were cold for some cold roast beef or cold mutton. Had a little of the latter & a little of the veal cutlets. Bad gooseberry tarts. Very bad dinner & the waiter so busy (the house full of noisy people – the master had been with company all day & was drunk, & every now & then ringing just under us as if he would pull it down). We had to ring & wait, & be as patient as we could, & were nearly 2 hours before we could have done dinner. The water thick & we could not drink it. Each had a glass of negus. The people very civil but we have no wish to stay all night here again. They can make up 26 beds of 1 sort or other. Mine in a shut up cabinet which just holds it, in our sitting-room. The beds smell fusty for want of air.

Monday 2 August [Ambleside]

Off from Pooley Bridge at 7 & stopt at Patterdale, a minute or 2 before 9 . . . Breakfast at 9½. Good bread & butter & milk. Most excellent potted char, of which I ate a great deal. They pot a great deal – get the fish best at this time of year . . . Off from Patterdale at 11¼ . . . About 6 miles to the top of Kirkstone, then about 4 of steep descent upon Ambleside present fine views of Windermere & Coniston water . . . The retired, pastoral beauty of the lake & village of Grasmere please me, or the magnificent beauty of Derwentwater – but the head of Ullswater – the pile of huge mountains pushed together is magnificently grand. But the scenery about here (Ambleside) perhaps better unites beauty with sublimity than anything we have seen hereabouts, except the vale of Keswick . . . Got here in 3¼ hours at 2½. So sleepy could hardly keep my eyes open. Ordered dinner & beds. The house so full only one double-bedded room for us. A gentleman & little boy, his son, left us the little parlour upstairs we had before. Slept from about 2¾ to 4¾, then looking at the book, picking our route home . . . Dinner at 6.40. Roast leg of lamb, <u>very</u> good. Boiled chicken with white sauce. Good potatoes & cauliflower, & gooseberry tart. Very good dinner. Pint of port wine – not good. Made negus of it after drinking one wine glass each at dinner . . . Fine day till between 5 & 6, then a couple of hours rain. Very thick this morning on the tops of the mountains. My aunt got a little cold yesterday in going to church & could scarce stir this morning. She is rather better now, tho', from her feelings of pain, auguring a change of weather. She went to bed at 10.

Tuesday 3 August [Kirby Lonsdale]

Good bed. Slept well. Dressed & undressed in our little sitting-room a story [sic] below our bedroom. Tolerably comfortable. Good water closet, rather a rare luxury hereabouts at inns. Rainy morning . . . We would make the best of our way home (by Kendal, Kirby Lonsdale, Settle, Skipton, & Keighley) . . . Very good breakfast. Good bread & butter, & oat-bread, & tea-cake, and very good boiled milk. Potted char, too, but less strong of mace and too much pepper'd & not so good as that yesterday at Patterdale Inn. Off from Ambleside at 10.40. Caradoc's bandage would not stay on & he was obliged to go without it. George rode him. The little horse in the gig. Foot's pace the whole way . . . The little horse off his food. Could not eat his corn. I wish we were all safe at home again . . . Pursued the direct road to Kendal, and stopt there at 3.10. Ordered George to get a leather boot made for Caradoc. Slept or dozed on the sopha at the inn ½ an hour. Baited the horses 1 hour, 20 minutes, & off to Kirby Lonsdale at 4.35, and arrived at 8 ... Rose & Crown or Roper's Hotel. Dinner at 9. Lamb chops, boiled chicken, potatoes & peas. Cold, boiled round of beef. Cold turkey pie. Apple, currant & raspberry tarts, & a pint of port wine, said to have been 6 years in the bottle. Better than at Ambleside but not to be compared with the wine at Penrith. We both of us enjoyed our dinner ... Went into my bedroom at 11½. Had the bed made over again to put the mattress on the top. Helped the chambermaid to do it. Extraordinary I did not then observe the sheets were not clean.

Wednesday 4 August [Settle]

Ordered breakfast at 9¼. Sat down to it as soon as it was brought in at 9¾. Very bad tea for my aunt. Good bread & good potted trout, but not so good as Mrs Hartley's at Settle. Indifferent butter & the milk not so good as I have had elsewhere. Made a rowe [sic] about not having had clean sheets on my bed last night. Mrs Roper herself declared they were clean, but so much worn it made them feel so soft & tumbled (i.e. not well got up after washing), & I therefore gave the chambermaid a 2nd shilling, saying I was sorry to have made her uneasy by my mistake ... Stopt at the Golden Lion, Hartley's Hotel, here (Settle) at 4¾. Ordered beds & dinner ... Dinner (good) at 6. Boiled salmon, Scotch collops, veal, cold fore-quarter of lamb, & cold duck, & a cold roast fowl all uncut. Potatoes & peas. Very excellent potted trout, & rhubarb tart. Very good dinner. We had each a glass of negus afterwards.

Friday 6 August [Halifax]

Got home at 12½ ... Scarcely spoke to my uncle but went upstairs immediately to read my letters ... A large kippered salmon, split & fixed flat on a board cut to the shape, had arrived for me on the 2nd inst. sent by Isabella ... After reading my letters, came downstairs for near an hour. About 3, went upstairs again. Put by all my clothes & finally settled our travelling account. Our expenses have averaged, including the hack-horse, about 2 guineas a day.

Saturday 7 August [Halifax]

At 2½, went down to see Caradoc bled. Mr Gill took a full gallon from the toe of the off hind fetlock ... My aunt came to us. Her journey has done her good – but she will soon, I fear, be as bad as ever again. Her habit is confirmedly gouty & she becomes very feeble in her limbs ... M— *told me my back was getting round. Got the yard wand & held it at my back with pain & difficulty, when undressed, near ten minutes this morning & above five tonight, meaning to continue this plan till I get my shoulders properly back.*

Wednesday 11 August [Halifax]

Letter from Isabella, dated 'Edinburgh. Sun. 8 Aug. 1824' ... 'Berwick-upon-Tweed is a good town & here I sent you a kippered salmon ... It is to be dressed upon the gridiron & sent to table in small oblong pieces.' She has sent me, from Edinburgh, 'a cloak made of the Maclean plaid' and 'a pot of Scotch marmalade' which I am to get in a few days.

Tuesday 17 August [Halifax]

Called with my aunt for ¼ hour on Mrs Catherine Rawson. Miss Bessy Staveley there. <u>Very</u> smart & vulgar. Bowed so slightly she saw I meant to cut her, & instantly got up & went away ... Found the bank door shut. Mr Saltmarshe's servant gave the technical 3 raps with the end of a key & I got in & got my concerns settled. *Took the whole of the balance due. Twenty pounds, nineteen & sixpence.*

Friday 20 August [Halifax]

Walked direct (down the old bank) to Halifax. Made several shoppings. Ordered about my basket oil-case cover mending at Furniss's. A light trunk, covered with leather (a small imperial) the size of my basket, would cost £1. An oil-case cover for it 10/–. I think I shall try this plan another time. Returned up the old bank. A long while talking to Jackman, giving orders about the farmyards & sheds.

Saturday 21 August [Halifax]

My aunt gave me one hundred and twenty-five, from my uncle, that is, 150 altogether, pounds for my journey to Paris. Came upstairs at 10.40. All the day till 6¾, looking over my writing desk, writing drawer, books & papers & arranging so that I can leave them tidily. Dinner at 6.40. In the evening for about 1¼ hour, writing out travelling memoranda.

Monday 23 August [Halifax]

Disturbed sleep last night. Gave Hotspur oatmeal & water. Came upstairs at 8.50. All the day, till 6¾, packing & siding my drawers . . . Letter from . . . Madame de Boyve (Place Vendôme, 24a Paris), merely a civil acknowledgement of my last & to say all is ready for me. Dinner at 6.50. My father & Marian called in the evening. Then wrote the above & dawdled over arranging the contents of my writing desk . . . My aunt rather low at parting. My uncle looked an anxious look, & I felt the sickly feeling of going.

The extended trip to Paris became, in some ways, a watershed in Anne's life. She had much to leave behind her and, at the same time, much to look forward to. She had succeeded in distancing herself from the hurt of her affair with

M——. Anne had become more critical, less easily swayed by her emotions and thus more firmly in control of her life. At home, the death of her Uncle James in 1826 and her aunt's failing health meant that she became the prime agent in the business affairs at Shibden Hall.

Anne's life, from her return from Paris onwards, took on a more serious aspect and, as her work at home increased, so did her desire to find a life-partner. The new woman in her life, reasoned Anne, would have to have both rank and fortune to bring to the partnership and, looking back over her old loves, Anne decided that she could do better for herself. The story of this quest, as also the story of her adventurous travels, lies outside the scope of this volume, but it reveals that Anne lost none of her zest for life nor her talent for acute observation of the scenes and people around her in later years.

She did not, however, discontinue her old friendships. Nonetheless, her relationships with Isabella Norcliffe and Mariana Lawton were never again to have the same intensity. She continued a platonic friendship with each of them. Isabella died in 1846, at the age of sixty-one, having outlived Anne by six years.

The liaison with M—— was the more enduring of the two. M—— had been the truest love of Anne's life and never again was Anne able to invest any relationship with the ardour she had felt for M——. Anne continued to offer a place of refuge at Shibden Hall for M—— should her marriage become too difficult or should she become a widow. In fact, M—— did briefly leave her husband in March 1826, but decided to return to him. The short interlude, during which C—— appealed to Anne to intervene for him with M—— in an attempt to mend the rift, brought about a reconciliation between Anne and C——, and thereafter Anne paid visits to Lawton Hall, which she had hitherto vowed she would never do. As with Isabella, the friendship continued through letters and visits, gradually becoming less important to Anne as travel, business affairs and new friendships came more and more to absorb her time and thoughts. M— died in October 1868, in her seventies, some twenty-eight years after Anne's death.

Anne Lister's life was cut short during what she termed her 'wild but delightful wanderings'. In 1839, she and her new companion left Shibden Hall for an extended tour of Europe and Russia. Fifteen months later, still on their travels to the remoter parts of Russia, Anne contracted a fever and died rapidly. She was in her fiftieth year. Her body was brought back to Shibden Hall and she was buried in the churchyard of the Parish Church, Halifax. The local press reports were as follows:

Halifax Guardian, 31 October 1840

Deaths: On Tuesday 22 September, at Koutais, of *la fièvre chaude*, Mrs [Mistress] Lister of Shibden Hall, Halifax, Yorkshire.

Local Intelligence: The late Miss Lister of Shibden Hall

In our obituary this week, we regret to record the name of this respected and lamented lady, whose benefactions to our charitable and religious institutions will long be remembered and whose public spirit in the improvement of our town and neighbourhood is attested by lasting memorials. In mental energy and courage she resembled Lady Mary Wortley Montagu and Lady Hester Stanhope; and like those celebrated women, after exploring Europe, she extended her researches to those Oriental regions, where her career has been so prematurely terminated. We are informed that the remains of this distinguished lady have been embalmed and that her friend and companion, Miss Walker, is bringing them home by way of Constantinople, for interment in the family vault. She died near Tefliz but within the Circassian border. Miss Lister was descended from an ancient family in Lancashire, the main branch of which is represented by the noble line of Ribblesdale.

Halifax Guardian, 1 May 1841

The late Mrs Lister. The remains of this lady (who, our readers will remember, died at Koutais, in Imerethi, on 22 September last), arrived at Shibden Hall late on Saturday night and were interred in the parish church on Thursday morning.

NOTES

INTRODUCTION

1. Jill Liddington, *Female Fortune: Land, Gender and Authority, The Anne Lister Diaries and Other Writings, 1833–1840* (Rivers Oram Press, 1988)
2. Jill Liddington, *Presenting the Past: Anne Lister of Halifax 1791–1840* (Pennine Pens 1994), pp. 12–14
3. Liddington, *Presenting*, pp.15–16
4. Liddington, *Presenting*, pp. 16–17
5. Liddington, *Presenting*, pp. 18–22
6. Liddington, *Presenting*, pp.25–30

1816

1. The Crescent, designed by John Carr of York and modelled on the Royal Crescent, Bath, is an impressive piece of Georgian architecture. Built between 1780 and 1784 for the 5th Duke of Devonshire, the west and east wings accommodated two hotels, the Crescent Hotel and the Great Hotel. The centre of the Crescent was reserved for the Duke's town house until 1804 when he ceased using it and it then became converted into the Centre Hotel.
2. The Great Hotel formed the east wing of the Crescent.
3. Rev. Sir Thomas Horton, 3rd baronet 1758–1821, of Chadderton, Manchester, rector of Whittington and vicar of Badsworth. Thomas married in 1779 the Hon. Elizabeth Stanley (died 1796), daughter of Lord Strange and granddaughter of the 11th Earl of Derby; they had one daughter, Charlotte, who is relevant to Halifax as she married

(1808) 'Colonel' Pollard of Stannary Hall, with whom Anne Lister was acquainted. The baronetcy became extinct in 1821. Sir Thomas died in Halifax. From Anne Lister's diary: Friday 2 March 1821 – 'Sir Thomas Horton, Bart. [Mrs. Pollard's father] died some time last night, or rather early this morning, at his house at Barum-top.' [My thanks to David Glover for the above information.]

4. Calderdale District Archives (hereafter CDA). Ref. SH:7/ML/E/26/20.11.1816.

1817

1. Marian Lister, Anne's younger sister, who lived with their parents, Captain Jeremy Lister and his wife, Rebecca, at the family estate in Market Weighton, East Riding of Yorkshire.

2. Northgate House, belonging to the Lister estate in Halifax and occupied at that time by Anne's uncle Joseph Lister and his wife, Mary.

3. The Rawson family were amongst the most prominent of the Halifax families whose wealth derived from the burgeoning manufacturing trade. Their wealth enabled them to move into the banking industry. For a more comprehensive account of the Rawson family in Anne Lister's era see 'The Rawson Family' by Arthur Porritt, *Halifax Antiquarian Society Transactions* (hereafter *HAST*), 1966 (pp.27–52). Also *The Genesis of Banking in Halifax* by Ling Roth, H. F. King, Halifax, 1914.

4. Louisa (Lou) Belcombe, sister to Mariana.

5. In 1788 Lady Eleanor Butler and Sarah Ponsonby, daughters of Irish aristocratic families, caused a scandal by eloping from Ireland in order to pursue their dream of spending their lives together. They settled in a remote cottage in Llangollen, North Wales, where they remained until their deaths. Their reputations became greatly enhanced by the way in which they epitomised the Romantic image of a life lived simply, in harmony with nature, à la Rousseau. See *The Ladies of Llangollen: A Study in Romantic Friendship* by Elizabeth Mavor, London, 1971 (reprinted by Penguin, 1981) and *Life with the Ladies of Llangollen*, compiled and edited by Elizabeth Mavor, Viking, 1984. Although the Ladies stoutly rebutted any innuendoes about the possible sexual nature of their friendship, Anne Lister, who visited them in 1822, was convinced that they were lovers.

6. The Rev. Samuel Knight, a distinguished classicist and fellow of Magdalene College, Cambridge, became the Vicar of Halifax in 1817 following the death of the previous incumbent, Dr Coulthurst, in that year. See 'The Georgian and Early Victorian Church in the Parish of Halifax' by J.A. Hargreaves, M.A., *HAST*, 1990 (p.49).

7. Situated in Church Street, Halifax, the medieval Halifax Parish Church of St John the Baptist had been the place of worship for the Lister family for centuries. It was built in the fifteenth century on the site occupied by two previous churches, the first of which was thought to date from c.1120. The second church was built between 1274 and 1316. The present building incorporates remains of both these earlier churches in its structure. See 'The Evolution of the Parish Church, Halifax (1455–1530)' by T. W. Hanson, *HAST*, 1917 (pp.181–204). Also, 'Halifax Parish Church' by R. Bretton, F.H.S., *HAST*, 1967 (pp.74–91).

8. Manservant at Northgate House.

9. Maidservant at Northgate House.

10. Princess Charlotte of Wales (1796–1817), only child of the Prince Regent (later George IV). She married, in 1816, Prince Leopold (1790–1865) of Saxe-Coburg-Gotha, who later became King of the Belgians. The only child of the marriage, a boy, was stillborn on 5 November 1817. Charlotte died the following day, 'in the grip of post-partum haemorrhage'. See *The Unruly Queen: The Life of Queen Caroline* by Flora Fraser, Papermac (MacMillan), 1997 (p.297).

11. Mary Jane Marsh, an unmarried woman of outwardly genteel pretensions behind which lurked an astute and scheming mind. A clergyman's daughter, and sister to another clergyman, she had insinuated herself into the household of the benevolent Mr and Mrs Duffin as companion to the elderly and ailing Mrs Duffin. Her ministering duties also came to include fulfilling the sexual needs of Mr Duffin. In short, braving the discreet scandal-mongering whispers of York society, she became his mistress with an opportunistic eye on becoming the second Mrs Duffin. At this point in their lives, Mr Duffin was sixty-two and Miss Marsh was thirty-eight. It was to be seventeen more long years before Mr Duffin finally took her as his wife. Mrs Duffin died in 1823 and Mr Duffin and Miss Marsh were finally married on 20 September 1826 at Holy Trinity Church, Micklegate, York. See *York Gazette* 30.9.1826 and 29.10.1826.

12. Manservant at Shibden Hall.

13. A hatchment is a square or lozenge-shaped piece of material depicting the family crest or arms of a deceased person. Usually displayed on the outer wall of the deceased's house for some time after death.

14. William Duffin, formerly a surgeon employed in Madras by the East India Company, was an influential character in York. A medical practitioner, he had been appointed Director of the York Dispensary in 1818. He was a member of the York Philosophical Society. He lived in Micklegate, York and died in 1839, aged ninety-two.

15. Rebecca Lister (née Battle) was born at Welton Hall, in the small village of Welton, near South Cave in the East Riding of Yorkshire. In 1788 she married Captain Jeremy Lister, a man twice her age. Their marriage was not a happy one. Of the six children she bore him, four (all boys) died at an early age. Only the two girls, Anne and Marian, survived. Disappointment, illness and alcoholism hastened Rebecca's death at the age of forty-six.

16. Eliza (Eli) Belcombe, sister to Mariana.

17. Anne (Nantz) Belcombe, sister to Mariana.

18. Henrietta (Harriet) Milne, sister to Mariana. Married to a military man, Lieutenant-Colonel Milne.

19. Manservant in the Belcombe household.

20. Situated in Blake Street, the Assembly Rooms were built for the purpose of providing a venue where the élite of York could gather for social entertainments such as card-games and dancing. The building, designed on the lines of an ancient Egyptian hall, was begun in 1730, first used in August 1732, but not entirely completed until 1735.

21. The Rev. Dr H. W. Coulthurst (1753–1817). Vicar of Halifax 1790–1817. He established the first free dispensary to meet the medical needs of the poor in Halifax. See *Halifax* by J. A. Hargreaves, M.A., Edinburgh University Press, 1999 (pp.88–9).

22. The variation in the times recorded by Anne is interesting. Greenwich Mean Time was not fully adopted throughout Great Britain until 1855.

23. A notorious accident blackspot, even today, over the moors between Yorkshire and Lancashire.

1. Rebecca Lister's inheritance from her father had provided them with an estate near Market Weighton on which, in 1793, Jeremy Lister had built Skelfler House (or Farm). There were other older properties on the estate, such as the Grange Farm and Low Grange, which were rented out to small tenant-farmers. Jeremy's inefficient business methods soon ran the estate into debt and, by the time of his wife's death, his financial position seemed irredeemably hopeless.

2. The Halifax Circulating Library was originally established in 1768 in an upper room of the Old Cock Inn. In 1818 it was moved to premises at Ward's End, adjoining the Theatre Royal. Eventually, the library was housed in the new Assembly Rooms some time after they were built in 1828. See 'Halifax Circulating Library, 1768–1866' by E. P. Rouse, *HAST*, 1911 (pp.45–59) and also 'Libraries in Halifax' by Derek Bridges, *HAST*, 1999 (pp.38–50).

3. One of the first provincial theatres in Halifax was built at Ward's End in 1791, superseding the earlier venues in the old Assembly Rooms at the Talbot Inn, and the inn yards of the Old Cock Inn and the White Lion. See 'The Old Theatre in Halifax, 1789–1904' by A. Porritt, *HAST*, 1956 (pp.17–30).

4. Anne constructed four different indexes: a journal index in which she recorded a short abstract of each day's entry in her main journal; a literary index, in which she listed all the books, pamphlets, reviews, etc., which she had read or partly read throughout each year; a letters index which allowed her to track down the date, and the name of the sender or recipient of every letter sent or received during each year; and an extracts index listing the subject of each extract from her reading alphabetically.

5. The housekeeper at the Norcliffes' town house in York.

6. 'The Cornelian' is a love-poem by Byron written to commemorate the gift of a heart-shaped cornelian stone to Byron from John Edleston, a young Trinity choirboy, with whom Byron fell in love during his time at Cambridge University. See Byron's letter to a friend, Elizabeth Bridget Pigot, dated 5 July 1807, in which he expresses his love for Edleston. *Byron: A Self-portrait: Letters and Diaries 1798–1824*, ed. Peter Quennell, Oxford University Press, 1990 (p.30). The esoteric theme of this poem is that of the transgressive love between Byron and a young man who was poor and

socially inferior to the poet. The young man gives the poet a cornelian stone which the poet values greatly. This text would have allowed Anne to send two veiled messages to Miss Browne – that she was the object of Anne's unorthodox love but that she was also Anne's social inferior and therefore she could not be her life-partner. In the event, Anne gave up the idea and Miss Browne eventually married without ever having really understood what Anne's motives were towards her – at least not until after her marriage when she had become more worldly-wise.

7. Kallista or Callista derives from Callisto from the Greek, meaning 'most beautiful'. Anna Clark, in her article, 'Anne Lister's Construction of Lesbian Identity', *Journal of the History of Sexuality*, volume 7, number 1, July 1996 (pp.41–50), relates Anne's choice of this name to '. . . the myth, retold by Ovid, of the nymph Callisto, beloved of Diana, chaste leader of the hunt, who rejected male company. When Callisto rests while hunting, Jove comes upon her, and in order to seduce her, disguises himself as Diana. When Callisto becomes pregnant, Diana turns her into a bear in disgust and anger at her betrayal. If Miss Browne was Callisto, who did Anne see herself as: Jove or Diana, or one in the disguise of the other? As Jove, Anne could inflame her fantasies of "taking" lower-class young women in a masculine disguise. As Diana, Anne could imagine a comradeship of free, virginal young women hunting and loving in the forest and identify with her rage when Jove raped Callisto, just as she resented the marriages of the young women she admired.'

8. Langton Hall, home of the Norcliffe family in the picturesque village of Langton, near Malton, East Yorkshire.

9. The Piece Hall was built for the specific purpose of buying and selling the cloth pieces manufactured by the woollen industry for which Halifax was renowned in Anne Lister's day. Designed on the Classical lines of Italian architecture, incorporating Tuscan columns and arches which surround a great courtyard, this spacious Italianate building was opened on 1 January 1779 to a great fanfare of public rejoicing and civic pride. Now listed as a Grade I building of historical and architectural importance and interest, it remains the only one of its kind in the whole of Great Britain.

10. Housekeeper at Langton Hall.

11. This was to be the first time Anne had met the Norcliffe family since the deaths of their youngest daughter, Emily, and their son-in-law,

Dr Charles Best, husband of their daughter Mary Best. Both tragedies had occurred in 1817 whilst the Norcliffe family were on a tour of Europe. Anne Lister was understandably anxious about visiting a family in mourning for their recently deceased loved ones.

12. Charlotte Norcliffe, sister to Isabella.

13. François Joseph Talma, (1763–1826), famous tragedian of the French stage, patronised by Napoleon and influenced by David, the greatest French artist of the French revolutionary period. Talma's reforms in acting styles, staging and costume in the theatre led to him becoming one of the leading figures in nineteenth-century French Romanticism and Realism. For a short account of his funeral, see Philip Mansel's *Paris Between the Empires*, John Murray Ltd, 2001 (p.216). Anne Lister was in Paris at the time and she noted the occasion in her journal. 'Joseph-François Talma buried yesterday morning at 11½ in the cemetery of Père Lachaise, not far from Massena, being carried, according to his request, directly from his own house to the cemetery. The procession left his house at 10, consisting of between 3 & four thousand. About twenty thousand persons estimated to be assembled in the cemetery. His death occasioned by an obstruction (of about 1½ inch) in one of the bowels.' Ref. CDA. SH:7/ML/E/9. 22.10.1826.

14. The Manor School, Anne's old school. She entered the school at the age of fourteen, sometime between April and August of 1805 and remained there until the early summer of 1806. The Manor School was housed in a medieval building known as the King's Manor which still exists today. Originally a thirteenth-century house, built as an abbot's lodging house, the north wing of the King's Manor was converted into boarding-school premises in the first half of the eighteenth century. At this period, 1805, there were around forty-one pupils, drawn for the most part from wealthy North of England families. For an account of the history of this medieval building see E. A. Gee's 'The King's Manor', *Royal Commission on Historical Monuments, City of York. Vol. IV*, H. M. Stationery Office, London, 1977.

15. Charlotte Sophia (1744–1818), wife of George III. The German-born Princess Sophie Charlotte was married to George III on 8 September 1761. The marriage produced fifteen children, of whom the eldest, George (1762–1830), became Prince Regent in 1811 and then George IV on the death of his father in 1820. As King George's illness, diagnosed as 'madness', became ever more distressing, Queen Charlotte

isolated herself, becoming bad-tempered with her family and aloof from society. She died on 17 November 1818. See Christopher Hibbert's *George IV*, Penguin Books, 1976 (p.517).

1819

1. Clare Hall (previously Calico Hall) was the home of the Prescott family during Anne Lister's era. For a fuller account of the history of this mansion see 'Clare Hall, Halifax' by C. D. Webster M.A., *HAST*, 1967 (pp.123–137).

2. When Anne was seven her parents sent her to a dame-school in Ripon, North Yorks, run by a Mrs Haigue and a Mrs Chettle. The school was situated in Low Agnes Gate. (Ref. CDA. SH:7/ML/E/ 15/ 22.5.1832.) Anne was almost totally out of the control of her mother who was left alone for long periods whilst Captain Lister, a seemingly indifferent husband and father, was away on military duties. She admits she was a difficult child. In later life, Anne told a friend that she was whipped every day at the school in Ripon: 'I told her I was a curious genius and had been so from my cradle. She wondered what I was when little. I said, a very great pickle. Sent to school very early because they could do nothing with me at home, and whipped every day, except now & then in the holidays, for two years.' Ref. CDA. SH:7/ML/E/3/10.11.1819.

3. In Greek mythology, Lethe is a river in Hades whose waters, if drunk, cause forgetfulness.

4. Miss Watkinson's School for Young Ladies in Halifax.

5. John Locke (1632–1704), British philosopher, known for his work on empirical knowledge, religious toleration and anti-authoritarian theory of the state.

6. 'Are you dead? Are you ill? Have you changed your mind? Have any difficulties arisen?'

7. Elvington, near York, was the home of Ellen Empson (née Rawson. She had been an old flirt of Anne's in their younger days. In 1814, she married Amaziah Empson of Harrogate and moved to Elvington.

8. Thomas Edwards (1762–1834) of the firm 'Edwards of Halifax', the booksellers. The book-binding skills of William Edwards (1723–1808) of Halifax became known around 1750 when he

created some of the best examples of the art of fore-edge painting in which the edges of the pages of a book depicted scenes, usually of a pastoral nature. His sons carried on the business and the Edwardses became renowned for their elegant and unique bindings. The success of their business led to the opening of a bookstore in Pall Mall, London. See 'Edwards of Halifax' by T. Hanson, HAST, 1912 (pp.141–200).

9. The joke here is, of course, that in Anne's era, 'kiss', like the French 'baiser', contained a double entendre in that in addition to its more common interpretation it could also mean 'to have sexual intercourse'.

10. Lallah Rookh (1817) by Thomas Moore (1779–1852), an Irish poet, songwriter and biographer, whose romantic ballads earned him the title of national songwriter of Ireland. His long poem Lallah Rookh consists of a series of Oriental tales in verse, with linking passages in prose, told to the princess, Lallah Rookh, on her journey from Delhi to Kashmir, where she was to be married.

11. Bolus – a large pill.

12. The years from 1816 to 1820 were what E. P. Thompson called 'the heroic age of popular Radicalism', dominated as they were by repression, radicalism and reform fever and Britain was closer to revolution than it has ever been since that period. Halifax, because of its importance as a centre of the woollen manufacturing industry, was a kind of crucible in which all the elements of political, economic and social dislocation were mixed, making a potent brew of discontent which permeated the society of this small, insular, Pennine town at every level. With the increasingly vociferous demands for parliamentary reform, the government found itself facing an unprecedented wave of radicalism with the dangerous whiff of revolution about it. With scenes of the French Revolution of 1789 still vivid in the imaginations of nervous politicians, their frightened response was to introduce repressive measures of great severity such as the Seditious Meetings Act of 1817 and the Six Acts of 1819. For an extended discussion covering this period see the chapter headed 'Demagogues and Martyrs' in E. P. Thompson's The Making of the English Working Class, Penguin Books, 1991 (pp.660–780).

13. William Milne was the young son of Colonel and Mrs Milne, nephew to Mariana. He was a very sick boy, suffering from tuberculosis of the bone and died at an early age.

14. The Peterloo Massacre is the name given to a meeting held on St Peter's Field, Manchester, the main aim of which was to demand parliamentary reform. Jill Liddington in *Presenting the Past* expands on the relevance of this event. A crowd of between fifty and sixty thousand people gathered there. Although the meeting was peaceful the local magistrates took fright and ordered the arrest of the leading speaker, 'Orator' Hunt. The Cheshire Yeomanry was sent in, panic ensued and shots were fired by the troops, killing eleven peaceful demonstrators and wounding around four hundred more. James Wroe (1788–1844), a leading Manchester radical and one of the founders of the *Manchester Observer*, was at the reform meeting on 16 August 1819 and described the events in the next edition of his newspaper. He was reputed to be the first person to give the title of the 'Peterloo Massacre' to the events which took place in St Peter's Field that fateful day. He was imprisoned for twelve months for publishing a series of pamphlets entitled *The Peterloo Massacre; A Faithful Narrative of the Events*.

15. Sarah Binns was a fictitious person with whom Anne pretended to be carrying on a sexual affair. The girl was, according to Anne, of working-class origin and served Anne's fantasy of keeping a mistress. In 1816, talking to Mariana's sister: '*I was led into hinting at Sarah Binns, the feigned name of a girl to whom M[ariana] believes, & has believed for the last two years, me to pay thirty pounds a year.*' Ref. CDA. SH:7/ML/E/26/ 23.11.1816.

16. *The Pleasures of Hope*, by Thomas Campbell (1777–1844) a Scottish poet of Glaswegian origin, was published in 1797. An instantaneous success, it was followed by a new edition, with added lyrics, in 1803. Campbell was instrumental in the founding of London University. From 1826 to 1829 he was lord rector of Glasgow University. He is buried in Poets' Corner at Westminster Abbey.

17. Known in France during the French Revolution as the '*bonnet rouge*', the red cap of liberty was worn by the militant sans-culottes as a symbol of freedom from tyranny. Dating back to Roman times, its original name was the Phrygian cap (in French, *bonnet Phrygien*) and it was given to freed slaves at the moment of their emancipation. See Simon Schama's *Citizens: A Chronicle of the French Revolution*, Penguin Books, 1989 (pp.603–4).

18. Housemaid at Shibden Hall.

19. Gay did not, of course, have the connotations which it has today. Anne is referring to Mr Kelly's licentious behaviour with, possibly, women and alcohol. In Anne's era it was the custom to speak of the 'gaieties' of men who were living a dissolute life.

1820

1. Mr Horton – a Halifax magistrate.
2. George III died on 29 January 1820 and the Prince Regent, at the age of fifty-seven, became the new king, George IV. 'The proclamation of his accession was delayed for a day, however, as January 30 was the anniversary of the execution of King Charles I; and it was not until Monday 31st that . . . the aged Garter King of Arms read out the traditional formula in a slow and quavering voice.' See *George IV* by C. Hibbert, Penguin Books, 1988 (p.543).
3. Haugh-end, Sowerby, near Halifax, was the home of Henry Priestley (1790–1837) and his wife, Mary. He was the son of Joseph and Lydia Priestley of White Windows, Sowerby. The family were prosperous clothing manufacturers. Joseph Priestley was a J.P. and also Deputy Lieutenant of the West Riding of Yorkshire. See 'Famous Sowerby mansions. White Windows' by H. P. Kendall, *HAST*, 1906 (pp.105–15).
4. Hope Hall (now the Albany Club) is a Georgian mansion built in 1765; it became the home of Christopher Rawson and his wife, Mary Anne, in 1808. The couple had no children but their house, like that of his mother's at Stoney Royde, was the venue for lively social gatherings of the town's élite. See 'Hope Hall, Halifax: and its Past Residents' by A. Porritt, *HAST*, 1972 (pp.77–87).
5. George Canning (1770–1827), Member of Parliament for Liverpool 1812–1823, Foreign Secretary 1822–1827. He became Prime Minister in April 1827 but died in August of the same year at the age of fifty-seven.
6. Sarah Siddons (1755–1831), the most acclaimed English actress of the era, excelled in such dramatic Shakespearean roles as Lady Macbeth, Desdemona and Rosalind. Although she formally retired from the stage in 1812, she did appear on special occasions. A benefit evening for Mr and Mrs Charles Kemble on 9 June 1819 was her final public performance.

7. The 'black hole' – a place of detention where miscreants were kept overnight prior to appearing before a magistrate the following day. It was thought to have been located in Dungeon Street at the bottom of Pellon Lane, Halifax. See 'Notes on Halifax Gaols' by R. Eccles, *HAST*, 1922 (pp.88–104).

8. Mary Vallance was the twenty-five-year-old daughter of a Kent brewing family. She had met the Norcliffes during their Grand Tour of Europe. She and Emily Norcliffe, the youngest Norcliffe daughter, had become close friends. After Emily's tragic death at the age of eighteen, from tuberculosis, the Norcliffes became very fond of Miss Vallance and she was a regular guest at Langton Hall. During the house-party mentioned here, there was a great deal of flirting and sexual activity between some of the women. Miss Vallance, after a show of maidenly modesty, eventually allowed Anne Lister some sexual freedom. As Anne wrote in her journal of 8 March 1821, '*I care not about my connection with Miss V. She gave me licence enough.*'

1821

1. Cliff Hill and Crow Nest – two of the properties forming part of the Walker estate in Lightcliffe, adjacent to the Shibden estate. In 1830, Ann Walker became co-heiress, along with her sister Elizabeth, to the estate. In 1834, Ann moved in to Shibden Hall to live with Anne Lister as her wife. See 'The Walkers of Crow Nest', in *Female Fortune: Land, Gender and Authority* by Jill Liddington, River Orams Press, 1988 (pp.27–38).

2. Henry Stephen (Steph) Belcombe (1790–1856), brother to Mariana, was the only son of Dr William Belcombe. He followed his father into the medical profession. He married Harriet Bagshaw by whom he had three children. Initially he practised medicine in Newcastle-under-Lyme but later in his career he moved to York, living in the Minster Yard. He succeeded his father at the York Retreat in 1826 and also at the Clifton private asylum. Charles Dickens was a close friend of his and visited his home on several occasions. See *Clifton and its People in the Nineteenth Century: A North Riding Township now Part of York City* by Barbara Hutton, Yorkshire Philosophical Society, 1969 (p.25).

3. 'If I lose you, I am lost.'

4. A three-volume romantic novel by German author August Friedrich Ferdinand von Kotzebue, published in 1809. A French translation from the original German was published in London. The story, which Anne saw as a parallel to her own unhappy love-affair with Mariana, is that of an innocent young woman, Leontine (Mariana Lawton), who marries a debauched older man, Major Arlhoff (Charles Lawton), to please her father, Count de Blondheim (Dr Belcombe). A much younger, honourable man, Captain Wallerstein (Anne Lister) is in love with Leontine and, after many romantic and melodramatic twists and turns, including the death of the hated Arlhoff, all is happily resolved.

5. Immanuel Kant (1724–1804), a German philosopher of the European Enlightenment.

6. Isabella Norcliffe's uncle, the Reverend James Dalton, had been appointed the Rector of Croft, near Darlington, in 1805. Brother to Isabella's father, Thomas Norcliffe Dalton, James and his wife Maria had been married for twenty-five years. There were eight surviving children of the marriage.

7. These works, particularly Byron's *Don Juan*, Moore's *Lallah Rookh* and Little's poems were thought to contain sensuous material not fit for respectable people, particularly women, to read.

8. Newcastle-under-Lyme, Staffordshire, where Mariana's brother Dr Stephen Belcombe and his wife Harriet lived. Anne and Mariana had been invited to act as sponsors at the christening of their new baby.

9. Ann Walker – at this point, Anne Lister had no deep interest in her young neighbour. A decade later, however, there was a dramatic shift in Anne Lister's attitude towards her. [See n.1.]

10. Holy Trinity Church, Harrison Road, Halifax, was opened in 1798. See Hargreaves' *Halifax* (pp.99 and 221).

11. For an account of this royal extravaganza, from which the queen was excluded, see *A Queen on Trial* by E. A. Smith, Alan Sutton Publishing Ltd, 1993 (pp.186–91).

12. The berry of a shrub, native of Java, resembling a grain of pepper. Used for medicines or spices.

13. *The Confessions of Jean-Jacques Rousseau*. First published in 1782, Rousseau's *Confessions* are hailed as the precursor of modern autobiography and earned him the title of 'Father of the Romantic Movement'. Anne Lister took him as her model and certainly his

opening paragraphs in Book One of the *Confessions* could be applied to the spirit in which Anne Lister's journals were written:

> I have begun on a work which is without precedent, whose accomplishment will have no imitator. I propose to set before my fellow-mortals a man in all the truth of nature; and this man shall be myself.
>
> I have studied mankind and know my heart; I am not made like any one I have been acquainted with, perhaps like no one in existence; if not better, I at least claim originality, and whether Nature has acted rightly or wrongly in destroying the mold in which she cast me, can only be decided after I have been read.

14. A euphemism for the lavatory or water-closet, as it was then called. Shibden Hall did not seem to possess one at the time Anne was writing but this was her tentative plan for its location. Before its installation, the Listers used to go to 'the place', as Anne described whatever area was used for the purpose, at some distance from the house. Alternatively, they used what she called 'footpots', in their bedrooms, which some luckless serving-maid emptied.

15. Anne could be referring here to the small medieval (c.1500) parish church of St Michael le Belfry which nestles in the shadow of its bigger sister church, York Minster. Alternatively, it could be a reference to the York Minster belfry.

1822

1. Joséphine Duchesnois (1777–1835), star of the Théâtre Français. She had many lovers, including Napoleon, and was also pursued by the lesbian Mademoiselle Raucourt (1756–1815), who was president of a distinguished lesbian club which flourished in Paris in the 1780s called The Anandrynes, founded by a Mme Furiel whose house was the meeting place. See Rictor Norton, 'Romantic Friendships among Women', *Lesbian History*, 23 August 2009. http://rictornorton.co.uk/eighteen/romantic.htm

2. It seems Anne was struck by the fact that, in a temper or in the heat of the moment, her friend had addressed her in masculine terms and had used the 'vulgar' word 'fellow'. Had her friend called her a 'gentleman', Anne would not have felt her dignity to be so much under attack. She was always rather pleased to have masculine qualities

attributed to her but did not relish being debased to a 'good fellow'.

3. Mariana Lawton (née Belcombe) was born in Vienne in 1790, during the time her father, Dr Belcombe, spent working on the Continent. At one point he was employed by Schweppes to promote the benefits of their 'new aerated water' in England. (My thanks to Janet Roworth for this information.) In 1827, Anne was travelling on the Continent herself and wrote to Mariana about her travel plans. '. . . mention having heard from Mrs Johnston – her admiration of Nice & the situation of Vienne. [I] must indeed see M[ariana]'s birthplace.' CDA Ref. SH:7/ML/E/10/7.12.1827.

4. The reference to Hotspur and Percy relates to Sir Henry Percy (1364–1403), who was known as 'Harry Hotspur'. He was the son of Henry Percy, 1st Earl of Northumberland. A famous northern warrior, Hotspur was immortalised in Shakespeare's *Henry IV, Part I*. Percy was also Mariana Lawton's middle name.

5. Individual banks issued their own notes prior to the Bank of England becoming the sole issuing authority in the twentieth century. For an account of early banking practices in Halifax see *The Genesis of Banking in Halifax* by Ling Roth, H. F. King, Halifax, 1914 and *Banking in Yorkshire* by W. C. E. Hartley, Dalesman Publishing Co. Ltd, 1975.

6. *Adam Blair* – a novel by J. G. Lockhart. First published in 1822, the book caused a sensation in that its theme was that of the fall from grace of a minister of the Church of Scotland. For Anne Lister's emotional reaction to the novel, see the extract dated Monday 8 December 1823 (p.342).

7. Mr Webb was the proprietor of the Black Bear Hotel, Piccadilly, which Anne frequented almost every time she visited London.

8. Eliza Raine was a young Anglo-Indian girl who became Anne's first lover. They were both boarders at the Manor School where, aged fourteen, they shared a bedroom. Their friendship quickly developed into a very intense and passionate love affair.

9. Hammersley's – the London bank and Bureau de Change which Anne used every time she travelled.

10. Meat purchased from butchers' shops situated in the Shambles, a medieval street in York which is still famous for its historical preservation.

1. In Greek mythology, Tiresias was a blind prophet whom the gods punished for his misdemeanours by changing him into a woman for seven years.

2. White Windows, Sowerby, near Halifax. The Priestleys were a large family of woollen manufacturers. At this time they had been the occupants of White Windows for around three hundred years. George Priestley (1786–1849) was the last of the family to live there. See 'Famous Sowerby Mansions: White Windows' by H. P. Kendall, *HAST*, 1906 (pp.105–15).

3. The Robinsons of Thorpe Green, near York, are famous for their connection to the Brontë family. In 1840, Anne Brontë became governess to the children of the Rev. Edmund Robinson. She was joined by her brother, Branwell, in 1842, when he was employed as tutor to the eldest boy. Both Brontës left their employ in 1845. Anne 'of her own accord', but Branwell because of suspicions that he had been conducting an affair with his employer's wife, Mrs Robinson. See *The Brontës* by Juliet Barker, Weidenfeld and Nicolson, 1994 (pp.456–70).

4. The costs of contesting for a seat in parliament were as high in the nineteenth century as they are today but, unlike modern politics, there were no party funds which a prospective candidate could draw on for his election expenses. As a result, the problems caused by money in politics could be ruinous. See 'Parliamentary Beggars' in *The Structure of Politics at the Accession of George III* by Lewis Namier, Macmillan Press Ltd (pp.402–25).

5. Germaine de Staël (1766–1817) was the daughter of Jacques Necker (1732–1804), Swiss banker and France's director-general of finance under Louis XVI. She was a flamboyant, highly intellectual woman whose literary salons, championship of women's rights and numerous love affairs brought her great notoriety. Her ongoing opposition to Napoleon culminated in her exile from Paris in 1803.

6. Juvenal's *Sixth Satire* was a particular touchstone for Anne when she wished to discreetly investigate the sexuality of women acquaintances whose orientation she suspected to be similar to her own. Anna Clark tells us that:

> When Juvenal refers to lesbian behaviour, it is in oblique and negative terms: for instance, when Tullia and her foster sister Maura pass the ancient shrine of Chastity.

> It's here
> They stop their litters at night, and
> Piss on the goddess' form,
> Squirting like siphons, and ride each
> Other like horses, warm
> And excited, with only the moon as
> Witness. Then home they fly
>
> (Clark, op. cit., pp. 33–4).

7. Located on the East Yorkshire coast and originally a small fishing port, Scarborough had become a spa in the early seventeenth century, when a local woman, Mrs Farrar, found water bubbling from a spring which was said to contain certain minerals beneficial to health. Later in the century, as sea-bathing became fashionable, the spa became a popular seaside resort, possibly the first of its kind in Britain. See K. Snowden, *Scarborough Through the Ages: The Story of the Queen of Watering Places*, Castleden Publications, 1995. Anne Brontë died in Scarborough and her grave lies in the field opposite the church of St Mary's just below the castle. For an account of her death and funeral, see Barker, pp.592–596.

8. The White Horse Inn (previously known as the Coach and Horses) is still in business and has stood on the site since 1671.

9. 'What is to prevent a man telling the truth with a smile?'

10. The date when Anne first became aware of Mariana's intention to marry Charles Lawton.

11. 'I know my own heart and I know men. I am not made like any other I have seen. I dare to believe myself to be different from any others who exist.'

12. 'Widish', meaning rather wide, which could mean well-spaced-out handwriting. In other parts of the journal Anne makes her writing 'very small' and uses many abbreviations, in order both to save paper and perhaps to deter curious readers.

13. Mariana's wedding night. Anne and Mariana's sister, Anne Belcombe, had accompanied the newly-weds on their honeymoon. Later, Anne confided to a Maria Barlow, her lover in Paris, how much she had suffered: '*I arranged the time of getting off to bed the first night. Left Mrs Barlow to judge what I felt, for I had liked [Mariana] much.*' CDA. Ref. SH:7/ML/ 8/10.12.1824.

14. Will o'the wisp, or the pursuit of an unattainable ideal.

15. *Glenarvon* is Lady Caroline Lamb's first novel. When it appeared in May 1816 it created a scandal because it appeared to be a kiss-and-tell (or as Byron crudely put it, a 'F— and publish') account of her affair with him in 1812. The characters are drawn from Lady Caroline Lamb's social circle, the pinnacle of British Society during the 'Regency' (1811–1820), when George III was declared incompetent to rule and the Prince of Wales acted the King's role as Regent. *Glenarvon* is set, however, during the brutally suppressed Irish Rebellion of 1798, and it strikes anti-establishment political notes. Paul Douglass, 'Glenarvon' in *The Literary Encyclopedia*, first published 19 October 2004 [http://www. litencyc.com/php/sworks. php?rec=true& UID=16597 accessed 11 August 2010].

16. *The Art of Employing Time to the Greatest Advantage, the True Source of Happiness* by Henry Colburn, London, 1822. Republished by Central Books, U.S., 2009.

1824

1. CDA. Ref. Sh:7/ML/E/7/6.1.1824.
2. Halifax became infamous for retaining the Gibbet Law long after it had fallen into disuse in the rest of the country. John Hargreaves tells us that: 'The establishment of a prototype guillotine, or gibbet, as it was known locally, gained notoriety for the town, with some sixty-three recorded executions between 1286 and 1650. An apocryphal beggars' litany prayed: "From Hull, Hell and Halifax, good Lord deliver us."' See Hargreaves' *Halifax*, Edinburgh University Press, 1999, pp.18–19. Also *The Story of Old Halifax* by T. W. Hanson, The Amethyst Press, Otley, 1985, pp.168–172.
3. Sibella MacLean was a thirty-four-year-old Scottish woman of good birth and breeding whose influence, eventually, was to significantly alter the trajectory of Anne's life, weaning her away from her old friends by introducing her into the aristocratic circle with which Sibella was connected – a world which Anne's ambitious heart had long wished to embrace. The MacLeans were an important clan or family in the history of the Inner Hebridean islands off the west coast of Scotland. Sibella's father was the 15th Laird of Coll, a small island some four miles west of Mull, which is itself the second largest island of the Inner Hebrides.

4. Despite Anne's seduction of Anne Belcombe in 1816, the affair was not resumed. Anne Belcombe never married. She died, aged sixty-two, at The Grove, Lawton, Cheshire.

5. *Night Thoughts on Life, Death, and Immortality: In Nine Nights* was a poetic meditation by Edward Young (1681–1765). It was an instant success when it was first published c.1742–45 and, due to its melancholy introspection, gained the reputation of a classic in the era of the Romantic Movement.

6. Mme de Boyve – proprietress of 24 Place Vendôme, Paris, where Anne was a paying guest from 1 September 1824 until 15 January 1825. See *No Priest But Love* by Helena Whitbread (ed.), Smith Settle and New York University Press, 1992 (pp.10–72).

7. 'The Maid of Buttermere', as she became known, Mary Robinson (1778–1837) was the daughter of a local hotelier. Her beauty attracted the notice of many tourists, including the Romantic poets. She is mentioned in Wordsworth's *Prelude*. Novels have been written about her life, the most recent of which is Melvyn Bragg's *The Maid of Buttermere*, Sceptre Books, 1987.

INDEX

VIRAGO
MODERN CLASSICS
707

Helena Whitbread was born in 1931 in Halifax, West Yorkshire, into an Irish-Catholic family. Due to ill-health, her grammar-school education was cut short at the age of fourteen. After a series of unskilled jobs, she married and had four children. Always conscious of her unfinished education, in her thirties she began a programme of self-education via the local College of Further Education, which qualified her to enter the Civil Service. In 1975 she enrolled in the Open University and in 1976 went to Bradford University to study full-time. After gaining a Joint Honours degree in Politics, Literature and the History of Ideas, she went on to study for a Postgraduate Certificate of Education. Once qualified, she was employed as a teacher by Calderdale Education Department and also began to work on the Anne Lister journals. The two books of edited extracts which resulted from her work are published in Britain and America. Now retired, Helena is working on a biography of Anne Lister.

Also available in Virago

No Priest but Love:
The Journals of Anne Lister 1824–1826